T0368495

# THE
# SWINEHERD

## JACK M. HEITZ

authorHOUSE®

*AuthorHouse™*
*1663 Liberty Drive*
*Bloomington, IN 47403*
*www.authorhouse.com*
*Phone: 1 (800) 839-8640*

*Published by AuthorHouse  09/04/2015*

*ISBN: 978-1-5049-2954-7 (sc)*
*ISBN: 978-1-5049-2953-0 (e)*

*Print information available on the last page.*

*Any people depicted in stock imagery provided by Thinkstock are models, and such images are being used for illustrative purposes only. Certain stock imagery © Thinkstock.*

*This book is printed on acid-free paper.*

# PROLOGUE

Life in me village went from day to day with me paying little heed to the tumultuous happenings across England and Europe.

The great famine had just ended five years past. It had affected us greatly but me da's strength had been instrumental in bringing us all through with less loss than others. Me new little sister Ann died from a wasting sickness. No amount of mam's milk seemed to help her. Others were lost as well but it had been much worse in other towns. We learned of depleted livestock and household pets. One minstrel even told us of rumors of cannibalism, which was shocking to hear.

Ugly minded people pointed fingers at the Jews, finding it easy to be blaming them fer their misfortunes. Many of our bishops supported this persecution, making them scapegoats and in 1290 the crown had enacted a law that all Jews were to leave the country. Wealth and lands were expropriated and many went into hiding.

We took no truck in such goings on and tried to help those passing our way...sharing food and giving shelter.

Monks going to Whitby Abbey brought news of war. We learned that Queen Isabelle was fighting to put her son, Edward the Third, on the throne. La Louve de France, 'The She Wolf' as she was affectionately called by her countrymen, had the full support of her lover, Sir Roger Mortimer and was turning southern England upside down.

Her husband Edward the second was imprisoned while civil war raged. Some say that he somehow managed to trip on a perfectly flat surface and died of a broken neck. There were other rumors that he had been buggered by a sharp pointed lance. He had been garroted and thrown into the Thames. He had been beheaded, and so on. The first seemed most likely, with a little help from his loving wife and friends.

The Scots, who had won their freedom at Bannockburn, were raiding throughout the north. The Welsh, though not in total uprising, were very annoyed with the English monarchy. And Edward the Bruce, Roberts brother, had crowned himself king of Ireland. During his short rule, 'he was killed in battle' he left Ireland fractured by civil war and famine.

Plundering armies were still looking fer food and didn't care if the serfs went hungry. Idle mercenaries were killing and pillaging as they pleased. To say the British Isles were in political and economical chaos would be an understatement and as always, poor people took the brunt.

Anarchy would find me all too soon.

# **ME LIFE, UP SIDE DOWN**

────── ✦✦ ──────

I sat back in the leafy shade of old willow and looked out over Krill Pond. Da had told me to mind the pigs on me own, this day and that is what I was doing, with me hands behind me head and laying back nice and easy. Da was a shadow of his former self he had lost a lot of his strength, working himself to exhaustion, helping everyone until the end of the great famine. Our whole village had survived it quite well thanks to his efforts and those of some others who backed him like Brian the smithy. Being isolated on the edge of the moors had helped us too. The past three years had been ones of growing bounty and life was getting to be much better.

I loved late summer, a time of haze, cobwebs and drowsing. The loud humming of insects almost drowned out the soft grunting of me pigs. Da and me usually did this together, once a week, and threw in a little fishing on the side.

Pigs have a way of looking after themselves. If'n they're happy they don't stray far. I bin looking after pigs since I was a bairn and knows me stuff. I turned me head as old Snoot came snuffling over and shooed her off with an idle foot. 'There ain't no truffle or acorn under me yer dumb old sow now scat.'

Then me ear picked up something, something….but what? I came up on one elbow, looked around and listened. The pigs had stopped making their usual noise and Tusk, our boar, was standing quiet, not moving a muscle. His nose was up, snuffling the air... and I could tell he weren't happy.

'What's upsetting yer Tusk?' He turned his head enough to let me know he heard, and then turned it back again. He and I had always had a truce and got along. He had bin a wild foundling shoat I had raised, his mam being dead from some Lord's spear. I heard something again, sort of like a faint scream. Then I smelled the smoke and parted the veil of willow branches to see thickening black clouds above the trees. I was up and running back towards the village with Tusk on me heels. I don't know what I planned, I had nothing with me, but I was scared fer me mam and da.

Tusk was suddenly between me feet instead of behind me, and I went down like a stone. I was about to curse him when I heard voices, very unpleasant voices.

'Did yer hear er squeal when I cut off er tits? No one else will be shaggin er.' There was a growl of cruel, vicious laughter.

I rolled off the path and peeked through a veil of leafs, Tusk lay quiet beside me, his namesakes gleaming in the half light. Two heavily armed men strode by with their heads together and more were further away finishing their bloody work. The village lay in a hollow between low hills and behind a stone fence. Some of the houses were smoldering, they didn't burn good with their fresh sod roofs.

Men pummeled a woman as they dragged her from a burning house by her hair. Her bairn, pulled from her clutching arms, was crushed to death under a mailed boot. Me brain froze as I watched poor Alice Sutter, shrieking fer her babe, dragged behind a wall by lusting men. Bodies were everywhere, men women, children, all me friends lying in a smoky haze. Then I saw mam, her chest a bloody mess, cast up against a stone wall like a raggedy doll. I shoved knuckles in me mouth so's I wouldn't cry out. I couldn't see da but guessed he was dead too. He would never let that happen to mam iff'n he were living. I was racking me brain, what could I do? Laying still was likely best. Tusk was one smart pig, smarter than any dog. He knew that laying still was best.

Three waggons rumbled by accompanied by a number of soldiers. Shocked by the scene before me I almost took no notice. The last one baled high with our barley, oats and vegetables. Other soldiers were mustering after their evil work, and waiting fer orders from an armored man on horseback. He pulled off his helm and threw back his coif, his hair plastered to his skull from sweat. It was carrot red and he was freckled all over his face and down his neck as far as I could see. That face was forever etched into me mind, the mouth nothing more than a thin crack and then them awful, wild light blue eyes. They glowed in his face even from a distance. He was young, not much older than me. He leaned down and wiggled his fingers over a dead girl. A soldier tore a scarf from her neck and handed it to him. Wiping down his blood slimed sword, a drop of blood got on his finger and he paused to lick it off. He said a few words and men jumped and started gathering to march off after the diminishing waggons.

Shadows fell over us. 'Look what we got here, two pigs!' The chuckling was cold and cruel. As I tried to rise, I saw a blur of something heading for me noggin. There was a flash of pain and as the world faded to nothing, I could hear Tusks enraged squealing....

I came back to the living, slowly. It took a while for me eyes to focus. One was like looking through a haze of red. I reached up and felt blood, a crusted puddle, in the eye socket. After scratching it clear, I turned me head only to come face to face with Tusk, still snarling in death. He'd bin some pig, smart, and brave as any ten men. Two men lay dead, one beside him and the other sprawled against a nearby tree. The one closest to him lay gutted they were spread about him, like a skirt. Boars were good at gutting people and Tusk was closer to his wildness than most. By the blood pool clotting around the second, he had bled out from a deep gash on the inside of his thigh.

I tried to get up. It took a couple of tries before I gained me feet and stood uncertainly on them. I felt like I might fall right back down. Tusk had two spears in him and I pulled one out, almost losing me balance. It was a short heavy spear, not meant for throwing and would make a good staff until I found me legs. A staff with a sharp metal point might come in handy fer other things too. I left the swords with the dead men. I didn't know how to use one at all. I was beginning to realize that me head hurt like the dickings!

Burying a village of people is no small chore but I did it. I'd found me da, they had tied him to a waggon wheel and had done unspeakable things to him. Death I sort of understood from butchering animals, and day to day living kept the reaper at yer shoulder but the cruelty was beyond me. I buried him with mam as it should be, and wept over them. I wept a lot over the next two days.

Fra Simon was a bitter sight too. They had hung the poor monk by his feet over a hot fire. Not much was left of his head, and only remnants of his brown robes made him recognizable. I cut him down right away, grimacing at the smell of burnt flesh. His crucifix had partially melted and burned into his flesh. I laid me fingers on it feeling tears well into me eyes. Nothing much was left of his robe so I found a discarded cloak to give him a measure of modesty.

I knew every villager by name. Alice Sutter her husband John and their baby boy, Nigel the miller and his wife Joan, the whole Dixon family had bin good friends and so many more. It was heart breaking finding those that belonged together. I finally made an accounting for all except one. The smithies son Tom wasn't about. He was a good friend so I searched high and low but couldn't find him. I found his da, he'd bin carved up pretty bad, but had given as good as he got. A dead soldier lay beside him with a crushed skull. It took most of two days before the burying was done. I said words best I could, including the psalm of David, which was me favorite, and then held me blistered, bleeding hands in the horse trough. I needed to be going, I had no more tears and dry sobs were tearing me apart. I let the dead soldiers lay where they were and watched the crows, daws, gulls and flies gather. They and other scavengers would scatter the dead men's remains into oblivion and I took some small satisfaction from that.

I went searching for supplies and I found da's butchering knife and took it, it was more comfortable in me hand than a sword. I took one of the dead soldier's kit bags and rummaging through the rubble got me a half wheel of cheese, some dry bread and an unspoiled pork pie, these, along with a large water jug, and two blankets. These brigands had not found everything.

Turning me back on the dead, smoking village, and shooing the blue bottles away with me hand, I headed back towards Krill Pond. The moors lay on the other side of the village and there was nothing out there until ye reached the sea and Whitby Abbey with a small village nearby. The pond was the way I chose to go besides I wanted to check the pigs one last time. They were quite capable of looking after themselves and would become wild in no time at all. Still I had a soft spot for them and wanted them safe.

I was circling the pond, more like a small lake, trying to get me scrambled mind in order. Looking fer eggs was a lost cause everything had hatched long ago. I looked about fer the geese and ducks, they were all at the far end, their late summer brood of youngsters nearly grown.

Sudden crashing in the brush put me heart in me mouth, and then I came face to face with a grand cow with long shaggy hair and wide horns. She came real close like she wanted company and I scratched her boss, or just below it, a place always dusty and itchy. By this time I could hear other cattle in the thickets.

'What's wrong, cow?' As if I didn't know. Animals sensed death from afar and they were on edge. The man that owned these cows was an Irish, who had taken up residence near our village several years before. He had built his self a fine stone house with a chimney and all. He kept

3

mostly to his own council but having met him a couple of times I felt he was a decent sort. The first time I crossed his path, the smith had given me a wrapped long parcel to deliver. The Irish, a big broad shouldered man, welcomed me in.

'What are you called, Lad?'

'Me names William Barrow sir, everyone hereabouts calls me Will.'

He nodded to me. 'I'm Darragh McAstor.'

He tore the wrapping from the parcel and a heavy looking sword came to light. It had a plain crosspiece a heavy round pommel and a broad blade inscribed with a leaping animal that could have been a lion and something that could have been words.

I stared at it in awe. 'What is that sword called, sir?'

He looked at me with a smile. 'Tis a broadsword lad and it was my fathers,' I just had the hilt rewired and the smith has done a fine job.' He handed me a purse that jingled. 'Give that to the Smith with my thanks and this is for your trouble.' He placed a bright sixpence in the palm of me hand.

I knuckled me forehead in salute. 'No trouble at all, sir.'

The second time I met him was when he needed help with a calf not wanting to be born. It was turned and I had to just about crawl inside the mother to get her unwound. I'd birthed lots of piggies and other beasts so it wasn't new to me. He had been very worried, and was grateful for me help and that got me another sixpence. It's always a treat to see a little one tottering around looking for a tit, so I didn't care iff'n he paid me or not. Me mam and da were all shiny faced and smiling when I laid a whole shilling in front of them.

I sighed and shook off dream land, those days would not be back. I decided to check on the Irish, it wasn't far to his home. When I got there, I got another shock. The stone walls were still standing but nothing else was left. The roof, blackened and still smoking, had collapsed. I searched high and low. The stable walls were scorched but unburned with one door ajar and the horses all gone. I found nothing else until I spied the sword, all charred and black. I picked it up from the dirt and looked sadly at it, I felt that he would never have left it to this fate, so must be dead. On some whim, I wiped it down. It went right back to shining steel so I rolled it up in a saddle blanket from the stable and then secreted it in a hollow tree. The cattle worried me a bit but then I thought, 'They are out to wild pasture most of the year, so they could take care of themselves.'

I found the pigs and old snoot wanted to come. That meant they all wanted to come and I couldn't be chasing pigs across England, so I had to be mean and shoo her off. Where she went, the rest followed. I really was leaving me old life behind.

# **TOM**

I was a couple of days out now, following a little used wagon road, it was quite over grown, though fresh ruts and hoof prints were showing. I marched along, the early morning cold air pulled at me nose a bit but the sun was warm on me back. Thought went to the pork pie I'd finished a day past, and licked me lips with wishing. Chewing on a piece of hard crust wasn't quite the same. Even so, I was enjoying the chew, the air and the sun when an apparition jumped out in front of me, just about making me shite me pants. Curly black hair full of twigs and leaves a face hidden in soot and wild round eyes. A knife glinted in his hand as he crouched low.

'Tom, it's me, Will! Ye scared the shite out of me. Why are ye attacking me?'

If anything, the eyes got rounder. 'Will? Me god it is ye. I thought ye bin following me the last three days, to do me in. I was going to put an end to it.'

'I didn't even know ye were about. I searched high and low for ye around the village.'

He slipped the knife back in his belt and stood straight 'Gods truef, Will, ye don't even look like yer self!'

I started laughing, 'Neither do ye.' Then laughing made me feel real glum.

He stepped close and squinted at me face we were much the same size and build. 'Ye got buckets of blood all over yer hair and face and a wicked gash above yer temple. I'm camped by a rill. Let's go there and get that cleaned up.'

I followed him to his camp, which was just a bed of leaves and a small fire. I was thinking I knew how I had survived. 'All the blood must have made me seem dead.' I sat quiet while he worked on me. For a hard working smiths' son his hands were surprisingly gentle.

He sat back and admired his work. 'There now, we can see yer face again. Ye must have a head like a brick. That wound needs to be closed, but after four days I don't know what'll happen. I'm surprised it's not festering already.' He got up. 'There's lots of hawthorn hereabouts, I'll try and find an old one and see iff'n I can make a needle.'

I understood why he wanted an old thorn the poison would have passed. The trick was to find one that wasn't too brittle. 'What are we using fer thread? I know, I'll unravel some of me jerkin.' By that time I was talking to meself because he was long gone. When he got back, I had a yard of coarse yarn laying out to dry. I had washed the dirt off in the rill.

After a lot of stinging and aching and a little whining on me part, the job got done. I studied me reflection in a pool off'n the rill. Hazel eyes looked back at me from under a thatch of straw colored hair. Where the wound had been there was a large fuzzy wad that looked like a giant extension of eyebrow. A wide mouth broke into a friendly grin. 'Ye did a fine job Tom, its stitching and bandage all in one.' I turned away from me reflection. 'Now maybe its yer turn to clean up, I have never seen a person as black as ye. What happened to ye that ye survived?'

He stripped down and waded into the pool I'd used for a mirror. The soot was greasy and didn't come off easily it just wanted to smear around. He looked up at me, water running down his face.

'When those soldiers attacked, we were all caught off guard. Da was hammering out horseshoes and I was scraping a hoof on Dixons mare. Mrs. Miller had just brought us scones and left, then we heard her scream. Everything became loud turmoil and two soldiers barged in. Me da stepped away from the forge with his hammer in one hand and the long pincers in the other. He yelled at me to run for me life and not look back. The urgent sound in his voice made me sprint fer the back, the frightened horse almost knocking me over, and then covering me retreat. I did look back. I saw me da catch the first soldier's sword stroke with his pincers and crush the man's skull with one blow. Then the horse, wheeling about, hid him from sight. I ran out the back and cut between two houses that were already burning. The choking black smoke hid me till I made the woods. People were yelling and dying behind me. Will, ye know I can fight but I would have had no chance against those armed men.'

He looked so remorseful and guilty, I put me arm around his shoulders. 'Ye did the right thing, Tom, only ye and me survived out of all of them.' I proceeded to tell him me story and when I was done his eyes were dewed with tears. He put his hand on mine and said in a trembly voice. 'Thank ye fer burying me da.'

When he had mentioned that he could fight, I knew it to be true. We had teamed up many times at summer and autumn fairs, wrestling all comers with few losses. We were both solid and strong, me from handling pigs and him from the forge. Bloodshed, however, was never who we were.

He looked at me, 'I haven't ad anything to eat except a few blackberries, for the last three days!'

I grinned at him, 'Its lunch time then, and ye are welcome to share.' I gave him a generous chunk of cheese and a dried crust. 'We have enough left for a light sup then we need to find more food.'

He nodded with a mouth full and then spoke around the bite. 'I hope we won't be stealing.'

I shook my head. 'No, me da would trounce me good for even thinking such.' Then I got real quiet, thinking about da and mam.

Tom studied me for a moment and licked the crumbs off his fingers. His voice was soft like he didn't want to intrude, 'We should be on our way ye know, but what way is that? I just started walking five days ago with nothing in me head.'

I shooed away the doldrums and stared at Tom, 'Me too.'

We both had a good laugh, almost giggly, and finally got serious. 'Where will we go?'

'How bout Twixmiddle, where the new ferry is? It's a bit bigger than a village and less likely to be molested. We might find work there, especially ye with yer skills.'

Tom looked flustered. 'Skills ain't much good without bloody tools. But ye are right, it's a place to go, better'n we have right now.'

# **DARRAGH**

Another day had passed and we were still plodding, almost dawdling. The sun was low and the shadows long when Tom grabbed me arm. 'Look here Will, Those newer waggon tracks they go into the trees here. I'm wondering why?'

'Maybe the owners are resting?' I studied the ground and pointed. 'Look there, much more'n one single cart horse came by here. I'm getting curious too, shall we look? At the very least we might get some nosh out of it.'

Tom gave me a little poke with his elbow, 'Let's do it, but real sneaky like till we know what we are up against.'

I gave him a nod and we flitted into the woods, that is, iff'n two husky lads can flit. We weren't gone far when we saw the flicker of fire and heard low voices. Hunkering down, we snuck in till we got a view. There was a waggon, several horses and about twenty men. Most of their faces were in shadow and then one stepped into the light. Me blood drained all the way down to me feet, it was the redhead, no mistaking!

He stalked across the clearing to his horse. 'Garrad, leave two to guard the prisoner, while we go collect some of life's better things.'

With a grunt of icy mirth a huge man in boiled black leather grabbed two soldiers by their arms and pushed them towards the waggon. 'Ye two guard the prisoner!' he gave each a shake, lifting them on their toes. 'Do ye like em fat or skinny? We'll bring ye one.'

One of the men grinned, as he rubbed his arm, 'Plump with big tits sir, more to go around.'

'Done!' Garrad clapped him on the back, staggering him, and stepped away.

The redhead pointed a stiff finger at the guards. 'You mind no harm comes to the prisoner. That's for my pater to do. Remember it well, or I'll have your guts for my lady's garters. We'll be back by mid morn.' While speaking, he had been tightening buckles on the girth straps and now he mounted his horse. 'Off we go, see you beauties in tomorrows' light.' The horsemen left at an easy trot, the men at arms double marching behind.

We studied the empty clearing, empty except for the two men guarding the waggon with a wooden cage on it. Try as we might, we couldn't see what was in it though a light was dawning. Tom caught me eye and pointed at me spear, then at the man on the right. I nodded and we snuck in. Me man was standing, scratching his arse, while Toms was by the fire. We froze as the arse scratcher looked about and said,

'Hope our sweet lord don't come back drunk. He scares the shite out o me when he's sober.'

The other laughed without looking up. 'Sure has a twisted way of killing folk. Takes it to a whole new level, he does.'

'The killing gets us what we want, that's good by me. It's killing me that's got me spooked.' He blew snot through stiff fingers and wiped them on his leg.

I used the spear like a quarter staff and gave me man a hard whack right above the ear. He went down in a heap. Tom's quarry was crouched by the fire with his helmet on, it got knocked off right smartly when Tom ran forward on soft feet, flipped his knife and gave the man a hard rap behind his ear, with the hilt. He had to catch him before he fell, face first into the fire.

I went straight to the cage and then couldn't wipe the smile off me face. 'Bloody hell sir, It's good to see ye alive!' It was Mc Astor, a little worse fer wear.

He opened his one good eye, the other was swollen shut and his upper lip was way too big for his face. 'It's nice to see you too, lad.' He mumbled. 'Would you get me out of here? I'm so cramped I could weep.'

Tom was already cutting the door loose and then we both worked on his bonds. We had to lift him from the cage he was too stiff to walk. We got him by the fire and while Tom massaged his legs, I ran for cold water. I rummaged through the soldiers packs and found cloths to use for compresses. Tom's guard was coming around so I wacked him again for good measure.

Mac Astor grabbed me water and drank a good swath into it. He gasped and mumbled. 'That might give me a belly ache, but I don't give a shite, thank you lad.'

After we had cleaned him up, he said. 'We need to be away from here, but I really can't walk yet'

'We'll use the cart horse but not the waggon, it's easier to hide without it.' I fetched the horse, and it took a bit to get the sore man onto it. Luckily it was a gentle nag and stood quiet. Tom made a torch to get away from the woods, by this time it was pitch black. I gathered all the food I could carry and was going to stick the men's sword hilts in the fire, 'Do ye want a sword sir?'

'Aye lad, bring them both.'

As we left, Mac Astor looked back. 'You should not have let them live, lads, they would never be as kind to you.'

'I know ye are right sir, but I've never killed a man before, and I don't wish to start now.'

He made a grumph sound. 'Their leader will likely do it for you.'

The moon glimmered through the thinning trees and Tom doused the torch by pissing over it. His teeth shone white in the dimness. 'Two birds with one stone. Aah that feels so much better.'

Already, next afternoon, Darragh had taken to walking short spurts. I had cut him a stoutstick for a cane. He demanded that we call him Darragh, 'we are all friends here,' he said. Being crammed into a cage the size of a tun and bounced on a rough road for all that time, had left the poor man in knots, never mind living in his own waste. He was lucky not to be forever crippled and it would be a while before he was right again. His spirit, however, was not crushed and he would show it in many ways.

Late in the morning, we heard horses and the chink of mail and had to take to the woods as a party of horse galloped by. It was our nemesis and his evil lot, along with three lassies hanging on behind. They all had horses now.

Darraghs eyes glittered as he watched them pass. 'God help those colleens, when those men are done, they'll be three more mice for him to play with.'

Later on that day, he finally told us how and why he was a prisoner and not just dead. We were eating supper and he had asked us about the village. He pondered the news fer a bit and said, 'God forgive me, it's my fault.' then he just started in on his story.

'My family was obliterated in a feud over a fine piece of land with good water.' He grimaced. 'Not that there's ever a shortage of water in Erin. I was away in Dublin when news came that my father and eldest brother were murdered. Shot from behind and killed in an ambush. I rushed for home only to be way- laid by well meaning friends, which saved my life. My other two brothers had died trying to avenge them. Incensed, I waylaid and killed Donal, the eldest son of my father's enemy, Krayan McOrdred. Krayan swore to obliterate my family, never mind that he had already almost succeeded. He burned our house with my mother and little sister in it. Being the last I was a hunted man, and the odds were certainly not in my favor since he had an army of cutthroat mercenaries in his employ. I decided to flee Ireland and make a home elsewhere. You know where.'

We nodded, totally enwrapped.

'Krayan McOrdred had three sons. The second is Brian and the youngest is that red haired butcher that you have all seen. They all have red hair. I remember when Skye was a bairn and liked to cut up living cats and dogs. His Pater encouraged him since he was cut from the same cloth. Anyway, he sicced that dog of a son onto my trail, and he found me quick enough. You know the rest. His name is Skye McOrdred and he is the scion of evil!' He sighed, a heavy sigh. 'It's difficult to believe that my father and his were once childhood friends. With a friend like that, none needs an enemy.' He sat a bit and stared into the fire then he hunched his shoulders and looked up, flames flickering in his eyes.

'We need to get off this path. He'll find us real quick. If he can track me most of the way across England then, under his nose, is no place to be.'

I looked at Tom for confirmation. 'Shouldn't we be in Twixmiddle before morrows midmorning? I thought we'd be there already. We would have been, two days ago, iff'n we were on the main road. Anyway, it will be a bustle and we should be able to go to cover in a crowd.'

Darragh nodded. 'That will be our best bet. I believe it's a Jewish settlement isn't it? Some that escaped persecution in the south. According to royal edict, they have been thrown out of England, so many are keeping a low profile.'

'I never could understand why people hate other people they didn't even know. I remember it bein a pretty little town.'

'You've been there before?'

'Aye, two years past, me da and me sold pigs there.'

'That's a long way to bring pigs.'

I grinned, 'Only in a waggon sir.'

Drarragh scratched a bristly chin. 'What would Jews be doing with pigs?'

10

I shrugged, 'Resell them I suppose, or maybe to keep them around and look like gentiles.'

Darragh looked at me in surprise and nodded slowly. 'No one would expect Jews to have pigs.'

The ferry wasn't busy at all and we crossed the Swale in short thrift. Twixmiddle wasn't quite the bustling place I remembered. There were still shops and the market but everything seemed subdued. The people we met were wary of us and spoke grudgingly when spoken to. One more gregarious person, a potter, told us that a battle was brewing between the local Bishop and the Scots, and they didn't want the churches attention drawn to them.

We passed a prominent inn and decided it was too conspicuous, then we came upon a pub named 'The Winds Harp', hidden in back of town and Darragh asked us to wait a moment. He sat on a horse trough edge and pulled off his boot. He shook out two sovereigns and me eyes did a double take.

'No wonder ye had a hard time walking!'

He gave us a quirk of a smile and a wink. 'Would you like some ale or not, let's go inside.'

The pub was dim but clean and we took a table in a back corner. The place was almost empty so the keep was with us in no time and had a friendlier attitude.

'Just passing through? What is yer wish?'

'Three of your fine ale, bar keep, and a mince pie to wash down. How much is yer lodging for... let's say a week?'

'I'll gather yer order, me wife will be with yer directly on the other matter.' With that, he headed to the bar. It wasn't long before a matronly woman with a friendly smile, approached us.

'I understand ye are looking fer lodging?'

Darragh nodded, 'Aye, but just for me, I injured my leg and need to rest up.'

She gave him a concerned look, 'Yer face says ye injured more than yer leg. Sixpence a day will get ye a room on the second floor away at the back, where there is less noise.'

'That will be just fine.' He pointed at us. 'These two can come and go as they please. They are my good friends. To anyone else, I am not here. He gave her a sovereign, here take two and six for five days plus the cost of our meal. If I leave early any remaining balance paid is yours with my thanks.'

She gave him a slight curtsy, holding back her curiosity. After all she was looking at a very motley trio. 'Here is yer key sir. I'll leave towel, chamber pot and blankets by the foot of the stairs. Please check first before ye dump yer pot out the back window.'

Our ale and pie arrived, leaving me drooling. Darragh pocketed the change for his sovereign and took me knife cutting the pie into three.

'Dig in lads.' He saluted us with his tankard and took a hearty swallow. He wiped his mouth with the back of his hand. 'Aah, that's' a good ale!'

I took a bite of me pie. It was sweet and spicy at the same time. It was very good and I washed it down with swallows of the dark brew. We ate and drank in relative silence until I looked at Tom.

'Darragh is staying here, what do ye and I do?'

'Let's get a feel fer the town, find out why it's so quiet.'

'I think we know why, War is passing this way and the people are terrified of Christian reprisal.'

'Aye, our village was lucky not to get caught up in any of that shite.'

I sighed and looked at the bottom of me tankard. 'Too bad the luck didn't hold.'

Tom's face scrunched and we all looked morose, until Darragh said. 'God's truth lads, snap out of it and get on with it. Ye can both sleep in my room, just not in my bed.'

# **SIR ROBERT**

We found out quickly to keep a low profile. There were recruiters at every square and the ferry landing. We had just missed them coming in. They were conscripting for the pending battle, and I for one, weren't ready to be fighting fer someone I didn't even know. Neither was Tom, because of his armor making skills he found some work right off. There was only one smith in town and he was overwhelmed, what with horseshoes, buckles and repairs on chainmail and weapons. Military types were passing through in a steady stream. Chainmail was a bother according to Tom, but it paid quite well. Being busy at the forge kept conscription off'n him.

I had to do a little more dodging, being prime for their uses. A day was gone when I met up with a butcher who needed some help. He spotted me way with animals right off and made me a Judas goat. The work had very little enjoyment what with leading cows to slaughter. His boys had the knack for butchering but someone, me, had to keep the animals calm. They wouldn't let me butcher, something to do with Kosher, whatever that was. I made five pence and swore I wouldn't be back. It's funny, I can butcher them meself but I didn't like leading them down the garden path.

I was standing in the shade of a building at the edge of town, munching a windfall apple and watching a man ride by on a very fine charger. Jet black it was, with a small white star on its forehead. It was high stepping along with its tail arched. The man sat on it like he was born there. He cut a fine figure dressed in a mail hauberk covered by a plain white surcoat and his helm hanging from the saddle. The hauberk was split to the waist so the he could sit comfortable and the shining oiled links covered his thighs, there were hooks on the saddle to keep the mail in place. Light brown hair, heavy eyebrows and a strong chin made him a fine looking fellow.

At that moment, the Scots attacked. They came swarming out of a ditch opposite me, and more from the forest a bit further back. Yelling and screaming their war cries they overran the charger and I was up and heading for the man, yelling 'alarm' at the top of me voice. Before I could reach him that beautiful horse went down from a spear thrust just back o the foreleg. The man had drawn his sword but now lay pinned by the dead animal. He managed to block a hard chop at his head but the pommel of his own sword smacked him in the face, stunning him. I leaped in so as to straddle him and drove me spear into the throat of the man threatening him.

I then laid about me using the spear as a quarter staff. One man slipped under me guard, with eyes only for me. He gasped and looked down at the sword stuck in his middle. Me new found gentleman had come too and saved me life.

It looked like the end of us both when a hail of arrows dropped Scots left and right. Twenty yeomen plus armed militia arrived to save the day. Scots further down the road had set a couple of fires but had not really got into it. The yeomen were as handy with a sword as with a bow and the battle turned quickly. Now that they had lost the element of surprise, the Scots hung their round shields over their backs and fled the way they had come. One took an arrow in the leg and two others dragged him along.

I tried to lift the horses' dead weight using the saddle for purchase, but to no avail. I could tell the man was in pain. A heavy set yeoman, wearing a kettle hat, materialized beside me. 'Here lad, maybe two of us can lift.' The two of us grunted and strained and then a third man pulled the pinned knight clear.

I knelt on one knee, beside the gentleman, trying to catch me breath. A hand grasped me shoulder,

'Thank you lad, you saved my life.'

I turned to look into the man's eyes. They were green. One was beginning to close from a swelling high on his cheek. 'I am glad I could help milord.' I gave no thought to the first man I had killed, not till much later.

Another yeoman wearing a kettle hat came up, tall and slim. 'Sir Robert, thank the stars we came in time!'

The Knight smiled, 'Tim Cross, you are a sight for sore eyes. Trust me my eyes are sore, I thought I had joined the angels and then I opened them to see a great pair of hairy danglers looking me in the face.'

All the men roared and I turned bright scarlet.

By this time, he was sitting up and another yeoman was checking his leg. 'It's not broken milord, but it is heavily bruised. Ye'll be using a cane fer a bit.'

I was feeling flustered. I had never seen a Knight before, never mind a lord. He looked me over,

'Are you fancy free? You are welcome to join my party, and be under my protection, lad.' He grimaced, a twinge must have gone through his leg.

'That would be wonderful milord, but I have two friends I can't abandon.'

'Where are they now?'

'We're all staying at The Wind's Harp sir.'

Sir Robert looked at Tim Cross. 'What say you we all retire there, I could use a sip of ale, and I wish to meet these lucky friends.'

The Jewish militia, after thanking the yeomen, stayed to clean up. The pub was brimming full what with twenty yeomen and me newly found Knight. The keep was giving me a friendly eye for bringing all this business. I went to fetch Darragh and after hearing me tale, he came directly.

Sir Robert had many questions for both of us and we told him everything, each in turn. It was then I found out that Darragh was a teacher of the sword, or weapons master. Sir Robert looked very pleased.

'Would you consider being in my employ, master Darragh? I apologize for all the questions but I need to trust those I bring into my house.' He looked up at a commotion by the door. 'Ah, this must be Tom.'

Using me directions, a yeoman had gone to fetch him. Tom looked bewildered until he spied us, then he relaxed a bit. Darragh introduced him to Sir Robert who was elated when he found out that Tom was a smith.

'Don't worry about tools lad, we have all you need. My old smith took a kick in the head and hasn't been right since. He's prone to blackouts and that doesn't mix well with a lit forge.' He turned to me with a smile. 'From what little Darragh has told me, Will, you have a way with animals. I have just the thing for you which you will discover when we get back home.'

I was in awe of this man, a Lord that treated us as equals, and I knew right then that I would give my life to him. I summed up the gumption to ask. 'Why were ye on the road alone, milord?'

'I wasn't very smart, was I. I stopped to visit my betrothed and sent Tim and the boys ahead to give me some privacy. As you know, they weren't too far ahead.' He looked over at his yeoman. 'And don't you go flogging yourself Tim Cross, this was my doing.'

A yeoman entered and spoke in soft tones to Tim who turned to Sir Robert. 'There are no chargers to be had, me lord, I'm afraid ye will have to settle for a palfrey.'

Sir Robert sighed, 'I hope the poor beast can handle the weight!' He got to his feet and stood on his good leg. 'Can someone help me outside?'

I was under his arm in a jiff.

He rested on me. 'As to my question, master Darragh, will you join us? I can guarantee eventful times to come.'

'Aye my lord, I would be most pleased.' He grinned. 'Someone has to wipe the noses of these two pups.'

Tom and I both gave him a doleful look that said, 'Watch it!'

Sir Robert mounted his palfrey, a pretty, white stocking bay, with my help. He gave me a nod of Thanks as he moved off.

As we marched out of town, I saw Skyes' troop stopped and watching their horses foam flecked from hard riding, trying to catch up. All he could do was watch, I could see the anger he was feeling by the way he sat his horse. We would see more of him, of that I was sure.

We were late into the third day on the road, following a river on our left. We had passed two abandoned villages, reminders of the great famine. Tom and I were marching within a group of yeomen and we found them to be very easy to be with. Darragh was resting on the supply wagon, he had already done his walking fer the day. Every day his circulation got better and his legs got stronger. I was walking beside the burly yeoman who had helped me lift when Sir Robert was pinned. His name was Rosschild, but he went by Ross. He told me quite a bit about where we were going, a place in Northumbria or Cumberland near the sea. Anyway, it was late in the day when there was an interruption up ahead. The column stopped and Tim Cross signaled us to stand down. He, and two others on palfreys, followed their master down the road.

I craned me neck to see, and could glimpse a party of horse approaching with an armored man in the lead. His helm hung from the saddle and he wore a bright green scarf around his neck, which contrasted with his black hair. Lord Robert and he came side to side and they grasped arms in friendship. Tim signaled for us to approach.

The other column turned back the way they had come and Lord Robert and this new knight rode stirrup to stirrup, speaking in soft voices. Sir Robert had to look up at his friend who was riding a charger, the spitting image of the one that died. Looking around I was realizing the land was wilder and higher. It might have been like this for a time, I don't know, that's how observant I am. Anyway, we were in mountains. Yorkshire is like that, up and down and everywhere. I asked Ross who the other knight was and was told he was Sir Gawain, a great knight and a man to be admired.

Well, I suppose we were not in Yorkshire anymore. We were passing through the gates of a fortified town, nestled against some crags with a mountain beyond. The wall was partially stone and partially some wood palisades. The stone was advancing and the wooden wall gave way to it. Once the troop dismounted, Sir Robert disappeared with his knight friend leaving us to our own devices. Tim Cross gave us permission to look around while he looked for a place for us to bed in. I was happy to have Tom and Darragh for company as everything was strange to me. The place was a bustle, with workers everywhere. Dozens of stone masons and other artisans were busy carving, chipping and placing rock in a haze of dust. We found the forge right off, since it was near the stables. Tom couldn't wipe the grin from his face, as he paced about it. An old man came dottering out of the shadows to see who we were. One of his eyes was turned and his head scarred and dented. Tom took his elbow.

'Ye must be the Smith, I'll be stepping in to help fer a bit and I'll see to it that ye have work if ye wish.'

The old man smiled, drooled and wobbled as Tom looked some more. The smile had never left his face.

'Gods truf Will, it's awesome. This is thrice the size of me das', there's room for three or more smiths here.'

I loved the smell of horses and was drawn to the stables right off. They were really well laid out with four long buildings, each able to hold forty horses plus night watch quarters. The first one held more of those black chargers but only ten at present. The other stalls were empty. I walked up to the first horse they looked even bigger in their stall. All I could think of was how beautiful they looked. He must have sensed me feelings because he jogged his head up and down and blew soft breath in me face. I cupped me hands and blew back and then stroked his velvet neck. He nuzzled me face and gave me hair a soft pull. I knew we would hit it off from that moment. Leaving him, I checked the other buildings two filled with palfreys, nice looking horses in their own right. Palfreys are the normal riding horses of our time, used by yeomen, Ladies, and anyone else with a need to ride. The forth building was still empty but ready to accept new steeds. Two square barns were in back, one for the waggon horses, two teams of oxen, waggons and plows. The other was holding bales of hay and silage vats along with more farm tools. There were foundations fer two silos, still to be built and a well for drawing water. The roofs on the stables were sod with plenty of soil mixed in and there were buckets within reach everywhere. There was less risk of fire with roofs like that and the pails were an added precaution. Down from the stable area, alongside a battlement, was the marshalling yard and training ground, a large open area with lists along the back. This was to become Darraghs' domain and when at work he was someone else entirely.

# **MEG**

My exploration of the town led me up and down cobble stone lanes and streets. I avoided the alleys they stank from the open sewers down their middle. Some towns had them in the streets so we were lucky.

I finally came to the main manor. If ye like, I guess ye could call it a fortified building, but manor sounds grander. It was grand, I had seen nothing like it, ever. There was a huge living or common room, and the biggest dining room ever. The table was a circle with paths at intervals for the servers to serve from the inside. It was fine fer minstrels and other entertainment as well. I could not count, but I found out later that sixty people could sit around it. I didn't climb the stairs as they led to the private quarters of Sir Robert and special friends. My travels finally led me to the kitchens, and they were gigantic. It was here that I met Meg Dardway, the finest cook in all of England. She was busy adding leek to a soup pot when I came in.

'Can I help ye young man?' Her voice was happy and musical and she reminded me so much of me mam except she was a little taller and plumper.

I smiled at her. 'Me name is Will, mum, I thought I was lost but now I know I am not.'

'Yer stomach led yer, did it?' She smiled and waved her knife. 'Sit down at the table there. I'll get yer some scones with blackberries and a nice mug o butter milk.'

Scones, fresh blackberries and milk materialized in a jiff. She sat down opposite me with a soft grunt, and started rubbing her knee. 'I get pain in me joints, some days worse than others.' She sighed.

'Ye must be Will? Everyone is already talking of yer.'

I think I might have blushed, just a little. 'Why?'

'Ye saved the Lords life. We are all beholden for that.' She smiled. 'Also ye are fair to look on lad, so I suppose I like ye for yer self as well. More milk?'

My face felt hot but I knew she was teasing. I grinned, 'Aye mum that would be good. I haven't had anything this good since I lost me mam.'

'Can I see that mess on yer temple? What is that anyway?'

'It's stitching mum, the best we could do at the time.'

'Men! I'll get me scissors and clean that up.' As she worked on me, I looked around for something to say. 'How do ye run this huge kitchen by yerself?'

'I don't, I'm just getting ahead, I like to be alone for a bit before me help arrives. They will come soon enough and this place will be organized chaos, never ye fear.'

I winced as she pulled wool out of me head. She continued, 'We feed well over two hundred people twice a day. Now Will, if ye need someone to talk to, I am here and there is always a mug of milk for ye. This time, on any day, is a good time.'

'I thank ye mum, I may show up more than ye might wish. Would ye mind if I bring a friend, sometimes?'

She gave me that warm smile once again. 'There, I think I'm done, and yer wound looks clean. It's nice to have some outside company, so yes, bring yer friend.' She looked over my shoulder, her smile never leaving her face. 'Why Tim Cross, It's so nice to see yer.'

Meg got up and gave him a hard hug. He smiled down at her and kissed her hair. 'It's good to see yer too auntie.' He looked over at me. 'I came to find ye Will. I found lodging that will keep ye three friends together. I thought ye might like that.'

I got to me feet. 'That was very nice of yer Tim. I'll come with ye right away.' I turned to Meg. 'Thank ye so much for yer kindness, I will visit again soon.' I risked a kiss on her cheek and walked away. When I reached the stairs, I looked back and she was fingering her cheek with a faint smile. I turned and chased after Tim, two steps at a time.

When I reached the courtyard, Darragh and Tom were waiting. The swelling was leaving Darraghs face though he was several different colors. I shivered a little this day was the first of several cool days to come. Summer was bleeding away fast, and there was a raw feeling in the air. Clouds were dropping showers on nearby hills but none here yet.

Our quarters was a small sod roofed hut with a stone fire hearth and chimney, and a sturdy door to fight the wind. I felt right at home and I think Tom did too. There were two cots on one wall near the hearth and one on the other. There was a heavy duty chest by each cot for stowing gear, and a rough table with four chairs in the middle of the room. Tim looked at each of us in turn. "I hope ye will be comfortable here." there's no need for cooking, ye'll eat yer meals with the yeomen. Sir Robert likes it that way, he says it makes people interact and getting on with each other is important."

Darragh went straight to the single bed and made it his. 'Thank you Tim, you have done well by us and I for one am obliged. Tomorrow I'll get a feel for my new haunts and start training. I'll need your help there too, pushing recruits my way.'

Tim grinned, 'Ye'll get more than just recruits, master McAstor, Sir Robert wants us all to go through the paces. Do ye know anything about pike men?'

Darragh shook his head. 'I've heard of such but I know little about their methods. Why?'

'It seems some may join us as allies in the spring.'

'Where from, do you know?'

Tim shook his head. 'I only know that a close friend of Sir Roberts will be arriving from the continent. At that time, he'll be bringing more Frisians and his own small army.'

'Frisians?'

'Aye, the black horses, they come from a place called Freisland, I don't know where that is, so don't ask!'

So! Now I knew the name of these majestic horses but it left me with so many questions.

19

# **GAWAIN**

T he wind was skirling through the woods and eddies of leaves were fluttering everywhere. I had six grooms under me care and three of us had the blacks out for their morning cantor. I was wearing a sheepskin vest under me wool cloak trying hard to keep warm. As I looked over the blacks, I spotted a string of Scots on their scruff ponies. They were a quarter mile off, coming from the woods and not looking our way. I warned me boys anyway. The blacks could easily outrun them but I wanted them no closer. I was thinking of turning us around and heading home when I spotted Sir Gawain approaching from the town with one other. He was conspicuous with his green scarf about his neck and he wore armor that wasn't seen in these parts very often. His mail had plate pauldrons over the shoulders and the back of his hands had metal strips, close together, forming a gauntlet rather than the mail mitten that was most common. His helm, hanging from the saddle, was a flat top, they had become popular during the last crusade and was still gaining in popularity. The eye slits were long and narrow, and with the welds, formed the cross of the Christ on the face. The whole front was full of tiny little holes fer breathing. His surcoat was plain white with a small harp emblem on the right breast.

He smiled as he rode up, his pale skin crinkling around eyes that were light grey. Iff'n he weren't a pure blooded Celt I'd eat me hat. 'I see ye saw the Scotties, Will. I'll ride back with ye, a show of force never hurt.'

'Thank ye milord yer company is most welcome.'

He pulled alongside me and rode stirrup to stirrup. 'We have never really met before, though I know who ye are. I am Gawain Cyllwillin and I hale from Wales.' He waved at his companion, who rode a little back at the blacks' quarter. 'This is Jarad Walster, me Squire.'

Jarad and I nodded greeting to each other, his florid face breaking into a smile. Once again, I felt flustered. Here was another knight speaking to me as an equal. I was a little tongue tied, not quite sure how to proceed.

Sir Gawain seemed to sense me unease. 'Ye know Will, ye saved the life of me best and closest friend, do not feel uncomfortable with me. I know ye were a swineherd, So? Me Pater ran sheep! He tended livestock same as ye, so ye see, we have more in common than ye think.' He gave me a shamefaced smile, 'Though we are rich and titled.' He leaned toward me, 'I returned two years past, from crusading and I saw things done in the name of the Christ that tore at me soul.

Sir Robert counseled me and brought me back from the abyss, he showed me a plan that I now live by.'

'What plan is that, Sir?'

'It will come to light anon, it is fer Sir Robert to explain.' By this time we were passing through the gates. 'I'll say this much Will, There is evil at work in this world but, I have learned, also great good. Look at yerself.' Gawain gave a parting wave and rode off, his squire in tow.

I smiled quietly to meself as I watched him go, and felt proud that people would be thinking of me in that way. Then I scratched me cheek as I remembered me da saying. "Be proud Will, even a little arrogance won't hurt yer but don't ever get smug." I sighed as I climbed down from me high horse. Truly, Storm was a high horse. He swung his head around and gave me a push on the shoulder as I loosened the girth. It was as if to say, get that silly thing off,n me and give me a good brushing. I shook meself out of dreaming and checked me grooms. They were all dismounted and tending their horses in a proper way. I was feeling hungry but first Storm needed his brushing.

One morning, I opened our door to be greeted by six inches of snow. It was still coming down and Darragh's prints were fading. He had left earlier. I looked about as large flakes came out of the dark to melt against me face. The air was so still sound traveled sharply upon it. The grumbling and whinnying of horses wanting attention, sounded like next door. I went and gave Tom's cot a kick.

'Get yer lazy arse out from under, Tom, it's time!' He greeted me with some incoherent grumbling as I left. I knew he would be along directly. This was the first of several days of light snow but it didn't change the schedule, first the horses, then breakfast and then training with Darragh. Me arms and shoulders were so sore, I didn't like him much. He soon realized that I showed little skill with the sword and so trained me with cudgel, quarterstaff and wood mans axe. I became a fair shot with a bow too, thanks to Tim's tutorship. Then it was the horses turn again. Each day, we ran the palfreys in a herd since there were too many to ride each one, besides some were not broke. Training them was me job and I loved it. It was like I could speak to them and they understood.

I tried to visit with Meg as much as I could and not as often as I would like. Each day was so busy. Supper was late, and once over the three of us would retire to our house, chat a bit over some cider and then fall into our cots.

# **RAGLIN**

This particular afternoon, the sun was shining bright and there was a bit of a melt. Two grooms were keeping me company and were walking off the palfreys after their run, the other grooms had gone to clean stables. The three of us were enjoying the warmth of the sun knowing it wouldn't last.

Sudden interruption came in the form of a frantic horse crashing out of the woods. It ran straight at me and I caught it straight off. I held its head and soothed it, its eyes were showing their whites and it was all lathered up.

'Easy horsey easy what happened to yer, hey?' I kept a tight downward pull on its bridle as I spoke soft and stroked its lathered neck. Slowly, it settled down. It was a scrub horse like the Scotts rode, small, rough haired and tough. One of the grooms was nearing and I called him over. 'Wipe him down, Joss, and walk him, would ye? I'm goin to back track him, something's happened.'

'Be careful, master Will.'

'Aye, I will be.' I was riding Storm, who was Sir Roberts' horse so I was very careful in the slippy snow. He knew how to handle it. The trees were thick and clumps of bramble and nettles were everywhere. The snow was covering everything like sheep's wool and every so often I would hear a plop in the woods as a branch released its burden. I'd bin backtracking fer a while when I felt a quiver go through Storm and heard low voices at the same time. I continued forward, loosening the laces holding me cudgel to the saddle. I heard someone moan and then saw a man standing in a hollow. It took a moment to realize that his feet were not touching the ground. He was hanging from a branch by his hair. I then spotted the others as they rose to their feet. Three young Scotts armed with shields and spears. The oldest looking, a burly lad, stepped toward me.

'Off with ye Brit, if ye knows what's good fer yer.'

'What have ye done to that poor lad?'

His grin was feral. 'He did it his self, and is our prisoner.' He raised his round shield. 'Now, piss off!'

'Ye have been torturing the lad, poking him with yer spears, hey? That's no way to treat a helpless man. Leave him and go yer way.'

He looked surly as he said, 'This was a sanctioned raid and ye have no right to interfere!'

'Sanctioned me arse!' I brought me cudgel up and rested it on me shoulder 'Don't test me Scottie, be off!'

He leveled his spear and I signaled Storm with me knee. He stepped forward and sideways at the same time, bringing me to bear. I swung the cudgel with an upward blow, smashing the shield edge back into his face. Blood spurted from his broken nose and mouth as he sat down hard on his backside. The other two backed up eyeing me, and the huge horse, warily.

'Pick up yer friend and get ye hence, there will be no more of this.' I said it with me most fierce scowl.

They did as they were told, and got their groggy friend to his feet, they half carried him to a nag and bundled him on it. Like shadows, they vanished into the snowy woods.

As I led Storm down to the hanging man, I realized he was not much more than a boy, perhaps fifteen years. He had a lot of hair, which got him into this trouble. It was cold, away from the sun and he was nearly unconscious. Storm took his weight and stood still while I reached into the tree. It was a bit of a struggle and I had to break some branches, before he was loose. He slumped forward in the saddle and luckily didn't fall off. I pulled him back against me shoulder and held him, letting Storm have his way. Me hands were getting sticky with his blood and I was worried that he would die on me. Finally, there was sunlight up ahead and we were back with the herd and very worried grooms.

'Thanks be that ye are alright, master Will. I was ready to send word to Sir Robert.'

'I'm fine Pat, Joss. Let's take this herd back home lads, this boy needs caring fer, right off!'

Not only was Meg a fine cook, she was a good nurse too. The first person we met, coming back, was Tim Cross. He saw straight away that the boy was in a bad way and fetched his auntie. She disrobed him and checked the wounds on his chest and shoulders. There were lots of them, some deep but none lethal.

Meg looked at me. 'What happened to him Will?'

I told her how I found him. 'They were poking and teasing him like some might tease a fox in a trap. I don't think they intended killing him, not right off anyway.'

Darragh joined us. 'Pat told me a little of what happened now I'd like to hear it from you.' He gave me shoulder a friendly squeeze. He watched as Meg carefully cut away the boy's hair all matted with bits of twig and branches and his scalp was bleeding and raw in places. I told him, in detail, what had happened. When I was finished telling, he studied me for what seemed like ages.

Finally, he sighed. 'What you did came out alright, but you were foolish to take on three unknowns by yourself. Never underestimate your enemy, Will. In the valley of Elah, a stripe of a lad brought the pride of the Philistines to his knees and beheaded him with his own sword. No Will, never underestimate an enemy, tall, short, fat or thin, each can fool yer just as vain Goliath was fooled.'

'Perhaps, like David, they underestimated me, Darragh.'

He laughed aloud and gave me a hard clout across the back of me head. 'Do it again and I'll have yer thrashed. Understand me lad?'

I rubbed me head ruefully frowning at Tims grinning face. He'd bin listening. I turned to look at Meg and the young man was awake, watching the goings on. Meg was just finishing putting ointment on his wounds, head and body.

I smiled down at him as I rubbed me head. 'How are ye feeling?' Meg looked up, she hadn't noticed him coming around.

His voice was a whisper. 'I feel like shite, could I have some water?'

She fetched it right off and he drank with relish. He winced a little when he moved and then looked at me. 'Am I a prisoner?'

'No, ye are not a prisoner, though ye may be here fer a while. Heavy weather is coming and ye'll be right sore fer a bit.' I looked over at Tim. 'Where will he stay? He could come in with us if Darragh and Tom can bear it.'

Darragh chuckled. 'It's fine with me and I'm sure Tom will go along. It will give me a chance to pick his brain.' He leaned towards the youth, 'What is your name lad, your full name.'

'Raglin Donclevy, sir.'

Lord Robert chose that moment to enter and his face broke into a smile. 'Will, Will, what have you brought me this time? You must be my guardian angel I'm sure. Since we met you've been my lucky charm.'

He beamed as he looked down at the young man. 'I've been trying to council with your father for some time. He's been very unreceptive till now. Taking care of you might put a wedge in his door.'

'Ye are Sir Robert aren't ye? Me Pater has some liking for what ye do but it is hard to gain his trust. He has been stung too many times. The last was a betrayal by the Bruce and me da foreswore him. With no faith in English royalty, either, he now stands alone, one more of the Border Rievers.'

Sir Robert nodded. 'Aye, the Bruce has been a thorn all over the north. After taking a ransom from the Abbot of Furness to leave off plundering, he sacked the abbey and the rest of the north anyway. Listen, as soon as this storm passes, I'll try to get word to your father that you are safe and decide how to get you home safely. In the meantime, I'll leave you in Wills charge, he will see to your comforts.' He turned to me, 'After supper, come to my quarters, I wish to speak with you.'

'Aye milord, I'll be there.'

Sir Robert was sitting near the fire with a shawl on his shoulders to fight the draft. His feet were up and toasting, his boots were laying beside him.

'Ah Will, come join me.' He pointed to a seat opposite him. 'Have a mug of mead and relax.' He poured with his own hand and passed it to me. It was hot and sweet with a strong but pleasant taste I didn't recognize. I could feel its warmth spreading through me.

He watched me sip at it for a moment. 'I have kept my eye on you, Will. You may be unlettered and unfamiliar with many things, but you are inquisitive, clever and forthright. Now tell me again of the circumstances leading to young Raglin being here.'

I told in detail what had taken place and when I was done, he stared at the fire, thinking.

'When you saw the lad hanging by his hair, what was your first thought?'

'I thought, its Absalom, the son of King David.'

Sir Robert smiled. 'So you know the Holy Bible?' He leaned towards me.

'Not by a long shot milord, I cannot read. Every Sunday, in our village, our friar, one Fra Simon, would give mass and then recite scriptures to us youngers. Sometimes it was stories from the Old Testament and sometimes the New Testament. I enjoyed listening to them and would repeat them to me da while we worked.'

'As I said, Will, you have a keen mind and I have a plan for you. I want you to learn to read and write, you will also learn geography and some history. Two hours a day during the winter months are to be allotted for this, besides your other duties. Spring and summer will be too busy. You will shelve the lessons during that time.'

I was stunned and couldn't believe me ears. Few men could read and write, even most knights and this was an unbelievable honor. All I could whisper was. 'Who will teach me, milord?'

'Sir Gawain has offered to teach you geography and history. Our friar, one Brother John, will do the writing and reading.'

'But Sir Gawain is a knight, why would he take the trouble?'

'It's enough said that he likes you and offered. You will learn that he is a complex man and his offer to you is unique. If he becomes too busy because of the times, the friar will take over' He sat back. 'So, Will, you will be educated and when you are I will explain more to you.'

'I have a question milord. What is this fortress town and why are we here?'

He smiled again. 'That's two questions Will! The town is called Haven and all I will tell you now is that I have a plan and when more friends arrive, we'll be moving. I will explain everything when that time comes. Go now and get some sleep, you are going to be a busy young man.'

I stood, bowed to him and left. My mind was spinning round and round and I didn't feel like sleep.

The first time I entered Sir Gawain's quarters, I was awed. He had things I'd never imagined, things from his travels. Tomes and rolled scripts everywhere.

He smiled at me. 'Please remove yer shoes Will. Feel free to look about, I'll be with ye in a moment.' I nodded and whispered, 'Yes milord,' as he vanished behind a curtain and spoke in low tones to someone, probably his squire.

I saw right off why I had to remove me shoes. Me feet weren't cold, in fact they were cozy. I looked down and was dazed by the beauty beneath me feet. I had never seen a carpet before, let alone one that looked like this. There were birds with long blue tails with eyes on them and large white birds with curved orange bills and groups of flowers with sharp petals were everywhere. They were all forming patterns on the floor and I had never imagined anything so grand. While I gazed in wonder at this beautiful thing I felt I was being watched. Sir Gawain had re entered and was standing quiet, watching me.

He frowned slightly, 'Removing yer shoes didn't make much improvement!'

I looked at me feet wondering what he meant.

'The carpet ye are standing on is from a place called Alexandria in Egypt. There are magnificent structures there, beyond our ken.' He saw the questioning look on me face and smiled again. 'I will show ye soon enough. He pointed to a wall. 'Look there!'

Once again I had me mouth gaping. I guessed the wall was twenty five feet long and twelve high. It was entirely covered by what looked like a tapestry, of what I had no idea.

I'll take a moment to tell ye of Sir Gawain as he steered me to the wall. He was an inch taller than me, I would learn later around five feet eleven, with extremely wide shoulders that almost made him look square and he had huge hands. His face was broad and flat with high cheekbones. light grey eyes gazed from under a strong brow and his skin was pale, not pinky white but the color of bone. His long black hair was tied back in a horsetail and He was wearing a loose blue robe a little like a habit and was bare foot. Looking at his feet and mine, I realized why he had said what he did. His feet were clean with trimmed nails and mine were filthy, the nails grainy and broken. He placed his hand on me neck and turned me head to the left. I could feel the strength in that hand.

'Ye are looking at a map of the world we live in, and where yer eyes are pointing is where ye and I abide.' He pulled a dagger from under his robe and used it as a pointer. There was an island with a slightly smaller one beside it. 'This is England, Wales and Scotland.' He pointed to each and then showed me where we were. 'There is Erin or Ireland with a vast sea beyond. Some say it tumbles away into the void if ye sail far enough. I don't believe that. Now look here on the other side of England, Will, that is where ye once lived and across that stretch of water, the North Sea, is Europe, a place of many countries, such as the Scandinavian group, and France, Germany, Holland, Italy and many more. Ye will soon discover how many.' He pointed at the south of England. 'France is the closest, just across that narrow body of water called the English Channel, and the straights of Dover.' He led me down the wall. 'This almost closed in sea is the Mediterranean and there, near its other end, is Egypt, home of the Nile, a vast river steeped in mystery. The empty looking area over here is mostly desert and Semite lands.' He pointed again. 'There is Jerusalem, the seat of our faith it is also claimed as a Holy city by the armies of Islam and the Jews. It is a stew pot and I think it will be so for generations to come.' He looked at me blank face and laughed out loud. 'I doubt ye'll remember a thing of what I said today. In time ye will and ye will know some history of these countries as well. Now hie ye to the chapel and find Brother John, he's waiting.'

I said me farewells to Sir Gawain and left with me brain spinning. I was walking on air, there was a big door in me small world and it was swinging wide.

# **BROTHER JOHN**

I found Brother John quick enough. He was at the back of the chapel sweeping the floor. I noticed right off that one arm was withered though he could use it to hold things, and he walked hunched and with a bad limp. It was his face that drew ye, Round with a button nose, eyes that sparkled and a mouth with a ready smile. I liked him right off. I found out later that he had bin crippled from birth and his mothers' love kept him alive. Later in his life, he chose to be a monk rather than a beggar.

'Ye must be Will. I have heard much about ye and am pleased to meet ye. Sir Robert bade me to teach ye to read and write. This I will try to do though I have never taught before.' He Smiled 'I expect, as time goes on, we will learn from each other? Over here, Will, I have a board set up, sit ye down there and we will start.' He made some scribbles on the board. 'This is what yer name looks like when it is written.' He handed me a piece of slate and a wedge of chalk. 'Now try to copy what ye see on me board.'

Me first line was a wiggly mess, even I could see that but I was so nervous.

'No no, Will!' He scratched his tonsured head. 'How do I do this?' He looked at me. 'Have ye ever tried to carve a piece of wood?'

'Aye I have and me da said I was fair at it.'

'Ye know how ye push yer knife for one thing and pull it for another? Yer movements are precise and controlled. It is the same here, ye pick yer angle and pull the chalk down and then push and then pull and so on.'

I'm sure me tongue was sticking out while I endeavored to do it. When I was done I could see the resemblance to the writing on his board.

He smiled and squeezed me shoulder. 'There Will, that is what yer name looks like in writing.'

I think I had a vacant grin on me face as I looked at me written name. Over the coming days me grin faded away as I did alphabets over and over and over.

Christmas was just around the corner when another mild spell of weather arrived, and Sir Robert knocked me up.

'Gawain said you were doing well in your lessons and gave his blessing, so you'll be riding with me Will. I'm taking this opportunity to return Raglin to his father. It will be about three days there and another three back so go get your kit together, I want to be back before the Advent.' He punched me in the arm with an almost mischievous grin. 'I'll be riding Storm, go find yourself another horse!'

I went to do his bidding, looking and feeling a little shamefaced I think. It was dawning that I was taking liberties that any other lord would frown on, even hang me fer. I discovered that twenty yeomen were going too. I raced about saying me goodbyes to Meg, Tom and Darragh. Darragh raised an eyebrow. 'Remember our little talk Will.'

I gave him me cheekiest grin. 'Aye I will.'

His look was ferocious. 'Remember, yer'll be back!'

I could tell he was trying not to smile.

I waited at the training grounds, with the twenty yeomen and Raglin, looking fer Sir Robert to arrive. Storm was saddled, ready and waiting. I had found meself a pretty, chestnut mare. She was swift and had a kind disposition. Tim wasn't going this trip. The burly yeoman Ross was in charge. Sir Robert finally came, accompanied by Brother John. He mounted Storm and sat with head bowed as brother John made the sign of the cross over us. He gave a customary benediction in Latin and then said, 'I pray that thy trip will be peaceful and successful and ye all return safely under Gods protection, amen.' With that he stepped back pulling his hood up against the cold.

With Sir Robert in the lead, our cavalcade passed through the gate tunnel with a clatter of hooves and the chinking of mail. A few people waved, sending us on our way.

On the trip, I took opportunities to speak with Raglin. Even though he had been living in the same house as me, I had seen little of him. Me day was taken up with so many things, I only had time fer eating and sleeping. Raglin had helped Tom at the forge and liked the work. Darragh had picked his brain as promised and spent a little time teaching him the sword. It was something he took to right well.

'Why didn't yer da come fetch ye? Word was sent.'

Raglin shrugged, 'He neer liked me much. Said I was a waste and born to hang. He'll be shocked when he sees me with me own sword.'

I couldn't help a small laugh. 'He got the born to hang right, but now that's over, ye are not a waste. Ye work hard and learn willingly, so what's yer da's problem?'

Raglin shook his head. 'Me big brother was killed in a Scottie raid and he died protecting me. Me Pater never forgave me, said it was me fault that Jamie died.'

'Grief often places blame in unfair places. I remember ye saying that yer da had become one of the Borderers, I've heard of them but don't know much. What are they?'

'There are a number of families on both sides, close to the border that got tired of abuse and heavy taxation by representatives of their crowns. They got nothing back and were always in the forefront, taking a beating, when there was fighting. They have withdrawn allegiance from their respective royals and now stand alone. They were soon called the Border Rievers and prey on each other and those nearby to make a living. Ye've heard of the Pardoones? one of the fiercest families, in their mountain stronghold. The respective Royals usually tolerate us because of our location. I told me Pater once that nothing changed with all the continuous fighting and we still stood in the way of invading armies. He didn't like to listen!"

# **ALEXANDER DONCLEVY**

We made good time and two and a half days saw us to Raglins home. It was a large blocky, four story house built from stone that almost looked like a stubby square tower designed to repel attack. Each floor had narrow slits for windows and the entrance consisted of a massive pair of doors with a sally port. As we neared, a sentry called an alarm and then there was silence. As we waited, the smaller sally port in one door creaked open, and three men on horseback cleared the building to approach us at a walk. The leader was a tall man with a cleanly shaven, long dour face, a hawks' beak of a nose and iron gray hair to his shoulders.

He spoke without preamble. 'Ye have returned me vagrant son to me. I thank ye for treating him well.'

Sir Robert pointed to me. 'You can thank him for your sons' life. He stood up to three and brought him back for healing. You must be Alexander Donclevy? I have a wish to speak with you. I am Sir Robert Arthur.' He extended his hand.

Donclevy nudged his horse closer and took Sir Roberts hand. 'Would ye join us fer supper and spend the night? We have not a lot but ye are welcome to what we have. We can talk the whole night through if ye wish.'

I took time to take in me surroundings while food was prepared. The ground floor was fer the horses and hay ricks, so there was always a strong smell of piss throughout.. One big bonus was that the horses threw off a lot of heat and kept most of the house quite comfortable. Men at arms and laymen shared the second floor along with a mess and storage rooms. The third was the main kitchen and dining room, and the lairds family and guest quarters. The forth was a large open area with archers slits and oil barrels to toss on an enemy and fire pits for burning arrows and torches. The inner walls were racked with weapons, sheaves of arrows and extra mail.

Supper was passed and the gentlemen had disappeared behind closed doors. Raglin and I had our feet up by the fire with mugs of ale in our hands. I studied him a bit, when he wasn't watching. He was a nice looking lad now that his hair was re grown proper. His wounds had healed though he would show the red scars for some time to come.

'How was it that ye were where I found ye? Ye were a bit from home.'

He raised his head from staring in the fire. 'There's a Lass I'm sweet on, she lives near to ye in a hamlet. I was making me way home after a pleasant dalliance, when I realized I was being followed. I led them a merry chase for a day and a bit round and round, trying to lose them in the woods. That's when I got meself into trouble. I overheard that they were a part of a bigger party returning from a raid. After that I must have passed out because I don't remember very much till ye came.'

I shook me head. 'Ye traveled that far to see a lass? She really must be special! The weather could have trapped ye too, never mind hostiles.'

He looked a little glum. 'I know ye are right!' His face brightened. 'But when ye are horny it overcomes all good judgment.'

I couldn't help but laugh. I took a swallow of me ale. 'Yer a knucklehead! Ye enjoyed working with Tom? I know he liked the help.'

'Aye, I really did! If me Pater would allow it, I'd return in the spring and ask Tom for an apprenticeship.'

Sir Robert chose that moment to enter. 'You lads still up? You'd better get some sleep Will, it's late and we leave early.'

I got up from me chair. 'Did ye accomplish yer mission Sir?'

Sir Robert smiled. 'Aye!'

That's all he said, so I hied it fer bed, trying not to wake anyone.

Next morning, at first light, I was on the fourth floor with one of the sentries. There was a soft mist on everything. I was watching sheep being herded by cleaver dogs when, in the distant haze, I spotted something unusual. It looked like an obelisk, disappearing high into the mist. 'What is that?'

'That monolith? It's something the Britons of yore put up, why? I have no idea. I think the Scotties hurdle it, too and fro as they do Hadrian's Wall, or what's left of it.'

I grinned, 'It would be quite a hurdle, even with the wind up yer kilt.'

He laughed. 'Aye it would!' He looked down the stairs. 'I just heard the bell, me relief is on his way and breakfast is waiting.'

'I'd best be off and get something to eat meself. Me lord will be leaving soon.' We nodded our goodbyes and I left.

I raced down the flight, and almost ran headlong into Alexander Donclevy. I avoided hitting him outright by spinning to one side. I could feel meself losing me balance when his hand caught me and steadied me up.

'Careful laddie, ye'll nigh sweep us all to our deaths. What's yer hurry?'

'I'm so sorry sir, I was in a rush to prepare for Sir Roberts departure.'

He hurrumphed and said. 'I was looking for ye anyway. I wished to thank ye personally for saving Raglin and this is for ye. We'll not be speaking of this again, I have me place and ye have yers. Now be off!'

I just about fell down the next flight staring at what he had placed in me hand, it was a dirk fit for a nobleman, with a bear head wrought in silver on the pommel. It lay in a sheath of black cowhide strapped with copper. It was the finest thing I'd ever owned. I looked back up the stairs but he was gone. I pulled it from its sheath, the blade shining softly in the twilight. It was razor sharp on two edges and tapered into a sharp point. Holding it at arms' length, I couldn't wipe the smile off me lips and then a sharp call galvanized me back to reality.

Ross was looking up the stairs, his fingers drumming on the rail. 'Hop to it lad, ye'll be late! Have ye had breakfast? Ye'd better find something to carry, no time to sit.' He saw what I was holding and his lips pursed into a low whistle. 'What have ye there?'

I held it out to him. 'It was a gift, isn't it fine?'

'Aye, it truly is fine, it looks to be Celtic.' He grabbed me neck and gave me a friendly push 'Now move yer arse, get grub to go and be outside in five minutes.'

I made it. As we turned our horses to leave, Raglin came running up. 'Will, Will! Tell Tom I'll be there soon after Easter. Me Pater has given his blessing.'

Sir Robert overheard and as I gripped Raglins hand, he raised an eyebrow and said, 'Another smith?'

I smiled, 'Aye milord.' I took a position just behind Ross and looked back. Alexander Donclevy was standing at a top floor arrow slit watching us go. I waved and I'm sure he gave me the slightest of nods even though he was half hidden in shadow. As we rode, one of the waggons right behind me and was making funny cooing noises from under a tarp. I raised an eyebrow at Ross and pointed with me head.

'They're pigeons Will, homing pigeons fer sending messages.'

Our trip home was uneventful and I was soon immersed in me old routine, studies and all. I was now careful to wash me feet and other things. Sir Gawain taught me much about things other than history and geography.

Personal cleanliness is not a priority amongst many throughout Europe and England but it is much more so in the near east, especially those in the noble and wealthy classes. He told me of houses and palaces filled with flowers and birds. There were pools for bathing and silken and fine linen robes for wearing. The ones he always wore at home were such. He had chosen to take some of their best customs for himself, even though they were the enemy.

'Always know yer enemy, Will. Not just on the field of battle but how he lives from day to day. He can teach ye much if yer willing to notice. A time may come when ye both wish to sue fer peace and if ye know his ways it gets easier. Bathing has become a pleasure fer me and I don't catch cold or the chills, as most would have ye believe.'

Brother John and me had become close friends as well as teacher and pupil. He was a kind man who tried every day to live in Jesus' light and he had a love fer animals, like me. He raised bunnies and chickens and was an accomplished beekeeper. He promised to teach me about them in the spring when they woke up. Me writing was improving every day and I could do some adding and subtraction. I even knew me multiplication tables and felt right proud of meself.

Christmas came and we attended Mass each day of the Advent. Christmas Day was devoted to a early long Mass celebrating the birth of the Christ child and then the preparing for a huge supper that would include everyone in the town. The courtyard was bedecked with holly and evergreen branches and a mistletoe arch was built in the center so those who wished, could snatch a kiss under the watchful eyes of everyone. Sir Robert and his personal friends and retinue ate at the round table but the food served was the same for everyone, in and out.

Outdoor kitchens had been set up, under the supervision of Meg and her covey of young women. Spits were turning with geese, ducks and pheasants dripping grease into the flames. Then there was beef, venison and wild boar. An abundance of fish was waiting to be broiled or boiled along with many vegetables such as beets, turnips mushrooms and carrots. Dried peas were turning into soup along with cut up hams. The smells were wonderful.

English cooking had changed since the crusades. Spicy foods and exotic flavors were much in demand amongst the gentry. The serfs did not benefit from this cooking renaissance they weren't even permitted onions, shallots or leeks. These were reserved for the lords table. All these could be found in the wild but ye broke the law under pain of disfigurement or death.

Sir Robert was nonesuch. He shared with all and frowned on the barbarism of his peers. Darragh, Tom and me were invited to his own table and I felt truly honored.

It was snowing again when we left our hut and made our way to the main house. The flakes were large and fluffy and seemed to muffle the sharp sounds of barking dogs and romping children. We were watching a sea of happy faces, when suddenly, Tom stopped dead in his tracks.

I heard the giggling of several girls and Tom said, 'That's Cora.'

How he knew that was beyond me, but it was. She was chatting and laughing with two other lasses that I recognized. Mary and Colette, a French girl, they both worked in the kitchen. As soon as Cora saw Tom they had eyes for only each other. I knew they had been off smooching with each other on other occasions and the mistletoe must have looked inviting.

I grabbed his arm 'come on Tom, we'll be late.'

Darragh was chuckling as he took his other arm and we lifted and turned him in the right direction.

Cora called after him with a cheeky grin. 'I'll be serving yer special after supper.'

We squirmed our way through the bustle with smiles and waves and finally reached the main entrance. We had just bin greeted by a friendly yeoman when the alarm horn at the main gate sounded. I think we all looked equally stunned and then galvanized into action. I raced to ready horses, if needed, and Darragh joined Sir Robert who strode out of the house with Sir Gawain and was closely followed by several yeomen.

Sir Robert spoke with Tim and a runner from the gate, giving me time to bring the horses round.

Pat met me with two blacks saddled and ready. Storm greeted me with a soft grunt. Running between those two high steppers, their hooves echoing off the cobbles, was a treat in itself. Sir Robert mounted Storm with a nod of thanks.

'Stay close to Darragh, will you? Watch his back, you and Tom both!' With that curt missive, he nudged the black into a cantor, towards the gate. Sir Gawain, mounted on the second, was close on his heels. Tom and I ran with Darragh and the yeomen, as we ran Tom handed me me cudgel and gave swords to Darragh. We accepted the weapons, gratefully. We had been dressed for dinner, not a possible fight.

# **Skye**

The falling snow partially obscured the party of horse standing before the gate. I had followed Sir Robert up the steps to the battlement and was now looking down on them. There was Skye in his armor and Garrad in his black leather, backed by forty men.

I whispered to Sir Robert. "These are Darragh's bane!"

He gave me a slight nod and bent over the parapet. "What do you wish at this time of festivity?"

That freckled face looked up and that slit of a mouth opened. "I bring greetings from my father, Krayan McOrdred and ask leave to enter at this time of celebration." His voice had a sibilant sound to it that gave me shivers.

"You may enter with five of your men. The rest will stay outside the gate and will be given food and drink in celebration of the Advent." Sir Robert signaled and the sally port was opened' it was big enough for men on horseback to pass in single file.

Skye and Garrad and four others entered and the port slammed shut. Sir Robert descended the stairs to give him formal welcome and then the whole troop headed back to the manor. We were careful to stay in the background so as not to draw undue attention to ourselves but Skye's eyes seemed to find us anyway.

Everyone seated at the table were well into dinner. Skye sat between Sir Robert and Sir Gawain, and I sat across the circle facing them. Black Garrad was right beside me, and I now realized just how big he was. At least six foot five and about seventeen to eighteen stone. His boiled leather reeked from his own sweat and the blood and tears of others. I instinctively knew this was a deadly adversary without qualms or pity. I could feel me hands shaking a bit as we ate in silence. Next to me, on me left, was Tom, then Darragh, who was watching Skye with an intensity that was felt by us all. Tom made a feeble attempt to strike up a conversation with him but was ignored.

He turned to me with a shrug and I whispered 'Let it be Tom, Just be ready- fer anything.'

He gave me a slight nod and got his fingers and mouth greasy with a piece of goose. If anything, the tension seemed to be growing across the room. Skye's voice was rising, high pitched in anger.

'My father has every right to arrest him and it's my sworn duty to act in my father's place.' He waved his hand in Darragh's general direction, 'That man is a traitor and murderer and will pay for his crimes when I return him to Ireland.'

'Darragh McAstor is an enemy of your family only and for good reason. He is not a traitor to his country and he is not a murderer.' Sir Robert leaned towards Skye for emphasis, 'He is under my protection and is going nowhere!'

'Then ye force me to take him!' Skye jumped up, spilling ale everywhere. His sword was half out of its scabbard when Sir Gawain grasped his arm in a vise like grip that made Skye blanch. Garrad crashed to his feet, chair flying, to defend his master. Two swords were at his throat before he could take another step. Tim and Ross had been ready. The other four were facing drawn bows. Darragh was on his feet with a dirk in his hand and Tom was pushing him back into his seat. I was still groping fer me cudgel under me chair.

Sir Robert was furious. I had never seen him so angry. 'You dare attempt to assail me and mine in my own home after I welcomed you in! We broke bread with you Mc Ordred, now take your men and go before I completely lose my patience and have you tossed into the goal.'

I could see Skye seething and fuming, as he, and his men were escorted to the city gate and put out like delinquent boys. He turned back towards the closing gate, his horse rearing up. 'I'll be back! I'll be back with an army, and my father. You will all burn! I will be back.' With that he turned and they fled into the dark.

It was mid morn the day after Christmas Day and I had just given Sir Robert a tally of newly tamed horses, when news of a dark crime came. He listened intently to the visibly shaken yeoman, who spoke in low tones to him. Sir Robert became quite pale, gripped the man's shoulder as if looking for confirmation and then disappeared into the house. The call to stations came about fifteen minutes later. Tim called out a list of men to prepare mounts. 'Darragh, ye are with me. Will, prepare a wagon. Load it with barrels of oil, four should suffice and bring Fra. John. We depart as soon as all is ready.'

Sir Robert appeared astride Storm. Pat must have prepared the horse because I hadn't had time. The party left at a canter, hooves clattering in the short tunnel, and I brought up the rear with the waggon, giving Tom a wave as we swept out the gate. Poor brother John was getting jounced around as I tried to keep up with the cavalcade. A foot of snow sparkled under a bright sun and blue sky and I was squinting against the brightness when the muffled drumming of horses hooves in the snow turned me head. Sir Gawain and thirty yeomen swept by at full gallop. His face was grim as he gave us a small salute. He caught up to the head of the cavalcade and slowed enough to say a few words to Sir Robert before continuing on.

We arrived at a cottage and everything seemed to become shadowed, it was as if God had turned His face from this place. Grim faced yeomen were guarding the perimeter, why, I didn't yet know. Ye could hear the frantic bleating of goats in the rear, they sounded so much like crying bairns. Sir Robert dismounted and went inside it wasn't long before he staggered out. A Yeoman steadied him and helped him sit, his face hidden in his hands. I don't know why but I had a need to see and yet I was so frightened. I jumped from the wagon, leaving Father John to his own devices, and went to the door. What I saw and smelled in the gloom will never leave me mind. Something cold and clammy brushed me and I pushed it aside with me arm. It felt like a sticky rope. As my eyes adjusted, I couldn't believe the horror I was seeing. I have butchered many animals, I have buried a village-family and friends, but nothing prepared me fer this. The ropes were intestines pulled straight and festooned about the interior with arms and legs tied in like decorations. Three torsos swayed up there, looking like grotesque plucked chickens, and three heads sat on a table in the center of the room. One was slightly forward, it was Cora, who's dead face was twisted in a silent scream of terror. I recognized her and sat down hard on the floor, me legs just wouldn't support me. She had been such a sweet young lass. The other two heads were her younger sister and her mother. I could feel me gorge risin and needed to get away. I tried to rise and found meself stuck in a pool of clotting blood. I tore meself loose and somehow floundered to the door. It swung a bit and I realized that a man was hanging from nails driven through his hands. He must have had to watch the cruel butchery before his throat was slit. I fell outside, into Darraghs arms. Seeing me stricken face, he pulled me head to his chest and held me. All I could mumble was, 'A foul demon did this it had to be a demon!'

Sir Robert came out of his stupor and clutched me arm. 'Poor Will, why did you go in?'

I stared at him, me eyes finally fillin with tears. 'Why should it only be ye that has to live with a vision so terrible, Sir.'

He studied me for a moment, made a slight nod. 'I will see to it Will, that you are at my side when justice is done. Try and clean yourself up, when we are all present I plan a service for these poor souls.'

A yeoman led me to a rill behind the cottage and I washed the blood off as best I could. If anything, the bleating of the goats grew louder and higher as they smelled the blood. As I washed in the icy water something changed inside me, a coldness settled in me to carry till a day of retribution came nigh. I returned to the throng by the cottage and took me place beside Darragh. The yeomen had poured oil over the entire hut, inside and out. Under the guidance of a visibly shaken brother John, we began to pray. Torches were set and fire engulfed the hut with a swoosh, flames reaching high into the sky. A hymn was sung and then we chanted the psalm of David. After, we all stood silent, with heads bowed, until there was naught but ashes left.

The goats needed to be looked after and Brother John accompanied me to their pen. Over all the bleating I heard some soft wimpering. A short search produced a large wolf hound with a long deep gash down its flank. He had crawled into a corner to die. I didn't want that to happen, I know it was only a dog but there had been enough death here already. I looked up at Brother John.

'He must have tried to defend his family can ye help me get him on the waggon?'

'Aye, I'll be back with it, directly.'

The dog was licking me hand when he returned and we lifted the dog into the waggon. I informed Sir Robert and he ordered a Yeoman to remain until we returned with dogs and horses to herd the goats.

As soon as we got back, I told Meg about what had happened, not everything, only that the whole family had been murdered. She was pale and in tears when she brought needle and twine. Brother John had given the animal a potion that had knocked him out and had shaved the hair away from the wound.

Meg immediately started stitching. 'We must tell Tom before he hears of it elsewhere. Shall we do it together?'

'Aye, I'll tell him. He'll need some comforting though and ye would be better than me.'

Meg finished her stitching and we got a bandage around the dog. In a moment of genius, Brother John got some of his bee keeping mesh and tied it over the wound so the animal couldn't worry at the bandage. Now we had to sit back and wait.

We found Tom straight off and sat him down. He took the news as expected, badly! Meg took his head to her shoulder and cradled him as he sobbed. I cried too, seeing me friend suffer so. We had lost so much and now he had lost more. Darragh came and sat with us, just quietly, saying nothing. His presence was comforting.

I wiped me tears away. 'I have to leave ye Tom. There are goats to fetch and a pen to prepare.'

Tim arrived that moment and said. 'Take them to Bartons' croft near the gate. He has sheep and can care for these too. I'll send him word. Three men and palfreys are ready when ye are, dogs too.'

'Thank ye Tim. I squeezed Toms shoulder. "See ye later me friend.'

He grabbed me hand like he didn't want to let go. I gently disengaged meself and Meg gave me a nod as I left.

The Yeoman was glad to see us. Being alone in that awful place didn't suit him, what with demons and awful things, and he was very glad to be leaving. The dogs were well trained and herded the goats back to the croft without much help from us. We just rode along giving a little guidance, once in a while. The yeoman stayed with us getting some comfort from our company. We did a count and came up with sixty nine goats. I marked the number down on a tally to give the quartermaster for his records.

Mr Barton was a portly man with a ruddy face and a salt and pepper beard. A woman and two young lads sat by their the huts door, watching. We were welcomed with a smile, though he turned grim at the news. He appeared a little nonplussed at the number of goats.

'I will have to build another pen.'

'Do ye have the material? If ye do, I will help!'

'Aye I do and yer help would be most welcome.'

We laid out a pen and I started digging postholes. I was surprised to see Tom arrive. He looked very grave and sad.

'Why are ye here Tom? Ye should be resting.'

'I need to do something Will. Please let me help. I want to be near a friend and I need to do something!'

'Would ye lay out the rails?'

Tom nodded 'Gladly.'

The pen was built in a short day and Barton was most gratified. He didn't have to help at all. We left him to pen the goats, and returned, in silence, to our house. Darragh was there, getting ready for supper.

'You have been busy, Will. It has been a very long day and you have filled it with a lot.'

'I welcomed being busy Darragh. Now I want to ask ye, will ye give me another chance learning the sword?'

Darragh stared at me. 'Why, this sudden change?'

'I have a feeling and I need to try'

'Come, let's all go to supper. You can start training tomorrow.'

Supper was quiet and subdued. Tom sat between us getting some comfort from our presence. Today's ugliness sat like a pall over us all. Oblivion in sleep would be good. I hoped Tom and me could sleep.

I did sleep, and after an early breakfast of porridge, Darragh and me walked together to the training ground. I learned from him that Sir Gawain had chased after Skye's band. There was little hope of catching him before he took to the sea but the main goal was to keep him moving so he couldn't stop to commit more atrocities along the way.

For reasons I can't fathom, the sword felt different in me hand. Darragh noticed right off, I could tell by his raised eyebrow. His training was stiff and he brooked no nonsense. First the presentation and the high stance, some called the falcon. Then came the strokes, leading off with the defensive ones, then the offensive ones. The sword I was using was weighted and by the time me session was over me arms and shoulders burned. I thought me self to be fit, and now I had found a different set of muscles. However, I discovered an affinity with the weapon that I would never have believed possible, I'd had no use for swords in the past.

On the third morning, I was deep in me training when Sir Gawain returned. He left his troops under the care of sergeant Ross and trotted over to us. I could feel his eyes as I went through me paces.

'I thought ye had no liking for the sword? Ye seem to be doing rather well!' He dropped down from his charger and landed lightly, as if his armor and mail weighed nothing. He walked over beside Darragh. 'Don't stop on me account Will, keep training, I want to see yer moves.' He turned to Darragh. 'A bit clumsy but shows promise.'

Darragh smiled. 'Don't let him hear you Sir, his head is fat enough already.' He sobered. 'How did your trip go, Sir?'

Gawain grimaced. 'Well enough I suppose. We chased him to the sea and were close enough to see his ship hieing fer the Isle of Man and then Ireland. That brutish fiend has much to answer fer and trust me, he will answer.' He turned back to me. 'Keep it up lad, I'll see ye tonight fer yer lessons.'

I managed to pant out an 'Aye milord.'

# **GORDIE**MIRIAM**

Days past and by mid January winter took us in a vise like grip. Temperatures dipped and everything froze solid. There wasn't a lot of snow, maybe two feet but what there was became hard and crunchy, slicing at the horses fetlocks something awful. We managed to clear the training ground and lists and ran them in circles for the time being. The cart horses wore wrappings around their lower legs.

It was the morning of January twenty first, I had reason to remember that date well. I was up on the wall enjoying the bright sun me eyes watering from the sparkling glare, when I was alerted by a guards challenge. I wiped me eyes clear to espy a waggon at the gate with three figures so bundled up ye couldn't make out who was who. The two horses were ready to drop and stood trembling.

The person with the reins threw back his hood. It was an elderly man with a long beard, likely in his early fifty's. 'My daughter and I and one other ask for your hospitality' then as an afterthought, 'We are Jews.'

A grating voice said 'I'm not!' and a second cowl was thrown back.

I was looking at a face that I would grow to hate in the coming weeks. The man looking up had yellow hair, yellow eyes and yellow teeth showing through a smile that was empty and twisted.

The guard signaled below. 'Open the gate let these travelers in.'

I hied down to help with the horses. They needed immediate attention. When I arrived, Ross who was watch commander was addressing the newcomers. The old man was trying to get down from the waggon. he was very stiff and Ross lent him a hand. I turned, to offer assistance to the third person, who took me hand and dropped lightly beside me. A woman's voice said. 'Father, are you alright?' She squeezed me hand in thanks and ran to him taking his arm around her shoulders.

Ross looked over at the yellow hair, 'What's yer name?'

'Gordon White, everyone calls me Gordie.' That empty simpering smile creased his face again.

I could tell Ross didn't like him any more than I did. 'Do ye have any money? No beggars here.' He turned to the couple. 'How is it he is with ye?'

The woman's voice was soft and melodic. 'His horse had died and he was nearly frozen when we found him two days ago.'

Gordie sneered, 'I didn't know they was Jews.'

I turned toward him but Ross was there first. 'Ye get one warning about that kind of talk. Any of us hears it again and ye'll be tossed out of town, cold or no cold! Now, again, do ye have money?'

Gordie tried to look contrite with little success. 'No! I have no money, but I can work and I know how to handle horses. I ask for sanctuary.'

All I could think was 'O shite.'

Ross glared at him. 'If it was me say, ye'd be back out that gate, but it's not me say.' He called a guard over. 'Take this man to Sir Robert's secretary, or Tim, whoever ye can find. He has asked for sanctuary and that's Sir Roberts say.' He turned back to the couple. 'Do ye have any money? I have to ask because we can't be swamped with beggars and freeloaders.'

'We have a little, enough to rent a small shop if you can point us in the right direction. My father is a tailor and I help him. His hands are stiffening up a bit.'

Ross smiled. 'And what is yer name sir?'

'I am Joseph and my daughter's name is Miriam. Our last name is Duselbaum but we rarely use it.'

'I can understand why. Look, if ye follow this road till ye are behind that very large fort like building, ye will find an area full of artisans and I know there are two or three shops fer rent. When ye get there ask around for Jack Plum, he'll assist ye.'

I piped up, 'I'll show ye the way and then take care of yer horses, A little warmth and some feed will perk them right up.'

I knew Jack Plum by sight, though we had never actually met. I was able to take them right to him and left them to haggle over a place. The woman threw back her cowl and thanked me for me help. She was beautiful. I had never seen anyone that beautiful. Me eyes were full of black shiny wavy hair. Dark eyes, red lips and white teeth as she smiled at me. Me legs felt like rubber and I thanked god I was sitting on the waggon seat. I stuttered something about feeding the horses and waggon and bringing them back when they were fed. I gave the reins a flick and fled down the street. Her sweet laughing voice followed me, 'Don't let the waggon eat too much.'

I fed the horses but they needed rest so I left them in their warm stall. I was walking on pins and needles wanting another look at Miriam. 'Miriam', her name danced around me head and I couldn't get her face out of me mind. All me chores were done, I had even gone through me paces with Darragh and I realized I had time to take the waggon back. After all, their possessions were on it and they would need them. I hitched up one of our teams and headed to the Wall Street, as it was called by the locals. I trotted out of the stable area only to bring the palfreys to a rearing halt. This Gordie fellow stood in me way.

'I was told to work at the stables, to run things when ye aren't around.' He smiled that ugly smile that was more like a leer.

'I don't think so, I have a man on that job already, and ye can report to him. His name is Pat and he is in the first barn with the blacks.'

He shrugged. 'I'm only repeating what I was told.'

'Who told ye?'

'Sir Robert.'

I think I must have look surprised but then realized what better name to bandy about. No one was going to trouble him and double check. This arse hole would bear watching.

'I see ye have the Jew waggon there. Wanting a free shag do ye?' He snickered.

I turned white with anger and jumped the palfreys forward, almost running him down. He skipped back to get out of the way, his smile turning to alarm. Now I was looking straight down at him and could have taken him by the throat. 'Any more ugly stuff spews from yer mouth and I'll stomp on ye like the vermin ye are.'

His hand dropped to his dirk. Tim chose that moment to show up. 'What's going on here?'

Gordie simpered, 'Just trying to do me job Sir.' He grabbed a nearby fork and headed fer the barn.

Tim gave me an inquiring look and shook his head slightly as if to say 'what?'

I grinned at him. 'Me bed of roses just grew some thorns.'

He chuckled, 'Good luck to ye Will.' and strode off.

I flicked the reins and got the horses moving. I was still fuming and certainly wasn't in the best of moods and tried to snap out of it. I arrived at the artisan area and spotted Jack. 'Afternoon to ye master Jack, where did the young woman and her da take up shop?'

He winked and pointed to a bend in the road, 'Just around the corner.' He turned back to chatting with some people sitting on a bench.

I came around the corner and there she was, leaning back against the door frame, catching a bit of winter sun. I could feel meself getting flustered and tried hard to get under control.

'I'm so glad you brought the waggon back, all we own is on it.'

I felt flushed, 'I'm so sorry, I should have left the waggon here and just taken the horses.'

'Do not concern yourself I'm glad you cared enough about the horses to look after them. They were flagged when we got here and wouldn't have lasted more than a few hours in that cold.'

'Ye were very much at risk too ye know.' I started to get down from the waggon and she took me elbow. I felt a thrill run through me and tried to smile me thanks.

'Would you be so kind as to help me unload? My father has not recovered from the trip yet. He is in the back room lying on some cushions the landlord was kind enough to lend us.'

'Of course I'll help.'

The next hour or so was spent unloading and placing stuff where she wanted it. We often brushed arms or shoulders passing each other in doorways and such and I loved it. I was surprised how much stuff was on that wagon, not just their belongings but furniture too. Two cots, a table and chairs a wardrobe and a loom along with other stuff. One of the last things I brought in, was a heavy chest bound in brass.

She opened it and showed me. It was his tailoring stuff, needles, threads and several pairs of scissors that I had never seen before, though I knew of them. There were bolts of cloth as well as a box full of fancy buttons that was fun to look through. One bolt caught me eye. I touched it,

'This feels like Egyptian linen.'

Miriam looked startled. 'How could you know such a thing?'

I proceeded to tell her about Sir Gawain and me education and she listened with rapt attention.

'I knew there was something special about you when we first met.' She grinned cheekily, 'You actually smelled good.'

I blushed and hid me confusion by saying, 'As days go by ye''ll find that Sir Robert and Sir Gawain are very unique persons who have brought out the best in those around them. I was a swineherd and now I am steward of horse and I am being educated by Sir Roberts' instruction.'

Miriam gave me a warm smile. 'I am very pleased to meet you, Steward of horse.'

I swallowed a lump. 'Would ye mind if I called on ye again?'

Miriam touched me hand. 'I love your Yorkshire accent. Yes Will, please do, and perhaps you could show me around town and, where you work. Now, can I bring you some cider to quench your thirst?'

I nodded, 'That would be nice Miriam.' Her name felt so wonderful on me tongue. Two meetings and I knew I was in love.

A quavering voice from the next room asked for cider too. I got up and followed Miriam into the bedroom. She had already put up a drape to divide the room in two. Pulling it aside, she said

'You're awake, papa! I'll get you some right away.'

She brushed past me with a smile and I realized how tiny she was. Her head came up to just above me armpit.

'How are ye today sir?' I grinned, 'Are ye warm yet?'

'Yes finally.' He shivered a little. 'Please call me Joseph. You have done us a great kindness young man and we are in your debt.'

I shook me head. 'No Joseph, no debt is owed to me, what I did is what we all do here, look out for each other. That doctrine comes right down from Lord Robert himself.'

Miriam returned to kneel beside her da and handed him a bowl of cider which he proceeded to sip with relish. 'I was very thirsty, thank you my dear.'

'We are so lucky papa. Ask Will how he arrived here, it's fascinating.'

I sipped me own bowl and started me story at the beginning, the death of me village. These were things she hadn't heard yet and they both listened intently until I was done. I didn't mention the evil at Christmas, not yet. There was time enough for that and they would likely hear about it from neighbors.

Joseph stared up at me. 'So, you saved Sir Roberts life?'

'So they say, though I think the yeomen saved us both.'

I realized the shadows in the room were getting long. I got to me feet. 'It's late and I have things to do. I'll take me leave now. May I call on ye again?'

'Certainly young man, come visit whenever you wish.'

As I left, I heard Miriam whisper. 'I definitely want him to visit again.'

I was walking on clouds, as I led the palfreys down the street. I grinned like an idiot at every one I met.

I fed and brushed the palfreys down and bedded them fer the night. As I was heading to me quarters I met Pat.

'Who is that shit head working with us, Will? He thinks he's running things just like that and I don't know where me and the others stand.'

'I'm sorry Pat, I should have dealt with this sooner but I'm not sure just how to go about it. You are still me second, no matter what he says. He is playing games with our heads but he is nowhere as smart as he thinks he is. He told me he had it straight from Sir Robert that he was taking yer place. I know Sir Robert, he would never have done anything that way. This Gordie is living in his own world of lies and deceit and we will have to trap him in his own words. Don't get into a fight with him, Pat, unless it is self defense. From now on we will have another groom nearby listening in, preferably out of sight. That way it's not just our word against his.' I rubbed me chin with me hand, I'd never talked this long before. 'So far no great harm is done but I have a feeling he'll be trying sabotage next so watch it.'

'I'm glad I met ye Will. I'll put the other grooms on alert. I know they are all loyal to ye.'

I took his arm. 'Are ye goin to supper? We can walk together. I'll let Tom in on it too, just so he'll recognize bullshit when he hears it.'

Gordie was just ahead so we shut up. He turned as we approached and gave us that blank sneer of a smile. 'Nice to see yer Will, I fed and brushed the blacks while ye were gallivanting about.'

I could feel me gorge rising but kept cool. 'Thanks Gordie but the blacks are me domain, me and whomever I delegate. I don't consider ye ready fer them yet, after all I know nothing about ye.'

His face turned sour. 'Fuck you! We'll soon see who is ready.' With that he stormed off into the mess.

I watched as he tried to sit with the yeomen and then with the grooms. There didn't seem to be any room. He wound up sitting with Darragh, poor Darragh. I gripped Pats shoulder. 'Talk to the boys, I'm goin to save a friend.' I left Pat grinning as I went to sit with Darragh-- and Tom,who had just arrived and was giving Gordie an odd look. The three of us were soon chatting while we ate leaving Gordie out on the cold fringes. He didn't bother finishing all his supper and left early. I soon brought Darragh and Tom up to date on the recent happenings.

I visited Miriam and her father as much as possible. With me work load, it wasn't as much as I would like. Miriam and I became close friends. I was definitely in love with her but kept it to meself for the time being. I found I could talk to her about private things that I didn't share with anyone else, not even Meg. Her father was a kind man and hospitable but sometimes I caught him looking at us with a sad expression.

Meg seemed happy for us though she too seemed concerned about something, what I don't know.

I got knocked up early one morning. It was pitch black out and Pat met me with a lantern.

'Ye'd better come along quick Will, one of the blacks is real sick. He's got the bloats and I can't get him to his feet.'

'Shite!' we both ran for the barn. We tried and tried to get the horse to his feet but it wasn't happening. 'What's the matter with him? It's not the bloats but something else.' I went and checked his feed. Firstly, way too much oats, and then I spotted a pale piece of something. It was a bit of mushroom. I ran me fingers through the feed and found other pieces showing red stamen underneath.. 'Son of a bi...Pat he's been poisoned! Check the other feed boxes right off, it's some sort of mushroom.'

Pat took off, calling to another groom in the aisle. He was back quite quickly. 'The others are alright, Will. Normal amounts of feed. The animals are behaving normal, no mushrooms. Joss has gone to warn the others and to check the palfreys.'

With Pats help, I tried to purge the horse but to no avail. Around mid morning the animal started to thrash about in pain then got quiet, then still.

I checked for breath and pulse. 'He's gone Pat, this was done deliberately and we know who. We can't prove it so keep yer council, just be aware and take nothing for granted. I'm going to tell Sir Robert that I lost one of his chargers.'

Sir Robert was very angry and just about bit me head off. 'You are in charge of the stables, Will. You are responsible for the well being of all my horses, now tell me why you shouldn't be severely punished for this dereliction.'

I hung me head, I hadn't told him yet why the horse had died.

'The horse died from eating poison mushrooms sir. I am still investigating how they got into the feed.'

Sir Robert seemed to stop in his tracks. 'Poison mushrooms in the feed and only one horse?' He turned away from me scratching his jaw. 'Sounds like a deliberate action on some ones part.' He looked back at me. 'You and all your grooms are to stand down while I have this investigated. Recent stories have come back to me how you seem to be losing your grip on things and spending too much time away from your duties.'

I think me mouth must have been hanging open in shock at what I perceived to be a gross injustice. Sir Robert almost looked like he wanted to retract his last statement and then he said. 'Leave me now. Stand by for an investigation and a search. Touch nothing under pain of death!'

Everyone was stunned, everyone, that is except Gordie. Each groom stood by his locker but not Gordie.

There was a commotion at the barn door and Sir Robert entered with Gordie by his side, speaking into his ear. Tim and Ross were close behind with five yeomen. Sir Robert turned to Ross.

'Go check, report back to me directly!'

Ross knuckled his forehead and went straight to Pats chest. He rummaged through it and it wasn't long before he returned with a sack in his hand. He opened it for Sir Robert to see. His lips pinched together until they were white. He turned to point at Pat 'Restrain him!'

Sir Robert held the open sack under Pats nose 'Explain this away lad'

I walked over and found meself staring into a sack full of poison mushrooms' 'Explain what sir those must be the same mushrooms that killed the horse.'

Pat yelled. 'This is bullshit! Will, you know I would never do what they are accusing me of. I'm being undermined by that asshole.' He lounged at Gordie, eyes full of hate.

Sir Robert turned on him as Ross yanked him back. 'Silence! you'll be given a chance to speak, in due time.'

Pat stood red faced with frustration but kept his mouth shut. Tim leaned forward and spoke at length into Sir Robert's ear. He listened intently and then, frowning, he spoke to Gordie.

'Tim overheard you threatening Will and abusing his relationship with Jews. You do know that kind of behavior is not tolerated here?'

He looked shocked. 'I've been misunderstood me Lord, I have nothing against them Jews. It was Jews saved me life.'

Both Tim and Ross looked like they wanted to throttle him but said nothing.

Sir Robert looked somewhat nonplussed. 'Tim, take groomsman Pat to the guard house and lock him up. I will speak with him later, perhaps tomorrow. Will, do you have another as a second?'

'Yes sir, Joss is up to it.'

Gordie piped up, 'But Sire...'

Sir Robert silenced him with a wave of his hand. 'You are new here and at the bottom. Your job is whatever Will or Joss delegate to you. You will be watched I'm not at all satisfied with what took place here. Will, you and your grooms are on probation. Especially you, you are responsible for what happens on your watch.'

'How can I be responsible for deceitful acts Sir!'

He stared at me, long and hard, Looked like he wanted to say something, then turned and left.

Tim gave me shoulder a squeeze as he and Ross walked past. An almost inaudible 'We are with you.' in his wake.

Gordie looked quite uncomfortable.

January bled into February with nothing untoward happening, except cold weather. Tom, Darragh and I still chatted together every chance we got, and I visited with Meg. They all knew all about Gordie and his sneaky ways and were watching me back as much as they could. Of course he was behaving himself. He knew he had overstepped and was keeping a low profile. Poor Pat was still stuck in a cell pending new evidence. Tim made sure his stay was comfortable and we were allowed to visit any chance we got. Me lessons continued, I'm sure Sir Gawain knew everything that had happened but we didn't speak of it.

I had told Joseph and Miriam everything, keeping nothing back. Miriam tried to comfort me. 'I'm so sorry Will, we brought that evil man into your life and I feel terrible.'

I gave her a hug, 'Don't be silly, dear one you were no more responsible than the horse that brought you here.'

She gave me a hard poke. 'Are you comparing me to a horse?' She poked me again with a mischievous grin and then we were struggling until she suddenly melted in me arms, her warm breath against me neck and ear. I moved me head to look at her and she planted her soft lips on mine. I was in ecstasy as I wrapped me arms around her and felt her body warm against mine. Her kiss became more demanding and I felt me hardness against her belly. She felt it too and even through her dress and such. She trapped it between her legs, her breath was hot and heavy, as was mine. I almost lost control and then whispered. 'We must stop.'

With a small groan she said, 'I know!' She pulled away from me, not much, just enough to look into me eyes. 'I love you Will, I love you very much. I have never known a man like you, strong yet gentle and kind yet my papa says we should not be together. He is very fond of you too, you know but says that the world we live in will destroy our union and over time, make us bitter.'

'Why would you think that?' though I already knew the answer because Meg had spoken to me about this very thing. The Jews would reject us because I was not a Jew and the Christians would reject us because she was. Our children would be social outcasts to most who knew. Many would look the other way or take no exception at all but it only took a few to destroy. The world harbored many nasty people even devout nasty people who hid their viciousness behind a cloak of piety. Meg had not minced words, she felt great affection fer me and had spoken to me like me mam.

I gazed at her beautiful face. 'I love you too and would protect you from that world.'

'Who would protect you? dear heart. I'm not as strong as you and I lack your love for all people. I have been hurt and threatened more than once, that is why we came here, to a safe haven. Look Will, I will sleep in your bed and take care of you and love you but we cannot marry in my faith or yours. I won't renounce mine and I don't want you to either.' She buried her face in me neck and I pulled her closer, suddenly feeling a great sadness that felt like an omen.

That conversation and the sad feelings lingered with me for several days. I did me work and watched out for Gordie and then the outside world came back with a clap.

# **MALCOLM**

---

n this particular day Gordie was one of the grooms running the blacks along with me
and Joss. It was the last day of February and the late morning weather was mild giving
us a scent of spring to come. Ye could see snowdrops and bluebells pushing through
the snow under protective trees. The sun glared against all the white and I was wearing a device
given to me by Darragh, to protect me eyes. It was a strip of leather with very narrow eye slits cut
into it. It worked very well in cutting down the glare and I could see much better than the others.
Joss vowed to make one fer hisself, Gordie just smirked his usual smirk. I spotted movement at
the other end of a long vale. Two men, about twenty feet apart, were coming towards us at a lope.
Gordie was closest to me.

"Looks like point men coming, could be scouting for a larger troop or army. Get the horses
back to safety and report to the officer of the watch what we are seeing. I'll stay back and watch
them fer a bit. Get more information if I can.

Gordie nodded and signaled Joss to turn the herd. They were soon gone from sight below the
hill I was on. I stayed low, watching the two men. They were coming straight at me and getting
bigger and bigger. I felt well hidden in the thick gorse as they came up, one on each side of me.
The man on me left got me full attention, he was Scottish and he was big. Ye could tell he had
been reddish blonde but was mostly grey now with a beard and a horsetail braid down his back
partially covering a huge two bladed axe hanging between his shoulder blades. An earring glinted
as he crouched not ten feet from me. He was looking ahead with his eyes squinted when he said,
'Do ye no think we cunna see ye, laddie? I know ye are a Brit but we mean yer no harm. It's just
information we're looking fer." He signaled the other man who moved on ahead. "Sit up now and
we'll talk.' He turned and crouched to face me.

I got off me belly, looking just a little perturbed. I could see a group of men, perhaps forty
or so, in the distance. 'I realize ye could have cut me before I could do anything, so why didn't
ye? I am curious.'

He chuckled. 'Are ye now, I'll introduce meself, I'm Malcolm Mackonigol and we are
searching fer an evil sod of a mon or demon who has left carnage in his wake. We have been
following a trail of horror for nigh on a month noo.'

I sat up at that. 'Describe to me what ye are talking about.' I held out me hand, 'By the way I am Will Barrow.' He reached out and we gripped forearms. I could barely get me fingers around his.

He frowned a bit. 'Ye seem to know something of what we speak? The first was just north of the border. A farming croft, everyone was dead and mutilated in bitter ways. I've seen lopped heads and arms in battle, even done me share of the lopping but what I saw turned me stomach. Men, women, children even little bairns cut and twisted in awful ways. I'll no forget it in a lifetime. Then another was discovered and yet another, all in Scotland. I didn't believe for a moment that Brit raiders did it, not that. So we got on a trail and found three more slaughtered crofts between the border and here. They had all been done some time ago but ye could still read the evidence.'

I leaned forward a bit. 'The one ye are looking fer is an Irish by the name of Skye McOrdred. He came to capture or kill a friend of mine in the name of his father Krayan McOrdred. As far as I know, he is back in Ireland after murdering a family close to home in retaliation fer a perceived insult. We won't get into that horror fer now, needless to say it was most similar to which ye spoke. He is out of our reach for the moment.'

'Finally, we have a name, he is not a ghost any.......'

Interruption came in the form of his man staggering back, holding his side. 'What's happened Titus?' He rushed to support him. Titus spoke in Erse and I didn't understand a bit.

Malcolm swore. 'Ye have bin taken laddie. One of yer men lies dead and the other tried to scamper with yer horses. Titus interrupted and got stabbed fer his pains. He says yer horses are still with us but the yellow hair cut and ran.'

'That born from shite Gordie, we need to tend yer friends wound quickly I don't know how filthy Gordie's dirk was. It was likely poisoned. Come back with me to me town, I can guarantee safe passage and a fine doctor.'

He nodded and addressed the men, who were arriving. 'Camp here till we coom back or send word to coom. Danny, yer da is wounded but he should be fine soon enough.'

Danny, a man my age, looked daggers at me and moved towards me. Malcolm stepped in front. 'Nay laddie, ye have it all wrong. Noo, wait fer me word.'

Danny turned away with a sour grunt and I ran down the knoll to find Joss. He was lying in the long grass, his sightless eyes open to the sky, and a second mouth gaping under his chin. Greenish darkness around the wound edges worried me as I knelt and closed his eyes. Looking around I found his horse. Grieving would come later, now it was time fer action. I led Joss's horse and mine back to where the men were. They were all on foot.

'Malcolm, take me horse and put yer friend on the other. I'll ride one of the others, bareback. Let's get going, and quick!'

With a nod, he helped his comrade up and leaped onto his own. 'Angus, see that these laddies stay oot of trouble. Be back soon.'

A short solid man gave him a wave as he galloped off. I whistled for Storm who was running free with the others and he came right off. I clutched his mane, swung up on him and caught up to the others quickly. The rest of the horses came behind, following Storm.

I shouted, 'I need to bring the herd to safety, they should be no trouble with Storm leading.'

Malcolms voice was muffled by drumming hooves. 'Aye laddie, we'll help.'

It wasn't long, about eight minutes, when we arrived at the field gates which led right to the stables. Seeing the herd fast approaching, the guards had them open and grooms were waiting. I could see by their faces, they all had questions.

'Malcolm, follow me.' I led them to the main gatehouse, and luckily Tim was on duty. 'We have a stabbed man, Tim, likely with a poisoned dagger.'

'What happened Will, who are these Scots ye have in tow?'

'Please get yer auntie I'll explain everything when she gets here. Oh, make sure she knows it could be a poisoned wound.'

With obvious trust, he sent a guard to fetch Meg and helped Malcolm and me to get the now unconscious Titus inside.

It wasn't long before she came hurrying with Sir Robert close behind. He took me shoulder and gave me a little shake. I couldn't quite tell if it was friendly or agitated. 'What are you up to now Will, are you turning my town over to the enemy?'

'hese are not yer enemies or mine milord. They want Skye McOrdred's head on a pike just as we do.' then proceeded to tell them everything that had happened, including Gordies betrayal.

Sir Robert sighed and looked glum. 'Well there's the proof.' He held his hand out to Malcolm. 'I am Sir Robert Arthur and I bid you welcome even though politics say we are enemies.'

Malcolm bowed as he took his hand. 'Yer reputation precedes yer me lord, we knoo of ye even north of the border. Ye were just a young officer but ye ordered a stop to the slaughter of wounded Scots at Falkirk and as a Britt ye were the first to show consideration to us. Over the past years yer defense of the poor and persecuted has no gone unnoticed. Ye are an honorable man and that's why I happily came with Will here to talk with yer.'

Sir Robert nodded. 'You shall have your talk over dinner but first there is something that sorely needs to be done. Tim, go release Pat the groomsman, with my deepest apologies. Tell him I will speak to him as soon as I can. And Will, I am sorry I ever doubted you even a little bit.'

I Smiled 'I understand Sir, it's been a trial fer all of us but now, even if it's not over, at least we know where we stand.'

Sir Robert smiled right back and then turned to Meg. 'How is he doing, will he live?'

'I have me hopes Sir, I think the night will tell. Right now he has a fever that needs to break fer him to survive. I think I stopped the poison and hopefully no more damage is done.'

'Do ye need to bleed him?' Malcolm looked concerned.

'Forgive me, but I don't hold with church medicine. He has lost enough blood already. If they had their way they would bleed him and put a hot shite poultice on the wound and he would be dead in an hour or two. Leave him with me and he has a chance.'

Titus moaned and Meg felt his forehead with her hand and it came away, dripping wet. I handed her another blanket. She nodded her thanks and said. 'All of ye, please leave now and leave this poor man to me.'

I took Malcolm by the arm, 'He's in good hands, let's go sit and have a small bite.' We went to the yeomen's mess where there was always a cut of meat, cheese and bread for those unfortunate enough to miss a meal. As we sat down, Darragh came in and introductions were made. I lifted the wet clay cover from a large platter, and cut a thick slice of rare beef for each of us and made three platters with cheese and a slab of bread. Passing them around, I noted that those two were hitting it off already. I pointed me knife at Darragh, 'This is the man Skye is after. Oh, I heard ye say ye fought with William Wallace at Falkirk. That was twenty one years ago, how do ye still look so good? Ye must be fifty years or so.'

He showed teeth in a ferocious grin. 'I watch me diet laddie and eat a Britt every day with a dram of whiskey,'

Darragh guffawed, 'No wonder your teeth are so white, from chewing all that gristle all day long.' They were both grinning as Malcolm tore off a ferocious bite of beef staring intently at me.

He sobered. 'Aye, I fought at Falkirk and aided our victory at Sterling Bridge. William was a personal and close friend. We grew up in the same valley and liked to scrap with all comers including each other.'

There was a small smile pulling at his lips as he seemed to be remembering. He snapped out of it when I pushed a bowl of cider into his hand. I proceeded to tell Darragh about Gordie's betrayal and the death of Joss. Malcolm listened and confirmed what I said with small nods of his head.

I stood up. 'Have to go, need to talk to me grooms and visit with Pat, also there's a lass to see.'

Darragh waved his hand. 'Go do what you need to Will, Malcolm and I will be fine.'

Pat still looked a little angry at his treatment but was glad to see me. When I told the grooms about Joss's death at Gordies hand, Pats anger immediately transferred to him.

'That sheep shagging little prick, I hope he's still alive when I get me hands on him.'

I put me hand on his shoulder. 'Ye'll have to stand in line Pat.' The other grooms all nodded.

I went to me quarters and bathed, and with a fresh tunic and leggings on, went to visit me beloved. She was happy to see me, having been scared fer me welfare. She led me to a cozy little nest she had prepared and we made love several ways possible. Completely drained, I fell asleep with me face in her scented hair and her hand stroking mine. When I woke up, Miriam had food prepared. We sat cross legged, and watched each other eat. I got aroused all over again so I reached over and picked her up and gently sat her down on me erection.

She still had a goose leg in her hand and started to giggle. 'What do I do, eat or fuck?'

We made love again and fell asleep again. In the early morning, before sunrise I took me leave. I hadn't seen Tom fer ages and it was nice to have breakfast together and catch up. Malcolm had gone to see how Titus was doing. I was running behind and hurried to the training ground.

Darragh greeted me by throwing a sword fer me to catch. 'Get your guard up.' He circled me looking fer an opening. 'Titus' fever broke and it looks like he will make it'

'That's good news!' I smiled and dropped me guard a bit. A painful whack across the shoulder that numbed me arm brought me back to me senses. I lunged with a flurry of strokes making him back up several steps. I paused, letting him think I had tired. He took the bait and stabbed at me. I sidestepped and smacked his wrist with the flat of the blade making him drop his sword. He immediately presented the other and watched me warily as I circled. Then he stepped back and grounded his sword. 'That's enough Will, you did very well today.' He frowned looking at his wrist. 'I need to stick my hand in cold water, it might be broke.'

I stepped forward, concerned. He waved me off. 'Go do what you have to. This comes with the territory. My carelessness could have cost me my hand in a real fight.' He growled to himself as he turned away. 'I need to listen to what I preach.'

# **GWEN**

I had just mounted up with the other grooms to take the palfreys for their romp when Ross waved me down. "Sir Robert wants to see yer Will. Pat can take over. Ye'll find him on the wall by the gate. He's with Sir Gawain and that big Scot."

I left on the run, me thanks trailing behind me. When I got there I hied up the stone stairs to the waiting men and knuckled me forehead. 'Ye wanted to see me Sir?' Looking past his shoulder I could see Malcolm's men approaching.

He reached over and pulled me into their circle. 'The time has come to meet my friends from the continent. There is far too much unrest in the south and the Irish and Welsh corsairs are being pesky on the Irish Sea. They are coming across from Germany, keeping the landing as secret as possible. That means a trek on our part, back to where you used to live, Will. I am asking you to go because you know your way around there and you will take good care of my horses. It is arranged for you all to meet my friends at the seaside of the Yorkshire moors at the mouth of the Esk. Sir Gawain will be in charge with Tim and one hundred yeomen. Malcolm will accompany you with ten of his men. Take the supply waggons you need but remember, you'll be meeting a small army at the other end. Oh If possible, help those that need help on the way.'

I realized he wasn't talking to me directly anymore, just including me in the conversation. I was thrilled to be traveling with Sir Gawain and I was wondering about Malcolm, why was he coming?

Sir Robert directed himself to me. 'You'd best get your kit and affairs in order Will, you could be gone for a month, maybe even longer depending on weather and other occurrences. Darragh will be staying with me to train more men, and as soon as Titus has his strength back he will take charge of the rest of Malcolm's men. I'll still have a hundred yeomen under Ross and we will hold the fort here. You leave in a week.' He directed himself to Sir Gawain. 'I don't like splitting us down the middle but you may need some muscle on route, and remember, the Scots won't fight Scots. Once you have joined up with the visitors, send yeomen back ahead of the main party. There should be enough Palfreys to speed up their journey.'

A week passed much too quickly. I was thrilled with the idea of going but I was going to miss Miriam. The night before, I couldn't get her to stop crying. We said our goodbyes and I left

Courser the wolfhound with her he liked her and her da and would give them good protection. I went to visit with Meg, Tom and Darragh.

Pat dropped by. 'I'll try not to spoil yer nags too much' He chuckled and took me hand, 'Have a safe trip.'

Gawain looked up at the dark clouds, rain strickling down his face. 'I think we're leaving too early, the roads will be a quagmire and that will slow us down quite a bit.' He turned to Tim and me. 'The horses will tire quicker and as fer the men...well they'll be bushed.'

'Maybe, when the country is more open, we could fan out a bit instead of stepping on each others' muddy heels.'

He smiled a rare smile. 'It's good to know I haven't bin wasteing me time Will. Those were me thoughts exactly.' He turned to a yeoman handling a waggon. 'I hope ye packed lots of oil, we'll all be squeaking rust buckets before the week is out.'

We laughed at his jocularity and I looked around, spotting Malcolm. He and his men were on foot, along with eighty yeomen. Tim and nineteen yeomen were on horse along with Sir Gawain, Jarad his squire, and meself. I yelled over, 'Hey Malcolm, ye don't want to ride?'

He shouted back. 'I know how to, just don't like to.'

I grinned at him just as Sir Gawain moved us out. Well wishers had to jump out of the way as the cavalcade splashed through deep puddles and headed out into the soaking landscape with banners furled and capped. I pulled me hood up and tried to hide in me sheepskin. The cold was raw it cut like a knife and felt worse than the coldest day in winter.

The third day on the road, the air was warmer and we were traveling in thick fog, coming up from the Ure river. Everything was muffled and I could only see the shapes of a couple of riders just in front or just behind. The clink of mail and the clopping of hooves told me the rest were there. Malcolm and one other were scouting ahead to keep us out of trouble but how he knew where he was or where we were, I had no idea. Later in the morning, shafts of sunlight cut through the fog and when I looked up I could see blue sky. A fine doe stood in one of those bright spots and a yeoman put her down with a well aimed arrow. He quickly had her gutted and tied up onto the wagon, meat fer the pot. Shortly after, the fog broke up and slithered away to where ever fog goes to, and we were traveling in warm sunshine. Some of the horses got quite frisky and it took a bit of muscle to control them.

The next few days were slow in the mud. Reports came from the scouts that there was nothing untoward up ahead. The weather held and things began drying up. Patches of snow in the shadow of trees disappeared and were replaced by snowdrops, bluebells and crocuses. It was the middle of March and spring had arrived early.

It was the end of the first week of travel when Malcolm informed Sir Gawain that Twixmiddle was no more, just a burned out ruin and the ferry was gone. We would have to turn north and find a crossing on the Swale. We stopped at Boroughbridge a hamlet with a bridge across the Ure. We could have taken that crossing but common sense said otherwise. The Ure and Swale joined just downstream from us to become the Ouse and with spring thaw coming on, would be impassable.

Sir Gawain used the red, white and blue watch system, which proved to be a good one. We camped outside a local pub, the 'Plowman's Rest', to give everyone a break. The watches took turns to partake of the tavern's bounty. The barkeep looked like the happiest man in Yorkshire. No one was permitted drunkenness, just a nice mug of ale fer each of us, courtesy of sir Gawain. On the road, the watch system worked well. For example, after a day's journey, the red watch would set up the camp perimeters and dig the latrine trenches then stand guard for an hour while the others ate. The white watch would come on guard duty for four hours while the reds ate and slept through to the wee hours of morning. The blues would take the next four hours knocking up the reds for their breakfast, who would break camp while the others ate. The next evening would rotate one watch ahead so everyone got a change. I hated the midnight to morning watch because ye got no more sleep till next evening. It was a good system though, because a third of the camp was armed and ready for hostilities at any time.

The day came when we approached Twixmiddle from the other side. Not a building was left the town a blackened ruin. The stench was unbearable. Flocks of ravens, daws and seagulls were everywhere and there was to be no doubt why. We shot a few dogs. Running in packs and eating human flesh made them dangerous. Quite abruptly, we came upon an awful sight. Poles had been strung between trees at the edge of the forest and there were upwards of sixty men women and children hanging by their necks. The birds and other scavengers had bin doing them over and they weren't pretty. In front of the hangings was a large natural depression filled with rotting corpses.

Flies rose up in clouds when Sir Gawain dropped from his horse and stood at the edge with his scarf pulled up. I couldn't see all his face but by the lines around his eyes, he was very sad. I think I heard him mumble. 'Will they never stop?' He broke out of it. 'Put the horses to work and drag every log ye can find onto these bodies. Cut those poor souls down. Chop the poles, don't handle the bodies. Get deadwood, branches, gather every thin that will burn. Use up a couple of oil barrels and fire this lot.' He swatted at a blue bottle and turned away. I stared up at a swaying young lad, his empty eye sockets crawled with maggots and I suddenly lost me breakfast. I shuddered, wiped me mouth on me sleeve. Sir Gawain was calling to me so I rode over.

'Ride with me Will, ye too Tim.' We rode past the burned out town. Houses up on the nearby hills were also blackened ruins. 'Shite that is what I feared!' He leaned towards us. 'Sir Roberts' betrothed lived near this town, ran a farm and a care center fer children with her da. I pray she is still alive, we must find her. Get Malcolm, we need his skills. Her name is Gwenevive Mon Franc De Tours.'

'Who did this awful thing, Sir?'

He shook his head. 'Jew haters, Royalists, mercenaries, Scots, I don't know. Maybe Malcolm can read this better than I.'

All I could think was 'Thank god Miriam and her father got out when they did.'

After the unpleasant cleanup, squads went out to search the surrounding area fer survivors. The Scots found a young lad, about fourteen, along with his sister a year or so younger. On a separate pass, it was the Scots again who found a bairn, about seven years old. He was terrified of his own shadow. It took a bit to catch him and it took a bit to calm him down. He was cold and hungry and why he hadn't died from the night chills was beyond me. We found no sign of Mistress Gwen or her family. We did find a large burned out farm and the bodies of farm hands and several children. Sir Gawain said it was her family's home and Tim confirmed it.

I stared at the desolation. 'Who makes war on children?' I hunched down in me saddle feeling quite depressed.

Sir Gawain sighed in exasperation. 'We have to search farther afield. Malcolm, yer Scots are the finest trackers we have. Pick some of yer best and fan out. Oh, take a couple of yeomen, I don't want ye being mistaken as the enemy. Let us know what ye find, whether it be friend or foe.'

Malcolm nodded. 'If she is alive we'll get wind of her. Will, why not come along with me and I'll try to teach ye a wee bit o tracking.'

I looked to Sir Gawain, wanting to get away from here, and he gave his consent. 'Learning all this new stuff might go to yer head a bit but yes, go. Just don't get in the way.'

Malcolm was a charismatic and pleasant man to be with and I was enjoying the company. Early afternoon got quite warm and I was sweating in clothing too warm fer the occasion. Me fleece was tied around me waist blocking me sword hilt. I carried one now but also had me spear from the village, which I used as a staff.

Malcolm had been curious, so I was telling him me story and how Tom and Darragh were me friends. He suddenly put a hand on me arm and a finger to his lips. Pushing me down into the foliage, he stepped into heavier brush behind a tree. I could just see him listening and looking about then he waved me up. He held up three fingers and pointed the way we were going then he pantomimed fer me to carry on up the trail. He stepped into the dimness and was gone. How such a big man could move so quiet was beyond me. I understood his ploy and carried on up the trail as if I didn't have a care in the world. I even whistled a tune under me breath.

Then, there they were, three men with weapons at the ready. One, dressed in mail and wearing a steel pisspot cap, put his sword to me throat. His command was terse. 'Pay up or die!'

I looked at him pretending puzzlement. 'Pay what?' I was eyeing the other two, one with a filthy pitchfork that could kill yer with a prick and the other carried a charcoaler's axe.

He sneered. 'Ye stupid fuck, yer money, what else?'

I laughed in his face. 'Money, I have no money.' While I had his attention, I spun me spear cracking his wrist. The point tore into his throat before his sword touched the ground. The others were caught off guard and didn't see Malcolm rise up behind them. The one with the fork died with a dirk thrust in his back and the other was knocked cold, slammed against a tree.

A little face slapping from Malcolm brought the man around. With his scraped face dripping blood, all the bravado had gone out of him. The Scot squeezed his throat a little. 'How many are with ye and where they be?' The squeeze got a little harder, the man gagged, spittle running down his chin and I noticed, spreading wet at his crotch. 'Well?'

He wheezed, 'There be forty six of us.' He glanced at his dead friends, ' Forty four. They is camped yonder, just over yon rise beside a stream.'

'How did so few of ye scum destroy a town with a militia?'

He tried to fawn, almost licking Malcolm's feet, 'there were no militia Milord. They was taken to fight a Bishops war. Our leader knew the town was undefended and deserted that same Bishops army fer easy pickings.'

Malcolm placed his dirk on the man's cheek, just below his eye. The blade was still dark with the other man's blood. 'What's yer leader look like, and do ye have prisoners?'

He started to nod and thought better of it as the dirk pricked his lower eyelid. 'Five prisoners, two are women. One is younger the other a hag. Then there is a white haired old man, a knight, I think. The two others must have been personal retainers. Our leader is as big as you and wears a crested helm and mail.'

'So, ye destroyed Twixmiddle and raped and murdered women and children?'

If possible, the man looked even more frightened. I could see him trembling. 'Aye we did, I didn't coddle with what went on, our leader is a cruel man and a Jew hater. He lost his wife and daughter to sickness and blamed them.'

'Ye didn't coddle? But ye took part and are still with him.' Malcolm dropped the dirk a trifle. 'Thanks fer the information… scum' The dirk sliced through the man's throat as if it were butter. He tried to speak but bubbled and spit blood as his legs folded. I watched the life bleed out of him as his face contorted fer air. Malcolm showed me his ruthless side that day.

'Ye go fetch Sir Gawain, tell him what ye know. I'll reconnoiter their camp and have more information ready when ye get here. Now off with ye, I'll hide these bodies.'

I hied it back as fast as I could. I spotted Danny and another Scot the same time they spotted me. After telling them what was happening, they came along. Danny was a young hothead but now that he knew I had nothing to do with his da's injury, we got along fine, at a distance. I could even imagine him as a friend.

Sir Gawain moved fast, gathering his little army. "The mounted men will stay here with Tim in charge. The rest of ye will go in on foot. Make sure yer quivers are full. Now, let's get going. Sir Gawain wasn't taking chances. We were almost three to one and disciplined troops.

Malcolm met us at the trailhead. 'They are a lax lot. They haven't even missed their comrades. The prisoners are on the right side of their camp, going in from here. They are all lashed to a large oak, all except the younger lass with red blonde hair. They've got her peeling turnips fer the moment. By the lustful looks on his face and some crotch groping, the leader intends to bed her anytime."

After a council of war, Malcolm led thirty yeomen behind the camp. I went with another twenty to the right side and Sir Gawain, being on horseback, would take the rest in a frontal attack. It was my job to defend the prisoners at all costs. Sir Gawain was sure we had found Gwen by the description.

A flaming arrow arced over the trees and thumped into the lap of a man by the fire. He let out a squeal of surprise and pain and was frantically slapping at the flames engulfing his crotch and cloak.

That was our preset signal and we attacked. Archers swept the camp with showers of arrows many men died even before the yeomen charged. I raced forward and took me stance beside the beautiful woman. Ye could see her beauty even though she was scratched, matted and filthy. She looked confused and then absolutely dumbfounded when we materialized. Me yeomen made a barrier between the hostiles and prisoners. No one was going to get through.

The enemy was scattering everywhere with no place to go. Realizing their predicament, some stood their ground and several made fer the prisoners, probably hoping fer body shields.

I had dropped me fleece and fought with me sword. It tore out more than one man's life that day.

Sir Gawain on his black charger struck fear into the hearts of those facing him. Those that didn't run, died, crushed under his flail or his chargers hooves. Jarrad finished those on his masters shield side, a hammer in one hand and a sword in the other...and he always looked so easy going.

Malcolm's group advanced in a disciplined line, doing their own bashing. Swatting men from his path, Malcolm made a beeline fer the leader. He was big alright but slow and fat. Malcolm's axe bit into the junction of neck and shoulder and cleaved deep into the man's chest. It wasn't even a fight. The Scot used the weight of the falling body to wrench his axe free.

The battle was done and only two yeomen received minor wounds. We took only seven prisoners. They had thrown down their weapons and begged fer mercy. I had never seen such a motley bunch, from farm boys to mercenaries, all thieves, rapists and killers.

It was Gwen, the woman we saved, also her father and governess along with the two retainers.

She was delirious with happiness, and held out her hand to me, which I took gently and bowed over.

'Ye saved me and mine with great bravery. Ye were me own private fortress and I will be forever grateful.'

'Ye are most welcome Mistress, I am glad ye are all safe.'

Sir Gawain strode up. 'My heart feels good to see ye safe little sister.'

She threw her arms around his neck with a chuckle. 'Thanks fer coming big brother.'

I must have been looking at them stupidly because Gwen burst out laughing. 'We are not brother and sister, just good friends with pet names fer each of us.' She hugged and squeezed Gawain's arm. 'After all, my betrothed's best friend is also mine.'

Sir Gawain wrinkled his nose. 'Ye may be me friend but ye stink, go get washed up lass, we will talk later.'

The stream came in handy for everyone to clean up. There was plenty of blood to wash off and the prisoners were scratched, bruised and filthy. No one had allowed them to do their toilet in private.

We stayed put for that evening. One Scot returned to our other camp to give the all's well. He would lead them up in the morning. Our prisoners were tied to the same tree so that they could enjoy the shit and piss of those they had ill treated.

A light supper was prepared consisting of coarse bread, cheese and cold venison. Some winter apples also came to light. An enterprising yeoman had a sack full. They were quartered up and s hared around. After having some food and a warm fire, Gwen told us their story.

She stared into the fire fer a moment, holding tight to her da's hand. 'I had just gone out to help, and check our winter crop of turnips, when I saw heavy smoke above the trees. It got heavier, even as I watched. Me da joined me and we hurried down to a point where we could get a view. From there we knew it was Twixmiddle, we could even hear faint cries and screams on the wind. Then we saw small distant groups of people running and dropping as larger groups overran them with flashing steel. We could see right away that it was very bad and we were in no position to help so we retreated, back to our home. One of our men stayed on watch while we gathered supplies and equipment needed fer our survival. I had several children in me care and they were getting agitated, wanting their parents. When we were ready, I went to get our sentry.

He was sitting up against a tree when I called to him. He didn't answer so I went to him only to realize that he was pinned upright with an arrow through his throat. Before I could turn and bolt, yelling men came out of the trees, overrunning me. Four of me lads bravely tried to save me but were cut down. They were field hands not soldiers. As I struggled in their grasp, me da tried to fight them. They laughed and toyed with him until he was knocked senseless by the flat of a sword. Then I watched helplessly as they slaughtered most everyone in sight. My God, all those little children, that awful butchery took place nearly three weeks ago. Those men intended to ransom us but then the weather turned and it rained 'cats and dogs'. The road became muck, too muddy fer them to travel and they camped out here. They were all very unpleasant men, especially their leader He enjoyed tormenting me and groping me. He said that once they had the ransom, he'd fuck me silly, with me da watching, before killing us all."

Malcolm, who had been listening intently, said, "It's a good thin fer him I killed that fat shithead. If he was still alive I would have worked on him a bit."

Gwen looked up. "That tub of filth ye killed wasn't the leader! That's him over there, trying to hide his face in his cowl."

Malcolm was on his feet with one lithe movement. He almost leaped across the intervening space yanking a ferret of a man upright. His strength was such that the man's arms, tied to the tree, were almost torn from their sockets. His mouth opened in a howl of agony. Before he could protest further Malcolm reached down with his dirk and sliced behind a knee. We actually thought we heard the tendons snap back. The man's mouth gaped in a silent shriek, his eyes just about popping, as he fell onto his hip. He tried to get up and couldn't, his arms pulled back and his leg useless. The Scot reached over and sliced behind the other knee.

"Ye wee pathetic excuse of a mon, ye are too vile to kill." he hawked phlegm and spat in the man's face. 'When ye crawl about begging fer pence, ye can remember Twixmiddle fer the rest of yer miserable days.' With that he turned his back on the whimpering retch and never gave him another glance.

Gwen had turned her head away from the ugly scene and Sir Gawain wasn't quick enough to do anything. He closed his eyes for a second and then called a yeoman over. 'See to this man's wounds let's make sure he lives to beg.'

We were bedded down fer the night and I could see Malcolm sleeping soundly. I still liked the man but he scared me stiff. Gwen was nearby just staring at the night sky. I could see her eyes glitter in the fading fire light. I rose up on one elbow and whispered. 'Can't ye sleep mistress?' She shook her head 'Too much in me head.' Then she rolled onto her side. I lowered my head back onto me arm. 'Aye me mind is just about spinning right off, can't sleep neither.'

The six other killers were hung the next morning. Since there was no priest or friar, Sir Gawain gave them time to pray and repent, none did. Some begged fruitlessly fer their lives. The cripple was left to his own devices with a ration of bread and water.

# **DANNY**

We were back on the march, three days out and the land was beginning to look familiar. For the first time since I left, I gave some serious thought to the pigs and cattle. I knew they would likely be wild after cold months alone, though, it was also possible that they had been found by other people. Still I hoped and rode up to Sir Gawain. I passed Gwen who waved a friendly wave. She and the old lady were caring for the bairn and youngsters. Having a couple of women around had eased their fears greatly. Gwen's governess whose name was Iris was not a hag, as she had been so meanly called, her face was a big wrinkle but she was spry and loved a good joke and the children really liked her. I reined up beside Sir Gawain and told him about me hopes.

'Will, I think ye are dreaming. They'll be scattered hither and yon…if they are alive.'

'I could ride ahead and see, Sir.'

'Very well if ye are successful we will pen them up and I will leave yeomen to guard them. We will pick them up on the way back from the coast.'

'It's just a little less than half a day's ride, may I go now?'

'Aye, take one of the Scots with ye, but not Malcolm.'

'Thank ye milord.'

I took Danny with me, I don't know why. He was always a little standoffish and seemed to have a chip on his shoulder. As I said before, we got on alright but we weren't yet friends.

I took the time to ask him about his home and soon we were having a nice chat. When we reached Krill pond, nothing had changed except the season. Some ducks already had little ones around them. I called for old Snoot with little result. I headed for Darragh's old place, remembering the hidden sword. It would be quite the feather in me cap, returning it to him. As we walked we came upon a foul smell, something was dead fer awhile. Checking the surrounding brush we found a swollen cow. Danny looked her over, 'Bin gone some three days, looks to be she died from milk fever or something similar.'

I agreed with his findings. 'Somewhere nearby, there'll be a dead calf.' As we moved down the trail, I said. 'With her only three days gone, others might be nearby.'

'Aye, they will be hanging around, probably upwind from here.'

'This trail goes to Darragh's old place and I have an errand there. Would ye look about fer the cattle?'

'Aye Will, I'll be in touch right soon.' Danny vanished into the woods. It was the first time he used me name.

Darragh's farm looked the same as when I left it. The house in ashes and the barn scorched with one door ajar. A bent hinge brought it to that position no matter how the wind blew. The tree hollow produced the blanket wrapped sword. The blanket was rotten and full of little bugs. The sword was fine with the thinnest coat of rust, buffing off with a little oil to help would fix it. I would deal with it, back at camp. I stood in the courtyard and looked around and on a whim, I called 'Hey old Snoot, are ye about?'

There was a bunch of grunts and squeals, and the barn door flew to one side. The next thin, I had a very large sow standing up with her sharp forefeet on me chest. I laughed out loud scratching her ears and looking at her ugly face.

'It's good to see ye too, old girl. By yer tits ye have some youngsters about?'

It was like she understood and dropped to all fours with a loud squeal. There was a whole lot of squealing and six piglets shot out of the barn bowling each other over. Piglets love to romp and play and I always enjoyed watching them. I crouched down holding me hand out, but they stopped short of me and stayed close to their mam. One, more adventurous than the others, crept over to sniff me hand. I scratched its ears and it relaxed right away. Other pigs started to exit the barn until there were eight. I spotted the young boar responsible fer the little ones. He was watching me, warily. However it was Snoot who led them. I grinned to meself. Since she still remembered me and liked me, me job would be a lot easier.

Danny had been watching from one side. He sounded curious. 'Brood sows can be dangerous, how did ye manage that? Ye sure have a way with the beasties, do ye not?'

Snoot whirled at the sound of his voice and I put a hand on her shoulder speaking softly.

'It's alright Snoot, he's a friend." She seemed to relax. She must have understood the friendliness of our voices. I'll take a moment to advocate fer pigs. We eat them so many look down on them, saying they're dirty and stubborn and such. They root fer their food and their shit stinks and they ain't cuddly but pigs are way smarter than any dog. Something we like to forget.

Danny came over, watching them warily. The pigs went back to their rooting with no concern for us.

'I found some of yer cattle, eight head. I don't know if there's more. If there are, they are probably scattered all over. They've had a winter to run around.'

'I'm surprised they stayed close fer all this time. It's possible they sheltered in or near the barn like the pigs it's where the feed is. Anyway, I am very happy with all this, it's far beyond me greatest expectations.'

Danny shook his head. 'Ye use some very large words and it's hard to understand everything ye say.'

I grinned at him 'Sorry, but I've been educated.'

He grinned right back at me, 'Fuck off. What say ye we trap these blighters and get them penned up?'

I let the pigs be they had been around all winter long and wouldn't go far. Danny led me to where he had found the cows. They were all cows, no bull around. Bulls were solitary brutes anyway.

Danny looked around. 'Watch yer back when ye are driving them. If he's around he might get pissed at us.'

I nodded. 'I think he's already here. The bushes behind ye are shaking!' He spun around and then cursed me when he heard me laugh. He shook his finger at me with a shamefaced grin. The cows were wary of us at first but soon got over it. We got all eight back to the barn without incident, and found Tim with two other yeomen.

'Ye found us.' I said smiling. 'Are the others close?'

Tim grasped me hand. 'About an hour back, we've left markers along the way though those Scots don't need markers, they don't miss a thing.'

Danny laughed. 'Ye are right about that. There's a bull standing right behind the lot of ye.'

I wasn't falling fer that one but Tim and the other two jumped away with curses. I couldn't contain meself and turned to look. 'God's truf! Where the bloody hell did he come from?' Me heart flip flopped back into me chest. He was big, hairy and all muscle with horns near six feet across. I saw right off that his nose had been ringed sometime in the past but how was I going to get a hold without being killed. He seemed bent on keeping the cows fer hisself.

I glanced at Danny. 'I'm going to try and coax him into a stall, stay near to slam the gate.'

'How are ye going to do that?'

'I'll show him me arse and waggle it a bit, then run like bloody hell.'

He chuckled, 'Ye should let me do it, I can run faster with me kilt up than ye can with yer pants down.'

'He's all yours then, I can't argue with common sense.'

The yeomen got the barn doors open wide and stayed out of the way with looks of anticipation. Tim went inside. His voice sounded hollow when he yelled. 'The first stall on the left is ready!'

The bull was facing me, huffing and puffing, so Danny picked up a stone and with a yell hit the beast right on the nose with it. It was a perfect shot, he must have spent time pegging birds. The bull spun towards Danny, snorted, dropped his head and pawed at the ground. Danny lifted his kilt, waggled and let fly with a monstrous, loud fart. That was too much fer the bull and with a bellow he charged. Danny raced into the barn and then the stall with the bull right behind. He almost took flight over the side rails as the beast skidded to a stop. The yeomen collapsed, laughing and I was laughing so hard, I barely made it in time to slam the gate. Tim had found a tether and another longer rope. I made a noose and looped it around those horns. Danny and I and the other two yeomen used our weight to hold the bull tight to the rail. We were all giggling and it took a couple of tries before Tim slipped the tether through the ring and the animal was safely tied to the rail, with enough slack to eat and drink. I snatched up a wooden bucket and went to fetch water fer the thirsty beast. I was still chuckling as I came outside, and I realized we had an audience. Not just the cows and pigs but Malcolm and several men were standing there grinning.

'Did I hear something about common sense? Ye laddies having soom fun are ye? I see ye have found what ye were looking fer, Will.'

I realized he was holding the sword and I held out me hand as I greeted him. 'How are ye Malcolm? May I have that?'

'Where did ye find this blade laddie?' He passed it to me.

'It belongs to Darragh. I hid it last year when I was on the run. At the time I didn't know Darragh was alive. I thought it would be nice to return it to him since it belongs in his family.'

He gave me a friendly smile and nod and stepped back a bit. 'The others are here.'

The riders came first, making the livestock nervous. Sir Gawain seemed to notice as he dismounted. 'Keep yer mounts calm, lads and stand down.' He walked over to us in a haze of dust and gave me a grin. 'Are ye going to make me eat crow? It looks like ye got more than even ye bargained fer. He turned to Tim, Get some of yer lads and pen these animals up, ye have the rest of the day to do it. Tomorrow we travel to the sea.' He looked about. "This is too small fer making camp, do ye have any other suggestions, Will?'

'Back at the pond is one spot sir, or three minutes to the village site.'

He nodded, 'We'll go there, too many bugs hanging about the pond, and the frogs are too noisy.'

I thought frogs sounded pleasant and calming, but that's me.

Once camp was made and everyone settled into the evening routine, I got a chance to visit the gravesites of me parents and some of me old friends. Gwen saw me there and joined me. We both stood silent fer a bit.

Gwen cuddled a little deeper into the blanket around her shoulders. 'Am I intruding Will? I heard about what happened to ye and wished to pay me respects.'

I shook me head and realized she was looking down and not at me. 'Nay mum, I'm glad to have yer company.' I felt the presence of others and saw Sir Gawain, Tim and Jarrad and then Malcolm and Danny. They came up beside us and stood quietly. More yeomen arrived and I could feel a hot sob in me throat. I dashed away tears with me sleeve. I had made so many friends the feeling of wonder was almost more than I could bear.

A ragged sigh escaped me as I looked at them all. 'I thank ye, everyone, from the bottom of me heart. I'll neer forget this.'

As we broke up, many men stopped to give me shoulder a squeeze and Danny said. 'I never thought I would count a Brit as me friend but ye are and I'll cry with ye.'

That really got me going and Gwen found me her hanky. Malcolm smiled a soft smile and turned away so as not to embarrass me.

# **CHEVE AND URI**

We woke up to bright sun, some clouds were scudding in from the coast and promised later showers. However, it didn't look like serious bad weather and spirits were high. Sir Gawain commissioned ten yeomen and two Scots to care fer the livestock. I cautioned them about how swift and agile the piglets were and how they could get lost.

One Scot snorted at me. 'Never ye mind laddie, I dunna think Brit pigs are any different from Scottish pigs except Scottish pigs are more bonnie. Never fear, I'll keep a good watch on them.'

The moors are rolling open country with copses of wind torn trees and hedges of bracken, fine country fer hares, conies, foxes and many birds. There were traps fer man and horse on the moors too, bog holes that could swallow a rider in seconds, leaving no trace. Usually they were in hollows between hills but sometimes, to the uninitiated, they looked exactly like solid ground. I knew them well from hunting and fishing with me da. One river flowed near to us, the River Esk that drew the salmon every year. Even though it was against the king's law we capitalized on the runs. South of us the moors became more marshy becoming fens in places, due to another meandering river.

I led the cavalcade without mishap. Ye could smell the sea long before we saw it and then came a line of small dunes. We crested them and there she was, the North Sea. Me whole life I had never known it's name but I knew it now thanks to Sir Robert and Sir Gawain.

The sky out to sea was getting very black and scattered, large raindrops squelched in our faces as a cold snap of wind cut through our clothing. I looked fer the mouth of the river and recognized landmarks about three miles north of us. Ye could just see Whitby Abbey against the darkening sky. Many of us were pulling our hoods over our heads as we marched up the beach. It wasn't long before banners were spotted on a headland. Sir Gawain told us to stand down and wait. He, Jarrad and three yeomen cantered towards the camp and a small group of horsemen came out to meet them. I could see other activity. Men were forming up in rows across the face of their camp. The two groups met and after a short parley, a yeoman broke off and returned to tell us to move up. Tim set the pace and we followed in formation threes.

As we neared the large encampment, I got me first view of Pike-men, three disciplined rows of them. They stood six feet apart and six feet in the aisles, fifty to a row with their fifteen foot pikes upright and at rest. They wore a mail coif and a Norman style conical helm with nose guard and knee length mail rolled at the neck to repel sword cuts. Mail leggings protected their legs and their feet were booted. Each had a sword hanging on his left side and a dirk on the right. I sensed that they were equally curious about us but they never moved a muscle, only their eyes glinted, hidden in shadow.

There was a loud command in a language I didn't understand, and they turned left and right, split down the middle, to quick march fifteen paces. They stopped with a thud of feet and pike hafts then turned back to face front with another thud. They were even more disciplined than the yeomen and that was saying something. Our cavalcade rode and marched through the opening and me attention was drawn to the group up ahead that included three knights' and a number of men at arms. Each knight was impressive in his own right but one, a little to the front, really caught me eye. He was tall, even on horseback. His hair was white blonde and shoulder length and he was by far the most handsome man I had ever seen. I would learn, soon enough that this was Sir Jean Du Lac, a French-Swiss knight from Geneva. On one side and just back of him was his opposite. Also tall but very broad and powerful with black hair and beard hiding a scarred face. Sir Peitre Du Boors a Flemish knight. We would soon be calling him the boar. On the other side was a shorter man with light brown hair and a pleasant face, Sir Hans Frederick Lenzburg another Swiss knight. I would learn later that he was from the Canton Aarau, and these pikemen his and were trained by him. What I noticed the most was that the knights were all riding Friesians.

Sir Gawain dismounted as did the others and he embraced each of them. The way they shook each other and grinned, I knew they were good friends, especially he and Du Lac.

The wind was getting brisker making the flags and pennants snap. A Gust of heavy rain hit us and then was gone fer just a moment. I heard a flurry of hooves and another knight joined the rest. He spoke to Du Lac as he dismounted, and then grabbed Sir Gawain in a grinning bear hug. He was much the same size and build except he was a dark blonde. He was Sir Karl Spatzhein from Germany.

Sir Gawain called me up. 'Du Lac says that Karl is having some trouble off- loading the horse barges. Two grooms were lost in the surf. Would ye go see what ye can do?'

'Aye sir,' I looked about, the camp was big. 'Where do I go? I'll need the help of the Scots.'

Sir Karl had remounted and offered his hand. "Up behind mich, I vill show you."

I vaulted up behind him with the help of his strong arm and we were off at the gallop.

We arrived to bedlam. Many animals were already off and had scattered all along the beach. One palfrey was frantic, blocking the exit of others. She was rearing and screaming, as a groom stabbed at her with a long stick. He may have been frustrated and angry but that was no way to treat a horse. As I jumped down, he caught her just over the eye with his long sharp stick, tearing the lid away. I could see the dark red flesh of her eye socket and was infuriated. I ran and grabbed him by the scruff of his neck and smashed him into the barge wall. Leaping at the horse, I got me arm around her head and an ear in me teeth. I bit hard, letting me full weight hang on her neck. She squealed but settled quickly, I could feel her fear trembling through her body.

'Throw me a blanket!'

Sir Karl was right there with one and we got her head covered. I led her back to a hitching post as other grooms ran up.

'Please get her off the barge and put her in restraints. I have to look at that eye and she must be unable to move.'

Sir Karl translated and one groom knuckled his forehead and said something like 'Oui'

A rough hand grabbed me shoulder and spun me around, and I was looking at a man with a bad nose bleed and spitting fury.

'Who the fuck do ye think ye are, yer whores son!'

I snarled right back. 'I'm yer worst nightmare.' I snatched the angry man's stick from his hand and gave him a hard poke just below the joining of the rib cage. Both hands went there as he gasped in agony.

Sir Karl stepped between us and directed himself to the groom. 'Zi bist ein dummer ochse! You are ordered to leave now, not just here but zis camp. Be gone before I haf you stocked and whipped.' The groom scurried away with death in his eyes.

Sir Karl, that's what I'll call him, looked a little shamefaced as he placed a hand on me arm. 'I ride zees beasts, but I do not know zem very well. I haf mench to do zis fer mich. I speak a little bad English and a little French but not enough. I could not- how do you say- communicate well.'

I saluted him with a knuckle to me forehead. 'Don't worry Sir. I'll have them back in order quickly.'

There was a second barge not yet ashore and with the increasing wind gusts, needed me attention. 'Do ye know how many horses there are, Milord?'

'Zer are eighty, forty on each barge. The Friesiens are za ones out zer!'

The second barge was beginning to roll and bang dramatically in the shallower water. 'Shite, we need to get her in fast and I need help.' I yelled fer Malcolm or Danny or anyone! I saw them on their way and said. 'Sir Karl, there are pikemen and yeomen trying to help. The tide is coming in so keep them from the surf, with mail on they'd have no chance.'

Without another word, Sir Karl mounted his horse and tore away. I waved to a Frenchie and pantomimed that we needed to beach the second barge, fast!

Men rowing the towboats were aware of the problem and were pulling fer shore and fighting fer every yard. We met them close to the beach and laid hold of the ropes. Frenchie had been yelling in his gibberish and other grooms led three large gray horses in traces down to us. We tied off the ropes, and with the help of the horses and boat crews we managed to ground the barge.

The Scots arrived at the double, and after clearing the first barge, Malcolm came straight to me.

'What do ye need laddie?'

'All the blacks are on that barge and its getting rougher. We will need a man fer each horse to get them on shore as fast as possible. Some may balk at the surf when ye bring them out so keep a tight hold.'

The surf went from knee deep to waist and shoulder deep now, and the barge was beginning to move. I got the boat crews to keep the ropes as tight as they could with the help of the horse teams. Malcolm and his men already had the gates open on the side of the barge and men, Frenchman and Scot alike, were untying the first beasts from their posts. The loading ramps were immediately swept away by surging waves, so the men ran and jumped the first six through the surf without difficulty. Then one man lost his footing. Luckily, the horse dragged him ashore where he lay gasping and coughing. Someone got him out of the way. I was heading to the barge when another black spooked and threw his man against the hull. The man went under and with a little good luck I got me hands on him before he was swept away. The surf was getting higher and ye could feel the undertow rip and claw at yer feet. The rain was coming in sheets and one could barely see. Horses were coming past me like specters, one after another. I managed to climb on without getting bowled over. It was looking quite empty then I spotted Malcolm and Danny coming with their charges, Malcolm was last. Danny raced by giving me a soaking wet grin and a 'Good luck.'

Malcolm yelled in me ear. 'There's two left, one up in the bow shelter!'

I nodded and using the tether posts as help, struggled towards the bow. The barge was really bucking now and once caught me off guard. I drove me knee into me chin just about breaking me jaw and splitting me lip. There was little difference between the taste of brine and the taste of blood. Like a ghost in the rain, Frenchie was there, helping me up.

'Haut, haut, il nous faut aller vite!'

I didn't understand one word but I knew it wasn't an invitation to eat. That little accident made me realize how freezing cold and stiff I was getting. We got to the bow, and he untied the last black. In the shelter there was a horse like no other. He was the size of a Friezien but a spotted light grey with black mane and tail that almost touched its knees in length. He was fighting his tether and I could tell he would fight anything. Grabbing his halter with one hand I put the other under his jaw and talked to him loud, over the wind, so he could hear.

'Don't fight me horsey, I want ye to live!'

He threw his head about and tried to kick, but I held on, pulled his head to me chest and kept talking. He lifted me off me feet a couple of times then slowly calmed and stood trembling. I untied him and did a crazy thing. I leaped onto his back and gave him his head. We galloped towards the opening fighting the pitch and yaw and the slippery wood. Once he almost went to his knees but caught himself and then took a huge leap towards the beach. On shore he stood, trembling and I was afraid he had hurt himself. Jumping down, I checked his legs and looking under his belly saw the boat crews cut the ropes with axes before the traced horses were dragged into the raging surf. What with the torrential rain and wet sand, I got a load of grit in me eyes, and had a hard time seeing but I managed to lead me charge up the beach to safety. Hands took the halter from me and other hands led me to a horse bucket full of fresh water.

'Wash yer eyes out, Will.' It was Danny's voice.

'Did we get them all?'

'Aye, they are all safe now, we didn't lose any.'

Me eyes felt bloodshot and gritty but I could see again. The first barge had spun about, holing the second, which was now floundering. The first was fleeing out to sea chasing the ships that had raised anchor to get out of the shallows. The long boats were up on the strand and clear of the tide. There were lots of people around us. Sir Gawain came to me, fast walking with Du Lac. As they approached, I could see Tim and his yeomen putting finishing touches to rope corrals. They were getting help from the Swiss, who were using their pikes fer posts.

'Ye saved the day Will. That was fast thinking.' He gave me shoulder a friendly shake. Du Lac just watched, not saying anything. By his expression, I got the feeling he didn't brook this familiarity with the peasants.

Sir Karl came and spoke in a foreign tongue, French I think, to Du Lac. He answered with a grunt and turned to Sir Gawain. 'It seems that our German friend feels the same as you do. Your groom saved us all.' He sounded a trifle annoyed.

Sir Gawain took his arm, 'Come now Jean. With two deaths, control had been lost and a level head needed. Others could have done it but this time it was Will.' He started leading Du Lac away and his voice grew fainter in the blasting wind. 'I'll tell ye about him and others over a cup of that good cognac ye are so famous for....'

A tap on me shoulder brought me around to face a smiling Frenchie. I got me first, good look at him. About my size with curly black hair and a bushy mustache and wearing a woolen cap with a long tassel. He took me arm and said 'Tiens avec moi.'

I let him lead me to a group of grooms, sailors and a number of pikemen. They all gave me a boisterous round of greetings and a mug was pushed into me hand. I grinned back and took a mouthful. Choking and gasping for breath I felt me eyes brimming over. Frenchie gave me a good natured slap on the back. 'Ne vous savez comment biore?'

The others laughed and I looked at him with me dumb, I don't understand look. He sobered. 'Je vous remercie pour aider a sauver les chevaux.' and he gave me a hug by the shoulders. The others all raised their cups and drank.

A Swiss pike man, a man with a stocky, broad shouldered build, looked me in the eye. 'Do you want me to translate?' He laughed at me stunned expression. 'Yes I speak English. My mother was English.' He held out his hand, which I took, it was callused and hard. A scar down his cheek, from the corner of his eye to his chin, pulled when he smiled, making him look lopsided. "My name is Uri. The Frenchman is Cheve Bardaux and he said 'thank you for saving the horses'. He laughed, 'That's Kirsh you are choking on. Isn't it good? It's made from cherries.'

I wiped me eyes. 'Aye, it is good once ye get past the potency. Me name is Will Barrow and I am very pleased to meet ye all.'

Me comment passed on to pleased nods of greeting. It wasn't long before some Scots showed up and a boisterous party unfolded.

I had no time fer partying and got Cheve's attention. I pointed to me eye and pantomimed sewing. He gave me a nod and said something to another groom who pointed across the beach. Uri must have heard because he got up and followed, as Cheve came over. He took me elbow and we walked across to a pile of cargo.

Uri said, 'Why are we here?'

I told him about the injured horse and what I intended to do.

'If it moves, you'll take its eye out.'

'Look, there's the horse.' I grinned at him, 'Ye can help.'

'I know nothing of horses except sticking them with a pike.'

I glowered at him. 'Ye can help!'

A groom had tethered the frightened horse between two posts, and hobbled it front and back.

'Let's get this done, and give this poor beast a rest!'

Uri translated fer me. Cheve flipped a halter rope around her neck pulling it tight. Now her chin was against her neck and she could barely move. I got me a needle and strong thread from Cheve, who had pulled an etui from his jerkin, and with the two of them standing firm on each side of her neck, I moved the flap of eyelid into position and started to sew. The job was done quickly and I didn't even step back to admire me work, she was breathing in short high pitched squeals. We got the horse free as quickly as possible and tethered properly with water and some oats. The animal had had an extremely bad day from a horses point of view and it would take a while fer her to calm down.

Malcolm arrived with a bottle that wasn't full any more. 'What are ye up to now laddie?'

I introduced Cheve and Uri, and Malcolm passed the bottle around.

'That's very good stuff, our whiskey is better, but that's very good stuff.'

I could hear a slight slur in his voice and saw that it was the kirsh. 'Ye drink all that and ye'll be cursing in the morning ... very quietly.'

Uri laughed and told Cheve who grinned.

'So, now ye are stitching up horseys.' He hiccupped. 'There's no peace fer the wicked Laddie'

He smiled to himself, pleased with his witticism, and summoned the bottle with wiggling fingers.

I got up, 'I don't want to nurse what ye'll be nursing in the morning, so I'll be off.'

'I'll join you and show you the way.' Uri got to his feet and walked with me. Cheve was pulling the bottle from Malcolm's hand.

We passed several encampments until we reached the largest being the Swiss pike. It looked as if there were a hundred more than the ones that had been on parade.

'How many of ye are there Uri?'

'We number two hundred and twenty five plus twenty five senior trainees and our captain. Du Lac is our supreme commander and has one hundred heavy cavalry with him, plus support staff and some infantry. Du Boors has seventy men at arms and so does the German. Sir Lensburg is our mentor and we answer to him before anyone else, and he answers to Du Lac and no other.'

We had stopped in his camp and I was looking at a stand of pikes. "They are just like a spear or lance only much longer and thicker.'

Uri took one off the stand and tossed it to me. It was quite heavy, all fifteen feet of it. I held it out in front of me. 'How do you use it, it seems quite cumbersome.'

He grinned. 'You'll have to wait until we are in the field, I will tell you that the Austrians always yearned for our country. We threw them back out more than once but their pike-men gave us a bad time on a couple of occasions. Over time we adopted their strategy and improved on it.'

'Was passiert ist da unten?'

We both turned and Uri said, 'Guten abent mein kapitan.' He took me arm. 'Please meet my captain, Franz Swingely.'

I knuckled me forehead. 'I am pleased ta meet ye sir.'

Uri spoke with him in German or Swiss, I didn't know. The captain raised an eyebrow and looked me up and down. 'Do you vant to be a pike man, Master Will?'

I smiled and shook me head. 'No sir, I am very happy where I am.'

'If ever you vant a change, come see me.' Without further ado, he walked off.

I was feeling quite sleepy and still had me bedroll to find. "Thanks fer yer company, Uri, I'm off to bed now." We shook hands and I left. As I walked towards the yeomen's camp, I couldn't help thinking, 'So many of them seem to speak several languages.'

Early morning arrived with no trace of the storm though the wind was still brisk. The sky was still night black with dark and lighter blue edges. The last stars were still twinkling and just a few white cloud puffs were here and there. The sun became a bright orange glow on the horizon. I saw Tim and a couple of yeomen standing by a fire drinking warm water. Several more were going about their business in the twilight and lining up at the latrine ditches. There was a lot of coughing and farting going on.

Tim gave me a welcoming smile. 'How are ye this fine morn, Will? Did ye sleep well?'

'Like a log! And ye?' I looked around fer a cup and a yeoman passed me one already filled. I thanked him with a nod and a toast and sipped the hot water. It wasn't long before it did its work and I began to feel meself needing to go. I soon made me excuses and headed fer that awful stinking latrine, looking fer a relatively clean piece of plank to hang me arse over.

The wakeup call done, we lined up fer breakfast. The cooks had outdone themselves and we were having porridge again along with a slab of dry bread and cheese. I heard the cross between a moan and a groan and turned around. It was Danny, with eyes squinted and bloodshot, looking a little pale.

I grinned and whispered. 'How are ye? Ye'd best keep yer eyes shut so ye don't bleed to death.'

'Fuck off.! Ouch, don't talk or I'll stick ye with me dirk.' He covered his eyes with his hand.

'Don't try, it'll hurt ye a lot more than me.'

'Fuck off!'

A rather hard slap on me back, and there was Malcolm with a loud cheerful, 'Good morning laddie, where did ye get to last night?'

I stared at him. 'Unbelievable! Where's yer hangover yer big lummox?'

He laughed uproariously. 'I've neer had one laddie.'

'God have mercy, why don't ye all shut up and fuck off!'

I was nibbling on bread and cheese when I was told to find sir Gawain. I strolled through the camp heading towards a large group of flags snapping in the brisk wind. Sure enough, there he was, eating at table with the other knights. Jarad saw me and greeted me with his friendly smile. 'Morning Will ye are nice and prompt. Sir Gawain will see ye in a moment.'

'I haven't seen ye to talk to since the battle. I'm glad ye are me friend and not me enemy.'

'What do ye mean Will.'

'Ye were handling things right well out there, a hammer in one hand and a sword in the other.'

'So did ye Will, so did ye.' He turned. 'Ah, he's ready ta see ye. Come.'

'Good morning Will, are ye hungry?'

'No Milord, I have eaten.'

'Me friends now know who ye are and that ye will be in charge of the horses and livestock. I'll make yer job a little smaller. I'm sending forty yeomen on the palfreys along with the twenty already on horse, back to Lord Robert. Unhindered, they should beat us by a week. Ye'll have the blacks and take special care of the Andalusian he's a special gift from Sir Jean Du Lac to Sir Robert so guard him with yer life.'

'Andalusian?'

'It's a special breed from Spain, a place called Andalusia on the Iberian Peninsula. They used the swiftness and beauty of the Arabian and some other larger horse, perhaps a Friesian, needless to say, it is likely one of a kind here in England and of great value.'

'I understand sir. We have already had introductions.'

Sir Gawain looked me over, a slight smile flitting across his face. "Ye certainly are one with the beasties, it's magical. The French head groom Cheve Bardaux, is willing to work under ye, a testament to yer charm. His men will do as he says so ye can give the Scots a rest fer a while. They don't seem to care fer horses much anyway.'

'They don't mind them sir but they are more comfortable on their own two feet. I'm pleased that Cheve and I will be working together.'

He scratched his nose and nodded. Pointing a finger at me, he said. "We'll be leaving in the morning and make straight fer yer village to pick up the others. Ye will handle the herd as ye see fit. Now off ye go.'

I knuckled me forehead and left.

The dunes were begining to dry now though the surf still crashed onto the beaches. Dust thickened as camp was struck and men formed up. Cheve and his lads found me right off. He too didn't seem to have a hangover and greeted me with a cheerful smile. I mounted me palfrey and we rode together through the dust, passing soldiers filling in the latrine ditches. The first thing I checked was the mare with the injured eye. She fidgeted at first but settled down quickly as I stroked her and talked to her. The eye was quite swollen but she could still see out of it. I turned to Cheve his eyes sparkled with a look of approval.

'She can run with the others.' I pointed to her and then the penned horses.

'Oui, oui.' He took her halter and handed it off to another groom. 'Les preparer...' He paused as Uri came up with three other pikemen.

'Good morrow Will, We need to gather the pikes used for fencing, will it be alright?'

'Good morning Uri, no hangover? Yes, of course it's alright. We'll be moving them out, straight off.'

Uri chuckled. 'Yes, I have a bad head I just try not to show it. He shouted at an approaching waggon. 'Beobachten sie die radar, der sand ist weich!' He nudged me. 'Soft sand too soft for waggon wheels.'

I noticed that we had several onlookers as we packed up. They had walked from Whitby village which lay behind the abbey.

'I hope they don't think we are an invasion?'

'Sir Du Lac called on the abbey and made a donation. Everything should be fine.'

Forty yeomen came tromping down the beach, each carrying a saddle and gear. Tim was leading them, riding his palfrey. 'Will, would ye and yer men help us prepare the palfreys?'

'Aye, and in return, would ye pick a man with gentle hands I have an injured mare that is a little edgy.'

Tim looked over his shoulder, 'Humphrey, up front.'

A yeoman wearing a green cap and feather came up, 'Aye sir?'

Cheves' groom brought the horse forward and held out the reins which Tim took. 'Ye'll be caring fer this beast on the way home.'

Humphrey nodded. 'What happened to her?'

I told him, as he stroked her neck, 'Aye, she'll be spooked alright. I will look after her and keep watch on her eye.'

We kept the blacks parallel to the main column, while in open country. The Andalusian was tied to me horse with an umbilical cord. I wasn't letting him out of me sight. The others had been told to stay on me lead, because of the bogs. They had the same back home and knew what I was talking about. I needed to learn a little French and they needed to learn some English. I discovered that Danny spoke a little French and I asked if he could stay with me. He didn't like to ride, but the blighter could run all day.

We reached Darragh's farm without incident and everything appeared to be as before. The yeomen hadn't just been lazing about. There was a large hay waggon in the yard. Where they found it I have no idea but they had put carpentry skills to use and built sturdy sides on it.

A yeoman named Peter said. 'That will carry yer pigs, all we need are spare horses.'

'Thank ye, thank ye a lot.' I looked in the waggon to see a separated area fer the sow and her piglets. 'I think I know where to find some. Everything bin in order while we were gone?'

'Everything is fine here but the Scots have information fer Sir Gawain. We spotted distant dust two days ago. Good thing it was dry, if it had rained like yesterday, we would have missed it. The Scots went and took a look and told us it was an army, flying royal standards, heading north. About two thousand men, they said.'

'I wonder what's happening?'

Peter shrugged and laughed. 'They didn't stop to tell us.'

'Ha ha, I'm going to find horses.'

I saw Mistress Gwen and stopped to say hello. She was feeding porridge to her da and he was getting it all down his front. She threw the spoon down in frustration and blew a lock of hair away from her eye.

'Will, it's nice to see ye.' She grimaced. 'Me poor da has taken a turn fer the worse. Ever since the knock on his head, he's not been the same but now it's worse. He barely knows me today and yesterday was likewise.' She smiled. 'There's lots of talk about ye and it's all good.'

I think I blushed, 'People get carried away. It was a bad storm along with incoming tide and things had to be done. Lots of fine men helped me, and we managed to save the horses. Speaking of horses, I need to find some French ones. I am very sorry about yer da. Where are Iris and the children?'

'She took them to see the Swiss marching. Don't worry, she is well.'

'I must go, mistress, we are close enough to each other but duties keep us all far apart. If ye need anything, send word.' With a wave, I left to find Cheve.

'Cheve, Cheve.' He looked back, his tassel flying, when he heard his name and reined in his horse. 'Do ye have those big horses to spare? I have a cart that needs pulling.' He gave me a blank stare. I pointed to an oncoming cart, 'Chevaux to pull a cart.' I pointed to the team passing us.

Comprehension dawned, 'Ah, les Percherons.' He shouted, 'Rene, amener l'equipe, ils sont necessaires.'

I saw a groom acknowledge with a wave and then Danny came running. 'Are ye doing alright?'

'Aye, I think so, we'll see in a moment.' I saw the team I had envisioned coming our way, big, beautiful, grey horses with feathered fetlocks. I grinned at Cheve and gave him the thumbs up. He grinned back. 'Danny, tell him they go to the burned out farm to pull the pig waggon and hop up behind me.'

He spoke in French then looked up at me. 'I'll walk or run, as needed.'

'Ye'll have to get used to riding, sometime." He made a face, said something else to Cheve and took off fer the farm.

Including me, there were just five grooms, and four spoke French. So far, we were getting by on sign language but I made it me mission to learn some words. We cared fer the horses in shifts, splitting up, Cheve with two of his grooms, and me with one called Rene. Athos and Simon were the others. This gave us some rest though we were always on call. The Scots cared fer the cattle. They had the same kind in the highlands and felt right at home. Two yeomen were in charge of the pig waggon and the bull tied behind, everything was running smoothly.

Sir Gawain set a new route, slightly to the south west of our previous one. Not too far south as that would bring us too near York. No one needed to see Twixmiddle again. Besides, He did not want to run foul of the northbound army. The French and Swiss soldiers, plus the Scots, might be misconstrued as an invasion force by some. Sir Gawain wanted to pick his fights and not have one thrust upon him with over whelming numbers.

Malcolm chose a few men to run a skirmish line ahead and to each side of the main group.

We were following the Ouse River north when Gwen's da passed away. She found him dead on the waggon in the midst of travel. The column stopped for a few hours to bury him with a proper ceremony. Yeomen cut down a tree and made a cenotaph style marker right by the road. One spent all afternoon carving the name, dates and such. He did a wonderful job of it and Gwen was most appreciative. Sir Jean Du Lac was very attentive to her, and she rested on his arm throughout the service.

While looking for a crossing on the Swale, a Scot came back with grim news. They had come upon another croft and it was, once again, the scene of mindless slaughter. Sir Gawain asked Du Lac to accompany him, and went on ahead with the Scot and several yeomen.

We slowly followed and I took that time to tell Mistress Gwen about the atrocities and who was doing it. As I loitered by the waggon, Sir Karl rode up and caught the last of our conversation.

'Mein Gott, zer are men and women of great evil everywhere. At home, in za swartz, ah, za black forest, there was a starving woman who killed and ate her sickly husband. She vent on to luring young kinder to her house with promises of food and sweets. Her reign of terror ended ven a brother and sister pushed her into her own oven.'

Gwen glared at him, mockingly. 'Sir Spatzhein, must you? My appetite for roast meat is forever ruined.'

Sir Karl grimaced and grinned, 'Mein apologies Lady' He turned his attention to me. 'Tell me more of zis miscreant.'

I told him about Skye and how he was hunting Darragh, and how he liked to torture and maim innocents every chance he got, be it families or whole villages. I told him about Garrad the Black, his bodyguard and likely assistant in his obscenities, or so I believed.

Arriving at the site, Sir Gawain told us to make camp. He intended a service fer these poor souls.

Sir Karl joined Sir Du Lac and they spoke together in low tones. I didn't need to see another catastrophe and so I went looking fer Uri.

Me luck was with me as I found him off duty and planning to eat. "Take an early supper with me Will I haven't seen much of you on the march, besides, some of the other men would like to meet you.' So, I ate with the Swiss pike, and it was good food too. A spicy lamb stew with slices of heavy black bread called Pumpernickel. Many of the men were friendly and curious and I discovered that more than one spoke some English. I asked Uri about it and he said that Switzerland faced four countries, Italy, France, Germany and Austria. Each part chose to speak that country's language plus the native Swiss or Helvetian that sounded a lot like Erse.

'Learning languages is like a second nature,' Uri said, 'And many of us speak three or more. I learned English because of my mother. Others learned it from the English occupying parts of France.'

I scratched me head. 'I need to learn some French and German I find it difficult to understand things in this international group.'

Uri finished mopping his bowl with the last of his bread and spoke around a mouthful. 'I don't mind teaching you. I speak good French and fluent German. You seem educated to me anyway. I've seen you writing on a tablet and most of us cannot write. I can't, I took up soldiering at ten years and fought my first battle when I was twelve. That's how I got this," He pointed to the long scar. 'Couldn't eat properly for days.' He shrugged. 'I had no time for the higher things.'

'You mean you handled a pike at twelve?'

'No! I got my pike when I was sixteen and strong enough to master it.'

I smiled, 'I have an idea. Look, ye teach me and I'll teach ye. Do we have a bargain?'

He grabbed me around the neck in a sleeper, giving me a friendly squeeze. 'Yes, we have a bargain.'

There was a blast of a horn, calling them to muster, so I left to find the other grooms.

Our entire compliment formed three sides of a square around the croft, all facing Sir Gawain and the other knights. Once again, I watched yeomen fire the place. Sir Du Lac that took charge of the service and it was a lot longer than when Brother John did it. After an Hour we were called to ease. Sir Gawain looked us over and it felt as if he looked at each one of us individually.

'We will be back at home in three or four days. At that time, things will be revealed to ye though most of ye have made some good guesses.' He smiled. 'I just wanted to say that I am very pleased with all of ye. Ye have all behaved like good Christian men, to each other and to those passing. I may not get this chance to have all of ye in one place again and I wanted to speak me piece.' He paused a moment. 'That will be all dismissed!'

Tim stepped forward, 'Three cheers fer Sir Gawain!'

The whole company, including meself, gave three rousing cheers.

A party of travelers stopped to see, since their way was blocked. They looked frightened and acted like they wanted to turn back. Yeomen spoke to them and put them at ease. They were three families traveling together, fifteen of them with really nowhere to go. While feeding them, we discovered that they were farmers that had abandoned their crofts. 'Just fields of stone.' One dour man said. 'Naught will grow anymore except tares and bracken.'

Sir Gawain got wind of them and came to visit. 'If ye join with us, I can guarantee fields fer ye to work, and a safe environment fer ye to raise yer families.'

Our community was growing by leaps and bounds.

By the time we reached home, I could speak enough French to say hello, good bye, please and thank ye and let's eat. The last was an especially important praise to learn.

Homecoming was a spectacle. Sir Robert had mustered the troops including the rest of the Scots, Titus was using a cane but looked right chipper. The whole town had turned out and I spied Miriam and her father in the crowd. I managed a wave but then had to turn me attention to the horses. The gates to the barnyard were open and we herded them inside. Pat and his grooms were ready and the newcomers were stabled in short thrift. The first person I met, as I dismounted, was Tom. He looked thinner but his grin was there fer me as we threw our arms around each other.

'How are ye Tom, it's good to see ye.' I looked about. 'How is Darragh?'

'Darragh is fine he is mustered out front with Sir Robert.'

Pat was suddenly there with a bear hug. 'Good ta have ye back Will, Yer nags are fine. Who are these blokes behind ye?'

I looked around and it was Cheve and the other grooms. Introductions were made all around and they started hitting it off right away. Pat had hired two new grooms I didn't know, so I got to meet them too. Pierce was a slight lad with freckles and Henry was a little on the plump side but I would soon discover him to be a very able groom.

I got a wakeup call, the Scots had brought the cattle in and they were shitting on Darragh's training ground. The waggon was also there with the pigs and bull.

A yeoman jumped down from the waggon. 'Where do ye want these pigs unloaded?'

'I don't know let's leave them on the waggon fer now.' I turned to Malcolm, 'Would yer men help me get those cows down to the back? The grooms have to brush and feed the newcomers and this fine stallion needs a stall.'

When Pat saw the Andalusian, his eyes just about fell out of his head. 'What beast is that?'

I told him and he walked with me as I looked fer an empty stall. A loud whinny greeted me and there was Storms head hanging over the half gate. I walked up to him, leading the Stallion. He greeted me with a whole lot of face nibbling and hair pulling. I grinned, patting and stroking him. "It's nice to see ye too Storm."

The Andalusian grunted several low challenges and Storm snorted and blew into his face clicking his teeth. The other was right back at him with lips curled and I held a tight rein on his halter. 'I think these two need to be apart, is there an empty stall at the other end?'

'Aye, I'll fetch water and feed fer yer.'

'Thanks Pat, then I can formally introduce ye.'

The horses were finally comfortable and I took me leave. Pat stayed with the Spanish horse, getting acquainted. I needed to get the bull to suitable quarters. Cheve walked with me and I took the opportunity to show him around a bit. After the bull was penned, we stopped at the smithy and he got to meet Tom. There was a glad cry and I was getting buffeted by a very exuberant Raglin.

'So, ye made it lad. Are ye settled in?' I shook his hand vigorously.

He grinned and nodded. 'Aye everything is as I hoped and I think I'm even on better terms with me da.'

'How would ye know that?'

'He was here when ye were away, and seemed quite concerned fer ye. Anyway, we got on good and it felt great to have me da back.'

I gave his shoulder a squeeze. 'I'm glad yer happy.' I noticed someone else in the background and gave Tom a questioning look.

'Ah, this is Helmsley, Our new farrier. One was needed badly, what with all the new horses.'

'I can certainly agree with that.' I held out me hand. He wiped his on his apron before extending it. 'Welcome to the family Helmsley.'

His florid, pockmarked face brightened into a gap tooth grin. 'Thank ye kindly.'

'Would ye lads save me a drink, later? I really need to go see someone.'

Tom gave me a cheeky look as he punched me shoulder. 'I wonder who.'

As I left, I noticed how his face settled back into a sad repose. He was being game but it would still take a while fer healing.

The ceremonies had ended so I missed Sir Robert. However, I had the good fortune to see Ross who was on duty at the gate. We stood and watched Du Lac's cavalry making camp outside the wall, along with the Swiss pike. I made a note to look up Uri later on. The other hundred and fifty men were bivouacked around the corner.

'Welcome back lad. I hear ye have some tales to tell. Oh, Sir Robert left word that he would like ye to sup at his table tonight.'

'Thank ye Ross, I'm very pleased to see ye but ye are not as pretty as the one I really want to see.'

Ross guffawed, 'Get ye gone yer lummox. She's been pining all this time.' He gave me a mock boot up the arse as I hied it up the street.

When I took Miriam in me arms she was trembling and held tight to me neck like she never wanted to let go. Even though her body molded mine, I didn't feel arousal, only concern. 'What is wrong dearest I'm back safe and sound.'

'I am so glad you're at home, Will my love. I don't want to worry you but horrible, scary things have been happening.'

'Have ye told anyone?'

'It only just started, two days ago, so no, I've told no one. If you hadn't come home I would have reported it to the guard captain. They have all been very kind to me and father.'

'Well, what happened?'

'The worst was last night. Courser started barking and went out. Then everything was silence. I waited a bit and then got up to look. Our dog was hanging from the beam in front of the store with two arrows in him. A neighbor came when I screamed. She said she would be witness to the terrible act. She had seen two men skulking in the shadows. She is not sure, but she thinks one had yellow hair.'

Me blood ran cold but I held me council. 'What else?'

'The night before last, shutters on my fathers' side of the room were cut and open. He woke up surrounded by his scissors, all pointing at him. He shouted in shock and then yelled in pain, his slippers were full of pins. I came running but all I could do was to try and console the poor old man.' She pulled her head back and looked up at me, eyes brimming with tears. 'I thought we were safe here.'

I led her to her cot and sat down beside her. 'What happened to Courser is awful. I didn't save that dog to have him end that way. However I am equally concerned by the other. It was sneaky and vicious and I only know one man with a nature like that. Ye know him too, I think Gordie is back.' I got up and paced. 'He has to stay hidden there is a price on his head. That makes him even more dangerous and now it seems he has a helper. I am going to talk to Tim. He is captain of the yeomen and has even more authority than Ross. I'm hoping he will put an extra guard by yer shop and send a search out fer this dastard.' I got up.

'Please don't leave right now Will, I need you. I've prepared your favorite food. Fresh spring lamb chops and garden vegetables. Meg helped me get the things I needed.'

'I am staying right here.' I tried a smile though I was feeling grim. 'But ye are forcing me to eat two meals. I've been invited to sup at the lords table.'

'In that case, my love, you'd better have dessert before an early dinner.' She got up and pulled the curtain around the bed. She walked back, pushed me down and started undoing me britches. I helped by pulling off me jerkin and then tugging at the laces on her bodice.

I could still taste the minty crispness of lamb chops when I arrived at the lords table. I had made it on time and people were still seating themselves. Tim waylaid me and I was glad of that, taking the opportunity to tell him about Miriams' ordeal. He led me around the table, listening intently. When I mentioned Gordie's name his face tightened right up.

'Don't worry Will, I'll get right on it and put extra guards in that area. I have to report this to Sir Robert and see what action he wants to take.' He had me neck between thumb and fingers giving me little shakes fer emphasis. "Ye'll be sitting between Darragh and Jarrad.

I looked around the table and spied Malcolm sitting with sir Gawain. No other Scots were there. All the other knights were present. Gwen was on Sir Roberts left, Sir Du Lac and Sir Lenzberg were beside her. Sir Gawain was on the right with Malcolm between him and Sir Karl. Du Boors was next. Captains and other senior officers were scattered around the table mixed with many people I didn't recognize. I was very nervous and couldn't understand why I was in such exalted company.

A serving girl was at me shoulder asking if I would like wine. I was so tongue tied I couldn't get a word out. Darragh saw me predicament and laughed. 'Give him wine, I think he needs it.' He leaned towards me, 'I am very curious to see why a horse handler gets such special treatment.' He winked.

It got quite lonely in a crowd. I poked Darragh and tried to talk. Nothing would come and I fumbled and mumbled.

'What.'

'I think that Will wants to talk and can't think of anything to say.' Jarad leaned forward. He watched me with a smile, his chin on his hand.

Food came in the form of steaming platters of rare roast beef, venison, a suckling pig, sliced up and put back together and several ducks and pigeons in different sauces, some sweet, some peppery. More platters arrived with various vegetables as well as strawberries and raspberries. What a feast, and I had already eaten! I tried a little of this and that and settled on some pieces of honeyed squab. The pieces were small and a little sticky but easy nibbling.

Dinner was over and the loud hum of chatter increased, as the table was cleared. Ale, cider and hard spirits were brought to the table, even some wine courtesy of Sir Du Lac. I opted fer the cider something I was used to. One cup of wine had been enough and I didn't need to make a fool of meself.

A loud command fer silence echoed through the hall followed by a roll of drums that thundered in the closed room. Six drummers entered the hall striking a cadence fer marching feet. They moved along the perimeter wall until they were behind the knights. They were Swiss drummers wearing a two color tunic, white and red divided vertically and a dark blue floppy beret. Their stockings were blue too. Ten Swiss pike entered, their pikes almost touching the ceiling. They moved to me left to take position behind sirs Du Lac, Lensberg and Spatzhein. Then ten yeomen entered to me right to stand behind Sir Robert, Malcolm, Sir Gawain and Du Boors.

Darragh put his hand on me shoulder and said in a low voice, 'Follow me' He led me through one of the aisles to stand in the center facing the assembled knights. The drummers beat became a roll that vibrated throughout the room. Me heart turned into a lump in me throat and I was sure I was shaking enough fer everyone to see. Then I saw Miriam and her da. They had just come in and were sitting right behind mistress Gwen. Just seeing her began to calm me.

Sir Robert stood up and the silence was such, ye could hear a pin drop. His voice was deep and melodic. 'This day I wish to honor a young man. William Barrow has shown exemplary dedication to his duties ever since I've known him. He has been brave, loyal to me always and has been respectful and kind to those he has met. For those who don't know, he saved my life, fighting off the enemy till help arrived. He also fought for my betrothed, Lady Gwen. He has been groomed to take a place amongst us and now I ask who will stand for him and teach him, as a Christian Godfather, the values and obligations held by all in knighthood.'

Sir Gawain stood up. 'I will do so.'

'Who will teach him in all the ways of hand to hand combat that he may defend and protect the meek and downtrodden?'

Darragh put his hand on me shoulder. 'I will do so.'

'Who will teach him the way of the knights' weapon, the couched lance?'

Sir Du Lac stood up and me blood drained from me face. I thought he had no liking fer me. 'I will do so.'

Jarrad came up beside Darragh and handed him a parcel of folded garments.

'Jarrad, help him remove his jerkin.' he and I fumbled as Darragh unfolded the first piece of clothing which was a padded felt gambeson that buckled up the back, it fit me perfectly. I was sure I was sweating and looked at Miriam who was smiling. I knew instinctively that Miriam and her father had made it. Darragh unrolled a mail hauberk a little shorter than traditional. This was pulled over me head to fall with a swish about me body to just above me knees. It was beautifully made Saracen mail, light and fine linked. The last piece was a coif of the same material that split at the throat to cover both shoulders with added protection. I couldn't believe what was happening it was like a surreal dream.

Sir Robert leaned both arms on the table and smiled at me. 'I hereby appoint thee to be my squire, and to learn the ways of knighthood. You must foreswear all other duties and cleave unto me. Will you so do?'

I dropped to me knees 'Aye milord!'

'Rise Squire William Barrow and take your place at my side.'

Jarrad gave me a hard slap on the back grinning from ear to ear. There was spotty cheering and some table thumping. Darragh headed back to his chair with a barely heard 'Good luck Will, I'll see you later.'

Jarrad led me back to a chair placed beside Sir Robert. I was stunned, elated and definitely in shock.

Sir Robert spoke to me in low tones. 'I have a gift for you Will, Storm is yours. That steed and you have such a close bond and it is only fitting that you stay together.' He smiled, 'You'll need a war horse to learn some new skills.'

'Thank ye me lord from the bottom of me heart. Ye give me honors beyond measure.' I almost blurted out that he would be riding the Andalusian now but caught meself. I didn't know if he even knew.

Sir DuLac stood up and looked at me over Sir Roberts head. 'I have heard your story from my friend and now understand more of why you were given such a measure of recognition. You will meet me tomorrows' morn at ten. Bring a saddled mount for your first lesson.'

The man spoke perfect English so why all the interpreting? 'Yes milord, I'll be there and thank ye.'

'No thanks, soon enough they will be curses.' A slight smile crossed his face as everyone laughed. 'And now, to my dear friend Robert Arthur, here is my gift to you.'

There was a loud whinny and Cheve led the Andalusian, at the double, high stepping to the center stage.

He had a long soft whip in his left hand. He cracked it in the air and bowed to the assembled knights.

I couldn't believe me eyes, that dappled grey horse bowed too. Two cracks of the whip and the horse reared up holding the pose fer a moment and then came down on all fours. Without further ado it began a slow motion high step around the perimeter that was beautiful to watch. Front hoof and opposite back hoof rising high at the same time, the neck arched and the tail like a banner. After two full circles, he stopped broadside to the knights. A low command from Cheve and the horse leaped into the air, straight up, all four hooves leaving the ground at the same time. It seemed to float for a second before lightly touching ground. Cheve and the horse bowed again.

I gained a lot of respect fer Cheve at that moment. The man was a magnificent trainer. Everyone at the table rose to their feet, clapping, whistling and cheering.

Sir DuLac raised his hand and there was instant silence. 'Sir Robert, my dear friend, I give you this Spanish horse to carry you through battle and towards your destiny.'

Sir Robert stood up and they embraced. 'Thank you Jean, how can I ever repay you?'

Sir DuLac actually smiled. 'You have, many times over, my friend'

After some stroking, petting and admireing by Sir Robert, the horse was led away and a festive mood came over the table of people. Alcoholic beverages began to flow and many moved from their seats to speak to friends nearby.

It was like a blur as some congratulated me. Then Malcolm was there. 'Well, look at ye laddie, a Squire and I'll warrant, soon to be knight.'

I gave him a blank look, I hadn't even thought of that. It would take a little time to sink in.

It just dawned on me that Malcolm had been sitting in exalted company, who was he?

He poked me shoulder, 'Ye do know that DuLac is considered to be the finest jouster in all Christiandom. Noo one could teach ye the art better than he. I'm surprised he offered, he can be quite an arrogant prick on occasion.'

I grinned, 'I didn't think he even liked me much. Do you know anything about him?'

'Ye know he is from Geneva? Well, he is from a powerful family, but a bastard. He is of the House of Candia, Princes of the Holy Roman Empire. He was an embarrassment and sent on his way with a considerable endowment. He met Sir Robert and Sir Gawain on the last Crusade and through hardships and battles became staunch friends along with the other knights here. They were all disgusted with the atrocities committed by both sides in the name of religion but especially by their own Christian knights, foremost were the latter day Templers. Under their previous King John they had strayed from the path the original ones had chosen.'

'Why would these men be here now?'

Darragh sipped his wine and butted in. 'I don't know the whole story but I believe that Sir Robert had an idea that they all brought to fruition. Did you know that DuLac has leased Bamburg castle on the sea and many of us will be relocating there? Well, it will be happening soon enough.'

'What about this town? Will it be abandoned?'

'No not at all. Half the yeomen and DuLac's cavalry will be stationed here along with Sir Karl Sputzhein and his men at arms.'

'Why is DuLac leaving his cavalry here? All these foreign troops are sure to raise questions.'

'Bamburg is strategic but sits out on a spit surrounded by sea, mudflats and dunes, not optimum country for cavalry, heavy cavalry at that. The Swiss pike will control that area. You have a point about the foreign troops, ask Sir Robert.'

I tried to scratch through the mail with little success. 'So, all our horses will be relocated?'

'Yes, the stables will be turned over to the French cavalry.'

I wiggled me shoulders the itch was getting persistent. 'When is this all taking place?'

'As I said, it will be happening soon enough but I don't know when exactly.'

'God'struf, this itch is driving me crazy.'

Darragh laughed. 'Get used to it.' He and Malcolm wondered off to visit.

'Couldn't one of ye have stayed to scratch?' I searched around fer a stick.

Sir Robert was busy with his guests so I looked fer Jarrad.

'Do ye know who Malcolm really is and why is he cleaved to Sir Robert?'

Jarrad raised an eyebrow. 'Ye didn't know? He is a Laird in his own land and knows Sir Robert better than he tells. He's a man of secrets but is loyal to those he perceives as friends.'

I shook me head, just a little stunned. I had something else to think about.

I saw Miriam and her da only briefly. She knew I was tied up with things but put me mind to rest telling me that they were being quartered in Sir Roberts own house until the culprits were caught. She smiled as she kissed me. 'They are actually your quarters, so I think we all have a new home.'

I decided to spend me last night with Tom, Raglin and Helmsley. I'd not be looking after the horses any more, not the same way anyway. I mostly wanted to visit with Tom, me oldest friend. I may have forgotten to mention that Darragh had moved out to quarters more fitting fer a weapons master. That happened while I was away.

There weren't enough cots so Tom and I set up our bedding on the floor by the fire and talked fer hours before falling asleep. His grief was still raw within but he was coping. As I dozed off, I could hear the soft snoring of the other lads. It was a comfortable sound.

I awoke to a searing flame in me chest and then another. I realized I was being stabbed, and instinctively grabbed the hand holding the blade. I could feel me strength ebbing fast as I forced the blade from me. I struggled to hold it away and knew I couldn't. I yelled 'Help!' once and then me mouth filled with blood and I choked and spluttered. The weight was suddenly gone and I heard a sickening crunch against the fireplace. I vaguely saw Helmsley's concerned face looking down at me. Things were fadeing fast as I dimly heard Raglin yelling fer the watch. What of Tom? I turned me head to stare into blank eyes........

# **SIR JEAN DuLAC**

I tried opening me eyes but the light hurt too much. I heard Megs voice telling someone to close the shutters a bit, he's coming around. I opened them again and me vision was all blurry. Slowly, things cleared and I was staring up at Megs delighted face.

'Yer back Will! Yer back from the dead.'

I smiled at her and croaked 'I'm thirsty.'

She fetched me some water and was giving me small sips when Sir Gawain and Darragh came crashing in. Perhaps they didn't crash but it sounded like that. Noises were buffeting me.

Sir Gawain sat on the edge of me cot and took me hand in his. 'I am most pleased to have ye back, Will. Ye gave us all a great scare. Sir Robert has been a raging bear ever since the incident.'

I tried to lift me head but was too weak. I collapsed back. 'What happened? Tom is dead isn't he?' I felt a huge upwelling of grief in me chest and fought back the tears fer later.

'Aye, I'm so sad to say, and ye would be too but fer the grace of God. Ye have been gone fer three weeks, hovering on the brink. We think yer lung was nicked.'

'I took Megs hand, she was standing by me head. 'God sent his angel.' I smiled at her. Thins began going round and around and I closed me eyes.

Meg shooed everyone out. 'He needs rest and the next one here has to be Miriam. Off ye go.'

I was sitting up at last with Miriam sitting by me. She had me bolstered by pillows so I wouldn't fall over and could feel that it would be a while before I would be up and about. When I had to do me business, I needed a shoulder to hold on to. Miriam lavished attention on me feeding me washing me and making me do exercises that Darragh had laid out. Me strength was slow to return and during that time I discovered who had tried to kill me, it had been the groom I had humiliated on the beach, the one with the stick. Cheve had said his name was Percy and he had been taken to task fer cruelty on more than one occasion. Helmsley had left the man's brains all over the fireplace he wouldn't be up to no good any more. Raglin was sure there had bin two but the other had vanished into thin air. I knew it in me bones that it was Gordie, was he going to haunt us fer the rest of our lives? I Thanked the Lord it hadn't bin his dirk that was used on me. I was baffled as to how those two met. Gordie must have been shadowing us on our trek across Yorkshire. Didn't he have anything better to do?

Sir Robert visited several times over the next months watching me grow stronger each time. The last time he nodded his approval. 'I'll soon have you back and there is so much to do.' He smiled at me to take away the sting. 'You've been slowing us down you know.'

I had many visitors, Cheve and his lads, all me grooms led by Pat. Uri came and sat with me and we chatted. Brother John came once a day to continue me lessons and to talk about bees. Mistress Gwen checked in on me, once in a while, and brought me some confections she liked to make. I had never had anything like them, they were delicious. One of me last visitors was DuLac himself. He looked stern. 'You missed our ten o'clock appointment! I haven't forgotten.' His face broke into a smile and he actually looked friendly. 'I suppose we can make another and don't try to find some other way out of it.'

I laughed and it made me flinch a bit. 'I will be there sir, as soon as possible.'

Malcolm and Danny finally showed up. First they had been away tracking Gordie. They had nearly caught up a couple of times but he had eluded them each time and then they lost him on the coast. They thought that he had jumped a fishing boat and headed fer Man or Ireland. There wasn't another around so they called it off. While I languished in bed, several incursions by mercenaries and bandits had to be dealt with as well.

Malcolm had the chair and Danny was sprawled on me cot, just about pushing me off.

'God's truth Danny, will ye stop prodding me with yer knee. It hurts!'

'It's not me knee, dearest.'

'Piss off.' I gave him a shove and he fell off the cot, laughing and broke the water jug.

Malcolm watched the proceedings with a stupid grin on his face. 'It seems like ye're just aboot ready to have at it, yer lazy ingrate.' He looked up over his shoulder to see who was behind him.

Meg was standing there, arms akimbo. She was trying to look strict but it wasn't easy. 'I think yer right Malcolm. As of first thing tomorrow he is out of here. Now get yer imp and scram before he smashes everything.'

Malcolm sobered. 'Now that we know ye are alright, we'll be leaving fer a time. I'm taking the lads back to Scotland, we should be there before Christmas, I hope, some have families. Also there is word that the Bruce might be ailing and if so, his son David is only a bairn and there will be power playing and politics. Edward Balliol and the disinherited could make a play fer Edward the III's support. I don't care fer The Bruce but he is me monarch, and Scotland was freed under him, so I must goo. I hope to see ye, perhaps next year in the spring. I've made pacts with Sir Robert and ye are me good friend, always, lad.'

I sat up on the edge of me cot so I could take his hand to say goodbye. I would miss this very dangerous man who had given me his friendship and, had stood by me more than once.

Danny grabbed me hand without a word and pulled his dirk. He nicked me palm and before I could swear at him, he nicked his own. He took me hand in a firm handshake and looked me in the eyes, his own bright under curly hair.

'We will be blood brothers fer all time, I'll be seeing ye.' Then he turned and walked off

I could feel wetness on me cheeks as I watched them go.

Sir Robert put me on light duties fer a week or so with the requirement that I exercise every day under Darraghs instruction. He got me strength back in no time, with a lot of pain and complaining on me part.

A lot needed to be done arranging fer the moving of the horses and livestock. Over the months of me recovery, adequate quarters had been cleared and redesigned at Bamburg Castle, all the grooms would be there too. Du Lac's cavalry, would billet their horses in the barns at Haven and were building permanent barracks right by them. They didn't need grooms as each trooper cared fer his own horses and they had their own farriers.

Meg was a wreck. She loved her kitchens, they had been her home and now she had to move, since she was Sir Roberts cook as well as fer the yeomen. The cavalry cooks were getting her kitchen and were looking forward to it. Indoor cooking would be a special treat fer them. She warned them of dire consequences if they messed her kitchen up.

Even with the turmoil of moving, squadrons went out every day to check on nearby crofts, hamlets and small towns. The locals appreciated their protection and travelers soon learned that they were safe on our roads, even if their protectors were French.

Alexander Donclevy had made alliances with a couple of boarder riever families including the Pardoones, one of the most powerful. More of a clan or extended family, they could muster three hundred or more fighting men. They all patrolled down towards us and our men met them at prearranged points to collect news, hand over pigeons and do some trading before turning back. If additional man power was needed it could be arranged at short notice.

After a long, long time, a measure of peace and prosperity came to western Yorkshire, Cumberland and North Umbria.

I had just had breakfast and was walking to Sir Roberts' quarters when I stopped short. How could I have forgotten such a thing. 'Oh shite, I hope it was safe?' Darraghs sword, where was it? I felt very upset as I hied fer the smithy.

I spied Raglin beating on something. 'Have ye seen me sword, the one I brought back with me?'

He stopped what he was doing. 'Aye, it was leaning against the wall beside the fireplace, wrapped in a cloth. I put it under Tom's cot.'

'Oh thank the Lord, and thank ye Raglin, I'll fetch it right off.'

He yelled after me as I raced away, 'Next time stay a bit, it would be nice to chat.'

I found the sword right where he said, and breathed a sigh of relief. I'd had visions of Gordie stealing it. Holdin git to me chest I hied it to the training ground.

'You are late, where have you been?' Darragh walked over to me and looked back over his shoulder. 'Don't any of you kill each other.' He was speakin gto ten students, facing off with blunted dirks. He scowled at me. 'You're a squire now but that doesn't mean you can be late. Is that clear?'

'I'm sorry Darragh, I had an errand to run.' I held out the package. 'This is fer ye.'

He took it with a puzzled look on his face. He stared at me as he unfolded the cloth and then saw what he had in his hands. A look of reverence came over his face. 'My fathers' lost sword how did you...?'

'I found and hid it, Darragh. Back when everything was topsy turvy. I remembered to get it when we returned there.'

'Will, you never cease to amaze me. I thank you from the bottom of my heart.' He reached up to scratch his cheek near his eye. 'Now, get to your exercises.'

I went feeling real pleased with me self.

It felt like I had me old strength back and I could swing a sword without any pain. Me breathing was improving as well. I spent time with Sir Robert, helping him dress in the morning those gambesons all laced or buckled up the back. I also looked after his weapons and did anything asked of me.

Spending time with Sir Gawain gave me the most pleasure, and I felt a close friendship with him. A bond if ye like. One I didn't speak of, it wasn't me place. I learned much about our church and just how powerful and political it was. The present Pope's seat and several past ones too, was in Avignon in the south of France. I had always thought it was in Rome. I learned more of the Near East and then something perked me ears right up with interest. He had seen exotic, well armed, caravans arrive in Jerusalem and Gaza, places he'd been. Some of these caravans were led by men with yellow skins and thin eyes,who brought strange items from far away. The path these caravans traveled was called the Silk Road and was supposed to be three thousand miles, or more, long. I couldn't even fathom such a distance. Me head spun with adventurous thoughts but I knew they had to be put aside fer present duties. He told me how he had bought a new food called rice but had lost it all to some voracious insect and only had damp moldy husks when he arrived back in England. Then he showed me one of his prized possessions. It was a grey robe with brown squares all over it made from something called silk. It felt warm to the touch yet he said it was pleasant to wear, even in the heat of summer.

Me lessons with Sir DuLac were informative to say the least, and somewhat painful at times.

Of course we used blunted lances with balls on the ends, not the ones fer war. It still hurt a lot if he got past me shield or dumped me on the ground. Storm was a big help, he had been trained as a knights' horse and knew what was expected of him. At first I held me shield up too much with a slight tilt back. I was told not to but glancing hard smacks in the helmet taught me quicker. DuLac was a merciless teacher and was so good I had no hope of getting past his guard.

The day came when I did. We broke three lances on three passes, and then I dumped him on the ground. I rode to the end of the lists feeling jubilation and then apprehension. 'I'd dumped the greatest knight in Christendom on the ground? Fuck!!'

I turned Storm around and saw DuLac standing in the middle of the list with his helm off. His squire, one Christovan, was calming his horse. I nervously rode up to him and dismounted. I swallowed hard, 'Are ye alright Sir?'

With a faint smile, he knuckled me in the shoulder. He then held out his hand which I took. 'Your lessons are done, squire. Keep practicing but you won't need me anymore. You have done well. Remember young man, you have learned the couched lance but it is not for you to use yet. Once you become a knight, then and only then.'

The day of the big move came all too soon even though it was months late. It was already the middle of September and a wondrous day to travel. I dropped off at the Smithy with a lump where me heart was, thinking of Tom. Our lads were all packed and cavalry farriers were already setting up shop.

'Ready to go Raglin?' I nodded to and greeted Helmsley, 'Did I ever thank ye fer saving me life? I owe ye.'

He smiled, showing missing and blackened teeth. 'It was me pleasure sir, ye owe me nothing.'

I filed away that I did, and went to check on Cheve and Pat. 'Good morrow me friends, it looks like ye have the blacks where ye want them. Enjoy the journey.'

'Oui mon ami, you too.'

'I hear ye sat DuLac on his arse.' Pat was grinning. 'Good job Will, good job. Wish I had bin there. See yer at the other end.'

I was hesitant a bit as I turned away. I so liked being with the horses, that was one thing I would greatly miss.

We moved out mid morning and I cantered along the line of carts, cattle and horses. The pigs and bull were staying at Barton's croft. He had Sir Roberts' permission to collect siring fees. Yeomen were at the rear, all on palfreys. I soon rode abreast of the Swiss pike, I couldn't spot Uri but captain Swingley gave me a friendly but curt nod. I rode on to tell Sir Robert that all was well and everything was in place. He thanked me and let me withdraw to visit me family. Joseph and Miriam were with Gwen. Actually all the women were in a group, including Meg and entourage, who were leading ponies with panniers of pots and pans and other implements. I alit from Storm and holding his bridle, walked with Miriam, holding hands. She chose that moment to tell me she was with child. I couldn't wipe the silly grin off me face, except when I kissed her, perhaps, not even then.

The attack came in the late afternoon. The woods looked peaceful and still. Shield banging and yelling, all around us, alerted us, it was such a din. Yeomen divided on the double to each side of us, stringing their bows to face trouble. The Swiss pike took up positions covering the women, and Du Boors and DuLac with their infantry, took up position near the front. I shelved the wonderful news and raced towards Sir Robert, high grass swishing around Storms legs, to take me place. Sir Gawain and Sir Lensberg were already there, as I rode up and took position on me mentors shield quarter. I grinned to meself, just as Jarrad was doing fer Sir Gawain. I opted fer a weapon in each hand rather than using a shield. Two swords, as Darragh was wont to do. I realized he was close by when he raised his in salute. I returned the gesture. I checked that me coif was tied at the back so it wouldn't shift, tied off me reins and spiraled me swords to loosen me wrists. Storm, like most warhorses, had been trained to knee commands.

Armored riders appeared at the edge of the woods in no particular formation. They broke into a gallop, down the hill. It looked like every man fer himself. Then, there came the men on foot, many of them painted with woad. It looked like a lot of them. I still couldn't make out who they were. Picts maybe? Not a disciplined army, that's fer sure.

The Swiss had split their forces to face both sides. In one voice, they shouted 'Guten tag mein freund!' and their pikes dropped into position. The first row almost horizontal and the second at about a ten to fifteen degree cant. The cavalry facing them tried to break their headlong charge but to no avail. They were skewered on the pikes and there were milling, thrashing horses on the ground all mixed up with struggling men. A line of pike-men, their pikes set aside, had drawn swords and laid into the fallen without mercy.

On the other side the men on foot were able to stop their headlong rush and were milling about and hacking, trying to get past the pikes. Very few made it past the points only to be cut down by sword wielding Swiss.

The Yeomen let fly with a barrage of arrows and men fell everywhere. I really don't think the attackers had done their homework. When the knights charged with leveled lances followed by yelling infantry, the attack suddenly turned into a rout.

# **THORWALD FITZ PATRICK**

The rout was feigned. As soon as the running men reached the trees, arrows rained down on us. It was by the grace of God that none of our knights were seriously hit, even though the brunt of arrows fell around them. DuBoors was hit in the right hand and one skinned the rump of Sir Roberts' horse. He began kicking and bucking but Sir Robert managed to stay on and regain control. While this was going on, a line of heavy cavalry appeared on the side facing us, and more infantry on the other. I was now wishing fer a shield instead of two swords.

Sir Robert yelled. 'Retreat and form on the road!'

His command was passed on and I saw that he was not going yet. We were covering the retreating men at arms. I jumped down and helped a soldier to his feet. He had an arrow in his thigh. I handed him off to another man and got back on Storm.

Lances came down to point at the enemy. I looked over at Jarrad who gave me a wink before dropping his chin guard. As one, the knights charged, crashing into the enemy cavalry before they got momentum. After initial contact the knight's lances were discarded. We all fought with weapons of choice, back stepping towards the road.

Du Lac broke away, crushing three helms on his way by. He went to take charge of the other side his squire close behind.

I jumped to Sir Roberts' aid when a hammer crunched his helmet, twisting it so he couldn't see. I deflected a second stroke with one sword, dispatching the wielder with the other. Another man got past me, seeing me masters' dilemma and taking advantage. Suddenly he flew twisting through the air as Sir Roberts stallion grabbed his face with bared teeth and flung him, likely breaking his neck or back. I killed yet another and then Jarrad was there to help. I jumped Storm to Sir Roberts' side, and helped him get the helm off. There was a nasty cut on his forehead, filling his eye with blood and his cheekbone was turning blue. Sir Gawain was there, pushing between us, and the enemy. He must have seen our dilemma and sent Jarrad ahead. Sir Gawain was a master of the flail, which is three spiked balls on chains attached to a single handle. I never tried one in fear of hurting me self. Men were reeling around him and then Du Boors arrived swinging a morning star with his left hand, with Sir Gawain on his right, no one could get past that wall of death. Our personal retreat had been very slow, fighting fer every inch of ground. Swiss pike-men materialized all around us and formed in front of us. They were so efficient there was a buttress wall between us and the enemy, just like that. They deliberately stabbed horses in front of them, leaving the riders to sort it out.They moved back, covering us, to reform with the others.

I got a bit of a breather and then I spotted a huge man in black boiled leather. Me blood ran cold as I yelled. 'It's Garrad the Black Milord, these are Skyes men!'

He was making a beeline fer sir Arthur and I pushed me way past men to get between the two. He slashed at me and I parried. His blow was so hard it numbed me arm and shoulder. I managed a slash at his knees, making him jump back but I knew I wasn't doing well against him. Then Darragh was between me and him and Garrad stepped back to eye his new opponent. Darragh was big but not as big as his foe. Garrad recognized him and knew his reputation. He was willing to put his own up against it. Besides, his master would reward him greatly if he could take this man.

Fighting near us slacked off a bit as men stopped to watch those two opponents probing and feinting, feeling each other out. It was building up to be a fight to remember.

It ended abruptly! Fresh cavalry came, riding parallel to us, and smashed into the enemy. A man closing on me went down with a spear in his throat it was fletched like an arrow. I had never seen one before. To put it simple, the enemy fled and the new cavalry ravaged them as they fled, leaving groups of dead and dying all the way back to the trees. Garrad disappeared and I never did see Skye.

It was over, and we were left to lick our wounds. We had quite a few wounded but fortunately very few dead. The stranger horsemen guarded our flanks as they checked over and killed enemy wounded. A tall man trotted his charger over to us, dropped to the ground and removed his helm. His voice had a musical lilt to it.

'Fortunately we were in time.' He smiled through drooping mustaches as he shook out his long black hair. Extending a hand, he said, 'My name is Thorwald Fitz Patrick, at your service.'

Sir Robert took his hand. 'Your intervention was most welcome Sir. By your accent, you hale from Ireland?'

'Yes, I am a Dane but a patriot to Ireland. We go back a few generations. We stood against Edward Earl of Carrick. I suppose you knew him as Robert the Bruce's brother. His only goal, even as king, was to disrupt our country. After he was slain in battle, by Sir John De Bermingham, Edward left Ireland fractured into little bits. It took us these past years to do some healing. Lately we have been following Krayan McOrdreds army, trying to make him and his sons accountable for atrocities committed while supporting Edward. We finally placed Krayan McOrdred in chains, only to have him escape with the help of Brian, his second son. They have slipped through our fingers once again. Our spies brought word that Skye had hired an army and landed here in England. We chased him here, even though we are on enemy shores, and now he has escaped yet again.'

Sir Robert smiled. 'Well, at least you saved our arses. You are no enemy of mine, please join us for lunch?' I was tending Sir Roberts wound and was just finishing the bandage when he turned to me. 'Will, try to find us something to eat and drink. Even water will do.'

I went to do his bidding and was joined by Christovan, DuLacs squire. He wore a brown hooded cloak over mail and had a heavy cross hanging around his neck. His rather sinister face was long and narrow with heavy brows but when he occasionally smiled, it transformed him.

'I will help you English, we should bring food too.'

'Call me Will, I believe I know yer name, Christovan isn't it? Where do ye hale from?'

'Espania, Sevilla to be exact. My father sent me away to become a priest.' He shrugged, 'Here I am.'

'So ye didn't become a priest but a squire?'

He stared at me fer a moment. 'Obviously you do not recognize the garb. Yes I am a squire and a Dominican... more of a body guard placed with my lord, by his family.'

'Ah, warrior clerics, I have heard somewhat of ye.'

His eyes sparked with religious fervor. 'You will hear much more of us as we cleanse the Holy Church. We carry our swords as Gabriel and Michael did, to smite the heathen and the heretic and bring God to their hearts.'

I flinched a bit, hoping he didn't see. He was so different from Brother John.

I found Meg who was doctoring wounds along with Miriam and Gwen's help. I informed her of Du Boors' injury and then told her what I needed. She sent Colette to help us, the pretty little French girl soon found us a barrel of ale and some black bread with cheese and cold roast venison steaks from the night before. She placed the meat in a wet clay box to keep it cool. I thanked her, as Christovan and I split the load to carry back.

When we returned, introductions had already been made, and the knights had made themselves as comfortable as the terrain permitted. Jarrad came to help and we soon had a dining table of sorts, made from crates. The knights dug in with zeal. Fighting whetted the appetite. Sir Robert and Fitzpatrick soon had their heads together in deep conversation. We sat in the high grass and had our own bread and cheese. I introduced Jarrad to Christovan, though they had met briefly in passing.

As I chewed on the tough bread and sharp cheese, I watched the newcomers interact with the Swiss and the yeomen. One Swiss was examining one of those fletched spears with great curiosity. I found out later that many Irish still used the weapon even though it was antiquated. It had been around for a few hundred years but had died out everywhere except Ireland. The Swiss hefted it and threw with an exceptionally good, long throw. The missile held true without a wobble and it didn't tumble. It hit the target stump with a thunk and the Irish that owned it was thumping the Swiss on the back while the others cheered. I spotted Uri who was watching the proceedings. I excused meself and wended me way to him.

'Uri, my friend, I'm happy ter see ye in one piece.'

He grinned at me, his face pulling from the scar. 'It was a little workout. You look well, no wounds I see. Who were they that attacked us?'

I told him about Skye. 'He usually has about thirty or forty men with him, where he got this small army, I don't know. Paid mercenaries I suppose, I know some were Picts. They are pretty well lost in time but some still abide.'

'How do you know them?'

'They paint themselves blue with woad. Mind ye, some of the Scots do too.'

Uri nodded, 'Many of our mountain tribes do the same. The blue plant grows in many places. Look, some of your friends come.'

It was Cheve and Pat along with Pierce and Rene. Cheve smiled, 'I saw ye, mon ami, and wanted to see how ye were.' His English was getting quite good.

Pat cut in. 'The fighting was heaviest where ye and yer knights were and we were worried.'

'Thank ye fer the thought Pat. How did the horses fare?'

'Good! There were a couple of attempted thefts but we spanked them and sent them on their way.' He grinned. 'The yeomen helped a little.'

'I have to get back, I'm neglecting me duties.' I remembered the Andalusian got a slice on the rump. 'Ye should have seen Sir Roberts horse take out an enemy, it was brutal.'

'Doesn't he have a name yet?'

'Yes, always has had a name, its 'Taxeia' meaning swift in Greek.'

'An Englishman's horse, and with a Greek name what next.'

I shrugged and grinned. 'He was probably named by a Moor.'


Bamburg Castle was a huge, brooding, sprawling edifice, sitting on a black rock out crop that controlled both sea and land. Building had started back in the dim past, perhaps at the time of the Angles and had been tweaked with, and altered by Jutes, Celts, Danes, Saxons and Normans and the list goes on. Bamburg was one of three huge fortresses that controlled the north, and how DuLac got it, I have no idea. As I passed under a massive raised portcullis, I looked about me and saw Stone on stone and more stone. I shook me head somehow, it lacked the warmth of our old lodgings. But this was to be our new home fer a while and we'd better make the best of it. I grinned to meself, if we got an eviction notice it would be from the British king himself, and then what. Edward the third was on the throne, but his mother still ruled and wasn't known fer her kind disposition or fer keeping pacts.

Under a canopy of circling, crying seabirds, we made our way to a set of apartments reserved for Sir Robert and entourage. I discovered later that sir Gawain had lodgings near by though he would be there less than half the time. I had to admit that our apartments were very comfortable and Miriam got to work right off, to make them our home. From one window, ye could see a large garden, the greenery contrasted greatly with the stone. I found out later that there were many such throughout the castle grounds. Enough turnips, beets, vegetables and fruit were grown to help support those within during a siege.

Me first mission was to find out where the horses would be quartered. I bloody well found out where, it seemed a mile away, through a warren of stone. I then discovered that our suite had private stalls for our own chargers. Someone had thought of almost everything.

Being around Sir Robert all the time, I soon learned that DuLac's French heritage plus the Catholic power of his family had swayed Isabella to help him, ergo Bamburg Castle. I was curious to know what would happen if the Fench influence was gone. Me curiosity was growing about some other things too but I kept me thoughts to meself other than trusting me wife to keep things I spoke of in private, to herself.

Sir Robert would go exploring on most days with me and twenty yeomen tagging along. He told me that a pact had been drawn up, between Fitz Patrick and himself. Fitz Patrick would give the McOrdreds no breathing space when they were in Ireland. Their considerable estates were confiscated and they had to live like fugitives while there. On the reverse of the coin, they would get no rest while in England. We solicited the Crown and the Church in this endeavor, citing the terrible crimes that had been committed.

If they tried to enter Wales they'd get short thrift, but many Welsh were not cooperating beyond their borders. They seemed to be pissed off at just about anyone. And even though they were under English rule they were especially pissed off at the British thanks to Edward the 1st.

We would learn later, that the McOrdreds had created a stronghold on the Isle of Man which was a bit of a pirates nest in these lawless times.

When the tide was out, and even when the tide was in, there were vast beaches and mudflats, mostly to the south of Bamburg. They were home to hundreds of birds, shore birds, mud walkers and sea birds. Northeast of the castle there was a vast area of dunes, where one could lose an army. We needed to know the area like the back of our hands to form strategic battle plans.

Today he chose the beach and the wind was brisk but warm as I looked over the strand. It swirled making dust devils here and there. Sitting birds would spiral up with raucous cries only to settle down again. The antics of the birds were amusing to watch, when a query from Sir Robert shook me out of me dream world.

'Pardon milord?'

'Do you see those ships off shore?'

I squinted at where he was pointing. 'Aye sir, they have the rakish lines of the old Norse. They are Irish, most likely pirates, certainly not traders or fishers.'

'My thoughts exactly squire. Lets perk up the yeomen and have them gallop along the beach, and pace those blighters, a little show might deter them from landing hereabouts.'

I turned Storm fer home. 'Aye sir, and shall we put the pike on alert? We can't know but they might be allies of Skye.' 'I'll do that, you stay with Ross.'

# **MORGAN**

I rode with Ross and the men as we cantered along the foam line. The ships were being rowed, their single sail furled. They stayed parallel and matched us, except one who veered and was heading towards shore. Ross halted the yeomen and beckoning to me, got off his horse and walked towards the incoming vessel. Standing with wavelets lapping around our feet, we watched as the oarsmen shipped their poles and gently ran her aground. Two men jumped off into thigh deep water and waded towards us.

One cupped hands to his mouth. 'Do any of ye have authority to parley?'

Ross looked at me and called back, 'Aye, we both do and he speaks fer our Lord directly!'

I watched the spokes man as he neared. An inch or so shorter than me, he had a lot of hair. Hair spilling over his tunics' neck, and thick hair on his arms, a short cut but heavy beard almost hiding a crooked nose and curly strands sticking out from under a steel pisspot helm. As he rose up out of the sea, I saw how hairy his legs were too. He shook himself like a dog, spraying water glittering in the sunlight.

'We have a hostage up for ransom. I think yer lord would be most interested in this one.'

'What do ye know about our lord, who's up and how much?' I growled it at him and then looked at Ross, not really sure of me ground.

'We have a lass she is unmolested, no one has raped her.' He smirked, "No one would dare try. She is pure and I wager that yer lord would pay a hundred guineas for her.'

'We do not have any money with us ye would have to wait a bit.'

Ross cut in, 'And we would need to see her.'

I was watching the second man, nondescript in every way except fer the sword hanging from his shoulder and two dirks in his belt. Me attention was drawn back to the first when he said 'Bring the payment, we'll bring the lass.'

'Does she have a name?'

'Morgan.'

Ross stiffened. 'Will, go tell Sir Robert. If he grants it, bring the money.'

I hied it back and told Sir Robert about the ransom. When I repeated the name he looked momentarily stunned. He went straight away to a strong box and extracted a bag of coin. 'Let's go, lead the way Will.'

Ross and the two men stood up as we approached. The other yeomen had already remounted when they saw us approaching.

Sir Robert studied the duo for a moment and then jingled the sack. 'Where is she?'

The first man signaled the second. 'Fetch her.'

As we waited, Sir Robert fumed. 'I should have all of you eradicated for doing this.'

The man raised an eyebrow. 'We're just earning a living milord. Oh, ye should know that Skye McOrdred wanted her in the worst way.' He chuckled. 'And now he doesn't like me much.'

'So you don't answer to him?' I watched as a woman was dropped over the side and the man below, grabbed her arm. Her hands were tied behind her back and even from where I stood I could see that she was beautiful, as well as tall fer a woman.

'Answer to that butcher, never! He gives all privateers a bad name. Ye know, he is living on our Island now? And that's bad enough.'

The woman was pulled roughly to shallower water when she suddenly turned and drove her forehead into her captors' nose. He went down and came up spluttering and raging, pulling his dirk. Thin blood mixed with seawater leaked down his face. I leaped towards him with drawn sword.

'Sheath yer snee, she is with us now!'

Sir Robert tossed the bag of coin to the other who turned and restrained his friend with an upheld hand.

'They're right boyo, she is not ours anymore, take yer lumps.' He turned to us with a bow. 'It's been nice doing business with ye.' He looked at me with a devilish look. 'If ye ever need help with something, just bring money, ye seem to be free with it. Me name is Carver Merrell and this touchy fellow is me first mate, John Lynch.'

I nodded and pulled me dirk. Turning to the woman, I cut her bonds. 'Are ye alright Maam?' I was concerned, and then rather taken aback when her dark blue eyes coldly turned on me and she said. 'Piss off!'

I just watched as this auburn haired, mean minded sod of a Lady mounted a palfrey, leaving a yeoman to ride double.

As we rode back to the fortress, Sir Robert looked at me with the glummest look and whispered, 'God's truth Will, that's my half sister!'

When we entered the courtyard she jumped down, not too concerned that she was mostly naked in her torn garments. Her voice had a pleasing huskiness to it.

'Well brother, I suppose I should thank you for saving my arse. I hope I didn't leave you a pauper.' She stalked over to him and took him by the shoulders. 'Seriously Robert dear, thank you, I was on my way here when we were attacked by those pirates and our ship was sunk. The men with me were a bunch of curs, not one with spunk in the whole lot.'

'What are you saying Morgan. They all die on you?'

'Don't be clever, brother dearest, they ran or should I say swam or surrendered. There was this creepiest red haired man that wanted me. Not much scares me but he did, and he seemed to know who I was. Carver Merrell, the captain, said I was their booty and to back off. I'll say this much for him, when he was offered a large sum of money, he didn't take it. They rattled their swords a bit and the red head backed down, he was slightly outnumbered. I was only with them a few days and you know the rest. I lost everything Robert, including my weapons. Can you help me get settled?'

'Of course, I'm sure we can accommodate you in your own apartments. Now I would like you to meet my squire, Will Barrow, he negotiated your release.'

'Bullshit! That Merrill said give me a hundred guineas and this one said yes. That's not negotiation that's buying a woman. Something you men are so fucking good at. Anyway we met, I wasn't impressed the first time and not now.'

I had me hand out but I let it drop to me side. 'It wasn't me place to put a price on yer well being, mistress, so save yer vipers tongue.'

She just glared and turned away. This woman didn't seem to like me and I was beginning not to like her. I stepped back and looked at Ross who grimaced and shrugged.

I asked Sir Roberts permission to withdraw but he took me elbow and told me to stay. I think he was a little scared of his sister and needed moral support.

'Morgan, Will is married and Mistress Gwen is here, I'm sure the women would be pleased to help you settle in.'

She turned to me. 'So, you are a married man. Very well, you can introduce me to your wife. Now someone show me to my quarters.' She wrinkled her nose in distaste. 'I need to get cleaned up, being on that ship left me itchy and stinking of fish stew. That's all they seemed to eat.'

She was a completely different person when she was introduced to Miriam her disposition was actually sunny and friendly. She and Gwen already knew each other and began catching up on things right away.

I was trying to figure out what she was doing here in the first place. Why was she on her way here when she got captured? I was beginning to have a lot of questions about many things. Fer one thin, why had all these knights congregated here? Each of them could have improved things in their homelands, if that was their true agenda.

Next morning, after a wonderful breakfast of porridge with honey and pears, I went to work out with Darragh. Having breakfast with me wife was truly a bonus we had so little time together.

When I got there, he was already sparring with Morgan. She was bloody good, fast and cagey, and it was all Darragh could do to keep her off him. She even kicked him in the balls. He groaned but managed to keep on fighting. He had taught me that. Learn to fight and mask the pain, it will pass. If you don't, you'll likely be feeling nothing any more.

He saw me and grounded his sword, welcoming the respite. I noticed him massage his wrist it still bothered him, more than he let on. She stepped back and looked at me, not even breathing hard.

'You want a go?' Her voice was just possibly a little friendlier than yesterday.

I nodded as I took the falcon stance exercise was exercise.

'Oh, it looks like you know how to fight. Your wife tells me you are a really sweet man. I've never met one!' She lunged, almost catching me off guard. She was clever making me focus on meself rather than her. I parried, and a flurry of offensive cuts sent her tripping backwards. We circled looking fer an opening, and then she made her move again. I managed to force her back once more. I felt she was just a bit impatient and let her sour view of men cloud her best judgment.

92

I relaxed a bit, dropping me point just a trifle to give her an opening. She made the mistake of taking it. I stepped inside her steel and brought me sword arm across her throat as me knee went behind hers. She went down on her arse with me sword waving in her face.

I grounded me weapon and held out me hand, which she took.

'Yes! You do know how to fight.' She stood up, rubbing her bottom with a frown and then a slight smile. 'We must try that again, perhaps tomorrow?'

I bowed, 'Same time me Lady?' Her opinion of me seemed to have changed a bit.

'Yes, the same time will be fine. Now, if you wouldn't mind, be so kind as to take me to the smith? I have no idea where he is in this labyrinth.'

'Aye me Lady, it's a bit of a walk. I'll show ye around on the way.'

We walked together and I pointed out a few thins of interest, such as the Chapel, and the granaries and storage buildings. We passed another large open area where some of the Swiss were going through manoeuvres of some kind.

'Who are they? I've not seen their like before.'

'They are the Swiss pike, my Lady, very good at what they do.' I spotted Uri who gave me a nod and a slight grin. He was busy.

Morgan was very aware of things, 'You know him?'

'I do, he has become a good friend.'

We arrived at the smithy and Morgan looked at me with a slight smile. 'You seem to make friends easily, or so your wife says. I can even feel myself giving over to you. I never had that knack.'

I thought, 'I'm not surprised.' 'This is Raglin me Lady, he is as close to an armorer as we have. He was still in apprenticeship when our Tom was killed but he does do good work.'

Raglin bowed. 'Me Lady, what can I do fer ye?'

'I badly need some mail and weapons. I lost everything at sea.'

He looked startled, since women don't usually wear armor, then he caught himself. 'You might be in luck me lady.' Raglin walked towards the back, while he spoke. 'Tom was a craftsman and he left a suit of scale armor after the Danish style. It's a little tighter than most. Ah, here it is.'

He turned holding a handsome suit of mail with shining fish scales against black etching, dulled slightly by a layer of dust.

Morgan pursed her lips. 'That truly is nice I would like to try it on.'

Raglin looked around. 'There is a gambeson around here somewhere that should be close to yer size. Yes, here it is!' It came out of a pile in a cloud of dust.

Morgan wrinkled her nose in distaste and then sneezed. She seemed to wrinkle her nose a lot. 'I'm not wearing that filthy thing.'

I grabbed it and took it outside. I gave it several hard shakes, almost choking me self, and took it back in. "It's not perfect but better." I stifled a sneeze.

She pulled her tunic over her head leaving her upper body totally naked. She certainly had beautiful breasts, with no sag at all. Raglin was bug eyed and I heard Helmsley's hammer stop. I quickly stepped in front of her holdin the gambeson fer her to slip into. She did so with a faint smirk. She liked her power over men. I appreciated her beauty but I wasn't drawn to her. There was much not to like about this woman.

I turned her around, firmly by the shoulder, pulled away trapped hair and began buckling her up.

'This fits a little loose, I'll need one made as soon as possible.' She held her arms in the air as I dropped the mail over her head. It reached below her knees. 'Damn, it needs to be shortened.' She gave Raglin an almost worried look. 'Can you do that?' She turned to me. 'How does it look besides that?'

Raglin said 'Aye me lady, I can and right away.'

I looked her over and she must have seen me approval. 'It fits, does it?'

I smiled. 'Aye me lady, ye look the very image of a Valkyrie, now ye need a sword balanced fer ye, oh, and coif and greaves.'

'Greaves yes but I don't like wearing a coif, it plasters my hair. A padded helm is all I want.'

Raglin was taking it all in and had already marked the alteration. 'I noticed that new ties are needed on the mail, the old ones have dried out.'

'I noticed too, that's why I had it dropped over my head. Will, can you help me get it off?'

'That's easy me lady, since they have to be replaced anyway.' I pulled me dirk and slit lacings all the way up the back, and she was able to slip out of it. She spoke to Raglin with a teasing tone.

'Do you want the gambeson back?'

His eyes got all round again. 'No me lady, do with it as ye will.' He held a sword out to her. It was a little slimmer and lighter than most.

She gave it a couple of parries and thrusts, even a chop or two. She frowned a bit. 'The length is good but the blade is a little light and unbalanced.'

He took it and added two lead rings to the grip, one at each end, and a smaller one to the point of the blade.

She gave it a few more swipes and lounges. 'Yes, that's it, the weight is perfect, but now the grip is a little long and I don't like the leather. It gets slippery when wet.'

"I plan on making ye a whole new weapon me lady. The tang on this one is cracked. I just needed a model.'

'When will it all be ready?'

'Come back in two days, I have plenty of blanks already made up, fer dirks too.'

She nodded approval. 'I need one of those too. Walk back with me Will I know I've been keeping you from your duties.'

As we walked, I took the opportunity to tell her that me wife and her da could make her a fitted gambeson and anything else she needed. We arrived back and she cordially thanked me.

'See you at ten tomorrow morning.'

I reported to Sir Robert and told him where I had been.

'You are a bit late, but rather than admonish you I'll thank you. Two hours with her and she was still cordial? You never cease to amaze me. I suppose I'll have to come up with the money to cover all her expenses. Now I would like you to join me for a ride. I am meeting sir Gawain at that ruined monastery ten miles down the road and it's already late.'

'How many yeomen will we take Sir?'

'Twenty should do, our scouts have seen nothing untoward.'

I thought, 'discretion would be a good thing,' but didn't say anything. 'I'll roust up the men sir.'

The weather was fine fer traveling, warm with a bit of a breeze. A few windblown clouds cut out the sun, every now and then, giving a reprieve from its heat.

The monastery came into view. Several ruined buildings covered with flowering vines. There was honeysuckle and a lot of bindweed with its white, bellflowers. Seven palfreys stood with their reins hanging. The black charger belonging to Sir Gawain stood nearby. The sound of our hooves brought Sir Gawain out in the open with Tim by his side. The others stayed in the shade.

I stepped down from Storm and bowed to Sir Gawain. 'It's good to see ye sir.'

He smiled, 'I'm pleased to see ye too, Will. How do ye like yer new home?'

'Well enough sir.' I turned and embraced Tim. 'I've missed ye.'

He pushed me to arms length and gave me a light punch in the arm. 'Ye are looking right well, Will. How is yer family and me auntie?'

The two knights were wondering off with their heads together as I followed Tim back to the shade with the twenty yeomen close behind. There were greetings all around and then I turned to two of my men.

'Take yer water bottles and find spots by the road to keep watch. Yer auntie is beginning to feel at home but misses ye, Tim." I could tell by his face that he missed her too. 'Miriam is beginning to show now and her da is well but his hands are worse, if anything.'

'How are Darragh and Ross?'

'Ross is well but I'm a little worried about Darragh. I was instrumental in hurting his wrist and it's not getting better. He hides it but I know. By the way, did ye know that sir Robert has a sister?'

Tim grimaced, 'Aye, I know Mistress Morgan, a right piece of work, that one. How did ye know?'

'I've been showing her around, she's at the castle.'

'And ye are still alive? I'm amazed!' He grinned and then sobered. 'Have ye seen Du Lac and associates?'

'Ye know ?, I haven't, I have been so busy with Sir Robert and then his sister, I didn't give it a thought. I'm realizing, now that ye have mentioned it, that I haven't. By the way, where is Jarrad?"

"Of course ye didn't know. Someone injured his horse in ambush and Jarrad was thrown against a rather large tree. He badly bruised his ribs and we have him all strapped up. He is improving so don't worry. The culprit scarpered and we never did find him.'

I had visions of Gordie, though it could have been anyone. That face always came back to haunt me.

Our knights returned and said their goodbyes. Sir Gawain mounted and looked down on me. 'Keep him safe Will. Ye heard about Jarrad?'

I nodded, 'Aye, please give him me respects and be careful sir, God speed!'

He pulled the green scarf from around his neck and wiped his face, wearing mail was hot work-

He gave me a nod and said, 'I'll be seeing ye anon Robert, Tata fer now.' He left at a cantor with Tim in Jarrad's spot and the other six in the lead.

'Let the men snack, and then we will head back.'

'Aye sir, I'll go spell the two on the road, and join up when ye leave.' After sending the two back, I found a shaded spot and chewed on a piece of dried venison. It tasted like an old belt, but it was something to get me spit going. I was only there a bit when I saw a dust cloud and then a horseman galloping towards us. It was sir Gawain, alone.

He shouted 'I need yer help, me lads are trapped!'

I yelled, 'Alarm!' and jumped onto Storm.

Sir Robert was there right off, along with the men. As we galloped down the road, Sir Gawain shouted over the noise. 'A tree was felled and as we approached, we heard wood snapping and another was dropping behind us. Tim turned me horse and whacked him before it hit the ground. He saved me arse and now I need to save his.'

We covered ground quickly when he held up his hand fer us to stop. He kept his voice low.

'Just around that bend there's a cut between banks. That's where the lads are.'

Sir Robert said. 'Will, take twelve to the left. Try and slip into place. Gawain and I will take the others to the right.' We jumped from our horses, yeomen stringing their bows. We quickly fanned out and moved through the tall grass. A lookout was spotted and an arrow took him down before he could shout a warning. Now we could see others and they were concentrating on what was in front of them. Silent arrows took a couple more out before one turned and raised the alarm. We charged. I knew we were outnumbered but hoped surprise would help. A yeoman beside me broke his bow across the face of an enemy, and then drew his sword with the rest of us.

I saw me nemesis. Gordie was giving orders to nearby archers, and the skin on me face pulled tight. He was mine! I didn't even notice how many men I cut through, I only had eyes fer him. At first he didn't see me and when he did, I was on top of him. He reacted quickly and tried to draw me into a mistake going at me with a sloppy sword cut, I could see his poisoned dirk held low at his side. That's what I went fer, shouting into his face.

'This is fer Joss!'

I slashed, and his knife was on the ground, still in his twitching hand. He was already screaming when I bashed him in the face with the pommel of me sword.

'That's fer Courser!'

Me foot slammed into the back of his leg bringing him to his knees. As I stood in front of him, setting me self, he tried to sneer, his yellow teeth pink with his own blood.

'This is fer Tom!'

The sneer never left his face as his head bounced across the ground.

It was over. I felt a kind of relief flow through me as I turned to me duties. We were winning, I could see across the road and the two knights fighting side by side. The yeomen were taking the fight to the enemy who were looking fer escape. I jumped down to the road and took stock. Three of the six men were down and one was Tim. I raced to him and rolled him over. I almost got a dirk in the gut when he recognized me and stopped the thrust.

'Will, Will! Oh it's good to see yer face. I had given me self over to Gods Angels.'

I cradled him and saw he had taken two arrows, one high in the chest near the shoulder and one in the thigh.

'I am too ugly to be an Angel so ye must be still living me friend, and I have hopes ye will continue to do so.'

Sir Gawain came up beside me. 'How is he?'

'Alive sir but in bad shape, I think we need his auntie!'

The other two fallen were dead and dying. One soon died in the arms of a comrade, the other long gone with an arrow through the eye. Of me own twenty men, all were standing though a couple were limping and nursing minor wounds. The felled trees had been heavily limbed so the horses couldn't leap over them. It was those limbs that had saved the other three and they had given as good as they got in a battle with arrows.

Sir Robert stood with me and watched as a litter was made on Sir Gawain's orders. 'I saw you dismantle that Gordie fellow, remind me to never really piss you off.' He wiped the corners of his mouth with thumb and finger. 'Shall we get ready to go home? Sir Gawain will stay with us until Tim can travel again.'

Yeomen had cut the trees and pulled them aside so they wouldn't be hindering anyone else traveling the road.

Gordie's head was put on a spike by the road, as a warning. A written board let travelers know there was one less outlaw to worry about.

The litter was ready and two men carried Tim so he wouldn't get jounced about too much. One other went ahead to alert Meg. It was already late, and it would take at least two to three hours to travel on foot, we were prepared to arrive in darkness.

We heard horses approaching and tensed in readiness. Then we saw them coming through the twilight. It was Morgan, leading another twenty men.

'You are safe, brother dear.' She saw Gawain and rode over to him. 'I'm pleased to see you safe too, my friend. I brought some more men just in case you all were still at risk.'

He smiled, it's always a pleasure, Morgan. How are ye? I do not think the risk is great fer now. Will destroyed their leader and they scattered." He proceeded to tell her what had taken place and a little of the history between Gordie and me.

We arrived in the dark but Morgan had foreseen and brought torches. Some of the Swiss Pike had mustered at the gate and covered us as we entered the castle. Morgan stayed with us as we brought Tim to his auntie.

Meg was pale but ready to do what she could. Both arrows had broken off, which was a problem fer the one in his leg. Normal procedure was to push it through to the other side then flush the wound and then cauterize. Now the arrow had to be cut out, and so did the one in his chest. Having to do two, would put a lot of strain on Tim and he could die from the trauma. We didn't know how much damage the arrow in his chest was inflicting and wouldn't until Meg cut in. Morgan stayed and so did I, Miriam was there too. Meg sprinkled some kind of powder on both wounds.

'It will help numb things a bit, now pour some spirits down his throat, as much as he can take.'

She did the chest first because she knew it would put the most strain on Tim. We had to hold him down and still, as best we could. 'The arrow had punched through his mail and has gone in about four inches.

'I can feel the head and which way it lies.' She took a deep breath. 'Hang on to him, because here goes.'

Tim screamed and tried to buck. Morgan and I had his arms and held on tight. His legs were already strapped to the cot. Miriam was standing by with cloths and hot water to assist Meg. The work became easier after he passed out. She made two incisions in the form of a star and then cut deeper. Blood welled from the wound and Miriam soaked it away with cloths. Meg, sweating, brushed her sleeve across her forehead.

'We don't want the arrow to stick. The flesh has closed around it, holding it firm. These cuts should help. Will, I need yer strength. Wash yer hands with spirits. I want ye to pull steadily and straight up on the arrow. There is not much to grip so be careful.'

The short, broken haft was slippery with Tim's blood. I closed me mind to everything except fer gripping it firmly and not letting go. I slowly drew up on it and then Morgan gasped.

'I see the head, ye are doing well.'

I felt pressure release and I was holding it in me hand. It wasn't barbed, which was a blessin but blood was pouring from the open wound. Meg was still probing and removed some metal pieces. They were bits of chainmail punched into the wound. She threw them to the floor.

"I hope that's all! She took a needle and thread from Miriam, and did some stitching inside the wound. The flow of blood slowed down and seemed to stop. Meg selected a hollow reed and sliced it at an angle, making a sharp point. She then inserted it into the wound site through a new hole that she made.

'There that should help drain the wound.'

I looked at her, 'Aren't ye going to cauterize it Mom?'

She shook her head. 'Nay Will, it would certainly kill him. We will cauterize the leg.'

An hour later, all was done. Miriam had finished stitching the chest wound while Meg worked on the leg. Meg sat back, taking time to finally weep. 'Oh, me poor Tim!' She put her lips on his brow and then looked at us all. 'Thank ye fer yer help. Now we wait. If he can shake fever and lives the next day or two, he has a chance, barring infection.' She turned to Miriam. 'He's lost a lot of blood, as soon as he can eat, feed him broth. When he can keep that down, try him on beef and blood sausage, it may help to replenish. We must keep the wounds clean and change dressings frequently. Keep him on one side or the other so it will drain"

Miriam nodded as she put her head on me shoulder she was trembling. Morgan got to her feet and squeezed me other one.

'See you in the morning?'

I smiled at her and watched her leave. There was much more to her than one would guess.

I walked Miriam back to our apartments and told her I might be late. I then reported to Sir Robert who was trying to relax with Sir Gawain. He waved me to a chair and handed me a cool tankard of ale. He studied me as I took a swallow and then brought him up to date.

'I'm glad to hear Tim is alive. Your actions were exemplary today, Will. You are a fine leader and I have noticed you are also a natural tactician. You assume leadership without hesitation, the men listen and I am pleased with myself for the choices I made in your regard.' He actually grinned shamefacedly. 'That's enough patting myself on the back. I have decided, and Gawain concurs, that you will be knighted right after Christmas.. I am giving you two weeks to spend with your family your only duty will be your practice sessions.' He looked at Sir Gawain, who nodded. 'After your time off you will start your trials interspersed with prayer and meditation. This will be for the next few months. The night before the ceremony you will hold vigil with your weapons at the site of a tomb, in darkness for a period of contemplation that will last from sunset to sunrise.' Sir Robert sighed. "We have crypts within this fortress possibly even a king's tomb. Jute and Angle Knights and Celtic lords were all interred here at one time or another. Some were very ancient we just haven't found them yet.'

Sir Gawain chimed in. 'If ye fear ghosts and such, best steel yer self. Prayer will protect ye,' he grinned, 'but only up to a point.'

I took a deep breath and chewed on what they had just told me. It seemed to me that things were going much faster than normal. It seemed like only yesterday that I had become a squire. Me least concern was ghosts, I had not much belief in them since I had never seen one, or a fairy or a hob goblin.

'I am at a loss, Sirs. Ye give great honors to a swineherd. I cannot think of another instance where such a thing has happened.'

Gawain poured himself more ale. 'I know of several but one such sticks out fer me. There was a good knight by the name of Sir Kay.' He grinned to himself, 'We used to call him 'Clank'. He started as kitchen help, scrubbing pots and pans, and ended up looking fer the Grail in the holy land. He died in me arms in a Jerusalem alley, stabbed in the back by a cutpurse. It was such a bloody waste.' His eyes glowed in the firelight. 'I fer one will be thrilled to have ye by me side. Life is never certain so we must live it to the fullest while we can. I cherish the friends that I have and I count ye among them.'

Sir Robert looked at him thoughtfully, 'I remember Clank many called him the white knight because of his chastity. He took a vow of celibacy, didn't he?'

Sir Gawain rubbed his jaw. 'Aye, he never knew a woman and as far as I know, he never played with himself. He was as pure as driven snow and he drove me crazy.' He laughed aloud, 'Ye needn't take that route, Will. It's too late fer ye anyway.'

'Now go to your family, I'll see you in two weeks.... unless there's a war.' Sir Robert dismissed me with a friendly wave. I heard him say softly for sir Gawain's ears. 'Shit! Pretty soon I won't be able to order him around.'

There was an answering chuckle.

Spending glorious time with Miriam was simply wonderful. There were many untouched spots throughout the castle. One of our favorites was in a sunny alcove under the battlements, out of the wind, which was beginning to have a nip to it, and overlooking the sea. We took picnics up there and ate, made love and watched the endless birds. I loved to lay with me head in her lap. From there I could hear and feel the babe within, some days more than others.

On one such occasion, I looked up from Miriam's lap. 'What do ye think our bairn will be, dearest? Have ye chosen names, yet?'

Miriam smiled her wonderful smile. 'I believe it will be a boy and if you concur, I would call him Thomas in memory of your Tom.'

I could feel me self welling up inside as I smiled and gave her hand a squeeze. 'And if it's a girl?'

'I have always liked Ester, which means queen.'

'I lost a baby sister in the famine. Can we call her Ester Anne?'

She dropped her head down to mine, her hair screening us both, and gave me a kiss on the lips. 'Those are wonderful names, but I am certain it will be Thomas. My God, you are going to be a knight! How is that even possible? I am so proud of you, Will, so proud.'

We kissed again, long and hard and then made gentle love with her riding me to ease the weight on the babe. I lost meself in her eyes, her face and her hair.

I worked out every morning with Darragh or Morgan. She was a stickler fer exercising and never missed a day. She had noticed Darraghs difficulty and, one morning, gave him a pair of leather braces, which ye buckled on, and had a strap that could be made tight or looser.

'I had some similar to those, somewhere. Why do you give these to me?'

'A man I trained with, in Cornwall, told me that tightening them on your arm could relieve the pain in your wrist and make it stronger. Don't ask me why it works, I don't know. He said he learned it from a professional wrestler. They also tie cords on their upper arms to enhance strength.' She watched as Darragh put it near his wrist. 'Put it closer to the elbow, where the forearm is thickest.'

I watched the proceedings with interest, I had never heard of it when I wrestled, and I became even more interested when it began working.

One morning, Darragh came to me. 'You have no idea how much I was hurting and now it's gone, just like that. I don't even need the strap anymore.'

I looked at his wrist, it looked perfectly normal. 'I'm glad to hear that Darragh, I sort of felt responsible.'

'Don't be silly, Will. You may have irritated it but I already had moments when it troubled me, just not as bad as this last time. I think it might be some kind of rheumatism. Older soldiers often get something similar in their shoulders, elbows or knees. No one knows what it really is.'

Regular visits saw Tim grow in strength every day. He had avoided infection and, I believe, it was Megs' fastidiousness that diverted it. He certainly was a cheerful man and I am sure his attitude sped his healing. Miriam and I sat with him fer an hour, most days and the day came when I helped him outside fer some warm sunshine.

It was late October, once again. Miriam and I had taken Tim along to pick late blackberries and hazel nuts. They were both ripe along the roadside, in sunny glades not far from the castle. Tim liked the walk and light exercise was just what he needed. Next day he was to return to Haven with sir Gawain.

We were returning home with almost a bushel of each when we saw three figures, covered in grey dust, coming around a corner of the castle. It was Sirs Du Lac, Du Boors and Lensberg.

"Good day Mi lords, what happened to all of ye? I haven't seen ye fer a long while."

'Ah, squire.' Du Lac scrambled up an embankment towards us. 'We were looking for a bolt hole, most castles have one. We found a sappers trench from a former siege and were checking the castle foundation. The foundation was fine but we are still looking for that tunnel, if it exists.'

'But ye have so much dust on ye.'

He tried brushing his sleeve, sending a choking cloud into the air. 'The blasted trench tried to cave in on us, it's very old and fire scorched. Du Boors pulled us to safety.'

I pulled out me water container and passed it to him. 'Here, Sir, wash some of that out of yer throat.' I watched him as he raised an eyebrow in thanks and took a healthy swig. He then threw it to Lensberg. I wasn't buying any of it, not really. Finding a bolt hole made some sort of sense but why three knights together. Were they children playing games?" There was more to this than met the eye.

As this was transpiring, I held out me hand to Lensberg and helped him up the slope. I turned to do the same fer Du Boors but he was already there almost knocking me over. He supported me elbow and apologized fer the bump. Close up, his face looked badly scarred, from his left eye across his nose to his chin, giving him a menacing look. He looked a dour man, but he was a decent sort. He got the water next and finished it.

'Thank you squire I see you have been collecting berries and nuts.'

'Aye sir, If ye would join us I plan a concoction to please the palette.'

'Where?'

'In the kitchen sir.'

He turned to the others. 'Shall we? I think he plans something I loved as a child.'

Du Lac shrugged, 'Why not, but first I will get cleaned up.'

I smiled, 'Ye all have time.'

They were all cleaning their bowls and looking fer more. I had made a mixture that me mam made, A delicious blend of crushed hazelnuts, blackberries and porridge.

Du Lac looked up from his empty bowl with an actual twinkle in his eyes. 'From swineherd to squire, and you know how to make porridge too!'

Everyone laughed and Du Boors said, 'Just as I remembered it. Thank you Will, I had almost forgotten that feast.'

Lensberg patted his stomach, 'An Englishman made that?' He turned to Miriam. 'Don't lose that one, he is a treasure.'

She smiled. 'I know he is. Did you like yours Tim?'

Tim just nodded with a slight smile. I think he felt a little uncomfortable dallying in the presence of all these knights. He thanked me and Miriam, bowed to the others and took his leave.

I had some questions and summoned the courage to ask them.

'Sirs, why not look for yer bolt hole from the inside?'

Du Lac shrugged, it seemed to be a French thing. 'Usually they are very well hidden and I thought it might be easier to find the exit. Any partially hidden hole near the castle wall would be worth investigating.'

'Yes, but I would think that's when it would be very well hidden. If the enemy found it during siege it could be a Trojan horse.'

Lensberg piped up, 'A horse wouldn't fit, Trojan or otherwise.'

'Sir, according to sir Gawain, the Trojan horse was a ploy, a trick, but not a wooden horse as myth has it'

They all perked up. 'Do tell!'

'Aye, Hector, a prince of Troy, was commander of the finest cavalry of the time. They were the Trojan horse. Troy was reeling from blow after blow but their walls were impregnable. Hector was already dead at Achilles' hand, and his second in command was attempting to harass the enemy with exhausted and diminished forces. They were betrayed and trapped, facing insurmountable odds, the Trojan cavalry was cut off and slaughtered. The Greeks took the armor of the slain warriors, mounted their horses and pretended to flee from the pursuing Greek army.

The Trojan guards saw the plight of their cavalry and opened the gates just enough to let them through. They had plenty of time to close them again, only they were fallen upon by the enemy horsemen, and the gates were swung wide. Ye all know what happened next.'

Du Lac had a teasing little smirk on his face. 'You do like to preach, don't you ah, but it was a good story with considerable merit when you think about it. Now, what else do you have to say?'

Me face felt hot and I'm sure I was as red as a beet. 'Me apologies Sir, It was not me intent to preach. If there is such a thin as a bolt hole, wouldn't it be near to where the Lord of the castle and his family frequented?'

Du Lac nodded. 'Makes sense, so?'

'A hole to the outside would pull or push air, creating a draft. We might use torches to find such a draft.'

'Shit and this was a swineherd?' Du Lac shook his head and said. 'I task you to find it Will, I'm going for a nap'

Lensberg chuckled, looking at me. 'May I join you? My curiosity is peaked.'

Du Boors actually laughed. 'I will help.' He looked after Du Lacs receding back. You stung his ego, lad, but he'll get over it. We have been dancing around like children at play and you've come up with a useable approach. Now, where are some torches?'

Miriam, who had been collecting bowls on the sidelines, said in an accusing tone, 'I thought we were spending time together?'

I tried to look contrite, 'I'm sorry love. I'll be back as quick as I can.'

She shook her finger at me. 'Try not to be late for supper.'

I smiled, waved and took a torch from Du Boors. 'Let's start in the main hall shall we?'

Lensburg stepped close. 'I made my wife grumpy too many times and now she is grumpy all the time. Take a lesson from that squire, spend promised time with her.'

'Yes sir, me wife and I have an understanding.'

He grunted. 'Poor boy, you will learn.'

Things happened much quicker than even I expected. The main hall showed nothing and then we went to the assembly, which was a large room with a throne like chair on a dais. Here the lord would sit to take petitions or pass judgment. On the back wall was a large tapestry showing what looked like a pilgrimage. I was walking past it when me torch flared. I stopped and moved the torch about and it grew hot again at about shoulder height. Checking the lower corner of the tapestry I found it to be weighted but not attached. I moved it back enough to see behind and there was a slot in the wall in which a chain hung. The hole that the chain entered was the source of the draft. It was quite a draft and I'm sure that if the tapestry wasn't there ye would feel it on yer face standing nearby. I called the knights over.

'Who would like to have the honor?'

Du Boors grabbed the chain and pulled. There was a creak and a groan and a wall section pivoted just enough so one could get their fingers in the edge. He put a little weight behind it and with grinding stone on stone, swung it some more. There was a cavity big enough fer a man to squeeze through. Lensberg, being the smallest, went first.

His voice sounded muffled. 'We have a tunnel cut through the stone.'

Du Boors was the biggest and had to grunt and squirm to get through. He made it and I took up the rear. I was getting claustrophobic with that big man filling out the passage way ahead of me when I heard Lensberg say, 'Mein Gott!' He had stepped aside to let us all through. We were in a large cavernous room carved out of the bedrock. It was a crypt, and where the torch light was swallowed up, a number of sarcophagi in intermittent rows, could be faintly seen near the perimeter. There were three, standing alone in the center with the toes pointing inward. They formed a three sided star, or looking at it in another way, three triangles.

As we approached them, we could see that they were very old and pagan, not Christian. The effigies on the lids were two dimensional, and were dressed in scale mail with circlets on their brows. They were likely to be Chieftains of some kind but what race, Angles perhaps? We swept away layers of dust and now could see what each was holding. The one whose head was towards us held a small throwing ax in folded hands. The one on our right held a short sword across his chest and the other had what looked like a staff or crook. We searched the room for an exit and found none, which left us scratching our heads.

Du Boors said. 'Why would there be a hidden tunnel to a crypt? There has to be more to it than this.'

Out of curiosity, I went to the coffin with the staff and tried to move the lid. There was a 'ping' sound and dust cascaded to the floor. Lensberg leaped to the other side and we tried to lift. It wouldn't budge.

'Try pivoting it.' There was a creak and a hollow groaning, then a squeal of stone on stone that hurt the ears. The lid began to turn. Du Boors came and put his muscle to it.

'I think we need some oil.' He grimaced at the painful sound. We now had a hole with narrow stairs going down. A strong breeze was blowing up and ye could smell the sea.

At the bottom of the stair, we stood in calf deep, freezing seawater and could see muted daylight at the end of a short tunnel. We soon found ourselves in a small cave with ledges on one side. The decayed remnants of a boat lay on one. There appeared to be a maze of sharp rocks at the entrance, looking like dragons teeth, with waves surging through the gaps in a steady rhythm.

'So this is the bolt hole! Not much good without a boat.'

I looked at Du Boors who was watching the surging water. 'Aye and I'll wager it's difficult to find the entrance from the sea side. I'd only try on a calm day.'

Du Boors somehow looked a little disappointed. About what, I wasn't sure. 'You did what you said you'd do, squire, and I want to see Du Lac's face when he finds out, thank you young man.'

As we started back, I heard a very faint whistling moan that faded to nothing and started again. I looked around fer the source but could see nothing.

When Sir Robert heard our news, he had to be shown. When he came back through the secret door into the assembly, he also looked disappointed.

'You found our crypt, Will. I knew there was one and now we know where. Tomorrow your holiday is up and I expect you to get back into a routine. Leave exploring for some other time. I received word that Lord Alexander Donclevy will arrive shortly, to parley. He is bringing Cyril Pardoone with him Cyril is the eldest son in his family and acts for his father who is ailing. They will stop at Haven to pick up Sirs Gawain and Spatzhein...." A fit of coughing followed by a healthy sneeze, gave him pause.

I handed him a bowl of water. 'Bless ye sir.'

'Thank you. In a few days I may have an errand for you to run, so be prepared.'

I bowed and retired from the room. Morgan and Mistress Gwen were outside, chatting. When she saw me she called me over.

'I hear you find strange things, like crypts. I'd like to see it, would you show me some time?'

'Of course me lady, but I've been instructed to get back to work and leave off exploring. I could be free after Mass on Sunday, it wouldn't take long.'

'That sounds good for me.' She turned to Gwen, 'Do you want to see them?'

Gwen shook her head, 'Crypts are creepy, I don't need to go there.'

Morgan chuckled, looking at me, she was a much sunnier person now. 'See you at practice tomorrow?'

'Yes me Lady.' I paused. 'How did ye know so soon? I only just got back.'

She grinned, 'The walls have ears.' They walked off, with their heads together, laughing.

I took a moment to spend time with Storm and Taxeia. They had comfortable stalls but I think they were lonely. Storm was used to having other horses around and missed them. He and the Andalusian tolerated each other but they were stallions, ready fer a fight. The scar on Taxeia's rump had healed well but left a silver welt about nine inches long. Storm was being a little snooty I hadn't paid him enough attention the past couple of days. I brushed them both, really making up to me horse with a couple of carrot treats. "Let's go fer a nice ride tomorrow horsey." He was feeling better when I left.

After all that, I was only a little late fer supper and really famished. Miriam had made lamb stew and dumplings, which I wolfed down. While she cleaned up, I chatted with her da. Other than his hands hurting all the time, he was well. I had told Meg about his problem and she encouraged him to wear raw wool gloves with no fingers. She thought the greasy oil in the sheep's wool, with its natural warmth, might benefit him. He claimed it helped a bit.

On one of me errands fer sir Robert, I was able to see the lads at the smithy. Raglin was very talkative, almost nervous and I had to calm him down. He had found out that his da was coming and was excited and scared all at the same time. Helmsley laughed at his antics.

I watched Helmsley fer a bit, he certainly was good at his craft and horses accepted him. When he smiled, he had three blackened stumps fer teeth. One was on top and two on the bottom.

'Fergive me fer asking, but don't yer teeth hurt a lot?'

He looked at me oddly. 'Aye, sometimes, why would ye ask?'

'Ye could have them removed.'

He shook his head, 'There's too much risk of blood poisoning and I'm scared to have it done. I'd sooner live with some pain than not live at all.'

'Meg could do it and keep ye alive.'

'This Meg, she's the cook isn't she? What does she know about that sort of thing?'

'Ye'd be amazed at what Meg knows. She is fine at doctoring and knows a lot about healing. Some might call her a witch but I think she just knows a lot. Ye can trust her.'

Helmsley paused in between hammer strokes and stared at me, long and hard. He smiled. 'I'll take it under advisement, Will, thank ye.'

I collected a repaired dirk from Raglin. 'Ye wind wire as well as Tom ever did. I think Sir Robert will be pleased. Never fear, yer da will be proud. How's yer sword fighting coming?"

"Well enough, when I get time. I watched Lady Morgan the other day. She's good, hey?!"

I smiled, "Aye, she's damn good and likes yer sword. Ye did a fine job on it." I think he might have been blushing when I left. Mind ye, it could have been the heat of the forge.

Days of normalcy came and went. I was able to show Morgan the crypt and she was intrigued. Then one fine morning I woke up, had breakfast with Miriam and the 'usual' went away. I took the time to kiss me wife's lips and tummy, saying ta ta to both, and reported to sir Robert. He waved me to a chair and told me to sit.

'Will, I have some things of great import that must be dealt with and I trust you to carry them out. Before I tell you what your duties are, I need to be a little more open with you. You are astute enough to realize that my friends are not just here to bring justice to the land. I have seen it in your face at times. The justice brought by us is a side product of our real purpose.'

I began sitting up straighter, me curiosity aroused. 'May I have some water sir?' Me mouth was dry as dust. He pushed a ewer and cup over to me. 'We are a Brotherhood, joined together with a purpose, which I cannot fully indulge. I will say we are in search of something that has led us here. Your friend Malcolm is one of us and has been long before you met him. He is a Laird in Scotland and an enemy of England, but not mine. It was in both our interests to keep our relationship a secret. Alexander Donclevy has joined the brotherhood by invitation because we knew him to be a pious man of integrity and we need allies throughout the land.' He paused to have some water too. Narration was thirsty work. 'Of course, we have been noticed, by some, who are indifferent, and then there are others.' Sir Robert paused to look out the window. It seemed he stood there for a long time before he spoke again.

'When you Tom and Darragh joined my party something unforeseen was introduced, and that was the vicious hatred of the McOrdreds, especially Skye. This vendetta has put a whole new dimension to things. Now, mark you, the blood lust that demon has, must be stopped so we never planned on, looking the other way. It is just something we had not prepared for. Now we must deal with it.' He looked at me and said, 'This is where you come in Will. I need a man I can trust implicitly to go to the Isle of Man and spy out the McOrdreds. See what they are up to. Then try to hire agents as an early warning system. From there, go to Ireland and give this letter to Sir Thorwald Fitz Patrick's own hands, no other, is that clear?'

I nodded, 'Of course sir.'

'You will be in danger at all times, never mind the lawlessness, there are Irish sympathetic to the McOrdreds, the former supporters of Edward the Bruce, and agents for just about everyone.' He sat down and leaned back. 'Well, can you remember all that?'

'Yes sir, but where will I look fer Sir Fitz Patrick?'

'Land near Newry and proceed to Armagh, his new home is there. Once you have done all that, return in due haste to report to me. You should have a companion to watch your back. Morgan offered but I feel she attracts too much attention. Darragh cannot go we have too much at stake for him to be recognized. Pick someone you trust and do it quickly. The time of winter storms is just around the corner and it would be prudent to avoid them if possible. I know it's my fault, I should have acted sooner.'

The first person I thought of was Uri, providing his commander would release him. I made me way to the Swiss camp and asked to speak to captain Swingley. I was ushered into his tent right away.

He greeted me cordially, with his feet up on a campaign table. When I told him what I needed and why, he was most helpful.

'Of course he can go my dear young mench. That is providing he vants to go.' He he called for his aide. 'Fetch Uri Hazenfell sofort.'

That was the first time I heard his last name. We chatted about the weather and not much else, until Uri finally arrived. I told him what I needed and he jumped on it with both feet.

'Of course I will go, it would be good to see some action again.' His face pulled into his lopsided grin. 'May I leave my pike here?'

# **Merrill and Lynch**

The sky was spotless blue right to the edge of the world but the light wind was cold. We had caught a ride on a fishing boat and were now almost at Man and the town of Douglas. Uri shed his helmet and wore his coif and mail under a calf length, brown wool cloak. Me cloak was grayish white, untreated sheep's wool full of oil. It had a hood against rain and so I could hide me face if the wrong people showed up. I had a feeling that Skye or Garrad the black would recognize me. For an extra sixpence, the fishing boat mate had told us where we might find the pirate captain Carver Merrill.

We landed amidst a bunch of bollards, pilings and old rickety wharfs and made our way past fish sheds to a filthy roadway. The stench was awful from dead rotten fish, seaweed, human waste and, who knows, what else. We hurried through that part of town, past taverns and bawdy houses filled with rough and ready patrons. I could feel hostile eyes on us and was glad we looked dangerous enough to discourage would be assailants. As we walked, A drunken whore, with almost nothing on, accosted Uri. He tried to shoo her off, but I coaxed her back, holding out a sixpence. She snatched it and made it disappear.

'Ye want me ta suck yer off right here in the street, or what.'

I cringed at the thought. 'Just give us information maam. Can ye point us to the Bowlegged Duchess?'

'Bloody fuckin hell, no one has ever called me maam. Just follow this road till ye can't go further, turn right, go ta the top o the fuckin hill and ye'll spot it soon enough." she belched and what a stink.

We left her muttering something about the easiest money she ever made.

We followed directions and yes, we spotted the Bowlegged Duchess right off. Ye couldn't miss the sign, it was huge and suggestive. We entered and the atmosphere was surprisingly quiet. There were eight patrons drinking ale and behaving themselves. I knew the barkeep right off it was John Lynch.

I bellied up to the bar. 'Do ye remember me sir?'

He grinned at me. 'We don't give refunds here.' He wiped a glass, filled it with ale and placed it in front of Uri, he then did another fer me. 'The first one is on the house. Now, what do ye want?'

'I'm looking to have a private conversation with ye and yer captain. It is important and could be beneficial to both parties.'

'He's not here right now, but I'll get word to him. I shall arrange a private supper for the four of us? Come back at seven. If ye are going fishing, the McOrdred camp is inland just outside the city. Scups get out here!' He leaned over towards me. 'He got his name from sleeping it off in the scuppers, but he is a good man and can show ye around.' He thumped the bar. 'That will be a hundred guineas.' He laughed uproariously and walked away.

I curled me lip a bit, 'cheeky bastard'.

'Good afternoon yer worships.' We both turned to face a very skinny man in a worn out kilt. He knuckled his forehead and I could see the dirt ingrained into his hand, which was shaking a lot.

'Ye must be Scups? Ye needn't call us yer worships. I'm Will and this is Uri. We would like ye to show us the McOrdred camp if ye are willing, preferably without us being seen?'

"He scratched his arse and grinned, showing scummy teeth. 'Aye, let's go!'

Scups led us across town, through back alleys, to an abandoned building ready to fall over' it had been frequently used by derelicts and there were things on the floor I didn't want to scrutinize.

Uri nudged me. 'I think there's a skeleton under some rags over in that corner.' He pointed with his chin.

I grimaced. 'I didn't really want to know that. Come over here and take a look.'

Scups was pointing, 'That's the McOrdred camp, its growing every day, plenty of rough nasty folk coming in a steady stream.'

We crouched down at an opening that might have been a window, once upon a time. The camp before us was very large, much bigger than I would have thought. A rough palisade surrounded the main encampment, and I guessed that at least fifteen hundred men were within. There were more bivouacs outside, all a bustle with people settling in. I never saw Skye or Garrad. I did see one man in a split surcoat and armored leggings. I thought him a family member with his red hair. It was square cut at the shoulders, along with a droop mustache.

'Do ye know who he is?'

Scups looked where I was pointing and hissed through his teeth. 'Aye, that's the father, Krayan McOrdred, a violent beast of a man without mercy. If he's nearby, don't make eye contact.' He giggled, Ye'll wind up pissing yer pants.'

'I think I've seen enough, and I'll tell ye this Scups, the only pissing will be on his corpse when he is dead and a friend of mine will do the honors.'

He gave me an odd look, probably wondering at me lack of humor.

'Have ye ever seen Skye's handiwork? His da is likely the same, or so I've been told.'

'Nay, I have never.'

'The first time I did, I might have pissed me pants... in horror. Ye don't ever want to see what he's capable of.'

Scups shrugged, not quite knowing what to say.

We arrived back at the Bowlegged Duchess and it was now full of men but still low key. No one was rowdy and conversation was a loud sonorous murmur punctuated by a few laughs.

John saw us and waved us over. 'I've prepared a room fer ye, first one on the left at the top of the stairs. Rest and clean up a bit or have an ale supper is at seven, like I said.'

I gave Scups a whole shilling and I think it blinded him. 'Have a fine supper on us and thanks.'

He grinned again, showing us his scummy teeth, 'Fer ye any time.' He knuckled his forehead and scurried away.

Uri whispered, 'You are bloody generous! He's off to buy rum you know.'

I grinned, 'Just making a reputation...and friends.'

John was waiting when we came down stairs. He seemed to take a closer look at Uri who always stayed back a bit. 'Follow me Carver will be along in a moment. He's always a busy man, that one.' He led us to a comfortable private dining room and waved us to a seat.

I was puzzled by the hospitality, after all, the last time we met I was paying out a ransom and he was nursing a sore nose. I resolved to stay on guard and saw that Uri was watchful. We removed our swords so that we could sit comfortably, and hung them on the backs of our chairs.

It was only about ten minutes before Carver showed up. He bustled in, looked directly at me and gave me a cheeky smile through his thick beard.

'Come to spend some more money, have ye?'

I smiled back and shrugged. 'I bring greetings from Morgan she wants yer balls on a plate.'

He laughed, 'I enjoy sweetbreads too but I prefer those of a young bull. Now, let's sit fer a moment, have some ale and eat some supper.'

Two pretty, young ladies brought us our food. We started with a fish soup that was quite good and the entree was rare roast beef with Yorkshire pudding, carrots and turnips all smothered in gravy. It was very good, the main course was followed by a shared platter of honeyed squab and fruit. The ale was plentiful.

When I finished I felt I needed to undo me britches but couldn't reach under the mail. I let out a belch and a sigh.

'That was truly delicious, captain, and I appreciate yer courtesy, but why?'

'Ye get straight to the point don't yer. Well I'll get straight to the point too. I'm sure ye are here about our mutual enemy and I'm here to tell ye that we are on yer side in this. Let me introduce me self properly. I am Captain Carver Merrill, to all purposes, privateer fer King Edward the third with letters of mark from the acting Regent, Her Highness Isabella. In truth, and this is a secret to be kept, I am charged to clean up the island and get it back under proper British rule where it belongs.' He chuckled, 'I'm supposed to be Governor but if anyone knew that me throat would be cut, even by some of me own lads.'

'Yer secret is safe with us, but why would ye put yer self at our mercy? We are still strangers to ye. Yes we have a common enemy and that is why we are here. I will trust ye now. I have a letter for delivery to Sir Fitz Patrick, for his eyes only. After we have concluded our business here we must go to Ireland.'

Carver swallowed a mouthful of ale and bit into an apple. Moving the piece to his cheek, he said. 'And what is yer business here?'

I looked over at John who was quietly watching. 'We are expecting a major attack from the McOrdreds, likely not before spring, and we are hoping ye would be our early warning system, when they start to muster.'

Carver leaned back, putting his chair on its hind legs, and stretching out his own. 'I'll go one better. Put this to Sir Robert, We will give warning and I'll see to it that McOrdred boats are fired while he is fighting. He'll have no escape and if Fitz Patrick will comply, we will fall on his rear. Being rid of his lot would go a long way to bringing law to Man. I know Fitz Patrick wants nothing from England, but he might choose the lesser of two evils.'

I could feel the excitement rise in me. This news was far better than any of us had hoped.

'I am sure that ye just made Sir Roberts day. I feel so much better going to Ireland on that note. I'll make sure that Sir Fitz Patrick hears of yer plan and bring word on the way back.'

John leaned forward with a slight frown. 'Now that's out of the way, I am curious about yer friend.' He spoke directly to Uri. 'Ye speak English fluently but I can tell ye are not. Where are ye from?'

'I am Swiss, from the canton Aarau and belong to the Swiss Pike.'

John raised an eyebrow. 'Swiss Pike, I've heard of yer exploits in France and Italy, yer a bunch of lads that don't believe in losing a fight. What are ye doing in England?'

'My corps came with Sir Du Lac who is a friend of Sir Robert.'

'So there are foreign knights and troops on English soil?'

I stepped in. 'Yes, there are several knights visiting us and their motives are private but pure. Sir Robert, Sir Gawain and I will vouch fer every one. Did ye know that Du Lac leased Bamburg Castle from her Highness? How long the term is, I have no idea. Just ye be assured that they are friends and will fight by our side.'

John chuckled. 'I already knew all that, I just wanted to be sure ye weren't hiding anything from us. Ye are being aboveboard with us and now we will certainly be aboveboard with ye.' He held out his hand, which I took. His grip was firm.

Carver got up and raised his cup. 'Here's to success and victory.' We all stood, raised our cups and drank the toast. He put his cup down, 'Ye looked over the enemy camp? At last count, he had more than three thousand men and more coming. He is collecting the scum of England and Ireland and perhaps even some Frenchmen with promises of blood and gold. Then there are those Irish that were loyal to the Bruce and unemployed mercenaries abound. I wish I could call on the crown but they have other commitments in Wales and now in Scotland. The disinherited are looking to reinstate themselves with Edward and Edward would relish having a puppet on the throne of Scotland again. In a nutshell, there is no English army available to us. We however, will be there for ye. Now, if ye wish, John will see ye to Ireland on the morrow. I have other business to look after, so I'll say good night.'

He shook me hand and then Uri's, and left.

'Do ye want fer anything?' John held the door.

'No thanks, we're tired but thank ye fer yer hospitality.'

He smiled with a slight bow of his head, 'See yer bright and early. I'll have ye knocked up by five bells.'

We entered a narrow inlet in light fog. Visibility was good fer about twenty yards. John stopped his rowers and listened. Nodding to himself, he signaled the rowers to start up again and hunched into his cloak.

He spoke softly. 'We'll be there very soon, when ye leave the ship, ye'll run into a road at the top of a bank. Bear right and ye'll be in Newry in no time at all. Ye can rent palfreys there and it's about twenty five to thirty miles to Armagh. Watch yer backs it's as unsettled here as it is on Man. We will return here in the morning, three days hence.'

The ship came up to the shore like a ghost. Uri went over the side first, with a soft splash, and I followed closely. I looked back up at John. 'Thanks fer everything, John Lynch, see ye in three days.'

He waved as the ship back oared and started to turn. I got up on shore with a hand from Uri, and watched as the long ship vanished into the fog. It wasn't long and we were squelching down a well packed road, our cloaks starting to steam.

'Those ships they use, they are like the Viking ships of old.' Uri glanced at me and adjusted his sword across his shoulder.

'Aye it's funny how the Irish stayed with that design when others didn't. They sail quite well, are very fast on oars and have a shallow draft. Those lads have always been pirates at heart and those boats are good fer that. English and French ships are clumsy and not good in heavy seas or the shallows.'

The fog went away and we were soon walking under partly cloudy skies. We passed a few people who gave us furtive, sidelong looks and silence. In a couple of hour's we crested a rise to see Newry in the near distance, we arrived without mishap. There was a livery and a coach station, right across the street from a pub. I took Uri's arm.

'I'm going to arrange fer the palfreys and then let's have the breakfast we missed this morning. We can get some food fer travel too.'

Uri nodded, 'I'm starved, I'll go order.'

Breakfast, or lunch if ye like, was delicious, Bacon, sausages, kidneys and goose eggs along with slabs of Irish bread. I looked at me friend.

'Damn, that was good, now we have to work it off.'

'I need a shit before we go. That good food brought it on.'

That's a good plan needing to shit and bouncing on a palfrey don't mix well. We'll leave in half an hour.'

Uri grunted, 'Make it a bit longer.'

Uri finally showed up looking content. I had arranged fer our transportation and bought food to go. Another loaf, some cheese and a couple of blood sausage, along with water jugs. I expected there would be food at the other end. I never noticed that we were being watched furtively until Uri whispered to me that there were some young toughs nearby, interested in our well being.

As we traveled through the late afternoon, I noticed five riders keeping their distance behind us.

Suddenly they weren't there anymore.

'I think our company has left.'

Uri looked at the sky, 'It's getting late in the day Will, and it looks like a perfect spot coming up to graze and water the palfreys.' There was a pleasant, grassy clearing by a small rill. 'If they are locals, they know this spot and may expect us to stop. They just disappeared to lull us.'

I shook me head. 'Now I know why I brought ye, there's more to ye than a pretty face.'

He gave me a hard knuckle punch in the shoulder. It hurt right through me mail. I grinned at him while I rubbed. We took the animals to water and then sat while they grazed a bit.

'Loop yer reins around yer wrist and hope horsey doesn't wonder off. We'd best be ready.'

We snacked on bread, cheese and sausage. We didn't speak and kept our ears open. Finally' Uri, a typical soldier, rolled up in his cloak and was snoring right off.

The woods were dim this late in the day. I watched and tried to listen as the palfreys snuffled or grumbled masking other slight noises. I wished they would shut up. Then I heard it, a slight snap like someone trod on a twig and paused. Another rustle drew me eyes to a shadow with in the shadows. I kicked Uri and saw his eyes open. He made no sound.

There was a sudden rush out of the woods and I could see the gleaming of blades.

'Up Uri they are on us.' Me sword met one of theirs with a clash and one horse spooked and Kicked out. With an woof of exploding air, a man went down behind me. Uri was at me side and we watched four men trying to outflank us. There was a flurry of blades and I stuck one in the side. He backed off holding himself. Another sank to the ground in front of Uri and lay not moving. The other two were looking around fer their partner who was moaning behind me. I turned and stuck him and that shut him up. The two cut and ran with the other limping after.

One yelled, 'We'll be back.'

I shouted back, 'Don't be stupid, save yer selves some grief and keep going.'

Uri checked his man and then bent to wipe his sword clean. 'Damn foolish boys not much more than sixteen. This one won't reach seventeen.'

I checked mine, he was dead too. By the looks of his twisted body, the horse had punched in his ribs. I had just put him out of his misery. We dragged the bodies away from the camp, nearer the road. We had no tools or time to bury them, let their friends do it.

We found Thorwald Fitz Patrick with no trouble at all. He lived in a walled manor and we learned he lived there just fer the moment. His real home was in Lucan, very close to Dublin. We were welcomed with courtesy and given a room to rest and clean up. I was looking out the window watching grazing horses in a paddock when there was a knock on the door. Uri, who was lying on a cot, sat up. I went and opened up. Sir Fitz Patrick entered the room in a rush.

'You have brought word from Sir Robert?'

'Aye milord,' I handed him the letter.

He took it with a nod of thanks and broke the seal. After reading it he folded the letter and slipped it into his shirt. 'Join me for a late supper, I would like to hear about your adventures, getting here, and I'll have a letter for you to take back.'

'Thank ye sir.'

After a light but delicious meal of sliced ham and pickled asparagus with more Irish soda bread, we waited fer Fitz Patrick's cue. He called an aide who came with a silver tray. He lifted a sheet of paper from it and read. Nodding to his aide, he held out his hand and was given a quill dipped in ink. He signed with a flourish, blew it dry, carefully folded it in half and then rolled it. The aide tied a white ribbon around it and Fitz Patrick dropped a hot blob of black wax on ribbon and paper and pushed his seal down on it. No one could read it without breaking that seal. He blew on it a couple of times and handed it to me.

'See that sir Robert gets that, no one else. If you are assailed and are losing, destroy it any way you can.'

I bowed and took it. 'As ye order Sir, may I speak?' As I spoke I took a leather tube, handed to me by the aide.

'Yes. I want you to tell me of your trip and you are free to speak on anything else, if you have a mind.'

I gave a detailed account of our trip and about our discussion with Carver Merrill.

He shook his head. 'There is so much lawlessness in this fair land.' He looked at the backs of his hands. I couldn't read much past his heavy droop mustache. 'I always felt that there was more to that man than met the eye. He was more of a business man, and much too lawful to be a pirate, always sniffing out a profit, and good to his men. English or not, I am inclined to trust him and will give you my full support when the time comes. Some of that is already in the missive you carry." He got up from his chair. "My staff will make your stay comfortable. I won't be seeing you again as you'll leave early. God speed on a safe journey.'

We stood and bowed as he left the room. I turned to me friend. 'Shall we find a hot drink before bed?'

Next morning, Uri and I helped each other with our gambesons and mail. When we were ready, I said. 'I'll meet ye at the palfreys, get them ready while I find breakfast.'

He nodded and I left to try and find the kitchen. I walked along a hall with a few openings to the fresh air along it. As I passed one, a low voice gave me pause, 'Squire!' I looked to see Sir Fitz Patrick standing tall in the arch.

He spoke softly, 'Listen carefully, squire. If you are waylaid, don't defend the letter but don't lose it obviously either. Tell Sir Robert that when the time comes I will help him. I have sneaks in my camp, that's why the subterfuge. Let them believe something that isn't." He leaned down and picked up a small domed cage with three pigeons in it. "Take these and give them to Sir Robert. He can get word to me within a day. They need your protection more than the letter." He took me elbow, "Now go and safe journey.'

'Thank ye Sir, I will do as ye say.' I looked about. 'Can ye point me to the kitchen?'

The cook was just shoveling scones out of the oven and told me to take half a dozen and to help me self to some cheese. The scones were piping hot so I tied them into me cloak, grabbed a fat slab of cheese, and went to find Uri.

We were riding along, just finishing up our scones and cheese, when a large drop of rain splashed me face. 'God's truth, are we going to get wet again?' and then it came, a real soaker. We hunched under our hoods and watched the road turn muddy in minutes. We had come to a spot with low stone, walls on each side, when a large flock of sheep came out of nowhere and filled the road. Me partner and I were separated by milling, bleating, muddy sheep with nowhere to go. Then I saw the men, at least seven of them, surrounding us.

One called out. 'Give us the letter and you can be on your way.'

'What letter is that?'

'Don't cheek me squire. Look to your friend!'

Two bowmen had arrows trained on Uri. Not the best of riders, he was trying to control his flighty palfrey who didn't like the seething sheep. I took the leather tube from around me neck and threw it in a high arc to the speaker. Eyes followed the tube as I kicked me palfrey in the ribs scattering sheep everywhere. The beasts tried to climb the walls and one archer got knocked over, shooting his arrow harmlessly into the sky. The other fired just as Uri's palfrey reared, taking the arrow in the neck. The beast went down and Uri jumped clear of the kicking hoofs. By then I had reached him, gave him me arm and he swung up behind me. Scattering more sheep, we ducked more arrows and hied it down the road for a good distance before I slowed down.

'Looks like no one is following, they got what they wanted.'

Uri was frowning when I looked back at him, 'Why did you let it go so easily?'

'Easily! They were going to fill ye and us full of holes. Besides, I had instructions to let the missive fall into enemy hands. It worked out very well they won't suspect anything after all that.'

He gave me a shove and a smack in the back of me head. 'Why do you always leave me in the dark?'

'I was going to tell ye, the attack came sooner than expected.' I rubbed me head ruefully. 'Keep yer wits about ye, there are enemies everywhere. At least that's what I've been told.'

'My wits are with me at all times, I'm not so sure about yours.' He chuckled, 'Instead of just rent, you'll have to pay for a whole dead horse.'

'Don't ye be laughing it's coming out of yer pay. Ye were the one riding it.'

We bantered back and forth for a while and then finally sighted Newry. The rain stopped just as we rode into town.

As we approached the livery, I had a bad feeling and then saw something odd. It looked like a foot sticking past the door a bit, holding it ajar.

'Something's off, step down and be ready.' After Uri jumped off I got down too, grabbed the cage of pigeons, and looked around. I glimpsed a frightened face peering out a window, over at the pub, other than that nothing.

Uri limbered his sword in its sheath. 'Maybe you don't have to pay for the beast after all?'

I grabbed the big door and swung it back towards me. Sure enough, it was the liveryman laying there. I put me fingers on his neck and saw blood on his head.

'He's bin bashed but he's still alive.'

A low nasty chuckle raised me head. 'After I bash yer, ye won't be!' Garrad the black stepped around the corner of a stall. Uri immediately put his back to mine as two men came out of nowhere to cut off our retreat.

I put the birdcage down and watched this born killer with a wary eye. In a taunting voice, that sounded braver than I felt, I said, 'Where's yer bairn? You know, that vile little beast in nappies that ye look after.'

His face tightened with anger. 'I'm going to give you a lot of pain.' He drew his sword with a rasp, it was a very big sword, and moved towards me, flatfooted. Others were moving in behind him and I had a feeling that our goose was cooked. Like a flash, David and Goliath came into me head and suddenly the trembles went from me body and everything took on an icy clarity. Realizing I was still holding the palfreys' reins, I slapped her hard on the rump and she jumped out of her skin, scattering those in front of me. The clash of steel echoed behind me and I knew Uri was fully occupied with those blocking our retreat.

Garrad lithely sidestepped the paniced palfrey and almost beheaded the horse with one blow. It was such a contemptuous act of violence. His mind was off me fer an instant and the animals' blood gushed around his feet. Raisin me sword to the falcon position, I leaped toward me enemy. He turned to meet me and our blades slithered down each other, hitting against the cross guards. His stopped inches from me face. We exchanged five or six blows the clashing steel sending sparks flying, and circled each other. Even though his face was expressionless, I felt his attack moves the instant they came. He advanced with several hard strokes that sent me backward only to trip over the dead horse. I rolled over the carcass hearin the dull slap of steel on meat. I sensed motion behind me and blocked a henchman's thrust who was trying to get his point across.

Me counter slash left his sword and forearm on the stable floor. He shrieked, clutched his gushing stump and fell away. I turned back just in time to block a vicious cut from the black. It was time to go over the horse again. I did a back roll and came up on me feet. I broke me wrists, dragging me blade from behind, and ducked. He had one leg over as his steel went whistling past me head, throwing him off balance, just a little bit. Me sword scythed into the side of his leg, just above the knee. He tried to step away to take stock of his wound and slipped in the blood pool he had created. The combination of slippery blood and the wound made him drop to his knee, one leg still straddling the horse's body. I took me opportunity and instead of swinging down at his head, which he could still block. I took advantage of the clumsy length of his sword and the awkwardness of his position and swung from the off side with all me strength. He couldn't block in time and me blade struck through the boiled leather and hard into his neck. I yanked it loose and his eyes flew wide with surprise as blood gushed over his shoulder and chest. Me second blow took his head right off. It all happened so fast it was like a dream.

I stood panting, me blade dripping gore. Black Garrad was dead and the others in front of me panicked, backed up and ran. The one that had attacked me stayed crumpled against a stall. All the strength went out of me just as Uri caught me elbow to steady me. He had won his fight too. In fact, by the bodies laying there bleeding, he had won twice.

He found an empty oats sack, grabbed the head by the hair, and pushed it in. I looked at him in puzzlement.

'We need to give Skye a gift.'

I nodded slowly, still in a daze. 'Aye alright, let's leave this place before somebody gets up the nerve to confront us fer this mess. We can camp by the water the ship should be here tomorrow morning. I turned to the unconscious groom and pronounced him well, except fer the headache he'd have when he woke. He was already starting to groan. I dropped some coin on his chest and seeing Uri's raised eyebrow, said. 'Fer the dead nags…and his headache.'

We made ourselves as comfortable as possible. Autumns' warmth was leaving fast and the evening air was chilly, especially after the rain. Fog was rolling in off the water, which was good fer us.

'Why was Garrad the black waiting fer us? He's Skye's personal bodyguard, I wouldn't have thought they would separate.' I scratched at me nose as I stared through the twilight at Uri, trying to make some sense in me own mind. 'Ye' would think they would have sent lackeys to do the job.'

Uri swore in Swiss, and shivered. 'Mail makes a poor blanket.' He hunched more into his cloak. 'Why was anyone there in the first place?' He chuckled, 'I never knew I was so important.'

Uri's countenance was fading fast as darkness closed in. With the fog and no moon, it was now pitch black. 'We were warned that there are spies everywhere. That other group knew I was a squire. I've never had much to do with things like this. I'm worried fer Fitz Patrick now, he is surrounded by danger. I think they could kill him whenever they want.'

Uri's disembodied voice came out of the dark. 'He knows that and I'm sure he has taken precautions. Look, I'm going to try and sleep a bit, why don't you do the same.'

I closed me eyes and tried, me mind spinning round and round and filled with rolling heads. I jumped out of me skin when one glared up at me and said, 'The ships coming.' Me eyes snapped open to Uri nudging me with his foot.

The ship was right on schedule and two cold shivering men climbed aboard.

'Glad to see you safe.' John actually looked pleased as he led us to a brazier to warm ourselves. 'Luke, bring something hot for these lads to drink, some food too.'

A deck hand knuckled his forehead.

I drank the last of me honeyed mead, savoring the sweetness. The bread and cheese was gone and me stomach rumbled fer more.' That feels so much better it's nice to feel warm again. It was a long night in that fog with little beasties scuttling over our feet.'

John chuckled and then pointed with his chin. 'What's in the sack?'

Uri held up the now bloody bag. 'Surely you can guess.'

'Oh, I should have said, who's in the sack?'

I nodded to him, and Uri pulled the bloody thin out by the hair. The barely open eyes showed white through all the red and black. 'It's a surprise fer Skye, but I wanted to save it fer a bit and it's going to spoil.'

John took a closer look and made a grimace of distaste. 'Now that's what I call a red feather in your cap...... Luke, I need you again!'

The deck hand appeared and stared. 'Is that who I think it is, Sir?'

'Yes. Fetch me a small keg and pickling brine.' John turned to me. 'How did you manage it?'

I proceeded to tell him about our trip. I finished the tale and paused a moment. 'I'm still puzzled why he came after us personally.'

John put his chin in his hand and thought fer a moment. 'You must be more important than you think. You killed a formidable Opponent. I thought he was bloody immortal. Skye is going to have fits. We must have a traitor in our own ranks for him to have been there, waiting.'

'How will ye ferret him out?'

'I'm not sure yet, but I will. By the way, we won't stop at Man, for safety's sake. I'm taking you straight home.'

As the ship ran aground, a troop of yeomen came to meet us. Ross jumped down when he saw us dropping over the side.

'Yer back safe, thank the Lord,' We gripped arms and then embraced, he clasped Uri's hand, 'How was yer trip?'

'Eventful!'

John interrupted from the boat. 'Do you want this?' He was holding the small barrel fer me to catch. I nodded and caught it.

'Thank ye fer everything, John. I'll give Sir Robert a full accounting.'

He smiled and waved as the ship pushed off. I watched as the ship turned, with oars dipping, and rapidly diminished, heading out to sea. I turned back to Ross.

'He's a lot better man than I would have supposed.' I put me hand on his shoulder and gave him a little shake. 'We now have more friends at our backs.' He smiled slightly and gave me hand a pat.

Uri was waiting by the palfreys as we walked up. Ross pointed to a yeoman. 'Ye can ride double with him. Will, jump up behind me. Oh, I'm guessing someone's in the keg, who?' I told him.

'Darragh's going to have a fit he wanted to be the one.'

'He gets Krayan. He can also give Skye a gift! I didn't have much choice, fighting fer me life. I know God was with me, because I won.'

'I remember the first time I met ye lad, ye have come a long way but I'm sorry ye had to lose some of that innocence I saw in yer.'

I thought about that as we approached the castle and it dawned on me that I had changed a lot.

Sir Robert listened carefully to me entire report then he called Du Lac to come listen too. I repeated everything, making sure to include Uri's bravery and loyalty. Sir Robert asked me many questions while Du Lac listened in silence. When he was done with me, Du Lac spoke first.

'You actually killed a man that struck fear into the hearts of all his enemies? I would have liked to have seen it, just to believe it.'

I just bowed, not knowing what to say. Sir Robert was staring at Du Lac his expression saying, 'why would you say that.' 'You can leave us now, Will, thank you.'

I bowed again and walked out of the room. As I closed the door, I heard Du Lac answer a retort from an angry Sir Robert. 'Yes the young man has good qualities, but I'm sick of your ' everyone is equal.' Rubbish, he's just a swineherd for God's sake. If God wanted us all equal He would bloody well have given them all titles and wealth....'

The door closed on Roberts answer and I went to find me Miriam. I was tired of being a squire. I was tired of fighting and killing. I was tired of chopped off heads, and having one in a keg. I needed me sweetheart fer just a bit.

The next morning, after a good cuddle, I felt much better. Me dearest was getting larger now and was checked on regularly by Meg, who pronounced her healthy and told her to be patient.

I walked Storm and Taxeia to the smithy to have their hooves looked after by Helmsley. They behaved themselves for once and it was a quiet, pleasant stroll. I decided to go visit the grooms it had been quite a while, so I left the chargers in Helmsley's capable hands. Cheve, Pierce and Simon were there cleaning empty stalls.

'Ah, mon ami, we thought ye had run away with a sheep.' Cheve grinned and slapped me on the back. 'We thought ye were too good for us, squire. Where have ye been?'

'Trust me, I've been everywhere. Every time I tried to see ye lads something else came up. Where's Pat?'

'He and the other lads are running the blacks. They should return very soon.' Cheve threw me a pitchfork, 'Here, ye can help while we talk.'

I laughed. 'And ye wonder why I don't visit often. Ye speak English like a Yorkshire man now, it didn't take ye long. I've had little chance to practice me French.'

The rumble of hooves accompanied the blacks as they entered through the postern and milled about the courtyard. Grooms jumped from their mounts and started leading them away to be brushed and fed.

Pat spied me and welcomed me with a huge grin. He wrapped an arm around me neck. 'It's bin a while Will ye are looking good.'

'So are ye.' I looked him over and saw none of the bitterness that had eaten at him.

He looked fondly at me. 'It's the good company, they are a great bunch of lads. They all have yer back, just like ye used to. Ye know, I run the chargers in the surf and they are getting stronger and stronger.' He smirked, ' I run with them now and look at me thighs, they're so big they hide me sausage.'

There was a collective chuckle. I grinned at me friend, 'Even when they were bean poles they hid yer sausage.' Chuckles turned to laughter and I got a punch in the shoulder fer me wit. I sobered. 'Careful doing it too much, Pat, they may get skin problems from the salt.'

He nodded. 'I thought so too, so we wash them down three times a week, at a stream about three miles from here. And that's beside their regular grooming.'

I looked at a couple of nearby horses and found them in fine condition. 'I think I might take Taxiea and Storm fer a run like that, they're getting out of condition.'

"We're out from eight to ten, most days, its darker now. Why don't ye join us fer a romp, the horses love it." A whine at Pats feet made me look down and there was a wolf hound, the spitting image of Courser.

I could feel tears in me eyes as Pat said, 'Meet Irish, the horses all like him but he usually sleeps with Sir Gawain's charger.'

'Irish? How original.'

'Piss off, it's a good name and everyone can remember it.'

I was petting the dog as we spoke and he was pressing against me leg, almost putting me off balance. He had a very nice nature, just like Courser. "Where did he come from?'

Pat shrugged. 'He just showed up one day. Cheve met him first and brought him in.'

Me face was tightly under control as I stroked him. I could almost believe in ghosts.

The following day, I brought the keg to Darragh. Morgan was there and I smiled and said 'Good morning me Lady, I have something for ye Darragh.'

He looked at the keg and then at me. 'I don't think I want to know what's in there, I don't care fer herring.'

'It's something ye can give Skye fer a gift.'

He just stared, at me, and then the keg. 'What?' He put his hand over his mouth and spoke through his fingers. 'Is it Garrad?'

'Aye.'

'How?'

Morgan chimed in. 'You men are disgusting. Is that a head in there?'

I nodded, It's Garrad's alright he is a head shorter now.'

'Damn you Will, he should have been mine!'

'Why? I was the one standing in front of him when he tried to kill me!'

'Sorry.' Darragh sat down. 'Tell me what happened.' Morgan sat down beside him and they listened quietly to me story. When I was done, Darragh said.

'They obviously were trying to disrupt things by killing you both. The question is how did they know about you? Do you really trust your pirate friends?'

'Yes.' I hadn't told him who Merrill really was but I did now.

Morgan said. 'I recognize that name now he's from Cornwall where I grew up. He was Knighted about four years ago, for services to the crown. He received a title and estates. He's Earl of something or other, I can't remember. I do know he is a patriot and a man of his word.'

'He's the hairiest gentleman I ever met.'

Morgan laughed, 'That's the one.'

Darragh had been listening to both of us. 'If you both say he's alright, then he must be and he has a rat or rats in his ranks.'

'That's what John said and if I measured him right, he will ferret them out.'

'I wonder how?'

'Pretend to scuttle the ship and see who swims fer shore.'

Darragh shook his head and chuckled, 'They should have you over there.' He picked up a sword. 'Let's see what else you have learned.'

I had a few hours to me self and I probably should have spent them with me dearest but I couldn't get that 'breathing giant' sound out of me head. There was somethin else in the crypt that had been over looked. I wanted to go exploring again, and on me own. I stocked up on spare torches and went.

I found some torch brackets in the chamber. Two had rusted so badly they were useless but three others were still functional. One was at the back over the rows of sarcophagi, allowing me to see them better. One of the three central ones had given up a secret, and I doubted the other two were anything more than coffins. First, I did some spring cleaning to get rid of eons of dust. I left fer a bit to let it settle. When I returned, I went over the rows in the back. Looking at them from the front, there were two groups of six, one group of four, a group of five and another of four. Starting at the left, I looked them all over, though me attention was leaning towards the odd number. The first six were simply marked with ax heads one had an actual bronze ax head cleverly inlayed into the stone lid. From me limited history lessons, I would guess them to be ancient Britons or even Beaker people of some status.

I was beginning to doubt that Bamburg was even here when this place was built. It came much later.

The next six were also quite simple with Circlets chiseled into the stone. They were of Briton design, and the circlet would have depicted a chieftain, male or female.

The next four were a later period and I thought they were Celts. They all showed the outline of a warrior or knight. One was a woman and it caught me eye because a broken Roman standard lay across the bottom with her feet resting on it. Time had softened the carving and it was hard to make out. With hard scrutiny, I could see what looked like IX under a Roman eagle. I guessed this woman had orchestrated the destruction of a legion.

Four of the next five were Celtic as well but one was just a plain stone box. I wanted to study it some more, but first I looked at the last four. I was puzzled because they were Jutes or Angles with two dimensional carvings on the lids, similar to the style of the prominent three. It seemed that hundreds of years were represented in this crypt.

Now I returned to the plain coffin, which was the most to the right of the five. Crouching down, I studied it from all angles. There were lots of shadows made by the flickering torch at the back. Then I realized that the torch was flickering while the other two were quite passive. I heard that breathing sound again. a whistling moan that faded to nothing and then started again. It gave me goose bumps. I think me bustling about had masked it and I heard it now because I was still. I lit another torch so that I could see the foot of the coffin without shadow. It also started flickering. Something faint caught me eye and I froze. I was looking at an image, almost rubbed out, but I knew what it was. Two slightly curved lines drawn to intersect each other making a tail. It was a simple fish.

Sir Gawain had told me of the first Christians in the Roman Empire. They were hunted and persecuted, during the reigns of three emperors, driving them into hiding. The sign of the fish became their secret symbol so that they could connect with one another.

I could feel me self trembling as I studied it. What was a Christian symbol doing in a pagan tomb? Fer that matter, why were there so many different times and races represented here? Perhaps it was an on going connection of people through time. Ancient people had believed in continuity of all things. I decided to leave things as they were until I could speak with Sir Robert and Sir Gawain. I knew Sir Gawain wouldn't be at the castle until two days hence. I would wait.

It was a long two days and as soon as Sir Gawain arrived, I asked to see him. Jarrad was back, looking well as if nothing had happened.

'I'm pleased to see ye looking fit. What happened to ye anyway?'

'Me horse stepped into a trap when we were at a cantor. Its front legs were broken and we cart-wheeled into a tree. They found me half a day later, the poor beasts screams brought them. When I awoke, I could hardly breathe fer three weeks. Now I am as good as new.'

'Ye never found the culprit?'

'Never.'

'We can hope it was Gordie and not another. He's no longer a problem.'

Jarrad laughed. 'I heard how ye chopped him up. If it was him, thanks.'

We stopped talking when Sir Gawain entered the room.

'Ye wanted to see me Will, what about?'

'May I speak with ye in private Sir?' I turned to Jarrad, 'No offence to ye.'

'None taken.'

Sir Gawain put his hand on me shoulder and led me out onto a balcony. 'Alright me friend, what is this about?'

I told him, in detail, what I had found. His eyes never wavered from me face as I spoke. Those light grey eyes that seemed to look right through ye. When I finished, he studied me fer a moment.

'Why didn't ye tell Sir Robert?'

'I mean no disrespect to Sir Robert, Sir, but I wanted ye to be in on this from the outset.'

He turned from me. I thought he looked pleased but I could only see part of his face.

'We will go to Sir Robert now, the other knights can be told later.'

Sir Robert listened intently without interruption. When I had finished, he looked at Sir Gawain and then back at me.

'Why didn't you come to me right away?' He looked a little miffed.

'Sir, ye and Sir Gawain have both changed me life fer ever. And I am fer ever grateful. I wanted to share this find with ye both together. It felt right to me.'

Sir Robert smiled. 'Well then, lets the three of us go and see this find of yours.'

Sir Gawain hadn't seen the crypt before so I took the time to show him the useless bolt hole. Now, that he was up to date, I led them to the stone coffin and showed them the fish.

'Listen to the breathing, can ye hear it?'

Sir Gawain squatted down and watched the torch. 'See how it flutters in time with the breath? It's air flow again.' He looked up at his friend. 'Shall we open it?'

Sir Robert was pale. 'Yes, let's try. Will, come help, this should be your honors.'

The knights went to each side and I took the foot. We all lifted, at first nothing happen and then there was a faint pop. The lid moved, it came up and stopped. It wouldn't rise up any further.

Sir Robert let out a sigh of exasperation as we put it back down. It was very heavy.

'Sirs, let's do that again, only this time I will push on the end.'

With nods, they lifted again. As I pushed, the lid moved and pivoted over the head of the coffin leaving a black hole without bottom. Sir Gawain took a torch and held it over the opening. Now ye could see a bottom, about eight feet down. It looked like the start of a tunnel.

I looked at them. 'Who wants to go first?'

Sir Robert smiled. 'You started this Will, you finish it.'

'Would ye hand me a lit torch and a couple of extras?' I slid over the edge, hung and dropped.. It felt slightly damp but not wet like the other. 'The tunnel seems to go quite far, at least the length of this chamber, after that I don't know.' I could hear the nervousness in me voice.

'Go ahead Will, we are right behind you.'

I moved into the tunnel and heard someone drop down behind me. The tunnel was getting smaller and ye had to half crouch so as not to hit yer head but other than that, there was a little more room than the other one. After a bit, it started to climb, not steep enough fer stairs but almost. At the half crouch, it was tiring. I heard a familiar voice behind me. It was Sir Gawain.

'Anything yet, Will?'

'With the torch light in me face, I'm not sure. I think there is faint light ahead.' I put the torch behind me.

'Watch it!'

'Sorry Sir, yes there is soft light ahead.' I moved more quickly as the light got brighter.

I exited into a small round chamber about sixteen feet in diameter. There were short slits, artfully carved through the rock fer about a third of the circle, they were angled in such manner, as to be almost invisible but still let light in. The breathing was the air coming through them in time with waves far away. What caught me attention was another sarcophagus right in the center of the chamber. By this time, Sirs Gawain and Robert were in the chamber too.

Sir Robert studied the stone coffin and then dropped to his knees. His voice filled with reverence. 'By God, Will, you have found it, after all these years of searching. I was beginning to believe it was a foolish dream.'

Sir Gawain put his hand on his friends shoulder. 'I do believe yer right Robert.'

I stepped up beside them and looked down onto the stone coffin. On the lid words were carved.

Longinus
Anno Domini LXII
Quaerite Primum Regnum Dei

The script was faint but legible. I looked over at Sir Gawain whose eyes shone in the soft light.

'What language is that sir? What is this grave site?' I glanced around the chamber and noticed something I'd missed before. On the right side was a stone block or table with things on it. I pointed to it, and went with them to the table to stare down at a bronze helmet with a crest running crosswise rather than front to back. Just strands of red dyed horsehair remained. The helmet, was sitting on a sheathed short sword and, though tarnished and pitted by salt air, they were both in quite good condition. Another item immediately caught ones eye. It was a leather tube about three inches in diameter and five feet long. The leather was peeling and rotten and one could see the dull glint of gold. Both Sir Gawain and Sir Robert stood as if petrified and almost as an afterthought, Sir Gawain muttered.

'The language is Latin, Will. I can't speak it but I know the name but please give pause as we reflect on our good fortune.'

Both knights dropped to their knees and prayed. Not knowing what else to do, I joined them. Out of the corner of me eye, I could see other things now destroyed, sacks or bags, almost crumbled to powder. From one there were bits that might have once bin food of some kind, and coin lay near the other. Finally, Sir Gawain stood and helped his friend to his feet. He picked up the cylinder and studied it.

'I think its gold leaf hammered over some other metal. It's quite heavy! This end looks like a cap, but how does it open?' He tried pulling on it but it would not budge.

Sir Robert took it, his hands dropping a bit from the weight. He studied it and shook his head. 'Have a look Will, you're the puzzle man.'

I took it, pulled and then tried to turn the cap. It didn't budge. I tried harder till me hand started to hurt and then, with a faint squeal, it gave and started turning easily. After a few turns it dropped into me hand and the cylinder was open. I studied the cylinder and the cap and saw that they both had raised lines that spiraled and melded to one another. How this had been accomplished, I had no clue. I could only admire the fine craftsmanship as I gave it over to Sir Robert. Sir Gawain held his hands out as Sir Robert tipped the case. A wooden shaft slid out, to become a spear with a slender leaf shaped blade about eight inches long. The blade and the wood near it, were both stained almost black, as if with blood. Further back along the shaft was a crude carving of the fish.

Sir Gawain breathed a reverent sigh and in a soft voice, he said. 'I do believe he never used it again.'

I couldn't contain me self. 'What is that spear, me lord, what does it mean?'

Sir Robert touched his friend on the shoulder. 'You know we have a problem. Our squire is not yet one of us and is in danger from the others, especially Du Lac.'

'They will have to go through me to harm him. Ye and I both know his honesty and discretion. I don't think swearing an oath would change things much.'

'I know all that but we do not want to alienate the others, not now.'

'Very well, we will keep Will out of it fer a bit but he is entitled to a story. We will go back to yer apartments where it is more comfortable. We will notify the others later.'

We ate in relative silence and when we finished, I watched the two knights with expectancy.

Sir Gawain smiled at me as he passed me a cup of wine. I took it, not much caring fer it.

'Ye know that blessed wine symbolizes the blood of Christ?'

I nodded.

'Now listen carefully to a tale I heard, just once, in Jerusalem. I befriended an old librarian who took an interest and was kind to me because of me love fer books and scrolls. He told me the following....... Longinus was a young legionary, one of several assigned to execution duties on a very special day. Three men, were dragged through the narrow winding streets to the summit of Golgotha, a place of execution, a place of skulls. One, a man called Jesus, was struggling up the winding road while being severely flogged. On his sweat dripping head was cruel crown of thorns. Weakened by torment, he stumbled under the weight of the cross bar he had to carry. So many times, he stumbled and fell and was prodded back to his feet by uncaring legionaries and jeered at by the mob crowding the way. Longinus supported him more than once and even gave him water. The Centurion in charge was furious with him. He had orders from Caiphas, a high priest who had judged Jesus, to make this man's passing long suffering and as unpleasant as possible. What he did not know was that Pilot, the Roman governor of Judea, had asked Longinus, quietly, to help Jesus to a quicker death. He knew his innocence and that his death was wasteful but a political necessity. He had already 'washed his hands' of the whole thing, but did this tiny kindness to ease his conscience even more. Longinus' father had been a slave and accountant to Pilot's estates. Longinus, who was known to him from early on, was barely out of his teens and saw promise of better things by obeying Pilot. The Governor had said he would protect him and promised him a change of venue.

He watched as this man was nailed through his hands and wrists, onto the crossbar with horseshoe nails, hands only might have torn through. The other two, convicted thieves and murderers, were lashed to theirs. The three men, were lifted by pulleys to seating blocks on the masts, their feet barely reaching a wedge to give limited teasing support to their feet. The pain in their arms must have been excruciating. The Centurion, with his own hands, crossed Jesus' feet and nailed them to the wedge. Longinus heard his groans of suffering and stayed near. The mob was becoming riotous and the Romans formed a circle around the site. Then Jesus was heard saying,

'I thirst!'

The Centurion gave Longinus a sponge soaked in vinegar. 'Stick that on yer spear and give him a drink.'

He wouldn't and was promised dire punishment. Another soldier did the Centurions bidding.

Masked by the unruly mob and soldiers casting dice fer the felons' meager possessions, Longinus took that opportunity to drive his spear into Jesus' side.

That is when something happened to change his whole life. He had committed the act to speed the man's death. Then he heard a voice above him, whisper.

'Forgive them Father, for they know not what they do.'

They say Longinus had a revelation. He fell on his knees, the spear clutched to his breast, and wept. He was in disgrace with the other legionaries but he was beyond caring.'

Gawain paused and stared into me rapt eyes. He placed fingers on me cheek and smiled.

'We believe that, besides the apostles and some others, Longinus became the first Christian. In a split second, he discarded his Roman gods and cleaved to Christ.'

Gawain cleared his throat and sipped his wine. 'The old man's story ends there and it became our task to prove it true. After all, at this point it was only a story. The rest of our tale was gleaned from Roman records in Rome itself. Du Lac and Spatzhein hired scholars to research fer them. The Roman army kept precise records, especially those of their governors and after months of searching this is what they found. After the Crucifixion, Pilot must have kept his word and intervened on Longinus's behalf. Records showed him to be a member of Pilot's staff and after a while, he was given the rank of Optio. He answered to a Centurion, one Caius Ostico, who was a little kinder than his predecessor but life fer Longinus was still difficult. Christian values were lost on Roman soldiers at that moment in time. He was often grist fer the legions bullies and suffered many beatings but he slowly made converts, one here, one there. Other forces, such as the Apostles, were also at work and a Christian underground began to spread across parts of Judea but mostly within Rome itself.

Pilot returned to Rome in some disgrace because he was unable to stop the continuous unrest in the Judean provinces. Longinus and his Centurion were reassigned to the twelfth Legion heading fer Gaul and later, Briton.

Years passed and he became a Centurion despite being a Christian. His former adversaries grew to admire his stubborn perseverance and his men were reputed to love him. It was rumored that he was an immortal and it had some credence considering he lived another Forty three years in the legion. When he retired, as a senior Centurion, he opted to stay in Briton and when he died at the age of seventy eight his many friends, Christian converts, buried him. We now know where, thanks to ye Will.'

'Ye heard that one story and followed it? I am amazed.'

'Are ye admonishing me squire? Ye see the proof before ye. Remember, we were knights in search of something other than killing. The Templers had their secrets and it was rumored they had found them in Solomon's Temple. Pilgrims were buyingg pieces of the one cross...The old man told me that enough pieces were sold in one year to make ten crosses. Jesus' shroud was also rumored to have been found and was hidden somewhere in Europe. We needed our own relic, the Grail was a prize fer others. We needed our own." Sir Gawain stared at the floor and sighed. "We had all committed acts we were not proud of and had seen even worse. I think we were all in search of redemption and we thought this story was ours alone. Find the spear that drank Christ's blood that, was a relic that vied with all the rest. We had all became friends in the first place, standing together against a common foe and saving each others' lives. There are many more stories we could tell. When I came to them with me tale they all jumped at it and we formed a brotherhood. We called ourselves 'The Brotherhood of Longinus.' We were each sworn to secrecy and new blood could only enter the brethren with a unanimous vote.'

I was mesmerized and now, a little frightened. 'I know yer secret and I am not a member.'

Sir Robert nodded. 'You were going to be sworn in when you became a knight. We don't want to break our oath to the others so I am going to speed things up. You will be knighted in two days.' He got up out of his chair and clasped his hands behind his back. 'I can knight a member of my own

Family, you have no family Will, so, with Sir Gawain as my witness, I adopt you as my son with all the rights and obligations of a son.'

I was in shock, and dropped to me knees.... I seemed to be doing a lot of that lately... 'Don't I have a say in this, sir?'

He put his hands on me shoulders and smiled. 'Not if you want to live! Now get up and embrace your father.' He spoke to Gawain. 'I'll have papers drawn up by Brother John and you and Morgan can witness them in the morning.'

Gawain nodded, smiled and held his arms out to me. As we embraced each other, he spoke softly in me ear. 'Life has a way, doesn't it?'

The meeting with the others was put off until after I received me knighthood. I had time to tell me sweet wife what was happening and she was flabbergasted. I had no time to tell anyone else, not if I wanted to spend a little time with her. She was closer now, just a couple of months, I wasn't sure.

Meg visited to check on Miriam. I swore her to secrecy and told her what was happening. It was the first time I saw her blank faced and speechless.

I chose to sit me vigil at Longinus's side. It was quite difficult getting me weapons there, especially the lance. It scraped and stuck more than once before I got it through. Before it got dark, I looked around some more. Partially hidden behind the helmet there was a heavy gold chain with medallions on it. I had seen Celtic craft man ship before, they were renowned fer their gold craft. One of them had honored this man, honored an enemy or perhaps a friend. This Roman was an enigma. I found a seat, on the ground with me back to the coffin and pondered him until darkness came.

The night was very long. I felt something brush me shoulder but it was only an itch that persisted. The breathing became louder like someone was here with me. I nervously knew what it was but imagination got the better of me. I heard movement in the darkness and me hair prickled. It was only me own foot. I was beginning to scare me self right proper, and so I prayed, recited the psalm of David and thought about me obligations as a knight. Then me thoughts went to me mam and da and the lost village. Tom came next and it felt as if he was there with me. I prayed some more and perhaps I wept a little too. Me arse really hurt so I got up. The rustling of me clothes was eerie in the pitch black, and I thought I heard a rat squeak. I put me hands on the stone coffin and felt calmness come over me. Even in death, I felt as if he reached out to me to comfort me. I laid me cheek on the cold stone and almost fell asleep.

At long last, light began to creep into the chamber and I could slowly see things come into focus. Me weapons, the coffin, the table. I suddenly realized how cold I was. The light became rosy and then golden. I knew we were somehow facing east or south east. Me vigil was over.

The knighting ceremony was simple. Morgan was present, and all the other knights were there, even Sir Spatzhein. He must have had a hard ride. They all stood stiffly with their swords drawn and points grounded.

I knelt before Sir Robert and he drew his sword. Sir Gawain stood on one side of me, and Lady Morgan the other.

I was clapped on each shoulder by the blade and then on the head. The whole time he intoned words I didn't hear until he said "Rise Sir William Barrow Arthur." I stood up stiffly a night in the cold had done that. Morgan unfolded a white surcoat and put it on over me mail. It hung to just below me knees and was split up each side, me belt held it together. Sir Gawain placed a helmet like his own on me head and I was looking through slits.

Sir Robert took me arm. 'We will step outside now. You can remove the helm if you wish. Carry it under your arm.'

As we walked towards the door, Morgan whispered. 'Don't you dare call me auntie.'

We came out into the small courtyard, which was full of cheering people. The grooms were there along with a bedecked Storm. He had a surcoat on too. Pats face was beaming as he waved.

Cheve came forward. "Mon ami, may I take this liberty Sir." He kissed me on each cheek and handed me Storms reins. He bowed and stepped back. Darragh was there, and Uri, so were Raglin and Helmsley, then there was Miriam, Meg and Gwen and Brother John, all me friends, it was over whelming but I soon found me speech.

After a bit, Sir Robert came over. 'We have to face the music, Son. The others are waiting.'

He called me son and it gave me goose bumps. I realized the other knights were no longer with us. My mind was close to blank as we came to the doors to the reception hall. I entered to stand before a somber group of knights. Du Lac sat on the chair of office and all the others stood on each side.

Du Lac spoke. 'Well, what a surprise. I am stunned. Now I must call you equal?'

Du Boors interrupted. 'Welcome to our ranks Will.' he laughed loudly. 'Anyone that can make porridge as well as you deserves Knighthood.'

That broke the ice and smiling men stepped down to congratulate me. One by one they clasped arms with me as an equal. Du Lac was last and he gave me a short bow as he gripped me forearm.

'Perhaps we will meet in the lists? I would like that.'

I was sure he would. He was an odd man, friendly one moment and not the next. He had his point of view and I would have to except it just as he had to except me knighthood. I was just beginning to realize that I truly was a knight, but the foremost thin in me mind was that I was Sir Robert's son.

Sir Robert called us to order. 'You all know why we are here. I believe that my son should be allowed to join our order and I wish to call a vote.'

Du Lac nodded with a frown. 'That is why we are here, isn't it? As I call your name, say aye or nay.'

One by one, they all voted 'Aye' until Du Lac himself. He voted 'nay'

Sir Robert was furious. 'You know the vote must be unanimous! Why are you doing this?'

Du Lac's face got red with anger. 'You think me a fool? You have some trickery up your sleeve, why this sudden rush, adoption, knighthood, and all before Christmas. You knew my feelings on commoners joining our ranks and you try to push this down my throat?'

Sir Gawain stepped forward. 'Jean, please calm yer self. There was no deliberate skullduggery here. I'll be blunt. Will led us to the very thing we were all searching for. We needed to protect him and hoped ye would all make him a brother. Fer any outsider who knew our secret the sentence was death. I fer one will never allow a hair on this man's head to be harmed and was hoping fer the easy way. Please, do not put a rift into the brotherhood.'

Du Lac glowered. 'What rift would that be, the one caused by you?'

Gawain stared at Du Lac with a slight frown. 'Robert and I stand with Will and we brook no attacks upon him.'

'You would break the oath?'

'On this, yes we would.'

Du Lac scrubbed his temples with his fingers and then let his hand drop over nose and mouth. 'Damn you Robert. Damn you Gawain.' He sighed. 'I change my vote to aye.'

Gawain smiled, 'When ye see what he led us to, ye won't regret it.'

# **CHRISTOVAN**

I led the knights to Longinus's resting place, pointing out details on the way. I was now one of them, a member of 'The Brotherhood of Longinus' and had taken the oath. The crowded chamber hummed with prayer as knights knelt with heads lowered. Sir Robert passed the spear to each of them, and each of them held it with reverend awe. Du Lac wept. They all were caught up in the moment. I felt eyes on us and turned me head. I had just a glimpse of a face in the tunnel, and then nothing. I was sure it was that of Du Lac's cleric.

I kept it to me self fer the moment and would regret it very deeply, later on. A day later, I realized I was breaking me oath already and went to Gawain. I told him my suspicions.

'Why did ye not speak right away? We need to trust ye and ye have already erred.'

I bowed me head in supplication and asked forgiveness.

He put his fingers under me chin and raised it. 'Ye are a knight now, Will, and me good friend. Ye need not bow to me. We must both go and tell Du Lac of this. I can just hear him saying, 'I told ye so.'

Du Lac listened quietly as I told him me suspicions. When I finished, he said. 'Why didn't you speak up right away?'

I looked him right in the eyes. 'I wasn't sure if I was seeing things or not and had to clarify it in me own mind first.'

He nodded, 'I'll accept that. Let us hope it can be nipped in the bud. I never have trusted my body guard he has always answered to my father.'

Christovan was summoned, and stood defiantly before his master, his face filled with cold distain.

'Did you follow us into the crypt?' Du Lac paced back and forth before him.

'Yes! I have already sent word to my Holy Father. He knows you for the heretics you are.'

Du Lac paused. 'Why would you call us heretics?'

'You blaspheme, and pray to a Christ killer. You are forever cursed in the eyes of God.'

Du Lac turned and struck him, knocking him to the ground. 'How dare you. We have found a relic with Christ's blood on it. That's what we pray to!'

Christovan got to his feet, smearing blood across his face with the back of his hand. 'The holy church will decide your innocence or guilt. I have sent for my brethren, the Holy Inquisitors, the

Dominicans. They will be your judges and your executioners.' He drew himself up haughtily. 'Do what you will, I am a sword of God and will see you driven into Hell.'

Du Lac drew his sword. 'You dare denounce and betray me? Lead the way, Judas!' He struck once blood spraying. Christovan collapsed dead at his feet, sightless eyes towards heaven. Du Lac spun to us. 'I give it no more than a month and then they will be here. Hide those you love, for they are merciless. Curse him, and you Will, for being so naïve.' He strode away his face a thundercloud.

Gawain sighed and put a hand on me shoulder. 'Oh Will, trouble is coming. Never before has the Inquisition been in England. Ye will see a side of our church that will test yer faith to its very limits. Come, what DuLac said is very true. We must hide those we love. Miriam and her father are Jews and fodder fer their stakes, and Meg will be counted as a witch. These men call knowledge witch craft and heresy. I think we must send them to Haven and perhaps even to Donclevy's stronghold. Remember, no one at Bamburg is safe. We must stand together to face this.'

'Can't we fight them?'

'No! Like it or not, they represent the Holy Catholic Church that we cleave to. We can't fight them. We can try and resist them but above all, we must convince them that we are righteous men. That is why, it is so important that there be nothing they can call heresy. We must not give them a foot hold.'

Miriam was too close to labor and could not be moved. I was at wits end, in fear fer her and the bairn.

Meg wanted to stay but I would have none of it.

'Ye must leave mom, if ye stay it will very likely be yer death.'

'What of Miriam and her da? It's their deaths too!'

'I'll hide them, there's a place, out of sight on the battlements. I can make a shelter there.'

'I'll ask Colette to stay, I taught her to be a midwife with clean habits.'

'She can only stay if she understands the risk.'

Sir Spatzhein was returning to Haven to warn them of coming events and Meg traveled under his protection. I was glad to see her safe. I knew Tim would protect her as would Sir Gawain.

Colette said she would stay, brave girl. Ross and a couple of yeomen helped me erect a strong lean to in our special place. If the sun was shining, even in cold weather, it was warm and out of the wind. Miriam was invalid now and couldn't get around fast, so we kept her there even though there was an element of discomfort. Her da was with her and Colette could fetch things.

The Advent passed and me sweet little Thomas was born December twenty eighth in the year of our Lord thirteen hundred and twenty nine. I held him in me arms staring at his dear face and soaked him in me heart swelled with love for him and me Miriam. She was still very weak and bed ridden and I worried fer her.

# **HIS EMINENCE GREGORIO SAN MARIANO**

The day came when they arrived. A train of waggons and men at arms, with eight Dominicans on horseback, tramped through our gate. Their leader wore black robes piped in red. A scarlet lined black cloak and a black cap on his head. A plain silver cross hung onto his breast from a chain. He dismounted without help and looked approvingly at the Swiss Pike that had turned out as an honor guard.

The knights all stood behind Sir Robert who bowed to him. 'We have been expecting your Eminence. Welcome, would you like to refresh yourselves?'

He stared at Sir Robert with hooded eyes. The skin on his face was like old parchment and his mouth deeply lined with an expression of disapproval, not a smiling face. He made a sign, giving benediction, tracing his hand over us. 'I thank you for your welcome. We will look to our own refreshments and there will be no communication with any of my retinue except when I will it. Now show my priests where we can set up our court.' His English was perfect but his accent was strong, Italian or Spanish? I wasn't sure.

He paused and turned. 'Where is Christovan? Where is my loyal priest?'

Sir Du Lac stepped forward. 'I sent him on a journey your Eminence.'

On a journey, a journey to where?' he stared at Du Lac. 'Ah, yes, Jean Du Lac, I know your father well, now what of my priest'

Du Lac compressed his lips. 'He went in search of God your Eminence. He must have felt some guilt at betraying my trust.'

With hooded eyes, His Eminence stared long and hard at Du Lac and then turned away. 'I hope he returns before we leave.'

The other priests dismounted. They wore simple brown robes with no ornamentation other than Rosary beads with a wooden crucifix, and black skullcaps. They quickly took charge of the train and had a camp set up in the courtyard. The men at arms took up positions to guard it.

Sir Roberts own quarters were turned over to his Eminence and he in turn, moved in to share me and Miriam's quarters. He put his arm around me shoulders. 'We can get to know each other better as father and son.'

I would learn later that all Inquisitions started the way this one did. All the people in Bamburg, were invited to the field outside the castle. The only place where there was room. It was voluntary but woe be tide those that didn't come. The Inquisitors seemed to know everything beforehand. Each person, was asked to admit some minor heresy or sin in return for a lenient punishment. If ye pointed out another sinner, yer punishment was even more lenient. Once guilty parties had been gathered together, the court went into session. There was no one to defend ye and ye pleaded before His Eminence and the other seven priests. Ye were put to the question, which involved interrogation and possible torture that was offered in degrees from mild to severe. The hand press was most common and usually enough to make frightened people say what they wanted to hear. The seven decided the severity of yer guilt and then passed their findins to His Eminence. It was all very formal and time consumin. I believe, it was engineered to put fear into the hearts of those to come. His Eminence could overrule the priest's findings and would mete out the punishment as he saw fit. Penalties ranged from something as mild as Hail Marys to floggings at levels of severity, branding and incarceration. Death penalties were rare and if ordered, were carried out by agencies other than the church, ergo the men at arms. Priests could not kill.

Things were orderly and swiftly, considering. After all, the Inquisitors were really here fer another purpose. There were perhaps a dozen singled out to appear in court, when Helmsley held up his hand. He was scared out of his wits. A priest went to him and, with a hand on his shoulder, forcefully pushed him to his knees.

'Confess my son I see Satan's torment within you. Let God's forgiveness cleanse you.'

Helmsley was crying. 'Father, I have sinned. I caused the death of melittlebrother.' He hung his head. 'I tipped the boat we were playing in. It was a stupid accident yer Grace but I feared me fathers' wrath and hid the body in the marshes. I pretended not to know anything. All these years, it's bin eating at me.' He threw himself on his face in the dirt. 'O God, forgive me!' His shoulders heaved. The priest crouched beside him and gave him a hard finger flick on the side of his head. 'Speak to me my son. Your crime is grievous but we see how you repent. Do you know of any who have sinned or commited heresy? Speak and give yourself to God's mercy.'

Helmsley raised his tear stained face and I had an awful premonition. 'Yes yer Grace, There is a Jewess here with her father.' His voice quavered, 'And a witch!'

I left before I heard anythin else. I needed to be with Miriam, to protect her. I realized later that I had bin watched. I was nearin the hidden spot when I met Colette. She was comin to find me and was smilin. 'Come monsieur, your wife is much better.'

She must have been startled that I didn't react with excitement. I clutched her arm. 'Thank ye Colette. Helmsley has betrayed us. Ye must leave this place fer yer own safety. Go now lass and thank ye fer everythin.' I let go of her with a push.

I rushed to Miriam and saw her shinin happy face as she held our bairn in her arms.

'Look at your Thomas my love, look how sweet he is.' Her face changed as she saw mine and she drew the little one to her breast. 'What is it Will? What has happened?'

I opened me mouth to speak when there was a sudden commotion behind me and rough hands grabbed me arms. Miriam grimaced with fright, as I was slammed onto me knees, me arms pulled up behind me forcing me face to the ground. I twisted me head and watched as a priest pointed at me beloved.

'Take the Jew for the stake, destroy the thing!'

Joseph almost stumbled in front of the soldiers advancin on the mother and child. That poor old man took a spear butt in the abdomin. It probably wasn't meant to kill, but he was so frail, it did, he collapsed in a heap.

Me blood froze as I watched, me wife climb out onto the battlement with me son in her arms. 'Come no closer!' she wailed. Little Thomas was now screamin too.

The priests' voice dripped contempt. 'Pull her down from there.'

The men reached and she simply vanished.

A guard in front of me said. 'Well! That'll save us the price of kindling.'

There was a terrible hollow moanin cry and I realized it was me. First I threw the man on me left arm from me and then the one on me right. I had both hands on that hapless wretch before anyone could move. I picked him up and drove his head into the stonewall. Then there were flashes and sparks and everythin went black.

I awoke to twilight, which was just as well because bright light would have been too much. Me face felt three times its size. They must have beaten on me as I lay unconscious. I groaned as I stiffly sat up. The decayin straw on the stone floor stank. This place hadn't seen use for a long time.

A rough voice growled, 'He has awakened father.'

Robes rustled as someone got up. 'Thank you my son. I will inform his Eminence. He may see his visitors for a moment.'

A burly guard stepped across me limited vision. 'You can see him now,' His voice was grudging, 'Just a few words.'

'You took a fair shit kicking Will. I'm so sorry.' I could see Darragh's face in the gloom. Then I saw Morgans. She reached through the bars and took me hand.

Her voice trembled. 'You poor sweet man, what have they done?'

I felt such hollowness inside me as I looked at her. 'It was me! I caused this. I didn't speak up soon enough.'

'What do you mean?'

'Christovan, he saw us and I said nothin right away.' I buried me head in me arms. 'I killed me wife and son.'

'You did not, Will. Narrow minded bigoted men did.'

'Times up,' The guards' voice was harsh. 'He is to appear before his Eminence.'

'Can we clean him up a bit?'

'Not necessary.'

'He's a knight for God's sake!'

'Not necessary. Now leave or join him.'

I stood in tatters and chains before his Eminence, Gregory San Mariano and stared into eyes that were pitiless.

'Are you strong enough for the question my son?'

I nodded. 'Yes yer Eminence.' I wouldn't give him the satisfaction of seein me grief.

'Very well,' He leaned forward in his high chair. 'Why did you fornicate with a Jew? Why did you give it child?'

I raised me chin and stared into his eyes. 'Because I loved her yer Eminence'

'You loved a Christ killer? God forgive you my son.'

'She was no Christ killer she was the kindest most lovin person ye could hope to meet.'

His Eminence sighed. 'Why do you argue against God my son, I want you to repent so I can save your soul. Evil comes in all guises and Jews are Satan's masters of deception.'

I held me tongue and stared at the ground. I was only just becomin aware of others in the room, many others. They were all so silent ye could hear a pin drop.

He was sittin back with his chin in his hand. 'Now, to another matter my son you are accused of harboring a witch. How do you plead?'

'I have never known a witch yer Eminence.'

'Would you so swear on your honor as a knight and before God?'

'Aye, I would so swear. I never knew nor do I know a witch!'

His Eminence rubbed his nose with thumb and finger and leaned towards me again. 'Now, one final thing needs to be addressed. Are you a member of the camarilla called the Brotherhood of Longinus?'

'Aye yer Eminence'

'You admit bowing to a heathen Roman who took part in killing our Lord?'

'I admit no such thing yer Eminence. I hold in reverence, the Spear of Longinus that has Christs blood on it. As we revere the Cross he died on, and the cup he drank from and the robe he wore! May I ask you a question yer Eminence?'

'That is most irregular my son. What is it? The question will decide the answer.'

'On the Tomb were the words...I quoted them from memory... 'Quaerite Primum Regnum Dei' would ye tell me what they mean?'

He pursed his lips. 'Seek ye first the Kingdom of God.'

I smiled defiantly. 'Is that the epitaph of a blasphemer a Christ killer?'

His lips compressed and without another word, his Eminence stood and took a black cloth from a boy standin just back of his chair. He placed the cloth on his head.

'Now you will be judged my son on your knees before God.' A guard stepped forward to push me down with a spear butt as he raised a finger.

'First, for fornicating with a Jew, you will receive fifty lashes. If you survive, God has forgiven you.' He raised a second finger, glitterin with a ring.

'Second, for not being repentant of your sins, you will receive fifty lashes after the scabs of the first fifty start to fall off. If you survive, God has forgiven you. There can be no incarceration, which is deserved, as we will be leaving all too soon.' He raised a third finger.

'Third, your oath as a knight is accepted and there will be no punishment for harboring a witch.' His hand clasped the crucifix on his chest.

'Forth, your words smell of heresy but I feel that only his Holiness can be the judge of this. In all humility, I must decline judgment against you in this matter. I already came to a similar conclusion with the other knights here, who answered in much the same way. I will take the spear back to Avignon for our Holy Father to judge.' He removed the cloth from his head. 'This Court of Holy Inquisition is closed.'

I was led back to me prison and was told to pray fer forgiveness. Me punishment would commence in the mornin. I was racked with feelins of guilt, how could I pray fer forgiveness when I couldn't forgive me self. No one was allowed to see me, and I was only given tepid water to drink. I flailed at rats in the darkness and finally fell into a fitfull sleep. Miriam came to me and I saw that her feet did not touch the ground.

'My darling my love, do not blame yourself for the wickedness in men. We are all weak vessels hoping for salvation, and you my love, must find forgiveness...' Me eyes flared open with a start and then I reached fer the water. Me mouth was dry as dust. The dream had been vivid and left me troubled. I didn't want to forgive meself.

There was a flash and I thought of Helmsley. For a moment, hate filled me and then it was gone. That pathetic man had once saved me life. I had to find it in me to forgive him. He had done a wicked thing but he wasn't a wicked man, only a very frightened one.

I thought of me tiny bairn and wept. His little eyes hadn't even focused yet. I think I wept the rest of the night, fer me wife, me little Tom and, perhaps, fer meself.

Guards came and rousted me out of the cell.

'One growled. It is lucky for you our comrade didn't die. It would have been the hot irons for you if he had. Only his helm saved him." His chuckle held cold menace. "We have a friend on the lash. He'll see to it that you won't survive.'

Outside was dreary and cold, the misting rain made everything surreal. It was a fittin mood fer the occasion. I looked about and saw all me friends. The knights stood in a line with heads bowed in prayer, their cloaks hangin drab and drippin. All the grooms were there and Ross, Raglin and Uri. I felt very aware, and when Darragh walked to me, I was surprised.

'I am permitted to be yer second my friend. I will count the lashes. I just wish I could take some of them for you. Not many men survive fifty and they will not spare the rod. Remember lad, we all love you.'

'I'll live to love ye back.' I smiled as they tore away me shirt and tied me to rings, high on a post, so that I could only stand on me toes. Me whole body was taut and when the first lash fell, I arched in pain and gritted me teeth. After a few more, I remembered nothing. I awoke on me stomach with gentle hands smearin black ointment all over me back. I felt a lot like when ye sit too close to a fire only I could not escape it. I turned me head to the side and Darragh crouched down to look at me.

'My God, you are still with us. Try to get used to being on your stomach for a bit. You won't like any other position.'

Then Ross's face was there. 'Yer one tough bastard...Oh I'm sorry sir.'

'Don't make me laugh, you prick!'

He grabbed me hand as I grimaced. 'Not me intent sir, we had to forcefully stop the arsehole whipping yer when he reached fifty. He didn't like it, that ye survived."

A flash of pain seared me back. 'God's truth and I have to go through this again?'

The next face I saw, was Morgans, she was holdin a bowl that smelled like broth.

'It's so nice to see yer face me Lady, may I have some of that?'

She turned to look at someone behind her. 'Thank God he didn't call me auntie.' She turned back to me with a full spoon, 'Ready?'

Another face materialized beside hers. It was me new pater. I never realized before, how much they looked alike.

'Hello da.' I took a spoon of broth. It tasted like heaven.

He smiled, 'Hello son, it's good to hear your voice again. You have done me proud, Will. You have done me proud. I am so sorry for your losses, son. We all grieve. Others want to see you, including Gawain. But it will be tomorrow. You need your rest.'

Morgan spoonfed me until the bowl was empty. Then she awkwardly bent to kiss me on the brow. 'Try to sleep, Will.'

Sleep, how was I going to sleep? the pain was excruciating, and got worse if I tried to move, even a little bit. Somehow, the night slowly dragged by. No one was here yet so I tried to see where I was and the faint things around me. The bed I was on was a wood frame with interlaced leather straps. It was much more fergiving than the wooden slat cot I usually slept on. I could see a small tub with a dark brown, almost black, odious smelling substance in it. I recognized it as the unguent we applied to horses' sores and knew it was all over me back. I turned me head slowly to look the other way. God, me neck was stiff. There was a man sitting slouched in a chair, with his head on his chest. I tried to speak but only a gurgle came. Painful coughing cleared me throat.

'Uri wake up, we all know old soldiers can sleep anywhere.'

He didn't move but his eyes opened. He smiled as he turned his head to look at me and got up.

'You are awake Will. Are you hungry?'

'Yes. What are ye doing here?'

'We've been taking turns during the night hours. Cheve had his turn and Pat left maybe two hours ago.'

'The night watch, to make sure I don't pass on, what's me back like anyway?'

'Like a mass of raw meat. That Papal prick of a guard had lead pellets sewn into the lash. You were not supposed to live.'

I grimaced as a flash of pain seared me back. 'I may not survive the next fifty, Ouch!'

He got up to crouch down by me. 'That has us all worried my friend. Your father is pleading clemency before his Eminence. It seems with little success.'

'Why are ye not with the Pike?'

'Mein Kapitan likes you and gave me leave. Besides, we are all keeping a low profile while the Dominicans are here. Did you know that Du Lac is spitting fire? Now that you are one of his brothers, he has become very protective of you. His family's influence doesn't even ruffle his Eminences feathers. Ah, here comes your breakfast, I'm going to leave now, be back tonight.'

Colettes smilin face appeared. 'I have bread pudding with chopped apple for you, sir.' She fed me slowly, dabbin me mouth every, once in a while, with her bib.

I watched her every move while she fed me. She was such a pretty, little thing. I groaned. 'Why aren't ye married yet Colette? Ye must have many suitors.'

'I have lost my mama and papa sir there is no one to find me a husband. My papa aways told me to use my head and not my heart. He said many men were greedy little squirrels and once they had picked the cherry they would abandon the tree.'

I had to laugh and it hurt. 'Yer father knew what he was talking about. Don't worry, the right one will come along and he won't be just a cherry picker.' It hurt a lot to laugh alright but I knew I was still alive.

After fifteen days, I was able to walk with a cane and found meself up on the battlement. I forced meself to look over at the thunderin waves and rocks below. I wept and let me tears join the brine of the sea. It felt like a unity with me wife and child. I had found out that Yeomen had risked their lives to retrieve the bodies and had taken them away from Bamburg. Sir Gawain had them interred at Haven, in a prettier much happier place. I knew I couldn't visit them for some time to come.

The day came when I had to stand before his Eminence, once again. Guards removed the loose jerkin I was wearin and he inspected me back.

'It is healing well my son. God must love you more than you know. You are ready for the second fifty.'

I heard me paters' voice. 'I ask your Eminence for mercy. Do not allow him to be whipped with the lead balls again. He will not survive it.'

'He stands before me with no signs of contrition. The punishment will be carried out as before, may God have Mercy on his soul.'

Me eyes opened to a place of fire. I was sure I was in hell. If I had had a voice, I would have shrieked as I burned. All I could do was sob weakly.

'By all that's holy, he's living!' I knew Darraghs voice and knew I wasn't in hell after all. I coughed and wanted to die. The pain was worse than anything imaginable.

Morgans face swam into view. 'Oh, what have they done my darling man, what have they done?' She touched me cheek. 'They are no longer here, Will. They left two days past. Word has been sent for Meg and she is coming. Gwen is bathing your back, that's why it hurts so much more. That vile man with the whip struggled to throw handfuls of dirt on you as he was forced to stop.'

I heard Cheve. 'The ointment is coming mon ami, as soon as ye are clean.'

This time I felt like I might die. There was a weakness in me that wasn't there before. I could almost feel the presence of Miriam and me little son, as if they were waiting fer me.

Meg came, and wept while she worked on me. The pain subsided somewhat as she applied her lotions and balms. I learned later that I took a high fever and Meg had to use all her skills to save me. Obviously she did, I'm still telling me story.

The day came when Darragh brought news of Helmsley's death. The man was so overcome with guilt and remorse, he hung himself and would never see heaven. I almost found it in meself to pity him.

This time I had to use crutches and me back pulled here and there as it stiffened with scabs. There was always pain and bleeding, I was getting used to it. I could only wear a loose smock and no pants because me flesh was raw from me buttocks to me neck. Darragh said there was no skin left at all, it was like I had been flayed. In fact I had been.

I healed more and more and me mind healed a little too. DuBoors counciled me as did Lensberg. I wasn't really one of them. I hadn't been to the crusades but now I had been whipped within an inch of me life they were more solicitous. I had so many friends looking out fer me, self pity had no room. The first weeks, I exercised by walking on crutches. I went the length and breadth of Bamburg, visiting all me friends. There was just a little snow on the ground now. The smithy was sufferin from all its losses and Raglin was swept off his feet, by too much work. He really needed help. Rene chipped in to help sometimes but had a lot to learn. His one advantage was that he knew horses. Perhaps he would be the next farrier. I had lunch or supper with the Swiss pike on more than one occasion. I was like a mascot to them and I made more friends, even ones that couldn't speak English.

# **Cyril Pardoone**

It was now late February and Alexander Donclevy finally arrived with Cyril in tow. They had been warned, and stayed away until it was safe. Alexander was even more dour looking than before, and his hair seemed even grayer. He saw me and came over. Lifting me smock, he looked at me back. This Cyril fellow looked over his shoulder and made a face.

'That's more than any man should bear.'

Donclevy looked at him. 'This is no any man.' He turned back to me. 'Much has happened since we last met. Ye are now a knight and no so long ago ye tried to push me down stairs.' The corners of his mouth twitched with a hint of a smile. 'Me prayers are with ye, young man now I need to speak to Sir Robert.'

I watched him walk away, tall, lank and as proud as a hawk. Cyril glanced back at me with a look that said 'I'd like to talk.'

I stepped to one side. I was still slow on me feet and didn't want to be underfoot as armed men rode by. The first were men wearing tartan kilts, pinned at the shoulder, with bits of mail glinting through. Most were armed with swords, though there was a smatterin of spears and maces. They all had small round shields like the Scots. I didn't recognize them so guessed they must be Pardoones. After fifty, they stopped coming. I went to the open portcullis and saw a small army setting up camp in the meadow out front, a lot more Pardoones and roughly a hundred of Donclevys men.

Once everyone was settled in Cyril came to find me. He was a big young man, tall and wide and he reminded me a bit of Malcolm.

'I shood introduce meself, I'm Cyril Pardoone.' He held out his hand.

I took it. 'Call me Will, that's what I'm used to. Why are ye knocking me up?'

He looked a little embarassed. 'I knoo a lot about ye from the Donclevys and I am friends with Danny.'

I almost fell over. 'Ye know Danny, when did ye see him last?'

Cyril laughed. 'It's bin a bit but last I heard he's doing well. Loves his mischief, I've bin caught up in his indiscretions moor than once. He spoke of ye fondly and I decided I'd like to meet ye. The ride here was a little boreing, Sir Alexander is noo a conversationalist.'

'I won't be much fun either ye know. I'm still hurting bad and I'm trying to train to get me strength back.'

'I noticed ye are a mess! I'm Gooin to find Raglin, we played together as laddies. I'd like to stay in tooch if I may.'

'Aye, we'll cross paths. I try to train every morning on the training ground. We have the best sword master here. Darragh McAstor, have ye heard of him?'

Cyril nodded and I realized he was looking at me with hero worshiping eyes. I think I reddened a bit.

'I wood like to practice with him. I'm noo the best swordsman. I learned from men at arms, a bit here a wee bit there. Me da hurt too mooch to teach me. Raglin beats me every time.'

'Keep yer eyes and ears open. With the caliber of people there, ye could learn a lot. The lady Morgan is a great fighter.'

'Lady Morgan?'

'Aye she is Sir Robert's sister, or half sister. She takes a bit of getting used to. If she snaps yer head off don't be surprised. Look, if ye like, meet me at seven and I'll introduce ye around.'

'I'll be there.'

I watched his receding back and shook me head. He knew Danny.

Next morning I ate with the yeomen. I hated being alone, I had discovered I was no fun at all. I heard something that pricked me ears. A little gossip was going on and the rumor was that Du Lac and Gwen had been seen together, the kind of together that involved skirts up and drawers down. I was sure I was hearing things so I got into the conversation and got an ear full. I had been too preoccupied to notice but it seemed that this had been going on fer a while. Must say I was shocked, did Robert suspect? I left breakfast with a lot on me mind and no one to talk to.

I got meself over to the training ground. I was the first there so I pulled Darragh aside and asked if he knew of anything.

'Only the same rumors you've been hearing Will. There is one thing I do know, While you were down, they had a fight.'

'Who had a fight?'

'Don't be dense, Yer pater and Gwen, that's who. Something to do with being betrothed for five years and no wedding plans. It seems Sir Robert had no satisfactory answers and now they are not speaking. That's all I know for a fact, the rest is still hearsay.'

While he talked, I did some slanted pushups and could feel me back pulling and tryin to tear. He stopped me and looked at the scarring.

'Have you seen a burn victim? That's what your back looks like. The scars are all ridged and twisted and there is no resilience to your skin. I don't know if you'll ever get some back but we will work on it.'

Morgan arrived. 'Good day, Will can you workout yet?'

'I'll try but take it slow, let's do some warm ups first.'

Morgan stepped beside me and looked at me back. She touched it and let her fingers linger there. 'I would love to take a whip to the man that did this to you.' Her voice was soft.

I heard someone else and turned. It was Cyril. I nodded welcome and introduced him to Morgan and Darragh. 'He wants to learn a few tricks, Darragh. He claims he doesn't know much.'

Darragh took a training sword from the rack and tossed it to him. 'Let's have a look.'

Cyril managed to catch it even though most of his attention was on Morgan. She was worth looking at.

She took me arm. 'Let's get at it, leave them to their stuff.'

We were soon goin through a series of movements designed to stretch. I could certainly feel them and pushed to the limit of me pain thresh hold. I'm happy to say, there was no bleeding. So we carried on with some sword play. I was still quite slow and Morgan beat me every time. It was me first real workout in a month and a half. I knew I was going to get a lot better.

After our session, I went to see Storm. Me horse had been totally neglected by me. Cheve had taken him and Taxeia to bed with the other horses, and cared fer them there. When he first saw me he acted a little huffy, then he came over and was nuzzling me back. I pulled up me jerkin so he could see it. I could feel him sniffing over it then, using his head, he pulled me against him. We just stood there fer a time until he stepped back and wuffled me face. I'd just had a horsey hug and it left tears in me eyes.

Ridin was one thing I could enjoy despite the pain and Storm and I went daily. The grooms had stopped galloping the waves, it was getting too cold but the beach was still a good place to exercise.

Me second day out, Cyril joined me and we started to get to know each other. I found out that he had few friends except fer a younger brother that was a pain in his arse as he put it...Stuck in that aerie they called home didn't lend to casual visits. I liked him and was more than willing to be a much needed friend. We raced each other up and down the beach, him laughing like a ten year old boy.

Easter was around the corner and Alexander wanted to return home before Good Friday. He was very disappointed at not seein the relic but at least, he had been taken to see Longinus's tomb, and now knew the story. The day he left I opted to go along as far as Haven. I needed to see where me loved ones lay. Both Alexander and Cyril were pleased fer me company. Me pater and Morgan saw me off. Robert squeezed me hand. 'Be careful son, you might be coming home alone.'

'Aye da, I'll be careful. See ye soon, ye too auntie.' I saw her face change as I shied Storm away. Her fist whistled through thin air.

'You have to come back you, you.....Man!'

The trip was uneventful. Alexander and I spoke a bit, he accepted me as an equal now. He was very happy with Raglin and his hard work.

'I think, next year he should marry and raise a family. Have a son he could teach. Blacksmithing is honorable work. I know of a lassie, with connections, if he is willing.'

I laughed, 'He's always interested in a lassie, is she pretty?'

Alexander snorted through his nose and hurumphed. 'Pretty enough last time I saw her.'

'Have ye had any word on Scotland?'

'Ye have friends there don't ye? It's a mess again. The disinherited have rallied around Edward Balliol and The English crown is interested in him as a puppet King like his father John. Some say he is reluctant but reluctance can sometimes work as well as wanting. They are all waiting like crows around the Bruces' sick bed.'

I shrugged. 'That's pretty well what Malcolm said would happen.'

Snow had started falling when we reached Haven. I said me goodbyes to Alexander Donclevy and to me new friend Cyril. I told him I hoped to get up to his home sometime. Tim met me at the gate and we stood together, watching the cavalcade disappear into a fresh winter landscape.

'How are ye Will?'

'I'm well and improvin every day, and ye, how are ye?'

'I'm as good as new me friend. I heard about the ordeal ye went through and was prayin for ye every day.'

'Thank you Tim that means a lot to me, is Gawain about?'

'Oh of course, yer a knight now, me apologies sir, I forgot.'

'Forget all ye like Tim, Ye are me friend above all else. Don't stand on ceremony with me unless ye really feel ye need to.'

He smiled, 'Sir Gawain should be in his quarters.'

Gawain and I greeted each other as old friends. He offered me some cider to rid the dryness of the trip.

'Ye have come to see the graves of Miriam and yer bairn? I thought as much.' He took me arm. 'Let's walk together.'

We walked through the cavalry camp towards the postern when a shout stopped us. It was Karl Spatzhein.

'Greetings Will, is your back getting better?'

I smiled at him. 'Yes thank you and so is yer English.'

'Do you think so?' He looked pleased. 'Is there any new news for me to hear?'

I thought of Gwen and DuLac. 'No nothing, things will likely stay quiet until late spring.'

He nodded, 'Enjoy your walk my friend. Perhaps we can all dine together having new company is nice.'

Gawain said, 'Me quarters, about seven?'

Karl nodded and walked off humming a tune.

'I'd swear that man twitches.' Gawain smiled.

We walked along a path patched with snow until we came to a grand old oak tree spreading branches over three gravestones, one a little apart from the other two. The skiff of snow gave everythin a quality of purity. Gawain stopped and gave me a gentle push forward.

'I will wait here take all the time ye need.'

I knelt before the two. Someone had carefully chipped 'Miriam – beloved,' into one and the other had ' little Thomas – In Gods Arms' I could hear someone weeping and realized it was me. The other stone simply said 'Joseph'. I stayed with them fer at least an hour, praying and speaking to them. Gawain waited patiently in the chill, the whole time.

As we walked back, I said, 'Ye picked a beautiful spot Gawain, I thank ye from the bottom of me heart.'

He just nodded and then said. 'All through spring summer and autumn, there are flowers, from snowdrops to asters. That great oak harbors birds and small animals who will watch over them. They will never be lonely.'

I got such a lump, I was unable to say anythingg and just walked beside him, thankful he was me friend.

I planned to return home the following day and was very surprised to learn that twenty Swiss Pike had arrived while I was at the grave site. I thanked Gawain and promised to see him fer supper. I was curious and went to see.

A grinnin Uri met me. 'I've come to see you safely home. I know how witless you can be.'

'Is that any way to talk to a gentleman and a knight?'

'No it's not, but I can talk to my friend like that. My kapitan put me in charge so I think I was promoted.'

'You think?' I clapped him on the back. 'I'm very glad for yer company, but I have to dine with Sirs Gawain and Spatzhein this evening.'

'That's just fine I have to look after my men. See you in the morning.'

Dinner was delicious and the company, pleasant. I spooned another mouthful of peppered hare in mushroom sauce and asked Gawain to tell more of things in the near east.

He chewed a moment, removed a small bone with his fingers, and swallowed. 'The worst part is the trip there. Right now, France is no place fer traveling Englishmen, so ye have to sail from Plymouth all the way down the French coast to Donostia San Sabastian in Spain. Cross by land to Barcelona and hope the Spanish don't hate Englishmen." He grinned. "Play it by ear, and ye can go all the way by sea too. Now ye can take a ship across the Mediterranian to Sardinia or Corsica and then Malta. Take a breath and board ship for Alexandria in Egypt. Get used to the heat for a month or two and stop sweating all yer fluids away, then sail to Gaza. From there it is just a stroll to Jerusalem. The whole journey could take up to eight months depending on weather, men and luck.'

'How would ye find the Silk road?'

Gawain laughed. 'Why, are ye planning a trip? I think by the time ye get to Jerusalem ye'll be looking to come home.'

'Humor me Gawain.'

'Well, I'd look fer a well armed caravan, heading east from Jerusalem or Gaza. Or, if ye have a death wish, ye could go on yer own across Persia to Basra by the Persian Gulf. I've only heard this mind ye and it would bear more research.'

Karl looked at us both like we were insane. 'I like the climate here or at home. When you are baking in the desert you'll wish for some cool drizzle. I hated it there, just a bunch of foreigners who do not speak German or English, and they want you dead. They also made you pay double for all you purchased.'

Gawain choked on his ale and burst out laughin. 'Karl, did ye ever hear of bartering? That's what they do there. Ye have to haggle or they will have no respect fer ye.'

I thought about it. 'We say how much? and pay. Ye know where ye stand that way. How do ye know when to stop?'

Gawain shook his head. 'He starts high and ye start low. Generally ye meet in the middle.'

Karl threw his hands up. 'What a waste of time!'

'It's all part of socializing it's a pleasant past time or game to them. When in Rome do as the Romans do.'

'Oh, how profound' Karl pushed himself away from the table. 'Thank you for a fine supper, I'm going to bed.' He held out his hand. 'Have a safe journey home, Will. I hope to see you soon again.'

I stood and said me goodbyes. As I turned to Gawain, he said, 'Stay a bit Will. I'll show ye a new game, it's called Backgammon. It came from the Pharaohs, and is played all over the near east. As I said once before, know yer enemy. Perhaps ye can make him a friend.' He grinned. 'Or take his money.'

Gawain seemed to be reading me mind better than me. I enjoyed the game, even though I lost several times, and hoped to play it again soon. After a pleasant evening, I took me leave and went to bed.

I took early breakfast, and went to the gate to find Uri. A contingent of French cavalry were just heading north on their rounds and I stopped to watch them go. I supposed the English were getting used to seeing them and recognized them as friends. I thought it would be smarter to have a few Yeomen along to show their good faith. Uri was waiting and we left right away. The snow had stopped but it didn't look like we would see the sun this day.

We were well into our trip when a soldier called our attention to smoke rising above the trees on our right. It was just white smoke but it got darker as we watched.

'I think that's towards Bamburg village, lets investigate. The village is a fair bit off but there are crofts all around this area.'

Uri set the Pike to a double march. With their pikes and mail it must have been hard, but they handled it without protest, tough men. We covered ground quickly and when we were close, I called a halt. 'One man to me and we will take a look.'

Uri sent a man named Claus, I knew him from the mess table, he spoke some English. We slipped into the forest just below, and quietly made our way up the hill. The scene before me gave me a feeling of dread. Everything was quiet except fer the crackling flames in what was left of the barn. The ground around the small farmstead was heavily trampled and there were some piles of horse shit. I crept forward and checked on one. It was still warm. I told Claus to go fetch the others and headed fer the house. I knew before I entered, I could smell it. Skye had been here, he didn't delegate this kind of thing. Me stomach was much stronger now and I was able to study the horror within. Six people, young and old, had been cut to pieces, and festooned about, I was white as a sheet when Uri came. I was speechless when I grabbed his arm, stopping him from going in.

He looked into me eyes and gently peeled me fingers off his arm. He went in. It was a while before he returned.

'Mein Gott im Himmel what Hellish beast did this?' He covered his mouth with his hand and spoke through his fingers. 'Parts were missing, I think he eats them!'

Me eyes widened, 'Eats them?' I turned away it had just got worse, if that was possible. 'Uri, prepare this house fer burning. We want nought but ash left. I'm hieing to Bamburg village, and I'll bring the Mayor and a priest.'

# **MAGGOT**

I knew something was off as soon as I entered the village. There was nothing moving, no bairns playing, no dogs, no people moving about. I caught the glint of armor in the corner of me eye and then another. They had come from behind a hut. I turned Storm around to leave, only to face a dozen armed men barring me way. Other grinnin soldiers were comin out of nowhere to surround me. Storm sensed our trouble and got fidgety, high steppin in a circle, he tried to see a way out. One man stepped too close and he kicked him in the face. The soldier crumpled to the ground.

Then I heard a familiar voice. 'Curb the beast or it dies!'

I dropped down from me horse and short bridled him. 'Skye Show yer self, I'd know yer voice anywhere.'

Skye stepped from between his men with that thin slit smile on his face. 'I finally have you, you shite, you're the one who stole Darragh from me and killed Garrad. I thought an anniversary celebration might bring results and here you are.' His eyes scanned his men. 'Perhaps we could make a trade, his head for Garrads?' there was scattered laughter.

'So ye know about Garrad. He died bleating like a lamb led to slaughter.' I sounded much braver than I felt. 'Who changes yer nappies now?'

Skye's face darkened his voice a hiss. 'You will pay dearly for that! The black is gone and of no consequence to me anymore.'

I thought, 'so much fer loyalty.'

'When I receive his head my men might have a game of football in his honor. Would you like to meet my new man?' He raised his voice, 'Maggot, where are you dear, come here!'

A shambling mountain appeared and men hurried to get out of its way. I had seen grotesque things but nothing prepared me fer this abomination. It was like an ogre of legend, standing near seven feet. It was all greyish white layers and folds of flabby fat. Its pink eyes.seemed unfocused as it opened its mouth. Drool dripped from one corner, and I could see its teeth filed into points. It obviously had the mind of an idiot.

'Master has food fer Maggot?' The voice was high and whiney.

Annoyance crept into Skye's voice, 'Soon, my dear.'

'Where did ye find that monstrosity? Maggot fits it well.' I shuddered, it looked and smelled, vile.

'I found him living in a cave in the lake country. He fed mostly on human flesh and had a small village in thrall. They were in such fear they left him sacrifices just like the trolls of legend.'

'How did ye get that thing to follow ye?' I watched how it fawned on Skye.

He sneered, 'I fed him. If you feed a dog a few times he'll follow you anywhere.'

The thought was horrible. 'So now he's yer dog?'

'No, he's my Maggot.' He patted the creature on its arm. 'Aren't you, you're my Maggot"

It was becoming agitated and was rubbing itself through filthy rags. 'Maggot wants to fuck, Maggot is hungry.'

Skye laughed and waved a man over, 'Find him a wench, he can eat her when he's done with her.' He pointed to me. 'Chain him in a waggon and keep a close watch.'

I shut me eyes trying to get pictures of appalling evil out of me head. I barely felt any pain as they bashed me about, chaining me to the bed of the waggon.

It was a long night. I tried to cover me ears to the horrible, tortured screams of a woman. The cries were awful and crawled up and down yer skin. Then Skye came to visit. He discovered me back and held a torch near it. The pain became excruciating and I almost welcomed it, as it took me mind from other things. He ran his fingers over the welts and pluckered bumps.

'What a work of art, it's a shame the artists are all lying at the bottom of the sea.'

I grunted through the pain, 'What do ye mean, at the bottom of the sea?'

'Oh, didn't you know? The Papist ship went down with all hands, somewhere off Lands End near the Channel Isles.' He smiled viciously, 'Why do you look so shocked? I thought you would be pleased at the news.' He chuckled. 'Their God sent a storm He must have wanted them at his right hand.' He walked off, laughin.

Longinus' spear was gone, somewhere at the bottom of the sea. No one would see it ever again. I felt sad fer me fellow knights. Skye didn't seem to know that I was a knight, it must be me lucky day.

One thing made the rest of the night much easier. I saw a face with a noseguard helm peering from behind a tree. A raised hand showed a thumb up and then it was gone.

The morning would have brought more horror but a war horn sounded nearby, putting the soldiers on edge.

Skye was in a rage. His fun had been taken away from him, and the villagers would stay alive. He ordered Maggot to pull the waggon. 'If bad men come, kill him eat him if you like, just save me his head.'

I was Thinking, interested in his definition of 'bad men' when Maggot grabbed the waggon shaft with one huge hand. I fell onto me side, the bonds cutting in, as he heaved on it to get it into motion. His vile stench wafted back to me, God, I'd have to smell it fer the whole trip? It was difficult to believe that this thing was whelped by humans. It likely was shunned and outcast its entire life. Why hadn't it been killed as an infant? a desperate mother's love had saved it? The village where it was born could very well be the one it had fed from.

Skye's column was moving double time. Most of his men had horses but twenty or so were on foot. The pace was too much and they began dropping back. A bend in the road put them out of sight, then I heard the sudden clash of steel and cries of men just behind us.

Skye was yelling orders as a man in steel plate galloped up beside the waggon. He was ridin Storm. I shouted, 'Storm, go home.' The stallion bucked once, throwing the man onto the road with a clatter, and took off past the column towards Bamburg. I credited that animal with a lot of intelligence and seemed to be right.

Sudden chaos swept the soldiers as Skye screamed 'Ride! Ride for the sea, Maggot kill him!'

The road before me was suddenly empty as soldiers spurred their horses into the nearest cover, the one in plate had managed to get up but was moving too slow.

Maggot dropped the waggon shaft and turned to reach fer me. The stupid beast seemed to have no understanding of the danger it was in.

Then Swiss were all around us. The man in plate died quickly and one Swiss drove his pike into Maggots eye.

He shrieked and wailed, 'Why you hurt Maggot?' And then he was attacked and stabbed from all sides, his high pitched shrieks were hard to take as he squirmed, swatted and floundered. A pike stabbed his throat, silencing him. A slashed tendon brought him to his knees and another man drove his pike deep into the creature's back. When they were done, all that was left, was a twitchin mountain of scabrous fat. It twitched fer a long time after it was dead.

French cavalry swept by as Uri tore at me chains.

'Ye are a sight fer sore eyes, ye have no idea how much I love ye right now.'

Uri gave me a stern look. 'None of that talk thank you.' Then he laughed, 'I'm happy you are alive.'

'Who's leading the cavalry?'

'Sir Spatzhein. Thank god for boredom, The German showed up just as we realized you were in trouble.'

About an hour later, Karl returned with his French troop. 'Zey had ships in a cove nearby and escaped us.'

'Not again! That man has more lives than a cat and the wiles of a fox.' I looked up at Karl, astride his horse, 'He's really pissed now isn't he? At least I hope so another of his sweethearts is dead. More like that would be hard to find. I just hope we will drive him into a mistake.'

Uri made a face. 'I do not think that abomination could be repeated any time soon.'

The French captain dismounted. 'Vous etes en vie mais vous poignets sont en sang et des mati'eres premiere's.' He grasped me shoulder and pushed me down to sit on a log. He signaled a nearby soldier. 'Trooper, apportez pommade.'

The man searched through his saddle bag and came with a small container. When he opened it, the stuff in it looked quite familiar. I held out me wrists as the soldier applied it gently. It was a relief and I spoke to captain and trooper both. 'Je vous remercie pour votre gentillesse.'

The captain smiled, 'Vous parlez francais?'

I grinned back and shook me head, 'No.'

Uri spoke to the captain and then turned to me. 'You spoke that like a Frenchman sir, do you know where your weapons are and your coif, for that matter?'

I shook me head. 'They might be back at the village. We need to go there anyway, we have unfinished business.'

Spatzhein was talking to a couple of men when I walked up. He smiled, 'Ah, Will, can I help you?'

'Yes Karl, would ye be so kind as to accompany us until we are back on this road? I don't expect more trouble but ye never know. I seem to be a bit of an attraction.'

Karl laughed, 'Of course ve will. You are going back to the village, why?'

I told him about the croft and what needed to be done. Then I told him about the lost spear.

He sobored and nodded, he even looked crestfallen. I found him to be quite boyish most of the time, treating every thing like it was a game but now he became serious. Orders were given, and we headed back around the corner to Bamburg town.

The mayor greeted us and was most appreciative he knew we had saved their lives. Townsfolk crowded around as I told them about the croft and what needed to be done.

'We have no priest, good sir. He was the first to die when they came. They hung him upside down and lit a fire under his head. It was horrible!'

I looked at him. 'Horrible, yes it was and what of the poor woman last night? That too was horrible. I will have to do the praying but ye must witness it. Did any of ye see me stuff?'

A small man stepped hesitantly from behind others. 'I have yer sword, Sir. They left it lying in the dirt. I don't know anything about any other stuff.'

'You've not seen me dirk? It was special to me.'

Several shook their heads. I sighed and turned away only to get a foul gust of wind in the face. "God's truth that thing reeked bad enough living. It's down the road a bit and still stinking up yer village. Ye need to get rid of it.'

'How?'

For some reason I couldn't fathom, I got angry. 'Hitch a horse to it and drag it a long way down wind. That's how!'

When we arrived back at the croft, I still hadn't shaken me fit of bad temper. I tried to think of a prayer and me mind was blank. What was wrong with me? I stood in a stew until Karl came to stand beside me.

'A lot happened to you, Will. May I do the service?'

'It's not what happened to me but around me...Thank ye Karl. Please!'

The psalm of David, was spoken in French. It, and prayer, calmed me and brought me back, a little. Swiss and Frenchmen set torches to the sad building and soon it was an inferno. We all stood in silence until it was ashes.

I turned me horse towards home, wishing it was Storm. Noddin goodbye to the Mayor and townspeople, we galloped back down the road. As agreed, Karl left us on the main road and rode fer Haven, his task was to tell Gawain. We headed fer home.

We had just passed the old abbey when we met Morgan and fifty yeomen. I dismounted as did she and we walked to each other. When we were close, she threw her arms around me neck and I thought I could feel her warmth even through our mail.

'Thank God you are safe.' She wrinkled her nose. 'You reek! When Storm galloped into the castle we all thought the worst.' I hugged her tighter and I think I sobbed. She pushed back from me and stared into me eyes. 'What is it Will? What happened out there?'

I led her to a log and we sat. After me story was told, she just sat speechless. She stared at me and I could see the fright in her eyes. At that moment, I knew I felt more fer this warrior woman than I dared to admit.

'I learned something else awful, Morgan, Did ye know the Inquisition ship sank with everyone aboard, including our spear?'

She looked incredulous, 'The others will be mortified! Then her mouth twitched in a small smile. 'I can see those priests standing at Heaven's gates wondering why they feel so hot.'

I laughed at her quip as I took her hand and she seemed quite content, not tryin to pull away.'

At least we know the truth about Longinus and have memories to hold in our hearts.'

She smiled. 'You are unbelievable, Will. You go through hell time and again, and come out of it with a full cup.' She took me arm in hers. 'Let's go home and get you cleaned up.'

The rift had become an open sore between Sir Robert and Jean. I could feel the hostility as I walked to me empty apartment. I found out that Robert hadn't believed the rumors, until he found them together, DuLac's cock was in her and Robert went into a rage. He attacked with raised dirk only Jean was faster and threw him against a wall, stunning him. He and Gwen fled the scene and now stayed in DuLacs apartments. The other knights were staying out of the affair and walking around Bamburg was like walking on eggs.

I went to me new da and tried to talk to him. He looked pale and forlorn. Other than accepting me report, he had no interest in talking. In fact, his temper showed itself as he told me to piss off. It was not his usual language, so I did.

I talked with Darragh and told him what had happened with Skye.

He just stared and then said. 'That man has a capacity for evil that is unbelievable. Why God hasn't smitten him, I have no idea.'

'I think God is leaving that up to us. When we strike him down it will have been God's hand.'

He grabbed me neck between thumb and fingers. 'You are getting rather profound. I barely know you anymore. You're not the sparkly eyed lad I used to know.'

I grabbed his neck in a bear hug. 'I'm still sparkly on the inside ye old goat.'

'Old goat is it!' He swung me off him. "Where's my bloody sword, ye need a hiding."

I laughed, jumped away to the weapons rack and met him sword to sword. Our blades flashed and clanged a bit before we paused. 'I lost much of me gear when I was taken prisoner, I'm missing me dirk, the one gifted to me?'

He grunted as he parried a thrust, 'Haven't heard anything about that. You should check your horse.'

A flurry of blows sent me skittering backwards then I felt the bang on me head. I hadn't even seen it coming. I grounded me sword and swore, with me head spinning a bit. 'Ye got me good.'

He was laughing. 'It wasn't me boyo, look behind you.'

I turned to see Morgan. 'Call me auntie, will you!' She was grinning.

I rubbed me head ruefully. 'Ye hit like a girl!'

Then we were all laughing.

I took Darragh at his word and went to find Storm. He came up to me right away like he was happy to see me safe. I stroked and petted him. 'Who took the gear off this animal?'

Rene appeared around the end of a stall. 'Good morning Sir, I did. It's over here.'

I found me coif and other sword, also me mace, and spear. I was glad of the spear, it had been with me since I left me village. Of me dirk there was no sign. Rene and I chatted a bit until Cheve showed up.

'Good day, mon ami, Pat and the others are running the blacks.'

'Why isn't Storm with them?'

'He thought ye might be by. Rumor says ye had a rough time again and, besides, the horse needed a rest.'

'True, but it was much rougher fer others. I'll tell ye about it sometime me friend, but now I need to take Storm fer a run.'

I met the blacks on the beach and joined them. Pat and the other grooms waved. Running with them and hearing the thunder of their hooves was exhilarating, some thing I'd missed since becoming a Knight. I came up beside Pat and we clasped hands at full gallop. He grinned as horses swept between us forcing us apart. I saw Taxeia, usually in the lead. He had become the leader of the herd, a position always to be disputed, since the herd had many stallions.

As we walked them down, going back to the castle, Pat and I caught up on things. I was pleased to see him without resentment, the old cheerful Pat I remembered before the Gordie episode.

'It's Easter in four days, ye know.'

I looked at him, uncomprehending. 'What! Oh shite, with everything going on it completely slipped me mind. Thanks fer reminding me, Pat.' I thought a moment, getting things straight. 'Ye know about Sir Robert and Gwen?' He nodded.

'I think I want to see her and Du Lac, and the other knights. Me da is hurt and angry but has himself to blame as much as others.'

Pat checked something on his horses' neck. 'He gets angry very quickly and while he is in that state, ye can't reason with him. I know that first hand. Perhaps he has calmed enough by now?'

'I can only hope. I wouldn't presume to approach Du Lac but maybe his friends can intervene. I want to talk to Gwen, after all she might have become me mam. I feel she is a friend.'

'What ye want to do would be called interference by many, so be careful me friend.'

I started to laugh. 'Listen to us, a groom and a new found knight lookin to correct the ways of our betters.'

'Exactly Will, ye are a knight and equal to them, they are no better. Go give them shite but don't say I told ye.'

I laughed some more. 'Can I fix things by Easter?' I sighed, 'I can't fix things, a truce is all I can hope fer.'

I found Du Boors and Lensberg drinking hot wine. It looked like they had been at it fer a while.

'Will, please sit with us. We are moping.' Lensberg burped through his nose and made a distasteful face.

'Why?'

'Du Lac wants to return home and we must leave with him.'

'Ye would leave us defenseless against a growing enemy?'

Du Boors handed me a cup of hot wine. 'It's not our wish young man but what else can we do?'

'Well then, ye might as well be the first in this castle to know. The Inquisition is at the bottom of the sea with our Holy relic. That really is another reason not to stay here.' I put the hot wine on the table. "I can't stand that stuff." I walked away feeling unreasonable and angry. I didn't tell them about the new atrocity let them find out from someone else. I looked back at their stunned faces and felt unreasonable anger again. What was wrong with me?

# \*\*Danny\*\*

Late the next day, I was talkin with Ross at the main gate, when we saw a lone man walkin down the road.

'He looks familiar,' I strained me eyes, 'God's truth it's Danny!' I was up and running to meet him.

He saw me coming and quickened his step. We embraced right outside the gate.

'Why are ye here so early we weren't expectin ye before Easter.'

'I needed to coom. Get me some food and drink and I'll tell ye all aboot it.'

He greeted Ross and others he knew, and then I led him to the Yeomen's mess. The usual food was laid out and we caught it just before it was taken away to make room fer supper. I sat, and watched, while he ate, the poor man was famished.

He looked at me oddly, and spoke through a mouthful of beef. 'Ye seem different, what's happened here?'

'Lot's happened!' I proceeded to tell him the main things that had happened. He looked stunned when he learned of the death of me wife and child, then about the Inquisition, and lastly me knighthood. I left the rest, it would wait fer here and there.

He expressed his condolences fer me loss and I could tell he was shaken and meant it. When I told him of me knighthood, he just stared a moment. 'Fucking hell how do I talk to ye now?'

I gave him a poke on the arm, 'The same as always. Nothing's changed between ye and me.' I got up from me chair. 'Ye might as well see this.' I pulled me smock over me head and presented me back.

He just stared, chewing slowly. 'Where is the mon that did that to ye, I want to feed him his balls.'

'He's already dead me friend, him and all the others with him. They are all at the bottom of the sea.'

'Good riddance.' He shook his head. 'God, ye are a mess that must have hurt like hell.'

'Aye. There is another new person here, Sir Robert's half sister Morgan. She's quite capable of turning ye into sauce, so watch yer tongue around her. Besides, she's become me good friend.'

'What, so soon after Miriam?'

I blanched. 'Oh of course, she's not that kind of friend. I was out of it fer a month and then some and she looked out fer me. Sometimes I ferget that they are dead, me Miriam and little Tom, everything is like a bad dream. Now I find me self getting angry fer no reason.'

'Oh, ye have reason.' He came around the table and sat beside me. Placin his hand on me shoulder, he said. 'I regret to tell ye, on top of everthing else but Malcolm is dead. I just couldn't think of an easier way to tell ye.'

I stared, dumbfounded and dizzy, and was very glad I was sitting, 'How?'

'After all he did and went through, he died in his sleep. He went to bed one night and never came fer breakfast. They went to look and found him sprawled in his bed with his arms and legs flung every way. Perhaps he wrestled with an Angel or something.'

'He was such a strong presence of a man. How could he die in his sleep?'

Danny shrugged. 'There's noo answer. There was noo sign of foul play. Noo wounds, noo poison breath or froth at the mouth. He just died.'

'I understand that he was a Laird.' Me voice was husky, I couldn't feel tears, I was all dried up.

'Aye, I always knew and I'm sorry I didn't tell ye me friend. But it wasn't fer ye to know at that time.'

'Never mind that, is that why ye came early, to bring this news?'

'That and I didn't like what was happening all over again in Scotland. I'm done with our stupid politics. We had our freedom for a fleeting moment and now it goes with the Bruce. I don't feel like fighting a puppet King and a greedy disinherited. It never stops and so here I am.'

'So ye are not planning to go back?'

'No!'

'Let's walk, if ye are still hungry, we can return fer more supper. There's lots else to tell ye.'

That evening I lay on me cot, thinking about Malcolm, and tears finally came.

Having Danny about was like a breath of fresh air. His total irreverence fer every thing even had Morgan chuckling. He actually sat quiet while I talked to Morgan about the quarrel and its ramifications.

'Can't ye talk sense to yer brother? He's not talking to me.'

'The only one that might get through to him is Gawain. Their affection for each other goes back a long way, and I do not think Robert would lash out at him.'

'I'm going to fetch him then. Something should to be done before bridges are completely burned. Will ye speak with Gwen? She's yer friend isn't she?'

Morgan nodded, 'I'll do what I can. Be careful Will take yeomen with you this time, at least twenty. Go get Gawain.'

With the exception of a few passing travelers, the trip was without incident and we arrived back on Good Friday eve. Gawain went immediately to Sir Robert's quarters and shut the doors.

I wanted to talk with the other knights again and asked Danny to keep me company. We found them sparring in their own courtyard. Du Boors seemed to be taking it easy on Lensberg. They paused when they saw us. Lensberg gulped some water and Du Boors wiped his face with a cloth. He scowled at me.

'You were a short little snot with us the other day, young man. It was not a good way to tell us of our loss.'

'I apologize to both of ye. It's no excuse but I've been getting moments of unreasonable anger, and I don't know why.'

He studied me face. 'Sometimes things just get to be too much and you blow up. It's good to take a day and walk by the sea or in the forest and do nothing else. Get your thoughts back together. He rolled his shoulders and flexed his hands. 'Now I would like to lose some anger. Will you spar with me?'

I gave him a dubious nod and stepped into his arena. Danny found a seat and watched with anticipation.

'Don't look so gleeful yer Scottish prick.'

He smirked. 'I think ye might get trounced.' He rubbed his hands together.

'Who's your disrespectful friend?' Lensberg was givin Danny the evil eye.

I grinned. 'He's me blood brother and has license.'

I returned me attention to Du Boors who was circling me. He was as big as Garrad the Black and I had seen him fight. He came at me with a downward stroke from the falcon position. I had learned not to take those strokes head on. A strong man like Du Boors could crush and numb ye. Ye'd be tired in no time. I slid it off to one side and came back with a couple of me own. He nodded approval and attacked again. This went back and forth fer a time and I was tireing. He was breathing evenly and showed no signs of folding.

It was time to do something new. He tried the heavy downward stroke again. I let it slide down me blade and rolled towards his off side, bounceing from his own hip and behind him. Me sword was at his neck before he could react.

He grounded his blade. 'Damn, young man, how did you move so fast? that was very well executed. It might not work so well in a melee though.'

'Yer right sir, in a melee ye keep things simple and quick. Take out the man in front of ye before the next one is there. Or ye'll have two to contend with.'

He laughed, 'Yes, or three.' He took me arm, 'Come, let's have some water, that was thirsty work.'

As we walked to the table, I asked. 'Does Sir Du Lac know about the loss?'

'Yes, we told him, he was devastated by the news. In fact, along with this discord with Robert, he looked almost crushed.'

'I brought Gawain to speak to Robert, if anyone can make him see sense, he can.'

Du Boors grunted. 'Don't forget, Robert has been made the cuck-old and his pride is stung. Now you want him to pretend nothing has happened.'

'No I don't, I want him to forgive he needs to recognize the blame that resides with himself.'

'What blame is that?'

'He and Gwen were betrothed over five years ago with no words about a marriage date. She got fed up and I think she might have renounced their union.'

Du Boors looked at Lensberg. 'I didn't know that, did you?'

'No I didn't, but that is a poor excuse to fuck someone else.'

I frowned, 'Ye're not very forgiving are ye Hans?' He looked startled at hearing his first name on me lips. 'Du Lac has shown her a lot of attention since they first met at Whitby Abbey, I think attention was what she needed and Jean is a very handsome man.'

'Look, I'll try talking to him again.' DuBoors stood up.

I nodded, 'Lady Morgan is talkin to Gwen. If she would just show a little remorse for what happened, this could all blow over.'

Lensberg smirked. 'Good luck with that, my wife would never admit wrong doing and I think most women are that way.'

I looked at Du Boors. 'Listen to the cynic.'

He smiled a lopsided smile and shrugged in answer.

Danny and I left. 'God's truth, first a swineherd, then a sheep shagger, then a knight and noo a matchmaker,' He tried to duck as I swatted him in the head.

Easter morning, Sir Robert came out of his self styled prison. Gawain was with him and nodded to me. I took the nod to mean all was well.

I approached them, 'Good morning Da, good morning Gawain.'

Me da pulled me to him. 'Happy Easter Will, please forgive a stupid man for slighting you.'

'I'm happy ye are back, da, I've missed ye, are we going to Mass this morning?'

'Yes we are, it's Easter of course we are.'

As we passed Morgan's apartments, she joined us and fell in beside her half brother. I walked with Gawain, a few steps back.

Gawain whispered, 'I gave him a royal speech and finally he saw the light. I only hope that when he faces them he can swallow his pride.' He knows his neglect and stupidity but there is always that rigid pride to get by. We'll see.'

We were approaching the chapel and I could see others on the steps. Foremost were Gwen and Jean DuLac. The other knights stayed in the background. As we approached, Gwen walked to meet us. She curtsied to Robert.

'I owe ye me deepest apologies me dear friend. I am so sorry ye had to find out in such a way. I should have come to ye a lot sooner, Robert. Please find it in yer heart to forgive me?'

Robert took her hands and raised her up. 'Yes I forgive you Gwen. Can you forgive me? In my stupidity, I've always thought of you more as a sister and a friend, not a wife. I never saw through your eyes or felt with your heart.' He bowed his head. 'Once again, forgive my thoughtlessness.'

Jean was approachin as Gwen stood on tiptoes and kissed Robert. 'Yes I do.'

The knight crashed to one knee in front of Robert, and hung his head. 'I betrayed your friendship and trust and beg your forgiveness. I beg also because I cannot change my feelings for Lady Gwen.'

He took Jean by the shoulders and raised him. 'You hurt me beyond measure Jean but I realize now that the fault also lies with me. We have been friends too long and seen too much for this rift to be between us. Let us forgive each other in Gods light.' He took his friends arm and Gwen's and led them into the chapel.

I took Gawain's arm and Morgan's, and did the same thing.

Morgan whispered. 'You are the cheekiest man I ever met, Happy Easter.'

After two weeks, we held a memorial service fer Malcolm, at me instigation. It gave a little closure to those that had known him and I for one felt better fer it. I was happier with me memories of him than seeing him dead.

Brother John gave a fine service, and we all left feeling better about everything. I haven't mentioned Brother John fer a while but ye should know we saw plenty of each other. I counted him amongst me best of friends.

I introduced Cheve and Colette to each other and sat back like a conspirator to watch the proceedings. It seemed to be going as I hoped. Being a matchmaker was catching.

This winter to spring period was milder than the last but also much wetter. In me mind this was a good thing as war would have to be shelved fer drier times. Few people had traveled through March and April because the roads were a quagmire. Overnight freezing and daytime thawing made them treacherous indeed.

The end of April arrived with all the March like things, hail, sleet, wind and short heavy downpours often starting as snow and ending in rain. Fer the first two weeks of May it was cold, raw and miserable. Then the sun came and it was finally like summer.

I went out everyday learning every detail about the surrounding land. Sometimes I would take Lensberg and captain Swingley with me to study terrain best suited fer the pike. The Yeomen were the most mobile they could fight on horseback, on foot and from ambush. The English longbow gave them a huge advantage over crossbows and spears. The crossbow had power and penetration but the short quarrel lost accuracy quickly. The yew bow had four times the distance. The spear or javelin was only as good as a man's arm.

It was going to have to be a lot drier before cavalry could be put to good use. Heavy cavalry like Du Lac's French, were losing ground, as units like the pike gained in popularity. The Scots at Sterling Bridge had devastated the English cavalry with chopped down saplings.

Out in the dunes, pits were dug in strategic places and stakes were driven and covered. Redoubts were erected here and there in the dunes, along with more pits. All had to be marked on maps along with distance markers fer the catapults on the battlements.

Rock piles were building all over Bamburg along with sand buckets and oil. Sir Robert had no intention to being besieged but ye had to cover every contingency. Other than all these preparations, life was boring.

Then Du lac called fer a fair and tourney to entertain the people. Sir Robert agreed, so things were made ready, including word being sent to surrounding villages and Haven, so that Sirs Gawain and Spatzhein could join in if they wished. The date had bin set fer the first weekend in May and a lot had to be done fer two days of entertainment. The lists needed cleaning up and the seating stands repaired. Then there was food, lots of food fer everyone. Spectating was best when ye had something to munch on.

Excitement was spreading, and even though it stayed cold, the doldrums were thrown off. I was looking foreward to trying me skills. I tuned me self up with Darragh and anyone interested in sparring. Danny was a good swordsman with a few tricks up his sleeve. He demonstrated his abilities with me and with Morgan, and won his share. I also practiced jousting at the Quintain. If ye were careless, ye could get clouted and dumped.

155

The weekend of the joust arrived and I woke up to a cold sunny day and felt a thrill of excitement run through me. I found Danny and we went fer breakfast with the yeomen. Today was a special one, scrambled goose eggs, bacon and kidneys with heavy seed bread. It certainly put warmth in yer stomach and a smile on yer face.

Next, with Danny in tow, I went to the listings board to see me opponant and time. Danny was me second and was charged with seeing to me lances and other gear. I was one of the first, and was tilting against Karl Spatzhein.

Where they all came from, I have no idea. There were Jugglers, Minstrels and Acrobats, Jesters and Puppeteers and a myriad of people. Fer the first time in a long time, the castle was alive with cheeriness and laughter.

The call to list sounded on a horn and I went to prepare. Danny was ready and waiting with Storm all decked out in his own surcoat. I got meself mounted and firmly seated. Danny handed me helm up and I put it on, making sure the laces were tied correctly through a chain link collar, so it wouldn't get knocked off. I mentioned the air was cold but I was already sweating as Danny raised me shield fer me to take. It was new, with the colors of me new name on it. It sported a white background with a wide green bar across it and a squat oak tree in the center. I almost fergot the couching cup, but Danny didn't.

The second horn sounded and Danny handed me lance up. I seated the butt in the cup and was ready. Now I looked down the list at me opponant in a black and white striped surcoat and shield with a crimson double headed eagle. The center rail diminished into the near distance as I dipped me lance in salute.

The final horn blared, the crowd roared and Storm surged forward into an instant gallop. Me movements were precise as me lance and shield dropped into position. Sir Spatzhein grew larger and larger as we came together. Then came the explosion as me lance hit, dead center on his shield, and held.

Me shield took his and it disintigrated into bits. I had barely felt the punch as Storm slowed. I turned me horse and cantored back to me tent. As we passed, I saluted Karl. He answered but seemed to be reeling a bit. I was deafened by the screaming crowd as I handed off me lance and took another. The first seemed alright, but it could be cracked.

The horn blew and I was galloping down the list. Karl was a little late and I was two thirds along when we met. I turned his lance with a flick of me shield and once again mine hit dead center. Karl cartwheeled off the back of his horse with a crash and I brought Storm to a rearing halt. I dropped lance and shield, as I vaulted the fence and rushed to his side. He wasn't moving when I removed his helm. I sighed with relief when those light blue eyes opened and his face became a grimace.

'Damn, Will. It feels like you broke a couple of my ribs.'

'Ye scared the shite out of me. I didn't know ye had practiced summersaulting off the backs of horses.'

He gritted his teeth. 'Don't make me laugh you ass…'

Two yeomen arrived with a stretcher and I whispered to one. 'Go gently on him there was blood on his teeth.' The yeomen acknowledged me with a curt nod, as we lifted him onto it. Karl waved as they carried him off. The crowd roared even louder.

I got to rest untill after lunch, when I would face the winner between Du Lac and Du Boors. Sir Gawain was tilting against Lensberg. Sir Robert and Lady Morgan were officiating. I hadn't even seen them during me first bout, I had been so into the tilt. I checked on Karl and found him to be fine except fer some bruised ribs. He'd be coughing and laughing gently fer a bit.

With a huge concoction of beef, cheese and mushrooms between two slabs of bread, in one hand and ale in the other, I looked at the sights. Some yeomen were shooting on butt at fifty yards, they had already done a hundred and Tim was leading by a narrow margin. Other Yeomen were shooting the cloth, which could be as far as four hundred yards. It was the type of shooting done on the battle field, and unless ye were an archer, it could be quite boring to watch. The Swiss pike were putting on a fine demonstration of their tactics. I chatted with Ross fer a bit he was shooting the cloth later in the day. Then I spotted Cheve with Taxeia. He was taking a break so we were able to chat.

'Are ye putting him through his paces?'

'Aye, mon ami, the crowd loves him. Ye should go to the next field, Pat and the other grooms are demonstrating Roman riding with the blacks. The next show is very soon and I saw Darragh going there.'

The grooms were good, standing on two galloping horses and jumping hurdles. The people were havin a great, boistrous time and most never noticed the bits of rain spit in the wind. I found Darragh with Gawain just as the horn sounded. It was time to get back and face me unknown opponant.

'Wait Will, I'll walk with ye, I'm up right after ye.' Gawain stepped up beside me. 'I saw yer tilt, ye did well.'

'Thank ye I thought I'd be rusty but it all came back in a flash.'

'Ye didn't go fer the helm that was friendly and respectful. Watch out fer Du Lac and even Du Boors, they are senior knights and can play mean. Du Lac does not like to lose. He is number one in Christendom for good reason.'

'I got to dump him once.'

'Aye and I'll wager he hasn't forgotten. If ye go against him it will be a grudge match, trust me.'

We reached the lists and I had just time to mount when the second horn sounded. I didn't even know who I was up against. Danny passed me the helm and the shield.

'Who's up Danny?'

The third horn blared and Danny almost threw me lance at me.

'It's Du Lac, watch yer arse!'

Storm was away and I just managed to couch the lance. DuLac was resplendent in yellow and black. He was one of a few knights that wore plumes on their helms the fad was just coming in. His were two yellow and two black. His shield was yellow and black stripes with a white swan in the center. Then black armor and a black surcoat bordered in yellow.

Things exploded as we slammed together, I hit his shield dead center and he just shrugged it off. His lance came over the top of me shield and smacked me helm. I was reeling with me head spinning as Storm slowed fer the end of the list. We turned and headed back and as I passed Jean DuLac he raised his lance in salute. I think I managed to raise mine.

Danny took me lance. His voice was concerned, 'Are ye alright Will, Count me fingers.' He held up three.

'Five.'

'Ye'll do!' He handed me another lance.

I was coming out of the spin as we approached each other a second time. I decided I could play dirty too. As we came together, I saw his lance raise I brought me shield up, knocking it harmlessly to the side. Mine took him in the helm, catching the upper weld and smacking his head back. He went arse over heels off the back of his horse but one foot stayed in the stirrup. I somehow spun Storm around and raced after him. We caught up right away and I managed to reach across the rail to grab the loose bridle. DuLac was bouncing and getting kicked by his mount but I managed to bring us all to a halt. His second and yeomen came running and I'm sure I heard Gwen screaming even over the roar of the crowd.

We got his helmet off. His face was pale and still and it frightened me. One yeoman touched the side of his neck and said 'He is alive.'

I looked him over. His armor was dented and bruised all over from the chargers hooves. It was a good thing he was wearing some plate and not just mail like me. A yeoman put something under his nose and he came too with a start. His eyes slowly came into focus.

'What happened?'

'Ye got hung up in yer stirrup.'

He grimaced. 'I knew it fit wrongly but I let it pass, stupid of me.'

'Do ye feel like ye broke anything?'

'Help me up and we'll see.'

I got his arm over me shoulder and he limped a bit. 'I think I got off lucky this time, no real harm done, just bruises and a wrenched knee.'

'Ye gave me a right scare.' I helped him back to his chair.

He gave me neck a squeeze with his armored arm. 'I taught you too well, so much for me getting even.' he laughed, put a hand near his ribs and then said 'Ouch.'

His second started removing armor and I got him a mug of ale. He took it gratefully and downed half of it.

'Thank you Will you don't need to nurse maid me, go have some fun you'll be taking on the winner between Lensberg and Gawain. Too bad for me, I wanted to go against Gawain we've never met on the list.'

'Ye are going to be alright?'

'Go.'

I decided to watch the match between Gawain and Lensberg, and made me way to where me da and Morgan and Gwen were sittin. Gwen moved over so I could sit in the middle.

Morgan gave me a radiant smile. 'You are full of surprises and making a real mark for yourself.'

Gwen butted in, 'Is Jean alright? Ye gave me a right scare with that one and if he is hurt I'll never forgive ye.'

'The last I saw he was drinking ale and getting out of his armor.'

Gwen sighed with relief, 'Ye bloody men can't ye take up needle point or something?'

Morgan burst out laughing, 'Really, Gwen.'

'Go ahead and laugh Morgan, ye are as bad as they are. I'm surprised ye aren't competeing.'

'I would, but no man will go against me, something to do with chivalry or some such. I think they don't like to chance getting trounced by a woman.'

The first horn sounded just as me da said something. I didn't hear but smiled and pointed to me ears.

He leaned forward, 'I said well done my son. Du Lac taught you well.'

'Thank ye da.' I turned back to look at the contestants. Sir Gawain was green and white. His horses' surcoat was green as was his shield, which bore a golden harp. His own surcoat was white and the green scarf was tied around his upper arm. Lensberg was blue and white checker and his shield bore a rampant lion in red.

Finally, the last horn echoed over the lists and they were off. Both lances broke on impact and the riders seemed fine. I perked up, it seemed that, even though he was smaller, Lensberg was quite capable and holding his own. They had both scored direct hits on center shield. The same thing happened a second time, broken lances and direct hits. On the third charge Gawain flicked his shield turning Hans' lance. This turned his body just slightly and put him off balance just a bit. Gawains lance hit his opponants shield dead center and knocked man and horse off balance. The charger staggered and went down on his haunches almost dumping Hans from the saddle. He held on and the crowd roared like thunder. Gawain had won but only by a hair.

It would be the next day, after Mass, before Gawain and I would meet. There would also be a match between DuBoors and Lensberg the biggest and the smallest, they would be up first, ours was the final match.

Lensberg won his tilt and I thought, ' Another David.' and grinned to meself.

The crowd swelled, fer the final match, other entertainment had come to a stop. I spotted Uri and other members of the Swiss guard, then there was Cheve and Pat and Darragh. I was beginning to have snakes in the pit of me stomach.

The first horn sounded and I began me readiness. I was going up against a man I revered and looked up to, and I could feel meself trembling. The blare of the second horn brought me back and unbidden, the Psalm of David entered me mind, calming me. I checked the lacin on me helm and me shield straps and tried a faint grin at Danny as he held up me lance.

'Go on, knock him doon too!'

The horn blasted one last time and I was away in a thunder of hooves. I felt no more nerves, only resolve to do me best. Our lances leveled, crashed and we were past each other. I realized I was lookin at a ragged stump. We turned and rode back to our own ends, saluting each other as we passed. I heard Gawains voice echo inside his helm.

'Well done.'

I tossed the stub and took another from Danny. He held up his hand.

'Hoo many fingers?' he held up two.

'Five, you ass.'

He laughed, 'Ye'll do.'

The second strike hurt like fire fer a moment and then eased off. I returned to me end with a whole lance. Gawains was a ragged stub. Danny handed me a fresh one and paused.

'Ye have a huge splinter through yer shield and arm.'

I looked down and yes, me arm and shield were pinned together. How did wood punch through steel? I grabbed the end and pulled it out of me arm but it stayed stuck in the shield. It was the size of an arrow and I broke it off so it wouldn't be in the way. Blood welled from the wound, and Danny passed me a cloth to wrap it just as the horn sounded. There was no time.

We smashed together one last time. Me arm was too weak and me shield rim drove into me helm. I kicked free of the stirrups as I went off Storm's rump and landed on me back. The air whooshed out of me and I lay there unable to breathe fer a moment. Then I heard the crowd chanting.

'Get up! Get up!'

I rolled onto me side and then to me knees. I saw Gawain advancing with drawn sword. What had happened? Then I knew, I had knocked him off his horse too and we were now fighting on the ground. I staggered to me feet and let me shield slide to the ground. I hated fighting with one. It might cost me one day but I still hated it. Gawain stopped and grounded his blade. He pointed to me arm, rolled his finger around and tossed me his green scarf. I wrapped it as best as I could tucking in the end.

With a nod, I raised me sword to the falcon position. The crowd shrieked as our blades struck, sendin sparks. We fought back and forth and I was weakening fast. Gawain was so strong, even more so than the black.. I decided to try the maneuver I had used successfully against Du Boors. It failed, Gawain turned it against me and it was his sword at me neck. Dropping to one knee, I grounded me blade. The crowd was jumping up and down and screaming 'Gawain!'

He took a step forward and raised me up. Turning to the crowd he raised me arm. Now I could hear me name on their lips too. With his hand guiding me, we walked together to the center stands where Sir Robert sat with Morgan and Gwen. Du Lac was now beside her. He rose as we approached and bowed to Gawain.

'You should have the title as the first Knight in Christendom.' He turned to me. 'I would be honored to have you by my side in battle, young Will.'

I bowed. 'Ye honor me Sir and I thank ye.'

Now me da stood. 'Gawain, my old friend, it gives me great privilege to give you the baton of First Knight at this tourney. You, Will, get second place. I felt a presence on me other side and turned me head. It was Lensberg and he took third place. He looked me up and down.

'I thought you were a knight for a day, but now I see you are here to stay.' He chuckled, 'I may become a poet when I'm old and grey.'

I Laughed' aloud, 'If ye do it will be without pay.' I felt quite giddy and staggered he grabbed me before I could fall. Gawain took me other arm.

'We had better look at that wound ye are losing far too much blood.'

The throng was cheering and on its feet as we left the field, Morgan hurried after us.

The lance shard had stabbed deeply and I had bled a lot. Meg was at the tourney and I had not even seen her. She got the bleeding stopped.

She shook her head, 'how do ye do it? Ye are not even half a year old as a knight and already have more scars than a veteran.'

'Some of them were before I was a knight.' I grinned and kissed her cheek. 'It's all fer ye me dear, so ye have somethin to do.'

She cuffed me head. 'Save yer sauce.' Then she kissed me forehead and I noticed a glint of tears as she got to her feet and left.

I looked at Morgan. 'Why was she crying?'

'You are dense. You keep her worried and you are like a son to her, just as you are like a brother to me.'

'I don't want to be yer brother I want to be yer nephew, auntie dear.'

She grimaced in mock anger and raised her hand to strike.

'I am wounded ye know.'

# **KRAYAN & FAMILY**

We had everything as ready as it could be. Then the day came when a pigeon arrived. Me da called me to him.

'Word came from Man. It seems that the McOrdred camp is stirring. I am sending messages to our northern allies and to Fitz Patrick. Send a yeoman to put Haven on alert and I want you to go to Man and spy out the land. Get all the information you can. Lord Merrill must have amassed quite a bit already and should be a big help. Do what you think you need to do to make plans battle ready. Take sergeant Uri to watch your back. You two are a good team. It's already arranged with his commander.'

I nodded and said. ' Da I was thinking, we should have some fire ships on standby. If the wind is right, they could be of great value. A south westerly or north westerly off shore wind would certainly be in our favor and we could damage his army before it even lands.'

Me da gave me an incredulous look. 'That is a good plan! I'll have to find and buy some boats right away.'

'They don't have to be good boats, but they need to be big enough to ram or bang into another ship.'

He nodded, 'I'll look after it. Ross will enjoy spending good money for trash.'

I laughed, 'Yes he will, da, I'd best be going.' We embraced and I left.

We entered Douglas near four bells and kept a low profile on shore. One or two bawdy houses were still making noise but fer the most part, the town was quiet and in darkness.

The Bowlegged Dutchess was in silent darkness. I took a chance and knocked.

A sleepy voice said, 'Fuck off.'

'It's Will!' I hissed. 'I need to see Captain Merrill right off.'

There was a dragged out silence and I was just going to knock again, when there was fumbling at the door. The door opened a crack and I realized I was facing a loaded crossbow.

'Pull yer hoods back, let's see yer faces. Do it now!'

Uri and I obliged and waited. The door opened wider.

'Get inside, make it fast. We have some trouble about.'

We stepped in. the door slammed shut and was bolted. I looked around at a half circle of men with bared steel. Then a familiar voice said.

'Stand down boys, ye know these are friends.' John stepped into the light and smiled. 'Sorry for the theatrics. You are both welcome.' He stared at Uri. 'Are ye still carrying that fuckin head? Come, follow me, we need to talk.' We followed him across the main room to a hall in back. 'Forgive the lads they have a lot of swagger because they're nervous.'

'What is going on?' We entered a room with table and chairs. There was food and drink laid out but only one place setting. John must have been preparing an early breakfast fer himself.

'Please sit.' He went to a wall shelf and got two more plates with knives and spoons. 'We were attacked yesterday and Captain Merrill was wounded and taken. We were all caught off guard and lost four men besides the Captain.'

'Who attacked ye?'

'Ye can guess who, it was Krayan McOrdred's doing. He knows what we are up to, to a point, and likes disrupting things. The Captain was a bonus.'

'Do ye think they'll ransom him?'

'I think they are going to hurt him and I want him back!' He motioned with his hand. 'Feed yer selves.'

Uri and I helped ourselves to bread, cheese and fried sausages, washed down with cool water.

John scratched his forehead. 'Their camp is a fortress and I'm trying to come up with a plan to extract the Captain.'

'Ye can count on us to help. Do ye know where they are holding him?'

'I can't be positive, but they do have a cell block on the far side of the camp, right in the middle of the camped out soldiers, a bunch of Frenchies. Three hundred came in two weeks ago. A real scurvy lot they are. Probably come from the back alleys of Calais and as far away as Paris.'

Uri stopped chewing. 'I speak French fluently I could infiltrate them with little difficulty. A little soot to make me look grubby and I would fit right in. I'm sure they gathered together because they are French, not because they know each other.'

'I could go with ye if ye do most of the talking.'

'No Will, your face is known to too many, soldiers as well as the McOrdreds. I'd like to have someone at my back but it's not necessary.'

John shook his fork. 'You need backup, how about Scups? why don't you take him along. He speaks some French, though quite badly, and he blends right in. That's how he gets away with being drunk, no one notices him.' He went to the door and shouted, 'Someone find Scups and get him in here!' He helped himself to another sausage and sat back down. 'Yer plan has merit it's certainly the best we have. So you find Merrill, how do we get him out?'

Uri shrugged. 'Let's take one step at a time. First we make sure that he is there. Don't forget, they may move him to torture him, that's something we can't plan for until we know where and how. Scups will do nicely as a go between and let you know what I plan, providing he has the courage.'

'Don't worry about him I've used him to spy out the land before. His drinking keeps him brave just don't let him have too much.'

From covering darkness, I watched as Uri and Scups walked nonchalantly into camp, without a care in the world. I saw Uri stop, with the barrel tucked under his arm, and talk to a Frenchie who pointed indifferently somewhere within the camp. Then they were gone.

I appointed me self as liaison and sat back to wait. It was pre arranged with John to send some men to cause trouble on the other side of the camp. Setting some fires would do the job, without confrontation if possible. Cook fires getting out of hand were always a problem in these ragged camps and didn't raise a lot of suspicion.

I waited all day and then, as it began to grow dark, Scups appeared.

'We found our Captain right off Sir. He is beat up pretty bad and we don't think he can walk.' He took a stone and tried to draw the camp. He certainly was not an artist. 'The cell block is here,' He pointed to a mark he had made in the dirt. 'There be only a couple of guards but always other men around.'

'Wait here Scups I'm going to get John and some lads to cover us if necessary. Ye can take me in to Uri and we'll go from there.'

Scups nodded and sat in a corner to wait. I hied it to find John.

Our plans were made, I'd dirtied me self up when John drew me to one side.

'Uri said ye shouldn't go yer too recognizable.'

'I have to go I have to protect his back just as he has always protected mine.'

'I don't think it's wise, but I'll back ye.'

Now Scups and I were making our way through the camp. I helped meself to a piece of goose and chewed on the tough meat. No one gave us a second look and I prayed no one would speak to us. Havin a layered camp like this, with so many different types about, made our job easier, and I was banking on no one knowing me in this lot. We spotted Uri talking to a group around a fire, the barrel between his feet. As we approached, I said.

'Bonsoir mon ami.'

Uri grinned. 'C'est agreable de vous voir a nouveau.'

One of the Frenchies looked at me. 'Vous parlez avec un accent ou est-tu?'

Uri frowned at him. 'Il est Hollandais.'

Frenchie shrugged and stoked the fire. I looked around and quickly spotted Carver Merrill in a makeshift wooden pen. He was slumped against the bars and not moving. There were two guards spending more time chatting with nearby people than watching the prisoner. This would make it difficult, we couldn't take out the guards without alarming everyone and I don't think we could just go in and free the prisoner.

I whispered to Scups, 'Go tell John we need a major disruption nearby but away from the gaol and tell him to be ready to cover our arses.'

Scups grinned, gave me a nod and vanished into the crowd.

I stayed a little back of Uri and honed me sword. I didn't want to get pulled into a conversation.

I was getting a little nervous when instantaneously, three large supply tents burst into flames with a loud whump. They were less than a hundred yards away and men jumped to fight the fires. All attention was off the pen except fer the guards. Uri and I, as one, leaped at them and they died before they knew they were in trouble. I cut me way into the pen while Uri kept watch. Carver was unresponsive but alive. I got him across me shoulders and we ran fer the darkness. I looked back to see Garrads head watching us go. How Uri did it so quickly, I have no idea. We were near the edge of the light, when we were spotted by four men,who gave chase. Uri stopped to face them. One went down with a crossbow bolt in him, and suddenly Uri had welcome company as some of Johns' men joined him. They quickly dispatched the other three and then we were pulled into the darkness, being led by men with night vision. Me eyes quickly adjusted and I could soon see in the dimness. It looked as if we had got away with it.

A shape in the twilight, and John was beside me. He helped lower Carver to the ground, which was a welcome relief to me shoulders. Carver was awake, likely from all the jouncing. He gripped me hand and squeezed, then was caught in a fit of coughing. It was racking his body and I could see his pain. After all, I'd bin there. Men brought a stretcher and we were soon hieing it to safety.

A couple of hours later, Scups returned to us.

'I stayed to watch a bit. Skye was like a spitting wildcat. Even though the guards were dead, he had them impaled on sharp poles. Right up the arse they went and exited at the shoulders right soon. He left his men cringing when he said. 'Try fucking with me if you want the same. I've got a hundred sticks, just waitin to kiss arse.' He stuck Garrads' head on a stick too. I thought it best to leave on that note.'

Some of the men laughed and John looked at me. 'Do ye think we are getting him pissed off enough?'

I nodded and grinned as I looked down at Carver. He tried to grin back, though his pain. The poor man's feet were smashed and all his toenails torn out. He had also taken quite a beating, probably early on when they captured him.

I smiled. 'We are girding fer war me friend, will yer lads still back us?'

John crouched beside us. 'Most definitely Will, Ye have me word on that. Ye are going to be facing between four and five thousand, how many can ye muster?'

'Not even close to that number, perhaps a third, not counting ye and Fitz Patrick. We are banking on surprises and tactics.' I didn't tell him about the fire ships. It was possible they couldn't be used, and besides, there might still be informants in their camp.

John scratched his chin. 'Ye realize he can land anywhere and march to ye. He doesn't have to land at yer doorstep.'

I think I paled, knowin he was right and the fire ships could be even more redundent.

'Ye did miss somethin? Don't worry, we will be right behind him and as soon as his army is ashore, we'll scoot in and burn his ships. That will cut off his retreat and the smoke will tell ye where he is.'

I thanked John and wished Carver well. 'See ye soon, on the other side.'

On me return, I went directly to me da. Sir Robert just smiled when I told him about other landin sites.

'I thought of it too Will, I've got watchmen up and down the shoreline. There are only a few places suitable enough to land an army. I have arranged for fire ships in all these locations' He looked at me' 'You do know that we are totally depending on the wind? They will just be on display if that doesn't happen.'

I nodded and said, 'The bad news is that Carver can't take part in the attack. His injuries are too severe. The good news is that John can and will handle it.' I then told him about the jailbreak and Skyes' fury.

'You certainly have a way, son. You make friends easily and enemies just as easily.' Sir Robert laughed. 'I would have liked to see Skye's face, when you two got him yet again. Oh, if you are looking for Danny, I sent him to meet our northern allies. They should be here within a day.'

Someone knocked on the door and me da said, 'Come in.'

It was Darragh. He smiled and nodded to me. 'So, you made it back in one piece. How are the McOrdreds?'

'Agitated!'

He laughed. 'Glad to hear it.' Turning to Sir Robert, he said. 'Good morning Sir. The northern party is about two hours out, a yeoman just reported in.'

'Help me with my gambeson, Will, and my mail too. We can go and meet them, I could use some fresh air and a stretch and it looks to be a fine day.'

They were slightly further away because we made it to the old abbey. We basked in the warm sun until we heard the distant jingle of harness and clopping horses hooves.

I got up, stretched and walked to the roadside. Me eyes just about popped. There was a double line of horsemen and marching soldiers, as far as I could see.

Me da came beside me. 'This is a spectacle.' He was smiling as he gripped me shoulder.

Alexander Donclevy was in the lead, his dour face almost breaking into a boyish smile.

'How was your trip?' Sir Robert extended his hand and helped the older man from his horse.

'The trek was good and there is noot much to tell. We picked up some friends at Haven, they are at the rear.' He turned to me. 'How are ye Will?'

'I am very well Sir. It is nice to see ye again.' Then I was getting buffeted by an enthusiastic Cyril. 'God'struth, stop, ye'll leave me bruised fer a week.' I pushed him off me with a grin. 'It's nice to see ye too.'

Cyril laughed, 'I was a fidget all the way here.'

Danny stepped out from behind him. 'God, he certainly was. All he could talk about was ye and the coming fight, and ye again.'

I sobered, as I clapped Danny on the shoulder. 'How many men did ye all bring?'

'Over six hundred and then those from Haven and surrounding villages, we must be mustering close to a thousand now.'

Sir Gawain rode up. 'Good day to ye all.' He waved back down the line. 'There are four hundred, give or take, farmers and other laymen coming to help. Those from Bamburg village have not forgotten what ye did fer them and there are others.'

He took me da and Alexander by the elbows and led them away to some seating.

I greeted Jarad who was hurrying by with a clay cooler. He nodded and smiled. I now had time to look up old friends accompanied by Cyril and Danny.

The day we had so long awaited, finally arrived. A large mass of sails, were spotted about five or six miles to the south of us. They were hoping to land their army before getting harassed by us. I smiled to meself, they were tacking on an off shore wind.

With Ross and thirty yeomen in tow, I galloped towards the black smoke now showing in the sky. We reached a low headland in time to see three fire ships being towed towards the fleet. Some boats had already landed and I signaled the yeomen to harass the massing troops. There was a rise of land all along that section of beach, perfect fer covering the archers. I sat astride Storm and watched as the rowers cut the first fire ship loose. Now a raging inferno, it bore down on an approaching vessel. Men rushed to take evasive action and got their ship out of the way, leaving another behind her exposed and defenseless. Men with poles tried to push the derelict away but it was too hot. The ship caught fire with a whoosh, wet wood started singing as men dove over the side in droves. Drowning was better than burning and any with mail or armor, drowned. Wet clothing with a sword and dirk in yer belt could drag yer under. The other fire ships were now taking their toll. Four ships, full of men, were burning to the waterline and screaming men were hurling themselves into the sea. The rowboats were heading back to shore and the enemy caught one in the surf slaughtering the five men withing. I lifted a horn to me lips and blew a prearranged signal. The yeomen packed up, and looked fer the other lads who had fired the ships. Doubling up, they rode towards home. I took a last look at the arrow, riddled corpses on the beach and joined them. It was time to report to me da and the other knights.

A horseman met us as we neared Bamburg. He swiveled his mount and closed alongside me. It was Pat.

'What are ye doin here?'

'There's another landing happening in the dunes, the townspeople caught them and are hard pressed.'

I yelled to Ross, 'Go with Pat! Our peasants are fighting fer their lives. I must report to Sir Robert. I'll send re-enforcements as fast as I can. Man the redoubts.'

Ross wheeled away with a wave and led his men after Pat.

I galloped Storm under the portcullis and almost bowled Du Lac over.

He grabbed Storms bridle. 'Slow down Will, why the haste?'

'The peasants found another enemy landing in the dunes and are out manned and likely out classed. Ross is going there with only thirty men.'

He gripped me shoulder. 'Go do what you have to do I'll take care of it.' Cyril was passing at that moment. 'Cyril, I need some of your men, my cavalry are too heavy for the dunes. A hundred should do along with my infantry. At least till' we know the situation.'

Cyril started yelling orders as I raced to me da's quarters. I found him with Gawain, Donclevy and Lensberg, looking over a scale plan of the area. They all looked up as I entered.

'Well what's our situation?'

I placed markers on the map showing where the arenas of conflict were. As I did so, I told them what was taking place. 'Du Lac has gone to support Ross with a hundred and seventy men in the dunes.' I grinned at me da. 'The fireboats took their toll, as good or even better, than expected. Distraction cost McOrdred more men on the beach. He'll be marshalling his forces now and is less than six miles south of us.'

Du Boors entered along with Karl Spatzhein and they were quickly briefed.

'Listen, my friends, we will go with plan one. Hans, take your Swiss down the beach until you see the enemy and form up. Du Boors, you and Morgan will take your infantry and Half of Donclevy's men and protect their sea flank. Will, you and Darragh will command the remainder of them and the Pardoones until Cyril gets back. Protect the left flank of the pike. One hundred Yeomen under Tim will back the Swiss. Twenty yeomen will bolster Ross's men. The heavy cavalry and fifty yeomen on horse will hold in reserve, under Karl. He will support either side as needed. Let's go, go go!'

The Pike spread across the flats in three rows of seventy five, each man was six feet from his neighbor and there was six feet in the aisles. The second row was off set to fill the gaps, and the men in last row, with swords, maces and axes were there to protect their comrades if breached. The pikes were not a melee weapon by any stretch of the imagination.

The yeomen were in position to shoot over their heads into the enemy. The rest of our army mustered on each flank. Du Boors had the sea on his right to protect him but we had more open country on our left and could, ourselves be out flanked. This was our main weakness besides the three or four to one odd's against us.

Darragh and I were looking over the land to our left. It could be a dangerous area for us if the enemy thought to flank us.

Darragh nudged me and said, 'Look Will, I want you to have my sword should something happen to me. You have become a part of it, and without you it would have been lost. I have no son to give it to and I could wish for no better man than you.' He compressed his lips. 'May God watch over you Will, I love you like family.'

I didn't know what to say and felt flustered so I just nodded and gripped his arm. We sat our horses side by side and watched as the massed enemy approached. There were more than I would have supposed after the initial fire attacks. I reached over, pointing at billowing smoke behind a headland. Darragh nodded that he had seen it. The enemy army stopped, many looking back. A ripple went over their ranks and we could clearly hear McOrdreds calling fer order. True to his word, John had fired the ships. All we needed now was Fitz Patrick.

We were still greatly outnumbered, and we didn't know the disposition of the other landing.

We did have good morale and good discipline, something they lacked. Then I saw about three hundred cavalry appear behind them and I hoped it was Fitz Patrick. It wasn't, the infantry closed together to give them room to pass. They formed in a mass in front of us and it looked like they would use sheer weight to crush us.

The pike had been at ease. Captain Swingley gave the order and a hundred and fifty pikes dropped into position as the men roared 'Guten tag mein freund.' I had found out that it was a friendly greeting like 'good day my friend' I had to smile knowing what was coming.

Our world exploded with the rumbling of hooves as the cavalry began its advance. They started at a trot then a cantor and then broke into full gallop. They were unruly and much too close together. Some came up the bank towards us yelling war cries. As I lowered me lance Darragh drew his swords. Hans rode up beside me with visor down and lance couched. I spurred Storm and the three of us crashed into the enemy, closely followed by the Pardoones.

After that, things became a blur of violence. The cavalry crashed like a breaker on the pikes, and like a breaker, was spent. Men died on both sides but the pike held as it always did. Dozens of the enemy and many of their horses died in blood and carnage. They had totally underestimated the Swiss.

Those left tried to back off, but were pushed back onto the pikes by their own infantry. The yeomen set flights of arrows into them. The archers were instructed to pick targets and make their arrows count, they did.

I had lost me lance it was embedded in a body somewhere behind me, and I had lost track of Darragh. I laid about me with a sword and mace and I saw faces and bodies turn to red ruin as I cut me way through. My eye was always on the distant McOrdred banners.

Storm slipped or stumbled amongst the blood and bodies and went down onto his haunches. I was thrown off, the breath knocked out of me. A leering man rushed at me as I gasped. Suddenly he was gone and Hans was in his place. There were alot of men coming, too many. A man stepped over me, raising his axe to strike Hans from behind. I pulled me dirk and drove it into his groin. He shrieked and fell half on me. I saw red hair and freckles but it wasn't Skye. His face twisted in rage and pain as he struggled to drive his ax handle onto me throat, somehow, I got me hands on the haft, and was stopping him. He was losing blood fast and I could feel him weakening. The spike back of the ax head started turning towards his face.

I growled through gritted teeth, 'Ye must be Brian?'

He hissed and spat as the spike plunged through his eye and into his brain.

As I struggled to get up, I saw Hans chop his way into a mass of men. I thought I was done when Storm was suddenly there, kickin and bitin to defend me. I managed to roll the red heads body off me and kicked another off me feet. Time stood still, as a man with a spear was looking to strike me horse. His head flew from his shoulders and Darragh was there. Pardoones were surrounding me and one reached down to help me up. He looked at me blood soaked clothing.

'Are ye alright?'

'Aye, most of the blood is not mine...I think.'

He grinned as he turned his mount away to fight. 'We're all in deep shite!' I looked around but me dirk was lost in the bloody mud. I mounted Storm, the enemy was all around us and we were, cut off. I could see me da in the distance and Du Lac close to him. At least we had won out at the dunes. they must have had to double march to get here so quickly.

Another surge of men had me fighting fer me life when the French cavalry arrived. They had done with their lances and were laying about with mace and sword. Karl was suddenly there, whistling a tune as he decapitated a man in front of me. We fought, side by side fer awhile, the battle turning back to our favor. His horse crashed, screaming to the ground, a front leg cut off by an axe wielding maniac. I saw Karl roll back to his knees, killing that maniac, and then killing his shriekin horse. He vanished under a seething mass of thrashing men.

I cut me way towards where I had last seen him and saw a mound of bodies where he had been. Jumping down from Storm, I began pulling dead and dying men away. I found Karl Spatzhein at the bottom. His helm was gone and blood welled from several wounds. His eyes opened and he grasped me arm, his smile showing bloody teeth. 'Ah Will, you're..... His smile froze and his hand fell away. A fine knight was dead. I closed his eyes feeling a real pang of loss, and then looked about.

I had lost track of Darragh. Six Pardoones were still with me, all mounted, along with several French. Remounting Storm, I pointed at the McOrdred banners and yelled, 'That's where we are going!' As one, we moved into the press, carving a bloody road through battling men.

Faint at first and then louder, I heard cries of 'Fitz Patrick', they filled the air and I could feel new strength flow through me. Many of our foes were turning away to fight a new enemy, leaving a clearer road to the McOrdreds. I could see me da again, at the forefront with Gawain and Du Lac.

We were getting much closer when in one awful moment I saw an arrow strike me da knocking him from his horse.

Skye McOrdred saw it too and advanced with triumph in his every fiber. He started rearing his horse to stomp me da. I was too far away and Gawain and Du Lac had not seen. I grasped the spear I had with me from the village. It wasn't meant fer throwing, but. With all me strength, I threw it and watched it smash broadside into Skyes helm unhorsing him in a flurry of arms and legs. I now had time to reach him. I didn't even notice that men were breaking and running away.

I leaped from Storm's back and stood over the man I had hated, it seemed like forever, and tore his helm from his head. He glared at me with those light blue crazy eyes, one ear hanging by a thread.

He tried to spit at me as he worried at his sword trapped under him. 'Do yer worst whoreson!' he hissed.

I saw me silver headed dirk thrust in his belt and dived at him grabbing fer his throat. I snatched that dirk and thrust it into his side as the fingers of me other hand wrapped over mouth and nose smothering him. I drove the dirk into him again twisting it and then again. He struggled and squirmed under me and finally I saw terror in his eyes just before they went blank. I had done me worst and hoped he had seen the Hell he was going to....fer all the victims he had slaughtered.

Sir Robert, me da, was dying. The arrow had punctured his lung through and through. I held him in me arms as I looked at Tim through tearfilled eyes.

'Go get Morgan, where is Gawain?' I looked down on me da's ashen face me tears wetting him. Du Lac came to kneel beside me and then Du Boors. Gawain finally came followed by a bedraggled Hans. I let Gawain cradle me da's head and stood to see Morgan being lead through the mounds of dead, by Tim. Her mail was splashed with blood so she been in the thick of it too. She drew off her gauntlet and took me hand as she knelt by her brother.

As if he knew, he opened his eyes and smiled. 'Ah, dear sister I am glad you are safe. We were always at odds weren't we but I have grown to love you deeply.' he closed his eyes fer a moment and she burst into a fit of sobbing. I had never seen her cry, not once, and it broke me heart. She kissed his cheek and he opened his eyes again.

He smiled at her and seemed to find a reserve of strength and called fer Gawain and then me and the other knights. I had never seen a dying man so at peace, with his friends and family around him.

Sir Robert, placed on a stretcher, was carried to Bamburg by mourning yeomen. I had to see to cleaning up the aftermath. Fitz Patrick came to me and we clasped hands. As I tried to let go, he held on and started leading me. He spoke no words as I followed.

There, under the fallen and torn banners of the McOrdreds, lay Darragh and Krayan, wrapped around each other like lovers. They had stabbed each other multiple times. The McOrdred family would never hurt another soul but I had lost a dear, dear friend. Tears were hard to find, I had shed so many already. I saw Danny coming towards me and I breathed a sigh of relief. He was unharmed. He put his arm around me shoulder and drew me aside.

'Ye have done enough, Will. Someone else can look after this.'

'Sir Karl is dead.' I pointed, 'Have men carry both him and Darragh back, in fact see that all our men are brought back. Don't bury the others, have them burnt its cleaner. Ye can use wood from the beached boats.'

Danny was solemn, 'I'll see to it.' He handed me Darragh's sword, 'Now ye go.'

Sir Robert Arthur died quietly in the small hours of the morning, with all of us present, and now we planned to take him back home to Haven. Bamburg was a cold place of stone, not of his making, and had served its purpose.

During preparations, Du Lac came and spoke with me. 'Will, after the funeral rites I will be returning to Geneve' with the other knights. The battle is won, the brotherhood no longer has meaning and....' He smiled ruefully, 'I am no longer welcome in England. Isabelle is under house arrest as her son prepares her for banishment. I received notice last week that Edward's advisers are planning hostilities with France. Geneve should be able to stay out of it, but you never know.' He looked regretfully at me. 'Gwen and I will marry in Switzerland and I am sorry that politics won't allow you to be there.' He held out his hand, which I took. He then pulled me into an embrace and gruffly said, 'You were the rallying point in this battle my boy and your pater would have been most proud.' He reached inside his jerkin and pulled out a gold chain. I recognized the one from Longinus's tomb. 'You found him for us, this should be yours. God be with you.' With a nod and a smile, he took his leave.

I watched him go with some regrets. Our relationship had certainly been a hot and cold one. I felt a presence beside me and turned to Gawain.

'He told ye?'

I nodded, 'Aye, he told me and gave me this but it's not mine to take.' I showed him the necklace of medallions.

Gawain laid his hand upon it, his face was gentle, 'I'm sure ye'll know what to do.'

'It's going to be very quiet around here. You are the first to know Sir, I plan to leave in a month or so and hope ye will take leadership of Haven. I would like to leave me inheritance in yer hands, to use for the good of Haven. I will have gifts for me friends and travel funds fer meself. What is left is yours to use as ye see fit.'

Gawain smiled. 'Ye are going to the east aren't ye? Ye have a flea that has ye hopping to the Silk Road am I right?'

I nodded, 'Yes sir I want to see the other side of many hills. I'm not made fer sitting still. Danny is coming and I hope Uri will be released from service.'

Gawain put his arm around me shoulders. 'Stop calling me sir. I'm yer friend not yer da. Yes I will look after Haven. I already promised Robert that I would do that, many years ago. I've had enough traveling and I'm too old to go with ye anyway. Go see the world, Will and as fer Uri, I will negotiate his release. There couldn't be two better men to watch over ye than he and Danny.'

Me da's funeral was all it should have been and he was laid to rest under the same oak that harbored me family. Brother John had blessed the grounds and they were now consecrated. Lord Carver Merrill was on crutches, but he came with John Lynch. Thorwald Fitz Patrick was there too.

We joyously celebrated Sir Robert Arthurs' life and honored him before laying him to rest.

After, there was plenty of food and drink and we compared stories of his exploits deep into the night. I was present when Carver singled out Thorwald.

'Sir, the next time we meet we may well be tryin to kill each other but now, I would like to shake yer hand.' They did so, vigorously and toasted each other with several ales.

Darragh was laid to rest with a few close friends present. Morgan and Gawain were there and so were Raglin, Meg and Gwen. After the service, when everyone had left, I spent some time, sitting by his grave and thinking of our times together, me and him and Tom, more memories to take and treasure.

Karl was to be returned to his beloved Germany and I knew he would have wanted nothing else.

I promised to drink a toast to him when I arrived, hot and sweaty, in Jerusalem.

I told Morgan of me planned escapade. She sat for a long time, lookin at me. Then she leaned forward and cupped me face with her hands, kissin me on the lips. 'I'm going with you, you blockhead.'

I gaped at her, flustered. To me it was as if 'blockhead' was the nicest thing she had ever called me. In a sudden flash of realization, I knew I loved her and had loved her since the first time she cursed me. I had pushed it away because of me love fer Miriam. I stood, took her hands in mine and pulled her to me. I trembled as I felt her warm body melt and mold to mine.

The Necklace went back to Longinus' Tomb. It was a gift to him, not me and I felt it belonged there with him. I sat by him one last time. 'Me one wish is that I could have known ye and I am so sorry we lost yer spear.' Gawain was right I knew what to do.

Cheve came to me hand in hand with Colette. He asked fer me blessing and she asked that I take her fathers' place to give her away. I felt humbled and truly honored. I hugged them both with a solomn yes.

The wedding was a breath of fresh air after all that had happened and gave me good opportunity to see all the grooms and say goodbye to each. I spent part of the evening with Pat and Raglin who had become good friends with each other. Gawain stopped by to wish the bride and groom well. The other knights did not take part.

The bride and groom got a generous gift from me and so did Meg and Tim, Ross and Raglin. Especially Meg, she could now have a comfortable retirement. She and I spent a morning together in her kitchen she fed me hot scones with butter and cheese and sat, watching me eat. We didn't talk much but I felt our closeness. I would keep her close to me heart all me life.

I gave Brother John a new hooded scapular for which he was grateful. His other was in rags. Cyril seemed quite sad and asked that I visit before leaving England. I wasn't sure that I could and hoped he would understand.

The warmth of the markers felt good to me as I lay flowers on the five graves. I knelt and said prayers over me Da and then Darragh. Finally, I paid me respects to Joseph before laying between Miriam and little Thomas. I felt a great peace as the blue sky and sunlight made a tapestry of moving branches over our heads, and birds sang.

# PART TWO

# The Silk Road

# **BABA**

The hot air was so still it sizzled. Morgan and I stared down at the glassy surface of the sea as sweat gathered and dripped from our noses. It had been like this fer two days now and I think me mail was beginning to rust from the inside. Me wife was smarter and wore her shift and sandals. She pointed,

'Look there Will.' A pale grey shape moved by languidly, a shark or dolphin? I wasn't sure. We had been playing this game of spotting sea life fer some time. Everything seemed drawn to the surface and enjoying the sun.

I felt me hair stir and a riffle flashed across the ocean's surface. We both jumped at a loud crack as the sail above us filled with air. Everything came to instant life as men jumped to their duties. We both turned to see a small but intense black cloud bearing down on us.

It was over as quickly as it started. Sitting on the deck with me back against the bulwark I closed me eyes and tried to catch me breath. I felt Morgan plop down beside me and opened one eye to see she was as soaking wet as I was.

She grinned and kissed me wet cheek. 'That was quite a burster, Will.' She tried to squeeze water from her long hair.

I laughed, 'Yes it was, and look how quickly the sky is clearing.' Me scarred friend was crossing the deck towards us. 'Oh Uri, ye survived, where were ye skulking?'

He gave me a mock scowl. 'Skulking? If you must know, I was helping to lash down cargo that got loose. Danny is still over there, tidying up.'

'What cargo was that?'

'It was the amphorae of oil, if they got loose and smashed we'd have a hell of a mess. We would be slipping and sliding everywhere.' He gave me leg a nudge with his foot 'There's land off our port bow, if you'd get off your arse you'd see it.'

I got up with a groan, I felt so stiff, and helped Morgan up beside me. The last of the cloud fled the sun and it was suddenly hot again. For the moment, it felt good, warmin our cold wet clothes but soon it would be stifling. I saw the captain across the deck.

'Captain Salmi, is that Egypt we're seeing?'

'Aye it is. We should see Alexandria in about three hours. Thank you all for your help during the squall. Without you, I might have lost a good deal. I had concerns about my judgment, taking on so many passengers. You might have been pirates. Now I'm glad I did.'

Morgan laughed. 'We are glad you did too, Sardinia was a very dull place. Do you have any fresh water captain? I need to rinse my hair.'

He smiled at her. 'For you Lady anything, your wish is my command!' He signaled a crewman, 'Give the Lady what she needs and see you mind your manners.'

Weeks past, we had landed in Sardinia with another ship, a small trader out of England. We no sooner got ashore, when the captain took a fit clutching his chest, and died. His mate and crew decided to go get blind drunk and thugs stripped the boat of cargo. There we were stranded fer several weeks and Sardinia was a very dull place. We hung around the waterfront and smelly taverns where we approached several captains they were mostly a surly, standoffish bunch. I think they feared our militant look perhaps thinking we were pirates. We were ready to give up when captain Baba Salmi sailed into harbor. He was there to add to his cargo with Fennel and artichokes. He was already laden with olives and olive oil.

He looked us over with a finger up inside his turban trying to satisfy an itch. I liked him right off, a short solid man with friendly eyes and a massive beard sprouting from under a large hooked nose. I think Morgan's beauty made up his mind. He spoke quite good English. 'I will take you on provided you work your passage when I have need of you. I am picking up more olives and oil in Sicily. You must find and bring feed for your horses and care for them. There is an enclosure for livestock on the forward deck, which is empty now. Use it for yourselves and your animals. We will discuss costs after you have shown your worth.'

I looked at me wife and friends and could see their agreement. No one wanted to stay here any longer. I held out me hand. Baba spit in his and clasped mine. We had struck a bargain.

Hot days came and went and we all settled into a dull routine. Morgan and I looked after the four horses. Me lads weren't horse lovers. They would ride them when they had to but Uri had spent most of his life sticking horseflesh on the end of his pike, and Danny? Well Danny was Danny and liked his own two feet best.

I taught them all to play backgammon, and sometimes, when the evening was quiet, captain Baba would join us, he didn't need to be taught and loved to gamble and really enjoyed taking our money. One evening, as he walked off, Morgan whispered. 'I'm glad he only plays once in a while. He'd leave us all penniless.'

I gave her a hug and chuckled. 'Don't worry we are still in good stead.'

Uri leaned forward holding out a bottle. 'Have you tried this Arabian Arak Will? I bought it from a crew man, it's almost as potent as Kirsh.'

Danny hiccupped.

Laughing, Morgan took the bottle and then choked on its contents. 'God, I thought Moslems didn't drink.' Her eyes were watering when she offered it to me. I think we all slept well that night.

Then came the day of the squall, it hit hard and fast and was over almost as fast, leaving us drenched and cooled down. The voyage was almost over and Alexandria was just on the other side of the horizon. Danny joined us and we four watched the expanding coastline in anticipation pointing out this or that landmark to each other.

As we drew closer, I realized we were staring at foggy whisps that grew into a huge brown cloud. It was hiding a lot of the shoreline to the east. I called to the captain again. He looked a little annoyed, being interrupted once more.

'Look, what is that cloud?'

'I don't know Will it could be a sand storm though they are very rare near the Nile delta.' He grabbed one of his crew by the shoulder. 'M'tobo, scamper up the mast and tell me what you see, quick now!'

A slim black man knuckled his forehead and climbed the mast as nimble as any monkey. He shouted down, 'I see the minarets of a Mosque, sir. Wait, one is missing. Now I can see the tops of some other towers, the palace I think,one of those is broken, why? The cloud is starting to diminish sir.' He grabbed a line and dropped like a stone only to stop inches from the deck. 'I think they had the shaking earth, I've seen it once before.'

Captain Baba nodded. 'It seems a possibility, yes, very much a possibility. Alexandria has been plagued by such, over the last few decades. The face of the city has been changing.'

We entered the harbour and saw the once famous lighthouse on our right, all but destroyed, only one story was left surrounded by rubble and a few slabs of stone. Most of it was at the bottom of the harbour. Everything looked eerie in a haze of dust.

A measured drumbeat drew our attention to an approaching Dromond, its flashing oars looking like the legs of a menacing black beetle. Two dhows accompanied the galley loaded with soldiers. The smaller nimble boats were tacking so as not to out distance the heavier war ship. As she drew closer, one could see her four catapults manned by soldiers.

A loud command echoed across the water and a dhow pulled alongside the galley. Crewmen helped a golden warrior jump aboard. He walked forward and stood staring at us. His military stance oozed confidence. Within minutes they were alongside us. He grasped a rope ladder that had been dropped over the side and climbed aboard. Since I was nearest, I offered me hand. He took it, barely givin me a glance.

His voice was deep with a pleasant musical quality. 'My dear Baba, I thought it was you.'

Captain Salmi bowed deeply, 'Welcome aboard my lord. What is happening here? Why are there so many soldiers?'

The man before us wore golden, scaled mail and a snow white cloak draped his shoulders. He wore no helm his lean hard face framed by long dark curls. A brand on the forehead was that of a stylized image of a hawk. I would later learn it was Horus, a god of Egypt. He grimaced, showing even white teeth. 'We have had a series of earth tremors and the city is being torn apart. Mobs are rioting and pillaging, that is why all the soldiers. We are vulnerable right now and on guard. Since travel through the city is restricted I thought it would be nice to see my friend to safety.' He finally acknowledged us with a calculating stare, his horsetail crop casually slapping against his bare leg. "I thought all you Franks were dead, but here you are again!'

Baba was quick to introduce us and gave a terse but complimentary account of our assistance to him. The man pursed his lips and gave a brief nod. 'I am Ramses Assami.' His lips twitched with a hint of a smile. 'Welcome to our beleaguered city. Captain, do not take your vessel to the usual place it is not safe at present. Do you know the location of the old Roman docks across the harbour? I will lead you.'

Ramses shouted orders to the Dromond and was answered. Drums beat and one side back oared. The galley turned ponderously back towards the city, the other dhow skittering beside her like a gad fly.

# **RAMSES ASSAMI**

W
e followed Ramses' dhow across the harbour towards the northeast side. The dust was recedeing and everything was becoming clearer now. Discordant sounds of rioting, could be heard from various locations and pillars of smoke rose here and there, adding to the dusty haze. Many buildings had collapsed and piles of rubble blocked roads and lanes. People were everywhere, many seemed to be searching for those lost and trying to help the injured. Then there were many more using these moments for other, more dubious ends. I watched as two men clubbed another and stripped him. Soldiers appeared and the looters, in turn, were cut down. Our destination came into sight. There were several low piers with stocky limestone buildings behind. A sharp rise of land protected their rear. I assumed they were old granaries. It was much quieter here. I got a nudge from Danny he had spotted two soldiers riding and leading horses along a road hugging the shore. They were coming towards our landing area...

Captain Salmi looked concerned. 'My lord, I have artichokes on board. They may spoil if they are not put in a cool place soon.'

Ramses turned on him. 'Don't you have other cargo? If your artichokes are lost there is nothing I can or will do about it.' He seemed to relent, 'your crew can unload into one of those grain sheds. They are unused and cool.' The dhow had pulled alongside a limestone quay. He spoke to a junior officer standing in the bow. 'Send four ashore, the rest of you back to your harbor duties.'

The officer bowed and singled out four. As soon as they landed, the dhow turned back towards the harbor its two opposing sails lookin like wings.

We helped tie off the Rashma, captain Salmi's ship. The four of us kept together, unsure of what to expect next, our host had not been all that friendly.

'Your ship and cargo will be safe here, for the present. My troops have this area cordoned off.' Ramses looked at me. 'Do you have horses on board?' His words were abrupt.

'Yes, we do.'

'Fetch them then, we must go. I have other duties besides nursemaid.'

Morgan scowled at him, I don't think he saw it, at least I hoped not. Danny and Uri were already at the bow and the lean to. I followed smartly and could hear wickers of greeting. Storm was very cooperative when I saddled him. He knew he was getting back to solid ground. Taxia was the same. I led them into the sunlight and presented Morgan with the reins to her horse. Ramses raised an eyebrow in approval when he saw our horseflesh. At that moment, the two men I had seen along the shore arrived with five Arabian horses.

Ramses instructed two of the landed soldiers to help the crew protect the cargo, and turned to our captain. 'You will come with me Baba. You can ride double with one of your friends. As soon as possible I will release your ship to the warehouse area.'

One of the new arrivals, held the head of Ramses' horse as he stepped into the stirrup. Two mounted soldiers took the lead, drawn swords resting on their shoulders, with their commander just behind.

Our party was following the harbor edge when another quake hit. It was a hard one and left the horses frantic and all of us disoriented. Danny was thrown off and when it was over, I saw him holding his head. Our captain was crushing me ribs he was holding on so tight. It seemed forever and then it stopped. It had only been seconds. A grim faced Ramses made sure of our well being. Danny had a large lump and a dark bruise above his forehead, on the left side, but seemed all right. Ramses Impatiently waved us on. He had a lot of worries plagueing him. Two of his soldiers were leading with him next, and I was just off his quarter as we neared an area of three story buildings. There was aloud rumble and a cloud of dust billowed around us. A structure was collapsing almost on top of us. I reached out and yanked Ramses out of his saddle me arm around his waist, turning Storm aside, all in one motion. The two lead soldiers and Ramses' horse vanished under a pile of brick and mortar. I lowered him to his feet and he gave me arm a squeeze of thanks. I opened me mouth to say something, when captain Salmi yelped in astonishment.

'By all that's Holy, look at the harbor!'

The water seemed to be receding, leavin a hole where the harbor had been. It was an eerie sight.

'We have to get to higher ground fast. There will be a huge wave.'

We didn't stop to ask how he knew. Morgan grabbed Ramses' arm and swung him up behind her. I led the way, weaving through piles of rubble, away from the harbor.

Ramses shouted, 'Try to go to your right, there is an open avenue going uphill.'

I did as he said and sure enough, came to a wide concourse bordered by slender Cyprus trees, those that were still standing. We gave the horses their heads and we flew uphill at full gallop, passing once stately villas and leaping over some deep crevasses. I looked back and me brain froze as I watched a wall of water refilling the harbor. It swept over the lighthouse and then the wharfs and lower buildings like a heavy fog, and kept coming. Ships out in the bay, were thrown about and swept along like sticks. There was no sign of the Dromond. The waters' rise seemed to be slowing and I knew we were high enough. The horses came to a halt, just about blown. Ramses jumped down staring back at the desolation. I helped captain Salmi down from behind me and got off meself. Roughly, four blocks up from sea level, the entire harbor were flooded out. Some places more than others depending on the elevation. The water was already begining to recede. A pall of deathly silence hung over the city.

Ramses breathed a sigh that was almost a sob, 'My men.'

Uri yelled, and pointed, 'There's some people and they need help.' He headed back down at the double closely followed by Danny. The two remaining soldiers raced behind. This time I swung Ramses up behind me and Morgan took the captain, who was weeping openly. I realized the poor man had lost everything, ship, crew and cargo. We arrived to a stinking bedlam. Sewage and garbage, stirred up had returned to the city, with the wave. The stench was incredible! Uri and Danny were running around dragging, half drowned, soldiers and civilians from the slop. For many it was already too late. Morgan crouched over a small boy, tryin to push water from his lungs. Ramses helped one of his men drag a very heavy woman to safety.

A horse screamed and the other soldier, who was riding it, was thrown, with bone cracking force, against piled up brick debris. A huge reptile, at least twenty feet long, had the horse by the nose. Shaking it like a rat it drew it into deeper water. Thrashing turned the water into foam. There were others lurking and then the screams began as other people were taken. That sobered us and we were much more careful of our surroundings after that. We continued helping exhausted survivors to dry land well into the evening. Uri and Morgan had found a usable punt and were rescuing people stranded on islands of debris...Much later we sat in a stupor surrounded by the diminishing stink. Actually, I think our noses were just getting used to it. I was so tired we had done all we could. Morgan was giving solace to the soldier who had been thrown, his back was broken and his comrade was standing by with a drawn sword. Ramses spoke briefly to the soldier, then came and sat beside me, his face drawn and his golden armor and white cloak filthy and more than a little tarnished.

I said, 'Those awful beasts are they around here all the time?'

He scubbed his face with his hands, and then looked at how dirty they were. He grimaced, 'No, the crocodiles have come down river for the feasting. I don't know how they know, they just do.' He looked sideways at me. 'I want to thank you Europe. Thank you for my life and thank you and your party for all your help. What is your name?'

I realized he was tryin to be polite, callin me Europe. After all Frank was a derogatory term used by them.

'I am sir William Barrow Arthur, that is me wife, Lady Morgan and those two over there are our close friends Danny and Uri.'

Ramses got to his feet and bowed to Morgan. 'My lady, thank you also.' He gave the others a cursory nod and turned to me, 'You will all be my guests for a few days, but now I must see to the rest of my men and find my ship, then we will leave this retched place for a while.'

After a small repast, we toiled through the night, helping where we could. Next day we found the dromond with most of her crew. The warship's captain told his commander that they had been near the harbors' mouth when it all happened. He had put out all his anchors and prayed. The dhows with all their men, were never found again. Fortytwo men lost, I could see that Ramses was upset. The dromond beached by the wave,had suffered little damage. The commander conscripted any men he could find to help pull her off and no excuses were accepted. Some men went to find fallen pillars and any other lumber to be used for rollers. Others were foraging fer horses, oxen, carts, anything.

One man came to us fer help. He had found oxen just above the flood line. He thought there were three yokes, that meant six strong beasts but a pack of ferile dogs had kept him at bay. Danny was looking pale. I told him to rest, and asked a soldier to keep an eye on him.

Uri and I went to help. I took me bow from me saddle and we went on foot. I didn't want to risk Storm with the dogs. The man led us to them quite quickly. They were still trying to find a way into the barn where the oxen were. They saw us coming and turned to fight us. There were at least twenty, some quite big. A couple looked like Jackals, smaller but wily with razor teeth. They were probably the leaders. The man had found a club and Uri had his sword. I told them to stand back the dogs could overwhelm them.

'Be ready to climb something, I'm goin to shoot a few from here and even the odds.'

Uri nodded. He knew a few would die before the rest got wise. Then they would either bolt or attack. I put down five dogs, with well placed shots, then the rest came at us. I dropped one more before drawing me sword. Uri killed two with as many strokes and then the rest became wary. They started circling and feinting, looking fer an opening. A large yellow dog attacked the man with the club, thinking him the weakest. The animal died leaving brains in the dust. The rest decided we were too much trouble and faded away looking fer easier prey.

The oxen did not look like any oxen I knew. These were Zebus and were a blessing and Ramses was very pleased. I told him who had found them and the risk he had taken. I guessed and hoped, the man would be rewarded, when this was over.

Rollers, almost a hundred men, the zebus and a few horses were enough to get the undamaged galley back in the water.

Bodies had been piling up and now lay in long rows along the shoreline. Every so often, a crocodile would claim one and no one disputed it. Ramses left ten soldiers to oversee the burning of the corpses.

'See that it is done as quickly as possible, commandeer others to help. Also! no one is to drink water within the city. Have it brought from wells outside. I will bring fresh men when I return.' He gripped one man's shoulder. 'You are now my lieutenant, see that you do well by it.' Ramses turned to us, 'It's time to leave, let us go aboard.'

The sun was a whitehot cinder in a pale washed out sky. It was stifling and biting flies were very persistant, even in the heat. We had all been given horsetail crops which helped to kill them or drive them away. We were onboard the dromond and watched the shoreline slip by as the heavy warship moved persistently up the Nile with just oar power. I looked down at the rowing benches and saw that mostly black men chained to the oars. All of them shone with a glossy sheen of sweat. There was no wind at all, not even a flicker.

Each of us sat with our own water, sipping frequently to counter the loss from sweating. We had been told that we would soon stop sweating so much and would need less water.

Later that day, Ramses gripped me shoulder and pointed off the starboard bow. 'See our ancient wonders, Will?'

Me jaw must have dropped as I gazed upon the three Pyramids, one even greater than the others, they were a long distance away and looked ethereal in the heat waves. Morgan came to stand at me side.

'My God, Will, who would ever have believed...' Her grip on me arm tightened as she stared.

For once, Danny was speechless, he had somewhat recovered from the blow to his forehead though it was quite colorful. He still looked like he wanted to puke. Uri just looked on with a still face. No one could tell what he was thinking.

Ramses' deep voice broke me reverie. 'We are nearing my home, the island of Rowdah.'

The large Island loomed ahead with fortifications facing us. It was in mid river, far enough away to still look like part of the mainland behind it. Pink and white clouds of ibises rose from reed beds nearby and then we saw our first flamingos. As we drew closer to the island, horses could be seen grazing and nearly everyone had one or more white egrets on their backs. The harbour came into view. Fellahin were irrigatin other fields across from the island. Along the near shore, five more dromonds were at anchor. The one river channel was narrow here. The dromonds were close enough to each other that you could jump from one to the other. From our viewpoint, some rows of long onestory buildings could be seen. A command was given and the oars drawn in. Our ship slipped fluidly into its space and dropped anchors. We tied off to the ship next to us. Several bargelike boats came from the island to take us all to dry land.

We were entering a military encampment, a big bustling one with a permanency about it. There were long rows of mud brick buildings with woven thatch roofs. These were the barracks and there were many other buildings for various uses. Marshaling yards and corrals fer horses were everywhere. Further away one could see pastures also full of grazing horses. There were some small but attractive single dwellings down a central avenue, probably officer's quarters. North of us, the fortress faced the lower river.

Ramses smiled and pointed up the island. 'My home is at the far end, please join me when you have settled in and cared for your horses.' He called a soldier over. 'Show them where they need to go and give them every courtesy.'

The soldier hit his chest with his fist and answered 'Yes Lord.' and I looked at Ramses with renewed interest. Several officers had approached saluting him and he walked off in deep discussion with them.

Our guide was curious but too polite to say anything out of turn so I took the time to get friendly.

'This is a huge garrison, why on this island? Oh, can we let our horses loose to graze, they are well behaved.'

He smiled, 'Yes they can graze. He looked up at Storm. They are big not like our Arabs.' He led us through a gate. As he held it open he said. 'This island is very defensible, we have hidden defenses all around it and then there's our galleys, they control the Nile from beyond the first cataract to the delta and Alexandria.'

'If an enemy attacks, ye could lose all yer galleys. Burn one, burn them all, somehow, they should be anchored apart.'

He stared questionably and said. 'Will you be telling my superiors of this?'

I shook me head. 'You tell them. Maybe you will make sergeant or something.'

He grinned at me and bowed. He walked away still grinning. There was a strut to his step and I prayed he would think on his wording so as not to offend a superior.

I made a note to find out more about this first cataract. We let the horses loose and they raced off, leapin and kickin their heels like frisky puppies. I had to grin this was their first real stretch of freedom since Sardinia.

We took our leave of the soldier, and I made sure he now knew who we were and where we came from, tit fer tat. He pointed us in the direction we had to go and wished us long life. We started walkin through the huge conclave. It was a three mile walk, maybe a bit more. We watched men training everywhere. The majority seemed to be cavalry and I estimated at least three thousand men. I guessed there were many more off the island carryin out daily obligations. Uri, very interested, was making mental notes, of everything he saw. The east bank of the river was fairly close to us and a lot of construction activity was apparent, encroaching into what had been farmland. I was not sure yet what it was. As we neared our destination, I was amazed at the beauty. A snowwhite villa stood on a small knoll, surrounded by gardens, they were shaded by huge wild fig trees and lower acacias. Tall palms towered everywhere. Small troops of monkeys were scrapping for the ripest fruit and many birds were flitting throughout the branches. We came face to face with that magnificent bird that I had seen on Gawain's carpet, the one with the eyes on its tail. One fanned its tail in our honor and uttered a high pitched wail. Morgan stared wide eyed, and had her hand over her mouth as they strutted across our path.

Coal black servants, dressed in white robes with red sashes, met us at the door and ushered us past the shade of a tamarind tree into a cool tile entry. One spoke to me in Pharsi, a Persian language often used by traders and one I had been learning, thanks to our captain.

'My master bids thee welcome and is sure thou would like to freshen up after thine strenuous journey.' He bowed low, 'Please follow me.'

The floors we now walked on were tile and then we were led to a suite of rooms,which were mostly covered with carpets, except an area around two pools fer bathing given privacy by ornate screens. A main living room with a myriad of cushions strewn about low tables dominated the suite and plates of figs and dates, sharp goat cheese and mild red onions along with flasks of cool water were placed, here and there, around the room. I poured two cups and gave one to Morgan, while sipping on mine.

Uri stepped through a door to the side and came back out. He pointed. 'Looks like there are four of them, its a bedroom with mats or couches to sleep on. I'll use the mat in mine.'

'I take it that you chose that one as yours? What about Baba and Danny?'

He gave me a half smile, easy to do with the scar on his cheek. 'I am going to clean my mail then have a bath. See you later.' That sounded like a plan fer all of us. I bit into a plump fig as I followed Morgan into our room. Danny stayed to sample the platters. He came out of his fog long enough to yell after Uri, 'I'm sleepin in your room you Swiss prick.' No diplomacy in Danny. Baba went straight to the last one. He wasn't speakin much. He had barely spoken to any of us since his losses, though he had worked hard beside us.

Morgan and I hadn't been really alone fer some time and we took full advantage of it. First we bathed of course and the help took our clothin and mail to wash oil and clean.

We were both sweating all over again and breathing heavily as we lay side by side.

'Oh shite, I've missed that!'

186

She got up on one elbow and nibbled me ear. 'Let's have another bath dearest. We can get all sweaty again later.' She gave me a sharp poke in the stomach that made me grunt, and I jumped up.

Later, a servant came with cool fresh robes fer all of us. 'My lord would like all of thee to dine with him.' He stood waiting as we prepared. I called to captain Salmi. 'Aren't ye coming Baba?' he had insisted we call him Baba.

'You go I'm not good company right now.'

'Our host might take exception.'

'I don't think so. We have known each other many years. I hope he will understand.'

I shrugged, to me self of course, and went to join the others. Morgan smiled, her auburn hair really shone, set off by the white robe. I soaked in how beautiful she was and took her hand in mine.

We were shown into a brightly lit room. Ramses, now dressed in a snow white hooded kaftan, was playing with a very large spotted cat.

I was flabbergasted. 'My Lord Ramses, is that a leopard?'

He stopped playin and looked up. 'No Will, it is a cheetah. We call them the friendly cats. They hunt with great speed.' The cheetah chirped, soundin much like an ordinary cat, and then flopped on its side watchin us with curious eyes. Lookin at it, I realized me mistake. Leopards were chunkier with shorter legs. This cheetah was a tall, lean, long legged animal with a smallish head, built like a wolf hound. I approached, showing no fear and it stretched out to sniff me hand.

Ramses nodded approval. 'She seems to like you.'

I grinned. 'I seem to have a way with most animals. How did you come about this one?' I scratched her ear as she pushed her head against me hand and looked about. Stands on one side of the room had several hawks and falcons sitting and preening on them. Ramses was quick to notice me interest. 'Do you hunt with birds in your own land?'

'Aye my lord we do, and with dogs.'

'Dogs? They are filthy, unclean beasts, like pigs.'

I decided now was the time to keep me mouth shut and scowled at Danny, knowing his ability for putting both feet in his mouth. His innocent expression said, 'What'?

Ramses waved us to a group of low tables surrounded by many cushions. 'Come, let us sup. We can chat at leisure.'

He picked up a round of bread which he broke apart. Handin a piece to each of us, he formally welcomed us to his home. 'You asked earlier how I got my beautiful cat. Baba found her for me. I raised her from a cub. She is three years now and I need to find her a mate, Cheetahs are family orientated animals, that's why they will link to humans quite easily.'

We copied our host in the way of eating. It was done with the fingers of the right hand and pieces of the flat bread used like a scoop. I made special note that only the right hand was used. The food was very good, includin a white substance full of vegetables and crusty cubes of lamb, rare and juicy in the middle. After the main course, platters of fruit and cheeses were placed before us, along with a strong dark drink called coffee, it was served in small cups, very hot and sweet with a sharp under taste that was pleasing.

Ramses was a very good host, making us feel welcome under his roof. I had already guessed that he was a person of high rank and I made a point of telling him that I was a knight in me own land, hoping it would put us on a more equal footing.

'I don't want to sound rude, Mi lord, but ye do not look like an Egyptian.'

He stared at me fer a while that Horus brand fillin me vision. I was just beginnin to feel uncomfortable when he smiled showin those even white teeth again. He leaned forward. 'I'm not. I am a Circassian brought here as a boy of fourteen and a slave.' He watched us to see our reaction, a small smile pulled at the corners of his mouth. 'Ninety percent of everyone here is a Circassian or a Kipchak Turk., all brought here as slaves. We are descended from horse cultures on the Steppes and are the backbone of Egypt's armies. We are the Mamluks and our horsemen are called Bakris meaning large river.'

I think we all stared at him, openmouthed, I know I did. 'But Sir, you said you were slaves?'

He laughed aloud. 'Not like any you have known. We were second only to the ruling class of this country.'

I had a strange feeling, almost an embarrassed feeling. 'You are the Lord of all these warriors, aren't you?'

'Yes! My rank is Emir, what you might call a General.' He took a handful of dates and nibbled on them. 'I am not usually this candid, however, I owe you my life and also, I have taken a liking you.'

I scratched me chin, 'You showed Baba Salmi courtesies not usually given by a man of your rank. That is what threw me off.'

'Enough said that Baba was kind to me at a time when I needed kindness. I was ripped from my family. Thrown into cages with other boys and treated quite harshly. He was my staff for a while.'

'How did it happen, milord?'

He looked at the dates in his hand and smiled to himself then his eyes met ours. For the first time I noticed they were grey. 'Are you ready for a story?'

'I was standing on a dock in Alexandria. There were about seventy of us, all boys from twelve to sixteen. I had been, singled out for punishment, not that I had done anything wrong. There had been unruliness in our group and the culprits were closed mouthed and threatening towards the rest of us. I knew who they were but our code prevented me from speaking out. The guards were harsh as they lead me to a bench. They hit and kicked me into the position they wanted. I was sprawled over it with my hands and feet tied together underneath. It was most uncomfortable, I had difficulty breathing and I was terrified. A crowd had gathered and I made eye contact with this man in the crowd. He stared into my eyes and I could read his lips. 'Be brave.' His eyes never wavered as they began to beat me with hippo hide kurbashes. The pain was colossal at first then I lost myself in his eyes.' Ramses sighed. 'That man, my Baba, later found my cell and brought me fruit and water he did so for days until I was healed, thumbing his nose at the guards.' He sighed again. 'I am most certainly in his debt.' His laugh was cold and I glimpsed the ruthlessness in him. 'Those men who didn't speak up, I bided my time then put out their eyes, cut the soles from their feet and left them by the river for the crocodiles.'

We sat and absorbed his tale, somewhat shocked. I had a lot to think on. Men of his station were usually cold and aloof. I had thought that I had met a man like me foster father and Gawain. I realized now that he was nothing like them. Here was a dangerous, ruthless man who happened to enjoy our company...fer the moment.

He leaned back and the cheetah came to lie beside him. Stroking the cats' neck, he said. 'Now it's your turn Will. Tell me your story.' I spoke long into the evening, leaving out the pigs and dogs.

When I finished he stared at me, his eyes glowing softly in the lamp light. "Show me your back!" it was a command. I stood and did as he asked. Morgan didn't look happy. He pondered me scars and then arose, as lithe as any cat. Dropping his Kaftan to his waist, he turned his back to us.

'We seem to have more in common than even I thought.'

Danny grunted, Uri just stared and Morgan had her hand over her mouth. His back was very similar to mine. Mine was worse from the pluckerin of two beatings but his was close enough to form a kinship between us. He summoned a servant to bring two small cups of Arak. He handed one to me and toasted with an almost boyish grin, 'To our backs.'

The toast went down like fire leavin me eyes watering,

A short time later we took our leave, thanking our host for an eventful evening. The big cat accompanied Morgan and I, staying close enough to me side so that me hand brushed her back as we walked to our apartments. She left us there with a purring chirp and went about cat business.

Some days passed, and we were left to our own devices. Ramses was busy collecting plans from architects and going over them with various artisans and other workers. Plans fer rebuilding the city were taking fruit. Seeing so little of our host, me wife and I got a pleasant reprieve and spent some private time together. . On one occasion, Ramses summoned Uri and took him along. He recognized a soldier when he saw one and wanted to pick the Swiss' brains. A different style of fighting and one that was catastrophic fer cavalry interested him.

It appeared that the soldiers had instructions to be courteous and helpful so our walks about the camp were, if not always enjoyable, at least informative. I discovered an area we had missed before and I almost wished we hadn't found it. I guessed right away that it was the training camp for the newly conscripted boys. Their training was harsh by any ones standards, Whips and rods were used and never sparingly. Their hours were long and punishments severe but at least, from what we could see, they got good food.

Baba started coming out of his shell and Morgan and I would take him fer walks by the river, a favorite place of ours. The quantity of birds was amazing. Danny was often nearby playing bodyguard sometimes a part of the group, sometimes not. On this particular day a wind had come up, which was appreciated by all, as it kept the flies at a minimum. There was a penalty though. We were forever wiping grit out of our eyes. I was watchin a long thin line of flamingos fly over, not paying much attention to where I was walking, when Baba grabbed me arm and pulled me back. He pointed out a snake coiled among the stones. He picked up a rock and crushed its head. 'That was an asp, they are very dangerous, Will. Watch for them. There shouldn't be many here, the soldiers kill them on sight.'

Morgan looked at it. 'They're quite small, really.'

Baba cut in, 'But very poisonous, my Lady, like their larger relative the cobra.'

I soon lost interest in the dead snake and espied the snout of a crocodile in the deeper water. It vanished in a swirl and I guessed it was hunting nearby storks in the reeds. Wonder filled me as I watched the life and death around me. Turning to Baba I said, 'Do ye have any plans? We know ye may have lost everything. We would like to help if ye'd let us.'

He placed his hand on me arm. 'Lord Ramses sent me news. He is going back to Alexandria to oversee the rebuilding. He is taking me in hopes that there is something to salvage. Word came to him that some of my crew lived and were looking for me. They were elated when they found out that I was alive.'

Morgan and I both smiled and she said. 'That is good news I hope all goes well for you. As Will said, if you need anything, call on us. We will do what we can.'

'I thank you from the bottom of my heart. What are your plans now? You came here for a reason.'

I nodded. 'It is our wish to explore the Silk Road to its other end. I'm just not quite sure where to start. Jerusalem could be one place.'

'Caravans come all the way to Egypt you know. A new city is growing across the river from here. A small village is rapidly expanding. I think it might become the new seat of government, Alexandria is taking too much of a beating from the quakes and could not withstand an enemy attack, never mind the fact that bureaucrats fear being there. Anyway, commerce is beginning to find its way to this new place. It won't be long before government follows the money.'

I laughed. 'You are a very astute fellow.'

He grinned back, the first time since Alexandria, 'I am a trader you know, and a damn good one.'


Ramses returned from Alexandria without captain Baba. When Morgan and I asked after him the Emir said that he sent us his best wishes. He had been, re united with a third of his crew. They had salvaged much of his cargo of olives and oil, though the ship was smashed and un-repairable.

He had a servant pour coffee I was getting quite addicted to it. 'I financed him into another ship for a percentage of the profits.' His face broke into that rare young boyish grin. 'One day I will retire from soldiering and need nest eggs.'

He tried to find time to be together with us. He seemed to enjoy the differences in his routine that we represented. He even took us hunting, and that's when I got to see the first cataract.

I also saw some magnificent ruins from ancient times, Thebes, the temple at Karnak and the village that had the ruins' name. Morgan liked it so much she wanted to explore not hunt. Rameses said she would be perfectly safe so we left her there with servants and a bodyguard of soldiers. Danny elected to stay with her too. I told them we would be gone for two or three days.

Morgan smiled, her hand resting on an ancient stone, 'You go enjoy your hunt, dear, I am happy right here.'

Ramses had accepted Uri as a friend too. I think he saw much of himself in the Swiss warrior who had been soldiering since he was twelve. We travelled a little further upriver near Ipsambul and camped the first night behind a Zareba of stones and thorn bush. We were introduced to our charioteers, who were permitted to join us fer supper. This was a hunting camp and formalities were relaxed. All three were young Egyptians. I was introduced to a new bow. Ramses said, 'Yours is too long for the chariot, this one is a horseman's bow, a Mongolian bow. Egyptian bows are also too long and a little flimsy. Let's go try it out.'

Butts were set up and I was supplied with a thumb ring I had never seen before and a sturdy arm guard. After a while I began to get comfortable with the bow, it was a short re-curved weapon laminated from wood, bone and god knows what else. You needed some strength to draw it, luckily I was strong. Ramses watched with approval.

'Remember, you'll have the added inconvenience of a bouncing chariot. The terrain can get quite rough.' He looked at Uri, who had opted for javelins, Egyptian style. 'Can you use those?'

Uri just grinned and thumped one into the bulls' eye, first cast. Ramses slapped his leg with his horsetail and laughed. 'We are going to have some fun.'

We finally said our goodnights. I rolled up in me blanket and stared at a myriad of stars, listening to the rivers' power until I fell asleep.

The First day we broke fast with figs and something called yogurt. It was very good. Ramses gave us a plan of action and we took our first ride in the chariots to witness the cat hunting. We galloped out into rough terrain with just a few tracks here and there. It gave us time to get used to the bouncing of the light chariots. Malchise, me charioteer, showed me how to place me feet and keep me knees slightly flexed. I had to train me self quickly to find me balance and his instruction helped a lot. After all, when it came time to shoot the bow, I'd have to let go of the rail. We jumped a herd of smaller antelope that bounded away in swift, high leaps. Ramses released the cheetah and her speed and fluidity were amazing. She selected an antelope and seemed to anticipate its every move. I had never dreamed that anything could be so fast. She ran down her prey and made her kill by throttling the animal till it died. She then let Ramses load it on my chariot. That evening, it was returned to her. and she ate from her kill while we had supper.

The following morning, after a breakfast of dhurra cakes and more yogurt we went to do our own hunting. The terrain we went to was quite different, canyon country with shelving slabs of sandstone. The shift of colors was beautiful. Ramses, Uri and I hunted several large antelope with the chariots. It was a sport of the ancient pharaohs and exhilarating. I got me self a fine beast, the size of a palfrey, with spiral horns a yard long. Ramses got one very much like mine, perhaps a bit bigger.

Uri was spectacular. They were chasing an antelope down a dry wadi when, out of nowhere, a lion leaped from a rock shelf onto one of the horses, dragging it down. The chariot flipped onto its side dragging the other horse down too. The charioteer was pinned by one leg but Uri was thrown clear, getting a mouthful of gravel and sand. Both Ramses and I turned to go to the rescue. The other horse was thrashing, the lion was getting interested and the charioteer was in great danger. Our intervention wasn't necessary. Uri regained his feet and dispatched the lion with a perfect cast. It leaped high in the air with a yowl and was dead when it landed. Uri watched closely, the other lance, held in readiness. Uri had a lion, a big black mane male, and I had an antelope. I think I curled me lip at him. Ramses was jubilant. His hunt had been a huge success.

We were able to rescue the one horse and except fer a bruised fetlock, it seemed alright. The other had to be destroyed.

After I dressed the charioteers' injuries, mostly some deep scrapes and bruises, we ate a lunch of dates goat cheese and sweet onions chased with cool water, sitting with our backs against fallen trees. I think we all felt the comradeship of a successful hunt between us. I leaned back squinting at Ramses. 'Yer name is Egyptian isn't it? How did ye get an Egyptian name?'

He spit out a date pit. 'As boys, we were encouraged to take their names. Some of ours are difficult for them to say. I chose Ramses because, to me, it seemed a name of power.' He smiled ferociously. 'Now I have power.' He leaned toward us. 'Mamluks rule Egypt outright. It was inevitable, after a decisive defeat of the Mongols thirty years ago, we pushed the Frank Crusaders into the sea at Cyprus and now we rule.'

Me mouth felt a little dry. 'Do ye plan to rule yer self?'

He shook his head, 'I am an Emir, a military man who likes action. There are political men who I support.' He got to his feet, held out his hand, to help me up and clapped Uri on the back. 'I've told you more than enough for one day, ferenghi.' He smiled takin the bite away and I prayed he wouldn't regret his candor. I decided, then and there, that it was time to travel on.

We arrived back in Karnak to meet Morgan and Danny. Ramses took his leave, 'I have official business to attend to. Please stay a day or two with your wife and see the sights.'

Morgan loved being me guide and showed me the temple at Luxor. A place of pillars that drew ye into antiquity. Danny and Uri went to see if they could catch one of the Nile's giant catfish.

Two weeks later Ramses invited us to sup with him once again. This time he had another guest. He introduced all of us to As-Salih Ayyub. A complex name fer an Englishman but one I tried hard to remember. I believed him to be one of Ramses' politicians or ranking nobles. This gentleman was very interested in Europe and the interaction of its monarchies. We all did our best to fill him in. He was somewhat cool with Morgan. I didn't understand why and it annoyed me.

Our Emir seemed a little put off when I told him me decision to leave but had the good graces to wish us well. 'You will be entering lands who were once my enemies and may be again. I hope you never will be!'

I looked him straight in the eyes. 'Never milord, I will choose other theaters to fight me battles.'

He pulled me into an embrace and then Morgan. 'I have a gift for you Lady Morgan. Please forgive the slight of my country man I am afraid you will get many more.' A slave stepped forward with an open long box. Within was a beautifully crafted scimitar. Morgan picked it up and twirled it.

Flower like patterns caught the light and swirled along the blade.

'It is perfect and beautiful Lord Ramses! I thank you very much. How can I repay you?'

'You and your husband saved my life and gave me much pleasure that is payment enough. The sword is 'Damascus steel', metal from the stones that fall from heaven folded many times by the smiths. You will find that it will hold its razor edge even in the fiercest of fighting.'

'You honor me Lord Ramses and you can always count me a friend.'

Ramses looked very pleased and he included Uri and Danny when he said 'I enjoyed our dalliance very much. Now go, start your journey, I must go to rebuild.'

I thought this could very well be the last time I would see Emir Ramses Assami, lord of the Bakris horsemen.

# **BO'ORCHU**

Cairo was the new name given to the village that was growing rapidly around Rawdah. We were probably the first Europeans to witness it. The Sauk or market place was already large with a myriad of merchant stalls and a tannery. Construction of buildings was going on everywhere, even on the far side of the river. One up and coming building had such graceful lines that I was sure it would become a Mosque. Many caravans were about but none came from any further away than a place called Syria. We were all fascinated with new beasts called camels. We soon learned that most of them were nasty tempered brutes that liked to bite and spit, so we kept our distance.

The day came when a dusty group of riders arrived. I watched these strange men from a distance, and soon realized, from Ramses former descriptions, that these were Mongols. I could feel me excitement rising as I told the others.

Morgan gripped me hand. 'What do we do, Will. We don't speak their language and they may be unfriendly.'

'Why are they here in Egypt? They are not in their usual haunts and they do not appear to be looking fer trouble.' I turned to the vendor beside me, and purchased a bowl of couscous with vegetables and lamb and shared it with Morgan. Uri got his own bowl and Danny said he wasn't hungry. I was worried about Danny he had never really bin himself since he hit his head. One day he seemed fine and the next day he regressed into moping again. Anyway, I ate and watched these newcomers with interest.

One saw us eating and nudged another. They made their way towards us, knocking off their dusty clothing with their crops. As they neared, one said, 'Is it good?'

I realized he had spoken in pharsi and was speakin to me. I smiled, 'Yes very good.' I looked him over as he ordered the same. He was as tall as me, a little broader and his eyes were narrow. His black hair was tied into a horse tail. His friend was shorter with a very round face and the same narrow eyes and he had several plaits descending from an otherwise bald head. The first had already received his order and as he turned back to us, he picked up a morsel with his fingers and popped it into his mouth. He chewed and said, 'You are from across the sea?' It was a question.

'Yes, from a land called England.'

He nodded. 'I have heard of this England. On occasion, we have met other men from across the sea. Why are you here?'

'We came out of curiosity, to seek the Silk Road and find its end.'

'It has two ends. If you start at this end you might live to reach the other.' He laughed uproariously his friend joining in.

He had me laughing too, and then the others. I didn't really know why we were so giddy, but we were.

'So, you are waiting for a caravan? He looked across the way at his fellows. We will wait too but we must not overstay our welcome in Egypt. My name is Bo'orchu and this is Sengge.' He waited fer me introduction.

'I am Sir William Arthur Barrow, this is me wife Morgan. These friends are Uri and Danny. I am pleased to meet yer Bo'orchu, Sengge, ye can call me Will.'

He bowed a slight bow to each of us and said. 'Come, meet my friends.' as we crossed the road, he said, 'We are far from home and looking to work our way back. The caravans always need swords, they go though some hostile country.'

Bo'orchu and his thirty followers made us feel welcome in their camp. They were all open, friendly and curious. I found Bo'orchu to be an intelligent man with an inquisitive mind and I felt we would become close friends in our mutual quest fer knowledge.

I thought I already knew but I asked anyway. 'What did ye mean about overstaying yer welcome?'

'The Mamluks do not like us much. They know that, even though they defeated us nearly thirty years ago, we will still pose a threat one day.'

'Why don't they just kill you on sight?'

He grinned. 'Politics, we did help them throw you back into the sea, though we were late.' That sounded a little sinister but he smiled when he said it.

The Mongols took to Morgan very quickly and weren't shy about asking to see her skills with arms. They were good scrappers and knew something of our way of sword fighting. She didn't win every fight but she put quite a few on their arses much to the great joy of the others. The new sword fit her like a glove and one of Bo'Orchus men taught her some moves more suited to the curved blade than our heavier weapons.

I had found, in a short time that the Islamic peoples looked down on women. Their women had no status at all outside the home. Now I knew why Morgan had received the cold shoulder, more than once. The fact that she carried weapons made them disapprove of her manners even more. I watched several eyeing her furtively and worried about her. I told Danny and Uri so that one of us always kept her within sight. I asked Bo'Orchu about it, and he just shrugged and said Mongols were not that way. He did say they would keep Morgan from harm. Danny was still ailing so I told him about me worries.

He looked over at Danny and then back at me. 'If you think it was from the time he fell from his horse and hit his head...well that is a long time. If you like, I could bring him to our healer for a consultation. He is wise about horse related injuries.'

I nodded, 'I'll have to get that stubborn Scot to agree, but I want him to.'

194

Uri had just sat down with us and caught the gist of the conversation. 'I'm worried about him too so you can count on my help even if we have to carry him.'

It was easier to coax Danny than I expected. He really wasn't himself and didn't put up much of a fight.

The healer was not with the Mongol party and we had to ride for two days to find him. We came upon a much larger encampment of two hundred or more men women and children, along with sheep, goats and horses. I saw their traveling homes fer the first time. They were called 'gers' a domed shaped tent like structure made from heavy layers of felt and often mounted on a waggon when traveling.

Bo'orchu was welcomed with sharp cries and waves. I noticed several young women eyeing him furtively. I found out he was a bachelor from good family and considered a good catch. He led us through the camp, at a trot to keep the dust down, to a large ger done in reds, blues and yellows. A slim, middle aged man with a wispy beard sat on the steps leading up to the abode. He got up as we approached and stood waiting. He had a fur trimmed hat on his head, his narrow, black eyes were unreadable. Bo'orchu dismounted and walked to him. They embraced and spoke quietly together for several minutes. It seemed the man was asking question after question. Finally, Bo'orchu turned and waved us up. Morgan was the first to dismount and I could see interest on the man's face. He said something aloud, lookin back at the ger and a woman appeared at the door, holding a stool. I watched as she navigated the stairs, a medium height woman, with a pleasant face and braided black hair coiled on top of her head. She was a little on the plump side, though it might have bin her quilted clothing. She placed the stool on the ground and waited to one side, quietly and without expression.

The old man led Danny to the stool and told him to sit down. The man explored Danny's head with gentle probing fingers and while he did so, asked questions which Bo'orchu related to me, questions about appetite, behavior and such. I answered to the best of me ability. I saw his probing fingers stop and go over an area again. He beckoned to me and spoke to Bo'orchu, who translated.

'Feel here, where my fingers are.' I did, and felt a small but sharp indentation in the skull.

'There is pressure on your friend's brain. There could even be a piece of loose bone stuck in there. If I can remove the pressure, your friend should be hale again but there is some risk, risk of death or permanent disability.' We all looked at each other then, Danny spoke up.

'I know how I feel, better than anyone, and I say lets do it. I feel sicker and weaker all the time.'

The woman returned to the ger and brought an apparatus I had never seen before. It locked to the stool and adjusted to fit. A padded ring fit around Danny's head holding it rigid and in place. The three arms that held it there were sturdy and stopped Danny from slumping. A table was set up, along with a felt bag covered with runes. The woman then proceeded to shave his scalp. Danny drank a dose of something that quickly made him drift off. The woman put an ear to Danny's chest and lifted an eyelid. Satisfied, she nodded to her husband.

First, the healer took a small sharp knife and made two incisions in the form of an x. He carefully flayed the skin back, pinning the flaps with small bone pins. He now had two inches of exposed skull. There was very little blood, considering. Next, came what looked like a carpenters' auger with a strange looking bit. It was about an inch and a quarter with a serrated edge and a small protruding point in the center. The center point was enough to stablize the bit so it wouldn't skip. He began cranking the auger with precise measured turns, watching carefully how deep he was going.

Danny chose this moment to start moving about so I jumped in to hold him still. The healing man nodded his approval as he removed the auger. His wife handed him a small chisel and mallet as he spoke to Bo'orchu.

In almost a whisper, Bo'orchu said, 'This is a moment of danger, hold him firmly!'

I held me friend's head between me hands and was frightened. I willed him not to move as the healer presented the chisel and made several light taps. He inspected his work and nodded in approval. His wife placed a small tong like instrument in his hand, which he used to remove a loose circle of bone. He inspected it minutely and nodded. He showed me the piece and the fracture in it. A broken bit was pointing down like a tiny needle.

'This was all that was needed to cause such stress to your friend.' He sliced the piece off and then inspected Danny's exposed brain. Bo'orchu's low voice spoke in me ear. 'Everything seems to be clean it is now time to close the wound.' His wife had glued two flat pieces of a reed like material onto the disc, which he now reinserted into the hole. He spoke again to Bo'orchu who interpreted.

'It is important that the piece of skull does not drop lower in the hole. It will bond quite quickly even though the piece is a little smaller.'

He used more of the sticky substance on the skull, and carefully put the disc into place, moved the skin back, applied a powder and then he covered everything with a leather skullcap.

'We are done! Now we wait and see. If your God will listen, pray to him.'

I withdrew me hands from Danny's head with a small groan. I had cramps in me elbows from standing tense and still. Morgan took me hand and we knelt side by side. Uri stood behind us like a sentinel and bowed his head. I am sure we all prayed, I know I did, and we waited. The healer's wife brought us tea and offered us what looked like butter to put in it. I smelled it and found it rancid. I chose to drink me tea black.

Ere long, Danny began to stir. We waited on, pins and needles, as he opened his eyes. 'Me head hurts, do ye have something to eat?'

The sighs of relief were very audible, even from the Mongols.

I grinned like a little boy 'Yer back me friend. Ye got anything cheeky to say?'

His retort was quick. 'If I could reach me kilt I'd lift it and give ye a whole lot of cheek.'

Me old Danny was back. Morgan helped the woman remove the apparatus and got Danny to his feet. He was a little wobbly, probably from the drug. Bo'orchu called to a woman at a nearby fire and she answered cheerfully. It wasn't long before she brought a platter of sliced lamb and vegetables with a large bowl of rice.

'I'm hungry, but I don't think I can eat all that.'

'Don't worry, we plan to help.'

The woman gave us five sets of slender ivory sticks. Bo'orchu laughed at our lack of comprehension.

'You use them to eat.'

'God's truth! How do ye eat the rice, one grain at a time?'

We received our first lesson using these new implements.

# **CHI'PIN**

A weeks rest did wonders fer Danny. At first, he had headaches but now he was his old self again and fit right in with the Mongols who were a ribald bunch in their own right. I took that time to speak at length to the healer. He knew how primitive Europeans were in the field of medicine and was curious why I knew more than most.

He was quite candid and said that the art of opening the skull, he learned in Egypt. It was still new to him and he had welcome'd the opportunity to try his skill.

'Ye took a gamble on me friend? What if he had died?'

'We all die in time and life is a gamble my English friend.' He chuckled, 'I was always lucky in gambling.'

'Well now, ye did succeed so I cannot fault ye. I am grateful that ye gave me a whole friend again. As to me medical knowledge, I learned from a fine woman who pushed all the boundaries in many things.' I felt a pang, thinking of Meg, I missed her.

He nodded sagely, 'Women are the staffs in our lives and all would end without them.' I would only be half a man without my Jiyatu.' He smiled fondly to his wife who was sittin near.

'Now I know yer wife's name and realize we have not been formally introduced. I am Sir William Barrow Arthur at yer service. Ye can call me Will.'

'I am Chi'pin.' He smiled as we grasped hands. 'You and yours are always welcome in our camp. I understand you will be leaving in the morning?'

'Aye me friend, it's time to find a caravan.'

We spoke at length on many things and I learned that Bo'Orchu was from a family of prestige. His great, great, grandfather of the same name had been a general and close friend to the great Khan himself.

When I asked who the great Khan was, I got another history lesson.

# **KAREESH AL SAUD**

Uri, Danny and I were ridin three abreast bantering back and forth. It was nice to have Danny back. Morgan and Bo'orchu were just ahead with their heads together, talking about something or other. A man, who had gone ahead returned in a cloud of dust and spoke to Bo'orchu.

He shouted back to us, 'We have our caravan Will!' He and Morgan spurred their horses into a gallop. We were quick to follow, and as we crested a low hill, Cairo lay before us, still a village but now a big one, almost a town.

I saw three caravans but one stood out over the others. Two dozen pack horses, as many camels, some donkeys and waggons drawn by zebus. There was a flurry of activity and a score of men mounted horses and left, just as we rode up. Bo'orchu stepped down from his horse and started conversing with a tall slender semite in black yellow trimmed robes. Bo'orchu acknowledged our later arrival by waving me up. I dismounted and took note of the man before me. As I said, he was tall and slender with deep set eyes a long nose and thin lips surrounded by a pointed beard and moustache. He watched us approach, his face expressionless. Morgan joined me and one eyebrow arched just a little when he realized she was a woman.

Bo'orchu took me arm. 'This is the Englishman I just mentioned, Sir William Barrow Arthur. May I introduce Kareesh Al Saud the owner of this caravan.'

I bowed me head 'Salaam Alaikum.'

A small smile touched his lips as his hand went to his heart. 'As-salaamu' alaikum' He studied me fer a moment. 'You speak well for a foreigner. Not many learn our greetings. Please, sit.' He waved us to stools and cushions.

'May I introduce me wife, Morgan and me close friends Danny and Uri.'

He acknowledged each with a bow and salaam and he did not slight Morgan, which pleased me immensely.

He made a gracious motion in the direction of the Mongols. 'We have worked together in the past, but I do not know you. There may come a time when you have to give your life for my property. Do you understand this? Bo'orchu gives you good references so I am inclined to hire you. There will be three weeks before I return to the east. I will use some of that time to make up my mind.' He clapped his hands and a black man appeared by his side. 'Bring us coffee and sweets.'

'Yes my lord.'

I watched as he walked away, wondering.

'So, you wish to see the Silk Road? I have moved caravans back and forth on it for most of my adult life and it never ceases to amaze me. Yes, it is fraught with dangers but I find it all worthwhile.'

'The whole world is filled with danger, Sir.' Morgan watched him from under her heavy brows. 'England gave us as much as we could handle and it was worthwhile. What makes this worthwhile?'

'Ah, here are our refreshments. Take pause a moment while you are served.'

I received me coffee in a small cup and chose a pale pink translucent confection covered in a white powder. I bit into it to be rewarded with a subtle fruity taste that was pleasing. Morgan's hand was hoverin over the plate as she tried to make up her mind. 'Try one of these.' I showed her mine. She nodded and took an orange one. Her expression showed her approval.

'What are these, Sir? Oh, and as me wife asked, what makes your dangers worthwhile?'

Kareesh Al Saud laughed aloud. 'I will try to answer both questions. These confections are made from fruit juices, the usual being apricot, peach, orange and pomegranate. We call them fruits of heaven. Now, as to your question,' and he turned to Morgan 'Its simple really. The changing country is beautiful and the many cultures fascinating, profits abound and all are worth a few risks.'

I liked him even more, a man after me own heart. 'Will you tell us how you will proceed? Do you go to Jerusalem?'

He sipped coffee. 'Yes, I must visit an old friend. From there we will pass through Lebanon into Syria, enter Iraq and go to Baghdad. From there...we'll see. Much depends on successful trading and news of the road.'

Morgan looked up. 'What news are you expecting?'

'Bands of rogues have been getting bolder, our riches enticing them. One group of outlaws in particular are being a major problem. They don't just rob but slaughter and rape along the Iraqi Iranian border. The rulers of both countries mustered a joint military campaign...to no avail.'

Uri grimaced. 'Looks like you need us more than you know. Hire some callow men and I will train them in different tactics than those, you are used to.'

Al Saud looked Uri up and down. 'And just who are you? What tactics do you speak of?'

'I am Uri of the Swiss Pike and I know how to repel horses. This I can teach and give you an edge over other caravans.'

He smirked as he said, 'I suppose I...'. I chose that moment to butt in. 'Ye should listen, he has saved me arse more times than I can count.'

Al Saud looked at Bo'orchu who nodded. 'Very well, you are hired. I will bring men for your appraisal. You can choose up to thirty. Their and your wages will be commensurable to your deeds.'

I looked again, to Bo'orchu fer confirmation. He smiled and gave a slight nod in assent.

Al Saud, Morgan and I sat in the shade and watched Uri who, with some help from Danny, was putting some young men and older boys through their paces. Under the Swiss' stern tutorship,

199

they were learning fast. He picked them young because they tended to be braver, had less imagination and less garbage in their heads.

There was a commotion at the corner of me eye that caught me full attention. A long line of black men, were shuffling down the road, making a lot of dust. Arabs on horseback were on every side. I watched closely as they went past us. A long chain ran through iron collars for at least two hundred feet. Another ran between their legs with ankle bracelets attached to it with short chains just long enough to shuffle.

I spoke to Al Saud. 'These men are obviously slaves, why so many blacks?'

'They are cheap and profitable to the slavers.'

'How so? Most slaves are prisoners of war and come with some cost attached. Are ye at war with these blacks?'

He smiled and shook his head. 'The slavers buy these people from their own kings, for the most part. A pound of salt will buy a hundred men. It is more valuable to them than gold or ivory, which they also sell to the Arabs, for salt.'

I grimaced, 'A rich, profitable enterprise but one I find not to my liking.'

'You are against slavery?'

'Aye, I am. Many of our serfs were as good as, slaves to their lords. They were, taxed beyond their ability to pay and then suffered outrageous punishment fer it. I was more than fortunate and now could be a lord at home. I learned from me second da that common folk can be treated fairly and with due respect.' I sighed. 'He was a lord of another sort, a very special man.' I lowered me head, thinking back.

Al Saud poured three cups of water laced with fruit juice and pushed one into me hands and the other over to Morgan who had been listening or nodding off. 'I would have liked to have met this man I would believe that you are much like him.'

I smiled. 'I can only hope so sir' I paused and looked up to a loud commotion. Three of the Arab horsemen were using their kurbashes on a slave, showing no mercy. I jumped up, reaching fer me sword when Al Saud gripped me arm firmly. 'No interference, English, you will die for it. You are a foreigner and a potential slave to them.'

I allowed him to stop me. Morgan came to me side and linked her arm to me sword arm.

'Don't be rash Will. Custom is different hereabouts.'

I looked at her, wanting to kiss her. 'It was a reaction, that's all' I looked over Morgan's shoulder at me host and on a whim I said 'Can I buy him?'

'I thought you were against slavery.'

'I am, but I want to buy him and free him.'

'You English are crazy. Go to one of the slavers, and give him a little gold. A couple of dinars will do. Ask that he be marked as sold and tell them to stop beating him, you do not want your property damaged. You'll be able to pick him up and pay for him tomorrow at the auction block.'

I did as I was told, and without mishap. I had a good look at me purchase as he glowered back, His shoulders raw and eyes full of hate. I was glad that he was chained and not near a weapon.

# **BEMBE UTA**

The night's coolness vanished with a hiss as the sun broke the horizon. Dogs chased an errant hyena as it headed fer cover. It turned at bay a couple of times, with its hideous laugh, scattering dogs left and right. Chasing was one thing catching was something else. Several early risers were laughing at the show and I asked one what a hyena was doing here?

'They sneak into town for an easy meal, dogs, cats, food scraps whatever. If it found you sleeping it would bite your face off.'

That gave me pause and I resolved to make sure tent flaps were secure in the future.

A sleepy voice said. 'What's all the fuss?' and Morgan hunched from our tent, shading her eyes.

I got up and took her arm to help her up. 'A little entertainment me love. Shall we find breakfast?' I looked at me beautiful wife in a snow white, cool kaftan and wondered why I was still wearin hot mail.

After we had eaten, Al Saud Accompanied the four of us to the auction, he nodded approval to Morgan who had veiled her lower face. She was learnin fast.

It was hot and dusty again and I pitied the long line of black men in their chains. Sheltering awnings had been erected fer the buyers and refreshments were offered, by a number of young boys, property of the slavers.

I could feel Morgan's finger nails biting into the back of me hand, she wasn't happy here.

Danny hunched forward, gave me a prod and pointed, 'That's yer man, Will.'

There he was tenth in the row. He'd been bashed and beaten but didn't look at all subdued. I gritted me teeth and waited. I felt Uri's presence just off me left shoulder. He had drawn and grounded his sword point, putting on a nice little show. I looked like someone of substance with bodyguards and all.

One by one slaves were removed from the chain. The hobbles stayed around their ankles but the collar was removed, leavin a raw red weal around their necks. First on the block was a handsome boy of about fourteen years. He staggered, as he was roughly pushed, up the steps. The auctioneers' voice began its intonation as a slaver shoved fat fingers into the boy's mouth, prying his jaws apart to show white teeth.

If anything, Morgan's fingers dug in even more.

His loin cloth was torn away leaving him naked and showing him to be already well endowed. A fat patron with slobbery lips made the first bid with three hundred gold dinars. The auction was underway and after some bidding, back and forth, slobbery lips got the boy. I cringed fer him, poor lad.

Finally, mine came up and Al Saud told me to present me self. There would be no bidding fer this one. A price of four hundred gold dinars had been set. I tried haggling but had to pay, though they seemed quite happy to see the last of him. I asked the auctioneer to have the man's leg irons knocked off. He looked at me as if I had lost me mind but shrugged and did as I asked. Two Arabs with drawn swords stood nearby.

Me black man was staring at me with puzzlement. His eyes never left mine as they drove the pins out of his shackles with hammer and awl. I knew it had to be painful but he didn't show it. He was tall with tight curly hair, broad shoulders and a deep chest. His legs were powerful too. He was a handsome man with deep set eyes a straight nose, and full lips. I put me hand on his arm and motioned fer him to walk with us. As soon as we had distanced ourselves from that awful market, I had him sit in a shady spot as I applied me special horse liniment to his neck, shoulders and ankles. He sat stoically through the whole procedure, watching us closely as I worked on him. Al Saud spoke to him with no results and turned to me. 'Perhaps one of my boys can interpret when we get back to the caravan.'

The language barrier was finally broken, at least a little. Al Saud's houseboy knew a few dialects. We learned that his name was Bembe Uta and his people were from far to the south. I explained to him that he was a free man and could return home if he wished. He told us, haltingly, that his king had sold him so he could not or would not return home.

It took some time before he fully understood that he was free and that his life was, once again, his own. When it finally hit home, his face lit up in a smile that was worth all the gold I had spent. He began singing in his own tongue, his voice deep and mellow. It was like a psalm and we all sat, transfixed.

Days passed, and Bembe, after being introduced to the Mongols, was accepted by them as an equal. Our food and water agreed with him and his wrinkled skin healed and smoothed out. With the help of Moto, Al Sauds' house boy, I began teaching Bembe some pharsi. I decided English was out. I needed to improve on me own pharsi and Mongolian anyway.

I say Mongolian but I should clarify. They have many dialects and other languages incorporated as their own, including Mandarin Chinese and Russian. I was learning a dialect called Bur'yat.

Bembe, though ignorant, was very intelligent and learned quickly. It was as if he needed to talk to us. To understand who and what we were. He had only brushed against this world, and in chains. Everything was new and exciting, even frightening.

The four of us made sure he felt welcome and was a friend, never property. He still could not fathom his good fortune. Finally, he was hale and fully healed and we took him to the market. He needed clothing and weapons. I felt these would be the very things to proclaim his freedom and status among us. Danny and Uri grabbed him first and took him to a smithies shop displaying weapons. Morgan and I sat, waiting in the shade, drinking sweet black coffee and nibbling on figs. The vendor was most solicitous I think he had fallen in love. I smiled at me wife, enjoying the impact she made on these people. I nodded towards the dim shop.

'You've captured another soul. What will you do with them all?'

She grinned cheekily I could see it under her veil. 'Save them for when you are away my dear.'

Me retort was interrupted, by the three men. Bembe was carrying a sheaf of javelins, a large double bitted ax and a dirk with nowhere to put them.

Morgan raised an eyebrow. 'You can't pack all that around like that. You need clothing, belts and straps. Now its my turn to take you shopping. Let us go and see what we can find, shall we?'

Bembe beamed, 'Yes Inkosi' kaas. These rags stink of iron!'

'What is that word you called me?'

'Inkosi'kaas, it means queen.'

'I am not your or anyone else's queen. You will call me by my name and if you wish to be more formal and polite, you can put Lady in front of it. Is that understood my friend?'

'Yes Lady Morgan.'

'Good, let's go shopping.'

'Do ye want Uri or Danny to go with ye? I'm going to find Bo'orchu. We'll be leaving in two days.'

'Bembe and I will be fine. You take them with you, I don't need them underfoot. We will see you later.'

As soon as we parted company, Uri went to find his lads and arrange a marching order. They were to be half way along the train. I found Bo'orchu quick enough and we went over our own marching plans, looking fer improvement. Danny, bless him, went to water our horses. When I was satisfied, I went to clean and oil mail and weapons. I took the time to oil Morgan's as well.

They returned near to supper time. Bembe was transformed, and it showed in his every fiber. A leopard skin kilt with a belt pouch, water bottle and sheathed dirk, girded his loins. The javelins were in a quiver across his back along with a rolled, red dyed blanket. The axe was in his right hand and looked like it belonged there, a statement of just who he was. Morgan looked very pleased with herself.

'You didn't buy him sandals!'

'He will not wear them. I tried.'

We could see the low hills of Jerusalem in the hazy distance. So far, our trek had been uneventful and we had time to get comfortable with our duties and routines. Bembe had taken to Morgan and had become her virtual bodyguard. I couldn't be any happier knowing she was being looked after.

Al Saud had confided that his friend in Jerusalem was holding a large bale fer him. It was saffron from Crete and worth a fortune. He explained, it was harvested from the stamen of a special crocus, only grown in Greece, Crete and a little in Turkey. It was to be 'protected' at all costs.

'What do ye use it fer?'

'It is a flavoring spice for cooking and is popular mixed with rice. It is expensive because each flower gives so little. My bale will probably represent twenty thousand flowers or more and could, alone, pay for half this journey.'

Bo'Orchu chose that moment to ride up and must have heard the last of the conversation, 'By all means, we must defend it. I have enjoyed its flavor in the past.' He chuckled. 'Will, ride with me, there is some commotion on the road ahead, we need to check it out.'

I nodded and took me leave of Al Saud. I nudged Storm to a cantor to keep up with the Mongol.

The sun blazed on a long disgruntled line of traffic stopped in its tracks. Being on horseback, we could get by most of them, taking a few muffled curses here and there. Women, hidden in their burqas, stood about. They must have stifled inside those things with only their eyes showing. Unhappy camels were groaning their lamentations and an ass kept on braying and braying and wouldn't shut up. A huge sinkhole or some kind of cave in had destroyed the road and men were gathering ropes to help someone within. There was no reason to stay, there were more than enough men helping already. I did notice several standing about that wore black headdresses, trimmed in red, that covered their faces. They weren't helping and nearby people seemed nervous, even frightened around them. I took special note of one, he was looking me over with his face uncovered. His was a handsome but cruel face sporting a slender curved beard. I whispered to me friend about him and he took note. As we returned to the caravan, I asked Bo'Orchu how a sinkhole would happen here in this arid place. He said that there were many underground streams and rivers, especially in the wet season. The water receded the sandy soil dried up and a cave in occurred.

As soon as we got back, Bo'Orchu spoke to Al Saud. 'Do you know another way? This one is definitely blocked and the land on each side doesn't look good either, too rough and rocky.'

The Arab gasped with annoyance. 'We are so near and now must go around? There is a path, about three miles back. We will have to take it, I do not like it but that is the nearest alternate route.'

I expressed me concern about the veiled men. 'They could be herding us to where they want us.'

'There is nowhere else to go. This truly is bad news. I don't need bandits at my doorstep this early in our trip.'

Bo'orchu placed his hand on me shoulder as he spoke to Al Saud. 'Let's take it one step at a time. We are forewarned and they will find us a dangerous adversary.'

Off we went, turning the caravan was chaotic but we got it done. Danny and one of Al Saud's men went to scout ahead. I trusted Danny he was a damn good scout, he had learned from the best. Bembe stopped me. 'Why are we going back?'

'The road has collapsed and is impassable. Keep yer eyes and ears open, there might be trouble brewing. I don't know the country ahead and our leader isn't happy. Bo'Orchu and I are putting everyone on alert.'

Bembe nodded, 'I will be vigilant.'

We were about three miles into new territory when we saw a rapidly approaching dust cloud, Danny returning at the gallop. He was leading the other horse with the Arab slumped over its neck. An arrow protruded from his shoulder. Men helped get him down and carried him into some shade as Danny reported to me.

'There's a canyon up ahead, Will. I spotted men in the rocks. They realized we had seen them and so began fireing on us. Tareed wasn't lucky and caught one. I don't think they followed but they will be waiting. They hold a position of power up in them rocks.'

We stopped to take council of war. Trying fer a run through them was folly and our retreat, well it was, probably cut off. I advocated fer a night raid to whittle them down and unnerve them. Just a few volunteers were needed, nine or ten in all, to raise some havoc. Uri, Danny, Bembe and Morgan were the first. I looked at me wife and realized she wanted this to prove herself to the men around her. Up to now, many considered her a female upstart playing in armor. Bembe was with her and I knew he would watch her back. He needed to learn exactly who he was guarding, anyway. Three Mongols and two Arabs stepped up. We had our number. Bo'Orchu stayed with the caravan. There was always a chance of a rear attack, or other unforeseen events, and the wounded Tareed needed doctering.

Crouching in the black shadows, Uri and I watched as two men spoke in low voices. They were relaxed, and hovered by a small fire, chilled by the night air. The fire was good for us it messed up their night vision. The rest of our party had spread out to cover other guards that had been marked. Now, we needed to take them quietly. It was always possible that we had missed one or two in the shadowy star light. There was no moon this night. I knew where Morgan and Bembe were, the rest were out of sight.

One man knelt to tend the fire while the other looked up at the night sky. That was our cue. Uri signaled that he would take the left. Two throttling arms and two flashing dirks left two men dead on the ground. I pulled mine away from the fire, the smell of burning hair stank and someone might notice. Uri pulled the burnoose from his kill and threw it around his own shoulders, taking the man's place. I did the same. This allowed us to stand in the open and look about.

I spoke softly. 'There's two more on our left, one up in the rocks the other resting below.'

Uri squeezed me arm to acknowledge, and I strung me bow. Morgan and Bembe made their move and two more died. The guard in the rocks noticed something was off and began to yell when me arrow took him in the throat. Uri sprang into the darkness to dispatch the other man, in the act of getting up.

The camp was awake now and we threw stealth to the wind. We chose targets and attacked, moving to join Morgan and Bembe. I saw Danny and two Mongols. They were slightly overwhelmed and I pointed to them with me sword. Uri and I moved as one, to help. Men were now coming from every quarter. We killed or wounded many but now it was time to retreat. Uri, on me signal, blew a blast on his horn to let our camp know we were coming. Forming a circle, we began our withdrawal. There was no sign of our two Arabs or the other Mongol, yet.

It seemed like ferever until we reached flat ground. Three men were running toward us with others on their heels.

I yelled. 'Let them in!'

One, stumbled and went down, it was the Mongol. Morgan who was closest ran to intercept with Bembe close behind. The surviving Arabs stayed to cover him as the two arrived, those chasing stopped short, not liking the odds. I heard a swishing sound overhead and arrows dropped out of the darkness. One bandit got skewered by a feathered shaft, and the rest retreated as fast as their legs would carry them. Another flight of arrows followed them into the rocks.

I grinned at Uri. We had not lost a man and had raised Cain. 'Let's go find something to eat this kind of thing always makes me hungry.'

Bo'Orchu had set up a line of archers to cover our retreat. The pike boys had set up to cover our rear. If anyone had tried to close, they had decided it was a lost cause and retreated, back into the night.

We ate as I brought Al Saud up to date. A conservative estimate brought their casualties to at least fourteen, six dead fer certain.

Al Saud was pleased. 'That went very well. You have all proved your worth beyond measure. What of tomorrow do you think we can pass safely?'

I nodded, 'Aye, We will scout as a precaution, but I think so.' Bo'Orchu concurred it seemed our joint leadership had come as naturally as our friendship.

We ate as the sun broke the horizon, and were ready to leave, soon after. The weather here never seemed to change. Hot and sunny with a few clouds from time to time. I asked Al Saud about it and he smiled.

'There are sandstorms than can bury us all, if caught unaware. It will get cooler in a few months and the rains, even some snow, will come. When they do we will be at a standstill. We need to be somewhere else and far from here by that time.'

'So, ye do have seasons.'

Danny returned to say the way was clear. The canyon abandoned. They had taken their dead too. He had also collected a large bundle of spent but unbroken arrows, which pleased the Mongols. I thought I heard Al Saud's audible sigh of relief.

Jerusalem! The sounds and smells were like any other city but there was a special feeling about this place. Steeped in history, coveted by three religions, this city was special indeed, filled with people from all over the known world. Al Saud granted us time to see the sights while he visited his friend. I set up a duty roster so everyone had some leave leaving the caravan still protected. Bo'Orchu sent four Mongols to watch after Al Saud.

Uri and Danny went off to find a sword Danny's was badly dented and ready to break. I trusted them not to find beer and get drunk. Morgan and I, with Bembe in tow, visited a market and she haggled over a hooded kaftan she liked. It was creamy yellow with green trim in the form of grape leaves. She got it at a very good price, me wife learned quickly. We bought three meals from a vendor and retired to a pretty, peaceful garden to eat. I asked around, from passersby, where places of interest were. One old man paused and sat with us. He liked to chat and pointed out the hill of Calvary and the Church of the Holy Sepulchre, for us. He told us how to get to the Wailing Wall and other places, churches and mosques. The old man's daughter showed up. At least I assume she was his daughter. She was somewhat perturbed that he was chatting with infidels.

'What are you doing? You must come away, at once!'

He got up with a groan, 'These old bones.' He took the girl's outstretched hand. 'Do not get flustered my dear. I am too old to get converted.' He turned to us. 'I enjoyed your company but must apologize for my daughter. Children today have no manners.' As he walked away on her arm, he turned. 'Oh, did you know that you might be sitting in the very garden where your Jesus was betrayed and arrested?'

Morgan and I just stared at each other, stunned. Bembe was looking a little puzzled and I knew there would be questions later.

I found out, later on, that the Garden of Gethsemane was actually an olive grove just outside the city. Al Saud set me straight. I should have asked him in the first place.

I gave Bembe some brief lessons on Christianity and they just stirred his curiosity even more. I learned that his gods were stern and steeped in magic and witchcraft. He finally sat down one evening after supper, and told us all, his story.

'I was a prince in my own land and I had fallen in love with a young maid from a rival tribe. My father, the King, was not happy at my choice and he forbade us to wed. We continued to meet in secret, defying his edicts. We were young with no thought to consequences. A baby boy was born out of wedlock, which we tried to keep secret. My love, Nindani, told her father in trust of what we had done. He turned on us and betrayed her because he feared the Kings displeasure even more than he loved his daughter. My father was a cruel tyrant, interested only in his own pleasures and lusts and using his people any way he saw fit, selling many into slavery for a handful of salt. His regiments assailed surrounding villages for more slaves. He and I had always been at odds about these things. When he found out about us, he saw an opportunity to rid himself of a thorny son. He had Nindani and our son put to death. In my grief and outrage, I tried to raise an army against him but all failed. His regiments were battle hardened and we were no match for them. He captured me and slaughtered my followers. Because of my popularity he sold me into slavery rather than have a dead martyr on his hands, inciting rebellion.' Bembe paused to stare into the fire and then looked at us. 'The only way I could return to my own land, would be at the head of an army to destroy everything my father stands for. My land is far away with many obstacles between. It is but a foolish dream.'

I thought a moment, the adventure enticing me, and then said, 'We could take a detour and help ye take yer throne.'

He smiled at Morgan and me, 'That would be a very big detour. The Silk Road is a much better option. I have found that I like learning and you are true friends who I would not risk on such a venture.'

Jerusalem was far behind us now as we crossed into Iraq, destination Baghdad on the Euphrates River. Once again it was bloody hot and I had discarded me mail and so did Uri. The hills ahead of us looked white under the blazing sun, looking as if they were covered in snow. Morgan sidled Taxeia over to me and took me arm. 'Look Will, over there.' Me eyes followed her pointing finger. 'What is that? It's a vortex of some kind.' Me eyes popped and I yelled, 'Al Saud, do ye see what's off our left hand?'

Yes, Bo'Orchu and I have been watching it for a while. It is traveling parallel to our path at the moment if it turns this way we might have trouble.'

Danny looked horrified, 'Turns?'

'They can be unpredictable if that cyclone gets near us we'll have a sand storm. If it hits us we will likely be dead. Ah, the wrath of Allah is upon us, it has turned!'

We all watched that growing, massive whirlwind with trepidation, now we could hear its howl and clouds of sand were rising to block out the sun.

Al Saud, who was looking for a haven, pointed to an indent between hills, about a mile away. 'We go there as fast as we can. Hut, Hut!' The command was to his camel. We followed suit and the ponderous caravan began to pick up speed. Sure enough the whirlwind had turned, not right at us but closing on our right quarter. Danny, Uri and all his men were on foot so I and the other horsemen started picking them up. Morgan lent an arm to a drover as Bembe ran at her stirrup and Bo'Orchu grabbed Uri. Danny was mine. The other Mongols were picking up men as quickly as possible. Some remaining men were shunted to the wagons, which were slower and bringin up the rear. Zebus were hardy beasts but not very fast. We were making our own dust cloud as we approached the indent which grew to be a dry, high walled wadi. The first wave of sand hit us as we entered its mouth, and we were all quick to cover our faces.

The wadi got wider further in and Al Saud was yelling for us to circle the caravan with animals and everyone facing center. Bo'Orchu was quick to act and I went to help. Waggons were circled and animals unhitched to be brought to center. Camels were quickly prodded to their knees.

The sand was buffeting us now and it was difficult to breathe. The horses heads were quickly covered with blankets or cloaks and those that we could we pulled down onto their sides. The howl turned to a shriek as the whirlwind neared and swirling sand blasted exposed skin makin it raw. The animals were amazing, staying still. Morgan and I cuddled each other and prayed.

It was over, the howl was diminishing and sunlight was making rays in the still dusty air. Morgan uncovered her head and I started laughing and then choking. Her face and nostrils were caked grey as was her clothing too. Everyone was the same. Getting up was difficult as we were buried past our knees. We started beating the dust from our clothing and were soon choking on it.

'Let's leave off till we have more space, I need some fresh air.' I heard several assents from around me.

Al Saud called out, 'Before all else use precious water and clean the nostrils and eyes of your animals. They must be protected at all costs.'

The animals had faired very well except fer one donkey who had succumbed to the sand. Its load was distributed around and we were thankful that it wasn't too big.

Danny went ahead to scout the land and returned in a jiff. He was as white as a sheet and it wasn't all dust. 'I don't fucking believe it! You have to come see! God, I don't fucking believe it.'

After that tirade, we all had to come see. The plain scoured by the wind had exposed a shocking sight. A swath of dead men thirty yards wide meandered across the plain for about half a mile. With me in the lead, we approached them. Tembe was too frightened and stayed back. 'Why are you scared Tembe?' Morgan looked worried. 'Ghosts, evil ghosts will live here. I pray you stay away.'

As we neared, Bo'Orchu rode up beside me. 'What do you make of this Will?' I stared at the mummified bodies, scattered and crumbled in heaps and singly, limp flags and pennants drooped on broken poles 'They are crusaders! Look there, three Hospitalier knights, more over there.'

'There are many more Templers and I see some independents.' Morgan knelt before a knight in scarlet and grey. The skin was like parchment over his skull like face and the dust left a patina on everything, making everything washed out and drained of color. Danny crouched beside her and reached out to touch the body. It collapsed into its self and the head bowed as if in prayer. Danny jumped back, a little startled. 'Shite! Crusaders yes but who are they?'

I climbed down from Storm looking over the army of dead men. 'I think they are some of King John's army. He stupidly marched out into the desert to fight the Saracens. They just played with his army until they were exhausted, separated and dying of thirst. John, was later captured, and his captains were put to death by Saladin fer crimes committed including the rape and murder of Saladin's sister. I'm not sure what happened to King John, perhaps he was killed or ransomed. These men all show wounds, they died here fighting a lost battle.'

Al Saud had come up beside us. 'I have seen this sort of thing before but never an army of men. A sandstorm covered them up preserving them and now a decade or so later, they are uncovered again. The sun and wind will decimate them more and more until either, they are turned to dust or are covered up again. I have seen a town appear and disappear in this way. This could be a place of Jins, Bembe might have cause for fear. Allah, have mercy on our souls.' He roused himself 'Let us leave this place we still have miles to go.'

The caravan was on the move again and I looked back several times at the recedin army of dead men. 'What a strange world we live in'. It took until Baghdad to get that image out of me head. It was all we had talked about over the next few days. The city was a roil with commerce of all kinds, sauks and slavers, and individual shops along the cities' wall. The minarets of several Mosques could be seen, gracefully poised against the sky, and on a low hill stood the royal palace. The guards at the gate were courteous but cool and didn't respond much to conversation.

Al Saud gave us leave to look around but warned us to be on our best behavior. These people did not like Franks, bin at war with them too long. Saladin was their hero and is still on the lips of many.

Morgan was very careful to wear her veil and have her hair covered, along with her floor length kaftan. We took in the sights without mishap, bought a few trinkets and ate cuscus and lamb from a vendor's stall. I had always liked lamb, especially chops and these kabobs were becomin a favorite of mine. I did miss a good pork roast though, not that I would mention it aloud. I wanted to hold hands with me wife but realized we couldn't even do that.

On our tour about the market places, we saw a large enclosure with many animal cages and went to look. We soon steered away from there feeling shocked and saddened by the retched animals within. There were lions, baboons, hyenas a leopard and two elephants, which I had never seen before. They were all living in squalor and it left me feeling guilty for some reason, perhaps fer me fellow man. We spoke of it as we went back to the caravan, I told Morgan about Uri's lion and how wild, strong and free it had been, not like those poor pathetic beasts we had just seen. We entered the confines of our caravan and Morgan hugged me arm. 'There's nothing we can do Will so let's cheer up and find something else to do.' We ran into Danny, he didn't go out into the city. I think he knew his limitations. I looked around fer Uri and Danny said he had gone with Al Saud and Bo'Orchu to arrange fer barges to cross the Euphrates.

'There is a perfectly good bridge there. In fact more than one, why can,t we use them?'

'They are restricted to the military and select individuals.'

I turned up me nose. 'What say we go fer an afternoon nap?'

'We could retire but don't expect to nap.' Morgan smiled saucily, I could see it through her veil, 'Dont you dare start snoring.' Bembe was honing his axe as we passed and smiled a greeting, which turned to a silent laugh when he saw what we were up to.

After crossing the busy river, our guard duties became a blur of boredom. Our routine passed from one day to another to another and so on. Danny had become a fidgety grouch, trying to pick fights with some of the men until Morgan yanked him to one side, and gave him what for and told him to get himself together.

One afternoon, just after lunch, the boredom went away. Something zipped past me face and a drover collapsed with an arrow through his neck. I yelled 'alarm' as a few more arrows fell among us without hitting anyone. Uri's men galvanized and the Mongols prepared their bows. We were all trying to get our bearings when a line of horsemen appeared up on a rise to our left, numbering about a hundred. Three separated from the main group and approached us at the gallop. Bo'Orchu Uri and I jumped on our horses and went to meet them. Al Saud came galloping up behind us so we slowed to let him catch up. The two parties reined to a halt about ten feet apart. I recognized their leader right off. The man with the spade beard I had seen at the road cave in. His hawkish eyes singled me out and bored into mine, and his greeting was rude, 'Salaam, infidel.'

'Salaam alaikum. Why do you shoot arrows at us and then want to talk?'

'To get your attention, Frank!'

I knew he was baiting me but didn't rise to it. Bo'Orchu glared at him. 'You killed one of our drovers.'

'He was of no consequence.' His face was an arrogant sneer, 'Soon I may kill you all.'

'You tried once before, before Jerusalem. You didn't fare well then, what makes you think you could do better now?'

'I have a hundred warriors on that hill and another hundred and fifty behind. If you pay my price you may yet live for a while.'

Al Saud spoke up. 'What is your name shufta, and what is it you want?'

Spade beard spat on the ground in front of Al Saud. 'You are of Islam and fraternize with cursed unbelievers from two sides of the world? I am Eban Samuli and I want your entire cargo of saffron then you can go on your way.'

Al Saud looked startled. 'How did you….? You will beggar me.'

Samuli's laugh was cold and humorless, 'Better a living beggar than a dead merchant.'

'What guarantee do we have that we will live?'

The cold laugh came again. 'None at all, it is possible that Allah will strike you all dead as we speak.'

'Enough of this prattle come and take it if you can!' Al Saud reared his horse onto its hind legs. 'Back to the caravan and make ready!'

As we raced back me shoulder blades tightened with anticipation of an arrow. Our Mongols had been ready all this time and had us covered. Uri left his horse at the run and took charge of his pike. I yelled to Morgan to get our mail ready. Bo'Orchu and Al Saud rushed to prepare the caravan for attack.

'Who is threatening us Will?' Morgan took me arm and turned me around she already had her armor on. 'I armored myself with Bembe's help as we waited. Here,' she helped remove me burnoose and fitted me Gambeson tightning buckles. I slipped me mail over me head. "I'm ready. Its the same group we had problems with before Jerusalem. They underestimated us back then but now they are wiser, worst luck fer us.'

The black clad bandits, or shufta as Al Saud called them, had disappeared from view. We had fifteen pike men on each side of the caravan with a cleared central space for one side to help the other if needed. Uri had trained all the caravan drovers and other personnel to fight with sword, ax, club and spear. They were to defend the pike and themselves if breeched. The Mongols were on horseback and ready to do what Mongols do best, mobile archery.

As suddenly as they had left the Arab cavalry was back. Two crescent shaped lines of roughly seventyfive warriors in each. I hadn't spotted the remainder yet. I shouted, 'Al Saud, There are a hundred not accounted for. Beware!'

He raised his scimitar in acknowledgement. Danny, Morgan and I mounted our chargers and Bembe took his place at Morgan's stirrup. 'We are in deep trouble dearest, outnumbered at least four to one. We don't have enough pike to protect the entire caravan.' I leaned down and whispered into Bembe's ear. 'If it comes down to our defeat, my lady must not fall into their hands. Do you understand?' Bembe nodded grimly and it was then I noticed movement on a rise to our left. It must be the other hundred. Squinting against the bright sun I tried to make them out.

Bo'Orchu let out a whoop and galloped straight for them. I could see better now and realized it was a Mongol army, how many I couldn't tell yet. As Bo'Orchu neared, one broke away and met him. They jumped down from their horses, embraced and spoke for some time. The watching shufta were getting agitated.

There was increasing activity amongst the Mongols and squadrons started forming ranks, five ranks in all.

Bo'Orchu returned at the gallop, whooping all the way. He piled off his horse almost into me arms. His face was one big grin. 'It's my brother, it's Subukii.'

I gave him a joyful shake, 'What's yer brother doing wondering around the desert with an army?' I grinned at Morgan and Bembe 'I've changed me mind dearest. We are not in deep trouble after all.'

The Mongols had been advancing and I could see them better. The first two ranks were heavily armored, their horses too and the last three were light cavalry with bows. As they approached, the shufta just faded away.

There would be no bloodshed this day. Subukii stepped down from his horse. He was wearing armor I had never seen before, made from slats of lacquered wood and some kind and bronze. He doffed his helmet, which was very ornate with stylized bronze wings and such, and greeted Bo'Orchu with another shoulder hug, and said something that had them both laughing.

Bo'Orchu waved to me, 'Will come meet my brother," he said something and Subukii sobered. The man I faced looked a lot like his brother but had a close cropped beard, and shoulder length loose hair. I bowed me head, 'I am Sir William Barrow Arthur at your service.' I spoke in broken Buryat and Bo'Orchu slapped me on the back with a grin. 'That was very good Will.'

The Mongol smiled and bowed, 'I am Subukii and pleased to make your acquaintance. He turned to Morgan who had just stepped up, and bowed again 'My Lady.' His smile was genuine.

I asked how we were so fortunate to have his men show up when they did?

'Just luck, we are in search of someone and now we have crossed paths. My brother knows my men and he may choose fifteen to stay with the caravan, providing you all keep your eyes and ears open. I need any and all information.'

Bo'Orchu draped his arm over his brothers' shoulders. 'Thank you brother now let's go and speak in private.'

I watched them leaving and then went to find the others and bring them up to date. Uri was fascinated, 'Look at that armor even the first two rows of horses are armored. They might even give the pike a bad time.'

Sengge was passin by and I called him over. 'Perhaps you can rid us of our ignorance. We need your assistance.'

He laughed, his pigtails stickin out all over. ' I am not a miracle worker, what is it you want to know?'

'How long have the Mongol armies adopted the formations we just saw?'

'Over a hundred years ago the Great Khan developed the Mongol battle array and conquered the world using it.'

'You always say the Great Khan, did he have a name?'

Sennge tried to look wise making us all laugh. 'He began his life as Temujiin and after suffering years of trials and imprisonment he became Genghis Khan, Lord of the thousand eyes. Much that was his has since fallen apart because of the inability of weaker men. His great grandson still rules the Golden Horde in Eastern Europe and the son of Kublai Khan rules the Yuan dynasty in China. His legacy still lives and now another comes to take up the reins.'

'Sennge stop babbling!' Bo'Orchu looked angrily at his friend, 'You must have duties to carry out? Please Will, no more questions for the time being. I have spoken to Al Saud and we are taking a more northerly route across northern Persia to the border with Turkmenistan. We will pause in Tehran for more trading.' He scratched his nose with his little finger almost absent mindedly. 'All of us must remain vigilant, the shufta will still be shadowing us, of that I am sure.'

We did not see the shufta over the next month. Winter swept in and summer fled before it. It wasn't icy like in England but still cold and we shivered a lot. The rains came down in sheets and ye could really believe ye were drowning sometimes. With the rain came the mud and we were not moving. We settled on doing chores, keeping the animals happy and our armor and weapons rust free. Morgan and I had an argument over somethin stupid, I don't even remember. We didn't talk for a couple of days. Ah, but then we made up and the whole camp had something new to gossip about. The backgammon game made its rounds and I learned a dice and tile game from the Mongols. Every evening after supper was story time. The Mongols were a bunch of hams and some of the heroic epics cited had everyone in stitches. We needed something to make us laugh, life was such a bore during that month. Despite the mud, small scouting groups of Mongols would survey the land every second day or so.

Finally, the weather turned fer the better. We had to wait the short part of a week fer things to dry up and then we were on our way. It was still cool but the sun let ye know there was heat to come. Flowers sprouted everywhere and the desert was transformed into a glorious garden.

Tehran was a fortress city of some scope. There were beautiful things to see, parks, mosques and palaces, and of course the usual souks or markets. There were exotic peoples from places unknown to us.

Morgan came to me one afternoon, all excited. 'Will I have heard about a great man, a scholar and poet, he died some time ago and is enshrined in a beautiful place not too far from the city. Kareesh said we would be here for two more days. Could we go see?'

I had to laugh at her excitement, Morgan wasn't usually that way but she had taken to the antiquities of the east. I thought, 'why not.' 'We will go tomorrow providing Al Saud or Kareesh as you call him says it is alright.'

Al Saud smiled when I asked. 'I would go myself if I had time. Yes and take four Mongols with you. It isn't far but could still be dangerous if the wrong people are about. It is a well traveled, area so you will not be alone. Remember it is the shrine of a venerated man, Omar Khayyam is his name a poet, scholar and mathematician.'

We arrived without incident in Nishapur and soon found the Mausoleum of Imamzadeh Maruq. The Khayyam garden was there, a delicate structure of open arches shaded his tomb. The surrounding gardens were truly beautiful. Many Moslems said prayers there so we tried to stay back a little. It was a peaceful idyllic place with no room for discord. Morgan was so happy we had come and I was too. Even Bembe, Danny and the Mongols seemed at peace. Strife was too common in these lands and this place refreshed one for a moment or so.

It was getting dark when we left. It was a short journey on horseback and still plenty of people were about. Danny looked back at us. 'I think we are being watched, be on guard, ye never know.'

I trusted his instincts and so did the Mongols who had come to the same conclusion. They gave no outer sign but were ready. Bembe was the only one on foot but holding Morgan's stirrup he could run as fast as the horse, if it came to that, no one would be, left behind. There was a lull in traffic as we got closer to Tehran and the attack came out of the darkening shrubbery along the road. Black clad forms materialized out of nowhere and glimmering steel met our steel. Danny dived off his horse onto an Arab trying to ventilate a Mongol. They rolled back and forth under the horses' hoofs each struggling to win. Danny came up and with a Scottish war cry leaped at another man yanking him off his feet. No time to look for Danny anymore, we were fighting fer our lives. I don't know how many there were. Bembe Morgan and I fought, shoulder to shoulder, killing or wounding several men. Things were getting a little rough when we heard a blast on a horn. A few minutes later, cavalry came thundering down the road from the city, resplendent in their chainmail and pointed helms. Once again, the black clad Arabs vanished into the darkness. This time they left their dead. Our saviors were the guard from the city. Travelers had seen our predicament and called for them. The young captain looked annoyed when he realized we were European but recovered a bit when he saw the dead men. As he stepped down from his horse, a Mongol spoke to him. He listened politely before nodding and with a foot he rolled a body over. He spat and muttered 'Shufta.' He turned to me and said, 'Do you understand me?' in pharsi.

'Salaam Alaikum, yes captain I do.'

He acknowledged me greeting with a slight bow. 'What happened here?'

'We were set upon on the way back from Omar Khayyam's shrine.'

'Why were you there?'

'He was a great man and it was a beautiful place.'

The captain seemed somewhat mollified, 'These men you fought were Shufta and a particularly bad bunch at that. Why were they so interested in you?'

'I am with Al Sauk's caravan and they beset us twice, once before Jerusalem and again after we left Baghdad. Mongols came to our aid the second time.'

'And the first time?'

'They underestimated us and retreated.'

He looked at Morgan in her mail and frowned. 'You all will return to your caravan but be prepared for more questioning. I will send someone to clean up this unsightly mess.' He mounted his horse and with a stiff salute headed back to the city his men following sharply.

Al Sauk sat back and sipped coffee as we related our adventures. 'This shufta leader seems to have developed a grudge against us. We are making him lose face and by the size of his small army, he is collecting smaller bands together and making himself an Emir of sorts. If he cannot prove himself, he may lose them again. There is no honor amongst thieves and he will only keep them with success and profits. I am amazed you did not lose any men in this encounter.'

'It might have been different if the cavalry hadn't shown up.' I grinned, 'They are a sharp looking lot.'

'They are very good fighters too Will, they are the Shah's own household guard. Did you get the name of the young captain?'

'No I did not he was very young though, not much more than a boy.'

'I believe I know him. He is a little older than he looks and don't let looks fool you. His name is Turin Nahib and he is the son of a good friend of mine. He knows me very well and I think we will have heard the end of it, he won't be back to ask questions.'

# **Timur**

## 🙎

We were on the border of Turkmenistan two days march to a city called Asgabat. Early summer had finally reached the high country and I was enjoying the warmth as I chatted with Bo'Orchu. There had bin no more incidences for at least a month and a half and then I heard the cry fer help. I heard it again, almost lost on the wind and looked about. High up in the rocks I saw an arm wave and then the body attached to it. I yelled fer Danny and Uri who were back apiece.

'Do not leave the caravan!' Al Saud was quite agitated, 'It could be a trap.' He had seen enough of traps this trip.

I looked at Bo'orchu who just shrugged and drew his bow from its saddle scabbard. 'I'll cover you.'

Uri and Danny arrived in a cloud of dust and I pointed, 'Let's have a look.' I dismounted, swung the broadsword to me back and began to climb. Me two friends were close on me heels when I heard Morgan's voice, making me look back down.

'What are you up to now?'

Al Saud spoke in her ear loud enough fer me to hear, 'Talk some sense to your headstrong husband, this is dangerous country.'

Morgan laughed, 'He won't listen to me anymore that I would to him.'

He threw up his hands. 'We cannot wait!'

'Of course we can Kareesh dear.' She looked up at the three of us. 'Go do what you do, I'll make them wait.'

Bo'Orchu grinned, enjoying himself immensely. 'I will help you Lady, guards be alert.'

The man I was approaching was tall dark and slim and by his garb I guessed he was Moslem. 'Salaam Alaikum, what is yer difficulty, friend?'

'As-Salaamu 'Alaikum,' he touched fingers to heart and lips. 'My brother in law is sorely wounded and we have been here for some time. I couldn't leave him for fear wild beasts or his enemies would find him.'

He stepped slightly to one side and I was looking down on a young man in a very bad way. An arrow had embedded just above his right knee and his right hand wrapped in bloody rags. I yelled back down the mountain. 'Morgan, would ye fetch the medical kit and tell Al Saud this is not a trap.'

I knelt and cut away clothing exposing the leg above the knee. It was a mess, swollen and mottled, pus would have to be drained and quickly. While I waited I checked his hand, there was no real infection yet but he had lost his little and ring fingers. One still hung by a thread so I cut it loose. The young man chose that moment to wake up. He stared at us with fever burning eyes becoming quite agitated at our strange faces. I turned to the other.

'Show yer self to him he needs a familiar face.'

He knelt by him, 'Timur, Timur, it is I Husayn. You are badly wounded and these men are here to help.'

He calmed down, his eyes focusing and watching our faces. A sharp surge of pain made him grimace in agony and he gritted his teeth making no sound.

Morgan arrived creating a bit of a stir they weren't used to seeing a woman in mail, let alone a beautiful one. I introduced her as me wife and opened the small chest. First I fed him a pain killer made from the poppy. As his breathing eased I turned to me wife, 'Would ye cleanse and stitch his hand? I'm going fer the leg.'

Uri was right there to help and Danny stood watch. I took a sharp lancet from the instrument case, washed it and his leg with Arak and cut deeply right above the knee. Pus boiled out like custard along with the broken off arrowhead. It was that easy! Uri wiped away the filth as I squeezed the thigh down towards the knee. More pus came until it was mixed with blood, then just blood. I inspected the wound and grunted, 'I think the leg is clear, there is no darkness around the bone, with a little luck and a prayer he won't lose it.' I bled it some more, washed the whole area with more Arak, put ointments in the wound, stitched it and bandaged with clean bandages.

The young man expelled his breath with a shudder. He had been watching the whole time. 'Most of your kind are butchers when it comes to medicine.' His voice was weak, 'Where did you learn to do all that?'

I gripped his shoulder gently, 'It's a long story lad, when ye are better perhaps I can tell ye about it.'

Husayn scowled at me, 'He is Lord Timur to you infidel!'

The young man pushed up on one elbow, 'Hussayn!' he admonished, 'Do not be rude to our saviors, they did not know me and now own my life.' He collapsed back, weakly.

I smiled down at him, 'Lord Timur, I am sorry to say ye'll likely have a limp fer the rest of yer days, if ye keep the leg. We will do our best to see that it is so. Let me introduce me self, Sir William Barrow Arthur at yer service, me friends call me Will.

Bo'Orchu chose that moment to approach. 'My Lord, there have been search parties looking for you nearly three months now. Know that you are safe in the hands of this man and you are safe in mine.'

After making a litter, four Mongols carried him into camp. Hussayn was weak from hunger and thirst so Danny and Uri supported him down the steep rocky hill. Me first impression of the man was one of dislike. It wasn't because he had been rude, that was of no matter, he gave off a bad aura and I didn't trust him. Danny made sure he had water right away and food was prepared immediately.

Lord Timur stayed among the Mongols it was as if they weren't letting him out of their sight. I waylaid Bo'Orchu at me first opportunity.

'All this bloody secrecy! He is the one you've all bin looking for, isn't he. Ye could have trusted me ye know. By the way he's bin missing fer almost three months and he received those wounds more recently than that. They are perhaps a week old maybe a bit more.'

Bo'Orchu sighed, I am sorry Will, Subukii swore me to secrecy politics demanded it. I knew you could be trusted along with your people but no one could know of Lord Timur's dilemma' there might be enemy agents in this camp. The shufta were also dangerous if they knew about the Lord's difficulties.'

'You are all lucky that it was me that found him then and not someone else. Now, I would like to know what is going on, don't leave me in the dark any more me friend.'

'Tonight when we stop, join us for the evening meal and bring your wife and friends. My trust extends to them all.'

The firelight cast ripples of light and shadow across Lord Timur's face. His eyes already sparkled with renewed vigor as he smiled at us. 'Join us for some food and I will try to explain a few things.'

I bowed, 'Thank ye fer yer welcome Lord. Where is yer friend Husayn?'

'Being a devout Moslem he has gone to pray.' He grinned, 'I must tell you, I'm only devout when it is political to be so.' Then he laughed.

Food came on the backs of shields, still sizzling hot and to be shared by all. I discovered that tradition went right back to the great Khan who called fer this way of dining. The Khan loved to hunt and at the end of the day his warriors would cook their game and vegetables on their shields.

Timur had his leg propped on cushions and his own physician was changing the dressings. The doctor nodded his approval, the wound was healing without fester. He nodded to a woman who applied ointments and new bandages. Timur looked over at us, 'Please come and sit with me Will, your wife too.'

Space was quickly, made for us and food was brought. Vegetables and meat, were thinly sliced and tossed together until piping hot then put on a bed of rice, it was delicious. The sauce was one we had never seen before, Dark and a little salty, it added wonderful flavor. Eating went slowly we still were not used to the ivory instruments.

Timur grimaced a little at a twinge of pain and then settled into a more comfortable position. 'Three months ago we set out with a small retinue on a campaign to raise more converts to our cause. We were a somewhat, brash and silly and walked right into a trap. My soldiers had tried to warn me but I didn't listen. Husayn and I managed to escape the initial attack thanks to the selfless loyalty of my men. As far as I know, they all died in a rear guard action. My brother in law and I made it into the hills where we played hide and seek with our enemies. We could never break through to allies but we avoided capture. They harassed us without mercy giving us little chance to hunt and living off the land was difficult. It was the end of winter and there was little to eat. We both became weaker and weaker and somewhat addle brained. At such a moment our enemies almost caught us and I was shot with arrows. Husayn was unscathed and managed to spirit me away. My wounds were severe enough to really slow us down, especially in our already weakened state. Husayn managed to hide us in a cavity in the rocks. We were there about ten days living on rain water and mice when you found us and saved our lives.' He smiled and grasped me arm. 'I owe you much Will and Bo'Orchu. His men think highly of you and yours. I hope you will stay with us for a while, I know you have an obligation to our friend Al Saud but he will be staying with us too, for at least a couple of months. As soon as I'm well enough to sit a horse, perhaps tomorrow or next day, I plan to visit my wife and then meet with another friend and potential ally, Chagatai Khan. I would like you to accompany us.'

I interrupted, 'My Lord what exactly are ye planning? Why do you have so many enemies and friends?'

Timur laughed and many nearby with him. 'I plan to unite Mongol and Moslem and take back what the Great Khan's heirs have lost. The entire Silk Road will be our empire again. My wife is a direct descendant of Genghis Khan and I will soon be the imperial ruler of the Chaghatay tribe which is rich and powerful.'

I bowed me head, 'I would be most honored to be at yer side Lord, Where is yer wife?'

'She resides safely in Husayn's city Asgabat near the Persian border. We are quite close, less than a day's march away.'

Saray Mulk-Khanum reclined in royal splendor on a cushioned dais. She was a plain older woman and looking at young Timur I guessed that this marriage was one of convenience and opportunity. She formally welcomed her husband to her side and they performed some sort of ceremony I didn't understand.

We learned later that evening that she would accompany her husband to Samarkand where the Khan of Chagatai would meet with them. Husayn was standing in the background with an unpleasant cast to his face. I gave Bo'Orchu a nudge and pointed with me chin, 'What is that man's problem?'

He whispered back, 'He and Timur have very different ideas on how to treat people. Husayn always, overtaxes his subjects to pay for his excesses he is also overly cruel in his dealings. Timur on the other hand, treats his people well and shares with all. He has gone after his brother in law on more than one occasion trying to change him. He did so just after we arrived. I believe Husayn to be a vain spiteful man and one day he will break apart from his Lord.'

'Why does Saray hold the reins of power and not him?'

'She is the direct descendant of Genghis Khan, Husayn is her half brother who she dotes on.'

I gathered up Morgan and me friends to have a 'council of war' so to speak. I wanted to make sure we were all aware and in agreement.

Uri had also noticed Husayn's attitude. 'We should all have as little to do with him as possible. It shouldn't be difficult I don't think he will be the one to approach us.' We were all in agreement.

'Exactly who is the Khan of Chagatai?' Morgan looked at me. 'From what I could gather Timur thinks a lot of him.'

'Bo'Orchu told me he is a true Mongol and leads a tribe that lives on the open steppes of eastern Kazakhstan, no city life fer them. He is looking for Timur's help to consolidate several smaller countries I can't even pronounce. We will find out more when we meet him. Now, the big question, do we support Timur or stand on the sidelines.'

Morgan frowned a little, 'We still owe Kareesh our loyalty we can't leave him in the lurch.'

I sighed, 'You are right, but I believe he is staying with Timur for at least two months. We will have to ask his permission.'

Danny stood up to get our attention. 'What of Bo'Orchu and his men, Timur is their leader isn't he? They might withdraw their services from Al Saud completely.'

'Good point, However Bo'Orchu is an honorable man and I think he will stand by his promises, if he has to, just as we will if we have to.' I looked at Bembe, 'Do you wish to say anything Bembe? You are always so quiet.'

He shook his head, 'I am lost in all this but you know that I will stand side by side with you all whatever you plan.'

'It looks to me that we support Timur circumstances permitting. Am I right?' There were nods all around. 'Good, let's go find Al Saud and Bo'Orchu.'

Al Saud was the first we spoke to and it saved us some time. He chuckled at our concern and put our minds to rest. 'I am a supporter of Timur and will be following him if there is a campaign. After all I am a trader first and meeting the Khan could be profitable for me. Yes you may come as well if Timur wants you to. Bo'Orchu will look after things in our absence.'

'Why isn't Bo'Orchu goin?'

'Timur doesn't need him there. All will be explained, at a later date. Get yourselves ready, we will be leaving soon. Oh,and pack for war.'

I don't know what I expected when we were presented to Chagatai Khan. 'I learned that was the proper way to say his name' this tall strongly built man was stern but welcoming and invited us to sit at his table. He and Timur were obviously friends and everything was very festive. Food came on platters and we helped ourselves to whatever we wanted. He asked us many questions about ourselves our origins and Christianity. He knew much more on that subject than I would have supposed. I discovered later that he had crossed paths with Nestorians on several occasions. The Mongols were tolerant of other religions and many had a fondness fer Christianity. Most were Shamanists and worshipped the earth and sky, sun moon and stars. Chagatai Khan had little use for Islam as he followed the Laws of Yassa a code of laws set down by Genghis Khan himself. However, he still seemed to practice tolerance.

We spent the evening in casual conversation and watching entertainment, with plenty of food and drink. Fermented Mares milk was not me favorite but I had to put on a good face fer the sake of our hosts. The others, had been warned not to show dislike fer things. Morgan and Uri handled everything well. Danny got kicked under the table a couple of times, once when he came face to face with a sheep's eyeball and had to swallow it whole., ye can't chew gristle. Actually our hosts seemed to take great glee at his discomfort.

Later in bed Morgan and I whispered to each other fer half the night. Everything was so new and exotic we couldn't stop talking about it. The following day we were free to wander around as we pleased. Samarkand was what I would call a beige and tan city and quite beautiful in its own way. We enjoyed the sights and shopping, Morgan never got enough of shopping. I noticed military camps outside the city. There were Mongols, who would not enter the city on principle. People who lived in cities were effeminate and weak. Turkic tribesmen had their own camps and I was curious about them. I grinned to meself, I was always curious.

The following day, we were summoned into Timor's presence. He walked towards us limping quite badly. At least he had his leg. As he came up he took me arm, 'All of you walk with me, I need some sun. Today we will visit Chagatai's camp and make plans for a foray into Transoxania. There are some rebellious parties to be dealt with.'

'May I ask, me Lord, why he doesn't deal with them himself? He has more than enough men.'

'The Khan would prefer to not ruffle feathers even more with Mongol troops. He hopes to eventually have these rebellious small countries as allies and not a thorn in his side, at some later date. I will lead this assault with Turkic warriors hopefully any later hostility, will be aimed at them. Chagatai Khan will appear sympathetic to their dilemma and offer financial aid in return for loyalty.'

Morgan looked skeptical, 'You mean they won't see through that charade?'

Timur smiled at her expression. 'They might but politically they will pretend not to, especially after receiving their punishment from us. They know Mongolian policy is to eradicate their enemies giving no quarter and will realize this action is punitive and not all out obliteration.'

'Where do we come into this me Lord?' I eyed this young man with respect and just a little awe. He was already reachin fer his star.

'I hope you will be part of my personal retinue. He grinned boyishly after all you are my lucky charms. You won't mind a little action will you?'

'Not at all me Lord we will welcome it. We are all getting a little out of condition.'

# **FARAD**

---

W e rode into the Mongol camp twenty strong, Timur and ourselves with a small household guard and some Turkic leaders. Two Mongols met us and escorted us to Chagatai's ger. Me eyes took a moment to adjust to the soft amber light within the large tent. When they did, I saw a campaign table in the center, covered with a detailed map showing the areas of interest. Chagatai Khan entered from the back of his tent adjusting his robe and without preamble motioned us around the table. The household guard quickly left, as nine of us positioned ourselves around the table. One Turkic warrior across from me watched us with more than a little hostility. So many in the near east had no love fer Europeans, no matter what nationality. It seemed every country visited by them wound up fighting them. German, English, Spanish, French, they were all arrogant pricks who thought the world was their very own oyster with no consideration for the original inhabitants.

The Khan pointed out the area of coming conflict. I want suggestions on how to attack swiftly with little chance of retaliation. This rebellion must be put down, with a minimum of casualties on both sides. I looked the map over and said, 'There are three passes across the mountains into our destination. A general, long ago, crossed mountain passes with elephants to fight his enemy.'

Timur looked at me with consternation. 'We all know about Hannibal of Carthage what of it.'

I grinned at him, 'Do we have any elephants?'

Everyone broke out laughing and Timur actually punched me on the arm. The ice was broken. The Turkic warrior who had bin scowling came over beside me and pointed to the model. 'There are guard posts all through those passes. Nothing will get by them, elephants or horses.'

'How do they relay a warnin? May I ask your name?'

'I am Farad. They use fast horsemen and signal fires.'

Timur grimaced, 'Our one hope of swift retribution is to rush those passes and beat their warning systems. It's a poor hope!'

'My Lord, there could be other possibilities. One, a surgical strike on their guard posts before our cavalry moves through. Just a few men who understand stealth, we did it once before to the shufta and were successful. It should all be done at night keeping the horses as silent as possible.'

Chagatai pulled Timur to one side and they whispered together for a moment or two. Timur limped back to his place beside me. 'Would you lead such a foray Will? How many men would you need?'

'Twelve to fifteen divided up fer the three passes. Divide yer army the same way. If one fails there are still two others.'

Farad and I with two other Turkic tribesmen closed silently on the first guard position. They were relaxed, not expecting trouble and died. No warning was given and one of our men took a messenger horse back to our cavalry to get them started on their decent. Morgan and Bembe were leading another group in the next pass as were Uri and Danny in the third. We quietly moved down to the next guard post. These men here were awake and troublesome but none escaped. I took a slight wound in the arm which Farad bandaged fer me.

Each soldier was responsible fer keeping his horse quiet. Hoofs, were covered with felt boots and cloths were tied over their noses. We waited at the last post, our job done, and watched the silent cavalcade of about four hundred pass in the night. All ye could see was the occasional glint of metal and the sheen of a horses hide. We joined the rear of the column with our own horses taken from the guard posts. Farad's teeth gleamed in the dimness. 'That went well English. Hopefully the others had similar results?'

'Call me Will. It went very well let's go join the others shall we?'

Farad gripped me shoulder firmly, 'Let's'

A thousand horsemen were ranked up in the pre dawn mist ready to attack at sunrise. The enemy was still rubbing sleep from their eyes when the assault came and had no chance. Some rallied and fought back as the day progressed.

I was with a group of warriors when we came face to face with a determined older farmer and I presumed his two sons. He stabbed at me with a hayfork which I easily knocked aside. I used the flat of me sword on the return blow knocking him senseless. The younger lad knelt by his Da, in shock and the older screamed as he tried to stick me with a makeshift spear. I cut it in half, holding me sword point to his throat. I could see an older woman, two girls and a bairn hiding in a hollow. The boy was trembling but stood bravely waiting fer the death stroke. I removed me sword and said, 'Take yer father, he isn't dead, and all of you get in the house. Stay there until this is over and we will not harm ye.'

The warriors, who had been advancing with death in their eyes drew back with some puzzlement. I looked at them, 'Don't harm them, they are not conspirators just farmers.'

Many died and as we advanced into the country. The people, farmer and soldier alike, started to surrender in droves.

Timur Came to me, 'I was told that you were letting my enemies live!'

'No me Lord, farmers are not yer enemies they just want to farm and raise families and increase yer economy. They will remember ye as a benevolent ruler.'

Timur started laughing, 'Will, my soldiers won't agree but I understand and will give you license in this. Just do not get carried away.' He galloped away with officers in tow.

Lord Timur's retribution was swift. By evening, the ring leaders were hanging and kicking as a warning to the rest. No women and children came to harm, and criers went amongst the survivors informing them of their one and only choice. Behave and live.

Next morning Timur's forces faded away and Chagatai Khan took over. During the next weeks he gave succor where needed.

Morgan made a face at the charade. 'You men, all of you love to play don't you. Danny Uri Tembe and I were all laughing and congratulating ourselves. I grabbed her in a bear hug. She struggled a bit and gave in. She could have tried to leave me lying in the dirt but instead she kissed me firmly. That was much nicer.

Timur's return to Samarkand was that of a conquering hero. Drums that echoed and re echoed off the buildings and city walls heralded his entrance, and then the deep groans of Mongol warhorns brayed out. The throngs screamed praises, the women yodeling their undulating cries. Saray welcomed her husband, with open arms. After congratulatory celebrations, Chagatai Khan's Mongols broke camp and headed back to the open steppes of eastern Kazakhstan. He ruled most of the area but was satisfied to stand in the background with Timur as figurehead and ruler. After all, he had no love of cities or thrones.

There was a great hubbub throughout Samarkand and no one had told us why. Timur was busy with husbandly duties and had no time to see us. Danny came to let us know that Bo'Orchu and Al Saud had arrived with caravan and all. We were elated and rushed to meet them at the city gates. Al Saud was busy with some unruly camels and waved greeting. Bo'Orchu lifted me right off me feet with a bear hug. 'Action becomes you Will, you are looking very well.'

'And so are ye. Why are ye here?'

'You don't know? And right under your nose. There is to be a coronation of sorts.'

'Coronation of whom, ye mean Timur? Where have we bin!'

Bo'Orchu was laughing, 'You know that his wife Satay is a direct descendant of Genghis Khan, right? Well she has given her blessing for Timur to be ruler of the Chaghatay tribe.'

'But what about Chagatai Khan isn't he ruler?'

'You are confused Will, You'll note that the spelling is different? The Chaghatay tribe is one of the most influential tribes, with Satay at their head. Now as a dutiful wife, she is relinquishing her leadership to Timur. She wants the same as him, re-establishment of the Mongol empire.'

"God's truth! Politics are confusin in this part of the world.' I looked at Morgan and the others, 'We had no idea. So, he will become Khan.'

Meanwhile Al Saud had joined us a round of welcomes in progress. Morgan linked arms with him, 'You look tired Kareesh dear.'

He smiled at her, 'I'm alright. We had some minor skirmishes with the Shufta. Uri was missed, but his pike men did well enough. He has trained them well. How are you my dear?' Al Saud was the only Moslem I ever met that allowed such familiarity from a woman. He was more western than he realized. He turned to me, 'Timur will be Amir not Khan, he is not the blood line of the Great Khan.'

'So he will be a General?'

'No he will be a King! Emir is a general Amir is ruler.' I nodded understanding.

Uri was quick to go see his charges with a pleased look on his face. They in turn were happy to see their leader. One pike man had been killed, and a replacement needed training.

'So, those damn Shufta are still around? Surely he has lost face and his men by now!'

'He's done some successful raiding on others. Cruel butchery and rape are his trademarks and he has left his mark in several places. Do you remember the young captain from Tehran? He has joined us in an attempt to bring this upstart down.'

'Aye I remember him Turin isn't it? Where is he now?'

'He is at the rear of the caravan with sixty of his men. He is a very serious young man with a will to succeed.'

'Was he with ye when ye were attacked?'

'No, he came shortly after. He had been tracking them for some time without catching up. He always had to stop to bury the dead.'

'I can feel fer him.' I remembered Skye all too vividly. 'You said he as sixty men isn't he slightly outnumbered?'

'Yes but the Mongols will assist him when the time comes.'

I nodded, took Danny and Bembe in tow and went to find Uri.

Uri was talkin to one of his men when we came up. He paused to look at us.

Danny said, 'Yer men did well I hear.'

'Yes I am pleased but sorry we lost a man. The others say inexperience cost him his life. He stepped out of rank to stab at a nearby enemy. I keep telling them that is what the third rank is for.' Uri frowned, 'At least he set an example. The others won't be so quick to make the same mistake.' He took me shoulder to steer me and said to the others, 'I was just going to have a drink with my men. Join us?'

I grinned, 'Its been a while since we all drank together what are we having?'

'Tej, it's a strong ill tasting beer and the easiest to get around here. These non drinking Moslems make enough of the stuff.'

We had just finished our first drink when Farad came looking fer me. I introduced him around. The other three had only met him briefly at the conference table. I didn't know why he had done such a turnaround from glowering to friendly, so I asked him, point blank.

'I liked your style Will and decided to find out more. You lack the arrogance so many of your kind have.' I think he realized he was bordering on rudeness and shrugged, 'We did well together, you and my men.' He looked at the beer keg and then at Uri who grinned and passed a cup to him. After a healthy swallow and a gasp he said, 'Our tribesmen are staying to support Lord Timur and more are coming. I think it would be of mutual benefit if we could be on friendly terms.'

I was a little surprised at his candor after all he had bin the one scowling. 'We are all following the same star so friendly is good. Where are ye from?'

'Far away from here, across the Caspian Sea, The Golden Horde over rules our lands, at the moment we are their allies and they look favorably on Lord Timur.'

I grinned, 'There is so much going on in this part of the world, but then again that's true of me part of the world too.'

Bembe and Danny both laughed and Bembe said, 'In every part of the world I think.'

Danny downed his drink and tried to focus, 'Fer a man who doesn't say much that was rather profound. By the way, where's Morgan?'

Bembe looked dismayed and got up to look over our heads trying to find her. I gripped his arm, "Don't worry she probably got sick of listening to us men and has gone shopping. Look, Al Saud has gone too.' Despite me display of no worry, I felt a prickle go up me back and then another. I got up, 'Bembe, let's take a stroll and go find them!'

Farad jumped up the same time as Danny, 'We will come too.'

I turned to Uri, 'Please stay with yer lads, she may return while we are gone.' He nodded agreement.

We fanned out as we entered the sauk, it wasn't a huge one but big and busy and it was difficult to see through the shoppers. I craned me neck trying to when I saw a group of people crowding around, near the entrance to one of a myriad of alleys. I pushed towards them calling out to the others. Parting the crowd I found Al Saud laying in a pool of blood. With a curse I leaped to his side. Bembe arrived, knelt and felt fer a pulse. 'He is alive Will but needs help right away. He must have been stabbed in the back there are no wounds in front.'

Bo'Orchu appeared at that moment with Farad in tow. He looked grim as he rolled Al Saud over to see three stab wounds all above the waist. 'We need a doctor!'

I started to do something me self when we heard Danny's voice behind the crowd. 'I have a doctor here and a stretcher.' Danny pushed through the crowd with a small man in tow. He crouched beside Bo'Orchu. Let's get him on it shall we?'

'Where the bloody hell did ye come from?'

'I heard someone yell fer a doctor and this man looked up, I took a chance and asked and stole a table top.' Thank God fer Danny.

The doctor, an Arab, applied pressure bandages to the wounds and we all lifted the injured man onto the tabletop stretcher. The doctor told us to follow him.

An icy chill settled in the pit of me stomach. 'Where was Morgan, where was me wife?'

Morgan was gone and I had no idea where to look. Al Saud hung onto life by a thread and each of us took turns on the deathwatch. Women came to wash and water him. Very slowly his strength and color improved. Three days later, his eyes flickered and opened. I was happy to be the one present.

'How are ye me friend? Do ye think ye can eat?'

He smiled and nodded weakly, 'Some soup would be nice. Where am I?'

I called out fer anyone near. 'Do ye remember being attacked? Ye were badly wounded and ye'll be in bed fer a bit.'

Al Saud's face became grim just as Uri and Bo'Orchu entered the room. They paused to listen havin heard the question. 'Where is Morgan? we were assaulted by Shufta and they were struggling with her when I felt a great pain in my back. That is all I remember.'

Me worst fears were realized, and I felt the edge of panic. What would they do to me sweet wife? Seeing me state Uri gripped me shoulder tightly. 'I'm sure they will ransom her.' He looked questionably at the Mongol. 'Don't you think so?'

Bo'Orchu nodded just as a commotion began outside the room. Two soldiers entered, taking position on each side of the door, Then Lord Timur limped in looking very upset, he was accompanied, by the young captain from Tehran. Timur came straight to me placing his hands on me shoulders. 'This is a terrible state of affairs, and right under my nose in my city. You will have every resource you need to find Morgan, Will. To start with, let me introduce you to Captain Turin Nahib he will be your ally in this.'

I bowed to the captain, 'Salaam Alaikum Captain, we met briefly on the road.'

225

Touchin lips and heart he said, 'As-Salaamu' Alaikum. I remember English.'

'Please call me Will, names get complicated around here.' Timur chuckled and the Captain smiled. 'We will keep things simple you can call me Turin except in front of my men then captain would be better.'

I bowed me head in answer and turned to Timur. 'Me Lord, I don't know where to start! Al Saud only knows they were Shufta, everythin else is blank.'

Turin took a step forward. 'May I speak my Lord?' Timur nodded. 'I believe they are hidden not too far away. I don't think they would have the audacity to hide within the city but you never know. We will search every cranny inside and outside. We should hear from them soon, after all profit is what they want so they will try to negotiate a ransom.'

Timur spoke up, 'We will pay whatever they demand to get Morgan safely back then we will crush them that I promise!'

# **CAPT. TURIN NAHIB**

aptain Nahib arranged fer a command center in a building beside the main gate. He didn't want too many men, not an army, too difficult to keep by the hour order. Bo'Orchu placed his men at our disposal and sent word to Subukii. The captain began to protest when Bo'Orchu said, 'He has an army at his disposal, enough to take on the shufta in force. If he finds them he'll keep a low profile until you get there.'

Young Turin nodded, 'That makes sense. We can concentrate on different areas and call for assistance if needed.'

I took the opportunity to say me piece. 'Soldiers would be a better presence within the city. Citizens would be more inclined to co- operate with uniforms. Me people could assist any and all, the palace guards and your soldiers could be bolstered by Farad's men, he has offered a hundred who are his to command.

Turin took it all in. 'Let us proceed, find a starting point both outside and inside and begin a sweep.'

I could feel meself shaking all of a sudden, I felt I was making a wrong choice and needed to act. 'Turin I can't face going door to door and would like to change me mind and join Bo'Orchu with my group. Is that alright with you?'

Turin frowned, stared a moment and nodded. 'I'll use Farad as second in command to search the city. Go with God, may he keep you and yours safe.'

We received information that Subukii was searchin from the main road to the west of the city so we went east. Danny and three Mongols searched fer tracks leaving the high road. We didn't have much else to go on. After only half a day, a trail of horse prints were found, leading up into the rugged hills.

'If they are up there, they will have lookouts too.' I rode knee to knee with me Mongol friend. 'How do we find them without detection? Morgan is in terrible danger you know.'

Bo'Orchu sighed, 'Yes I know and I don't know. If we could establish these tracks as theirs and not some other, we could start hunting at night. If these turned out to be some other, sneaking about would waste valuable time but if we don't act with caution it could be very problematic for your wife.'

'It's just as problematic if we do nothing!'

Danny returned looking pleased. "I believe these are the shufta tracks, one horse has a healed diagonal split in its hoof looking like a half moon. I have seen it before outside Jerusalem.'

'Are ye sure Danny? We cannot be wrong in this.'

'Aye Will, there is always a minimal chance that it is another horse but I don't think so.'

'I know ye are free and easy with yer own life but would ye stake Morgan's life on this?'

He held me gaze and said, 'Aye I would.'

I trusted Danny's instincts completely. 'Well, what do we do now?' Turning to Bo'Orchu I said, 'Could ye send a man to fetch Captain Nahib? He should be with us on this. We'll stay away from this trailhead and hide in the rocks. Perhaps shufta will pass and we can follow, if not, Danny and his lads can reconnoiter under cover of darkness and hopefully find their hideout.' I pointed to a highland half a mile away, we will hide there.'

Bembe crouched beside Danny, 'When the time comes I go with you.' Danny nodded agreement.

We all sat in the dark eating figs yogurt and some blood sausage. A fire was out of the question and that was alright since there was some moon and the sky was clear. I discouraged talking as sound could carry a long way in the darkness. Turin suddenly appeared a wraith in the darkness, accompanied by two others. He came and sat beside me, Uri made room, and I placed a bowl of yogurt and figs in his hands. He nodded gratefully and ate. In low whispers I brought him up to date which didn't include much. He listened quietly his jaws working as he chewed a stubborn fig.

He swallowed, 'No riders?' He spoke sotto voiced.

I shook me head, 'None. Danny and Bembe are reconnoiterin right now. I don't expect them back until early morning. Has there been word of a ransom demand?'

Turin shook his head and pulled his cloak tighter around himself. The air was beginning to cool and by morning would be cold till the sun rose.

Danny and Bembe returned before dawn with some news. 'About three miles in there is a village of stone huts, only semi occupied. The ones there may be guards, I don't know. They never knew we were there. We followed their spoor for another five miles and their tracks ended at the bottom of a cliff. It was dark and we didn't rummage around much in case of drawing attention. My guess is a camouflaged cave very close by but I can't be positive.'

I growled at him, 'Why didn't you make sure?'

He just stared at me making me feel stupid. 'There could have been a guard right under me nose and I wouldn't have known until too late. That part will have to be done in daylight.'

I put me face in me arms and worried. Uri's fingers grasped the back of me neck. 'We will save her Will!'

A Mongol sentry signed that there was activity on the road. Uri was first to move to the viewing spot with me close behind. I guessed he didn't like this sitting around he never had. About seventy shufta led by Eban Samuli himself entered the main road heading towards Samarkand. I looked at me friend, 'This could be our chance.'

Uri squinted against the sun watching them go. 'It could be Will but we could also get trapped between two forces.'

'Every minute Morgan is in their hands diminishes her chances of good health. I say we go!'

Turin had crept up beside us. 'I agree we go now. We will send a messenger to alert Farad. He can guard the road, the inside forces won't be needed any more.'

We moved slowly up the rough road, the decision, had been made to go in on foot. We were more maneuverable and could take cover easier if we needed to. Danny, Bembe and a Mongol tracker were ahead of the main party. We had been traveling fer a bit, the sun hot on our backs, when Danny appeared at a bend in the road and waited fer us.

'The village is just up ahead and there is something bad that I didn't see in the dark. Bembe and the Mongol have gone to the other end to prevent anyone leaving.'

I stared at Danny, 'What's so bad?' I didn't like the look on his face.

'A woman has been stoned to death. Wait, Will!' He grabbed at me as I pushed past. 'We don't know who it is.'

Me stomach felt like a block of stone and the pressure in me head almost blinded me. There at the far end of the village a dark figure sat slumped in the white glare of the sun. I approached feeling fear well up in me like never before. The woman was so mutilated by stones she was unrecognizable.

A stake, she was tied to held her in the slumped position. As I drew close I could see strands of auburn hair in all the blood. Then me heart crashed in me chest, one grey eye stared blankly from her shattered skull. A grief stricken howl escaped me lips as me legs gave out and I collapsed beside the bloody corpse. Uri and Danny both rushed to me. Then I saw a finger, an untouched finger with a scar that ran diagonally from one knuckle to the other. Morgan never had a scar like that. I whispered through dry lips. 'My God it's not Morgan!' Weakness overwhelmed me and I couldn't move.

Danny wasn't aware of the finger. 'Oh Will, me poor dear friend…'

'Look at that finger, it's not Morgan!'

Uri grabbed me shoulders to help me up. 'You are right Will it is not.'

Danny finally saw it and I could hear his audible sigh of relief.

Turin came and had an old man in tow. 'This is the village head man. There are just a few old people left and they hide most of the time. The young men and women have been enslaved.' He turned to the old man, 'Who is this woman, what did she do to warrant such punishment?'

The old man spoke hesitantly, as if not used to talking, 'She was an Afghan woman, a slave to the Shufta leader. She tried to kill him and this was her punishment.'

Danny was incredulous, 'But she had auburn hair and grey eyes.'

Turin said, 'It is a common trait in this part of the world, especially in Afghanistan.' He looked down at the crushed body. 'She died most cruelly at the hands of these evil men and I will extract a price.' He called two of his soldiers over. 'See that she is wrapped and properly buried. Catch up later and be careful."

I finally got some strength back in me legs and we carried on. I promised meself to say some words over her grave when this was over.

The road was becoming more of a trail and we moved cautiously on each side up in the rocks, we didn't want our tracks showing on top of the others. Danny signaled that we were getting close and we hunkered down while his trio went to scout.

Half an hour later Danny showed up. He nodded to Turin and me, 'Follow me and be quiet.'

He led us to a ledge where Bembe was waiting he acknowledged us with a slight nod and pointed. I could see a black clad figure leaning lazily against a rock wall. Danny whispered, 'There's another on the other side of the trail, higher up.'

I looked and looked, and finally spotted him, just his head showing. He was looking the other way.

Danny pointed at the cliff. 'Just beyond yer vision there is a large cleft that will allow horse and rider to pass in double file. I'm not sure if it opens into a cavern or a valley. Those are the only two guards and me other man is workin his way behind the higher one.'

I watched intently and suddenly the head vanished and the Mongol gave the thumbs up. I could see him donning black robes and headdress covering his face. He stepped out and started down to the other.

'What are you doing Calif? Why are you leaving your post?' All the time the Mongol drew closer. 'I need to shit and I don't want to foul my nest.' The guard laughed, 'Hurry up about it. Wait you're not Calif!'

The Mongol dived the last eight feet splitting the man's skull. He dragged the body back to the rocks where we were. Men helped him strip the dead guard but the head covering was sliced, soaked in blood and of little use.

I took his arm, 'Ye are the only one in black so get over to his post before someone realizes something is amiss.' I turned to another, 'Take what's salvageable and get back up in the rocks. Only yer head can be seen so ye can cope.' I nudged Bo'Orchu, 'Now we wait fer the changing of the guard.' The Mongol took up his post and, usin his foot erased blood stains as best he could. The other soon appeared high up and looked quite normal with black wound around head and face.

A low whistle from the man in the rocks alerted us. He signaled a single rider coming. Now we could hear the galloping horse. He sped into the cleft and loud shouts and curses echoed. A man staggered out rubbing his shoulder and he screamed back, 'May a thousand sores infest thy anus.' A second guard emerged chuckling, 'His anus already has a thousand sores.' The first growled, That pox ridden imbecile almost trampled me, get you up to your post and hurry, that passage will be full in a minute. I heard him shout that our Emir wants another hundred men and quickly.

A swelling clatter of hooves announced the departing shufta. As they exited two by two, Mongol and Arab stood side by side and watched, the Arab guard not knowing he had only seconds to live. I saw the other reach the aerie and disappear to a flurry of arms and legs. Finally, the last rider diminished down the trail and the Arab died from a dirk thrust in the back. Bembe raced out, threw the body over his shoulder and raced back. Another man clambered the rocks to get black robes from the guard who stayed at his post. We now had three serviceable sets of black robes.

Danny said, 'I'm going in we need to know how many men we have to face and the whereabouts of Morgan.'

'Ye can't go. Ye speak Pharsi and Mongol with a Scottish accent!'

Uri said, 'I'll go I can speak it well enough. Those men are from all over these parts and speak different dialects.' Danny looked a little miffed but nodded agreement.

It wasn't long before Uri returned. He drew a rough outline in the dust. 'The cavern looks like this and it's quite big at least a hundred fifty meters across. Horses are corralled to our right, bridled and saddled, and ready to go. From center to the left is the camp with cook fires and bedrolls. The place is well ventilated there is little smoke. On the extreme left nearer the back, there are rock ledges with many cages and, I think, some latrines. I did not see Morgan but there were prisoners under lock and key. It is not dark but shadowed, there are two large holes high up in the roof open to the sky.'

'How many men Uri?'

'Around a hundred, more than enough to give us some troubles.'

Armed with this information I called me main players together. 'Feel free to make corrections but this is what I have in mind. Danny and Bembe along with one of Turin's men will wear the black and circle past the horses to get back to the prisoners and defend them! After giving ye a slight head start, Turin's men will attack the camp area, and Bo'Orchu and his men will go fer the horses, with their archery skills and on horseback they should take the upper hand. Three archers will hold the passageway if any others return, three or more dead horses will slow any attackers down. Uri will stand with me let us see if we can turn this little fortress into a trap.'

I watched me friends race fer the back and then me attention was drawn to our immediate problem. The shufta weren't caught off guard fer more than a few seconds and were swift to retaliate. They swarmed us with war cries and we were suddenly fighting fer our lives. We needed Bo'Orchu and soon. Turin was on me right, and Uri on me left and the three of us left a swath of dead and dying around us. Turin's men were going down about one fer one and there were far less of them than bandits. I blocked a cut at Turin's head, as he was occupied with another, and back slashed across the man's throat. Uri dropped to one knee and sliced into a man's groin before he could get to me. The three of us worked well together. Our young captain was as able as I had been told.

I felt a pain in me shoulder and took a cut on the cheek and retaliated chopping me opponent across the ribs. 'God's truth! Where were the Mongols?'

Three leering men had singled us out when one dropped with an arrow through his eye and another was choking on a piece of wood. The third I cut down. The Mongols were finally here and the battle turned in our favor very quickly.

'Uri, I'm going to the back, cover me.' It didn't take long to realize that there were more men than I could handle alone between me and Danny. At intervals, I could see them fighting. All three were still standing. I was cut off, but only fer a moment. Four Mongols joined me and with horse power and archery opened the way. I reached me friends after skirting a heap of bodies which were Bembe's work.

He had stripped off the black and stood magnificent in his leopard skin kilt. He was bleeding from several wounds but all men that had attacked him had died under his ax. Danny took me arm and pulled me to him. 'Give him room! We have been defending his flank.'

'What about his other flank? Oh, it's the shit trench.' I looked around, 'It seems to be over. Did ye find me wife? Did ye find Morgan?'

Danny shook his head, 'We didn't see her but we can look again to be sure.'

Ice in me belly again! Me wife was not to be found. The other prisoners were released, from stinking cages, and questioned. One had seen her but, she had not been brought here. She was in the custody of nomadic warriors other than Mongols. Turin and I looked at each other incredulously. 'Have we been duped?'

One of the bowmen from the passage came. 'Farad is here, he is entering as we speak.'

In one voice, Turin and I shouted 'No!' but too late. A cavalcade of horsemen rode in circling the perimeter. Our surviving men looked on with no comprehension of our betrayal but we knew. I watched grimly as Farad approached us with a gloating smile on his face.

'Tell your men to lay down their arms or they will all die.' Turin signaled fer them to do so. Bo'Orchu was furious but kept his men under control and Bembe had to be, restrained, by Danny who was being sensible fer once.

I glared at him, 'I thought we had a friendship or at least mutual respect.'

He sneered, 'Friends with a Frank? Never!'

Uri spit on the ground in front of him. 'You swore an oath to Timur and I know he is not party to this.'

'I swore another oath before that. Enough! Emir Samuli comes, you will face his judgement.'

Samuli galloped into the cavern, a conquering hero, his followers thundered behind him screaming accolades at the top of their voices. Finally, he raised his arms and there was silence. 'At last I have you Frank. Would you like to visit your wife? She is a little used,' He laughed, 'But there's more for all.'

Uri grabbed me around the throat as I lunged. Bembe had to be, knocked to the ground and was almost senseless. Samuli looked at the heap of dead at the back of the cave. 'It looks like you killed at least twelve of my men.' He reached down and prodded Bembe with his sword. 'I promise you a mutilation for each one, slave.'

Bembe spit blood from his mouth, 'I am not your or any ones slave!'

'Enough! He pointed to the men holding him, 'Teach him what he really is.'

Farad laughed cruel and loud, 'Allah truly is merciful and we will taste lamb in paradise. All these non believers were cursed by their gods.'

Danny glared up at him, 'Allah had nothing to do with this. Don't ye know He has turned His face from ye? When ye go to yer paradise, yer lamb will be pork and yer houris will have no holes.'

Farad fumed, 'Silence that insulant Frank dog!'

A Shufta stepped up behind Danny and drew a knife across his throat. Danny spit blood and more gushed down his chest. 'Fuck ye….. He slumped onto his face, dead.

I cried out in horror and shock as I watch me dear friend die. Danny was immortal! I did not weep I wouldn't give these animals the satisfaction. Uri clutched me shoulder much harder than usual. I knew he was shocked too but gave no visible evidence of it. I looked at many stunned faces, especially amongst the Mongols. How were we going to get out of this? There had to be a way!

They roughly mauled and pushed us where they wanted us and we were a despondent bunch sitting in circles of twelve and roped together with slaver ropes. Through whispers and asides, Bo'Orchu got a message to me. The Mongol who had been in the aerie was still there. If he went un noticed he would know what took place and go for help. Me face remained still, giving nothing away but inside I felt a bright ray of new hope.

The following morning, we were whipped to our feet. Farad glanced down at me, 'We go now to Asgabat and earn our Lord Husayn's blessings.'

'So that's the one ye owe allegiance to, I should have known.' He didn't hear as he turned to other things.

The march, even to the main road, was cruel. Many of us had bin wounded, and our strength sapped. The shufta were not sparing with their kurbashes' the hippo hide tore exposed flesh to the bone. Men started to fall and, were left where they lay to die of their wounds, thirst and exposure. Bembe was a main attraction and how he stood up under their onslaught I will never know. I felt sorrow fer that man but also great pride, he never gave them the satisfaction of a moan or grimace. Samuli rode past once and curbed their enthusiasm, 'I want him alive for later if he dies prematurely I will have your heads.'

I asked permission from one of the Turkic warriors if I could take water to Bembe. He allowed it whereas a shufta may not have. So I got to visit with me friend and gave him water. I also cleaned his wounds, which were many and painful but none too dangerous. He just sat with his eyes closed and whispered, 'Thank you.' I whispered back, 'Don't give up hope, one got away.' A shufta guard loomed, 'Silence! You have given him water now go back to where you were and be quick.'

I passed Bo'Orchu and managed a wink. He gave me the slightest of nods. The shufta reattached me to me group.

Once more, we were whipped to our feet and forced to march. When one of Turin's men dropped he was stripped of armor and left almost naked in the sun. I looked at Turin, 'Why are they stripping yer men? I know why, you are the Shah of Persia's personal guard it wouldn't do fer him to find out what is going on.'

Turin nodded, 'Me and my men will all suffer the same fate eventually. My father is a close friend of the Shah and news of my death at the hands of Husayn, even indirectly, would mean war, a war the Shah would most certainly win.'

I spoke low, 'When Timur knows of his brother-in-law's betrayal Shite will hit the wind.'

'I don't know, Lord Timur would never permit these things but he may not want to make an outright enemy of Husayn, at least not yet. His marriage to Sarey is fresh and his coronation even fresher. She dotes on her half brother and it wouldn't do to have Husayn's blood on his hands.' A whip slashed Turin's shoulders and then mine, silencing us. I glared at the whip wielder and he smirked. 'Speak again Frank and lose your tongue.'

Later in the day I noticed a Mongol staring at me and as soon as he saw he had me attention he used his head and eyes to point up the hill behind me.

I tried to make sure no one was looking me way before I took a look and then I did it furtively by scratching me head and looking under me arm. I noticed an unpleasant odor and then saw a glint of sun on metal and then another. I squeezed Turins leg and then Uri's and pointed with me chin. Through stiff lips I whispered, 'We have company!'

We were very close to Askabat. I remembered some landmarks. I prayed the activity in the rocks weren't Husayn's guards. The head of our column rounded a bend in the road to come face to face with a Mongol array. Five rows of warriors on horse and then five more and five more again, the first two rows in each troop, were heavily armored and the other three armed with bows. They went back right to the city gates and blocked the entire road and out on each flank. There was activity on the wall, but no hostility could be seen.

Subukii walked his horse to face Farad and Samuli. 'You will surrender to our mercies and no harm will fall on your men. If you do not, you will all die in front of your master.'

I could see the two men look up at the wall and then I saw Husayn standing there helpless. Samuli pulled the black mask from his face, which was suffused with rage. 'We will kill all the prisoners you would not have time to stop us.' He looked back raising his hand. Then his fist clenched his arm dropping slowly and shock on his face. There were at least a thousand soldiers behind us with Timur calmly sitting on his horse in the front. Up in the rocks on our right, Turkic archers stood with drawn bows.

A desperate shriek from Samuli, 'Kill the prisoners!' Farad looked startled and all bedlam broke loose. Shufta and their allies attacked us. We rose up to defend ourselves as best we could. Uri and I used our fetters to strangle an attacker. Uri took a wound in his side. Turin and the man beside him used the same tactic and now the four of us had swords. It was so difficult to maneuver in that struggling mass. None of the prisoners were going to die passively. The archers in the rocks had an equal problem tryin to tell friend from foe and hit their target. Our fetters were ropes and we were able to cut them. More of our enemies died their swords were picked up, by prisoners around us. We managed to cut our way to Bo'Orchu and found many of his men already armed. The archers were also taking their toll as numbers thinned and now we were tripping over bodies instead of into them. Shufta started surrendering, as did Farad's men. We glanced about stareing through the dust and then realized it was all over.

Uri and I looked at each other, drenched in blood, and started laughing with releaf. Bo'Orchu smiled with a look that said, 'where are you two idiots coming from. I looked fer Turin. He was sitting with a couple of his men tryin to staunch blood flow from a bad cut in the shoulder. I went to help and Bembe materialized beside me. He also was filthy from other men's blood. I grabbed his face with me hand, 'I am so glad ye are safe me friend.' He smiled and wordlessly shook me by the shoulder. I applied a pressure bandage on Turin's shoulder and tied it with a belt from one of the dead. One of his men thanked me and I told him to make sure Turin ate and drank very soon to replenish his strength. It would help his recovery and he needed a surgeon to look at the wound.

Subukii stepped over bodies as he approached to embrace his brother. 'My thanks to the Mother that you survived, it was a sticky situation for a while there.' His eyes scanned all of us, 'If you all had not attacked your jailors all could have been lost, as it is, it is bad enough.'

I looked around to see what he meant and, was taken aback by the slaughter. Turin only had sixteen men left standing out of the sixty he started with. Bo'Orchu's thirty was down to half, most of them lost in this last battle. I felt a presence behind me and turned into Timur's embrace. 'I am so glad you are safe my English friend. Where are the others?'

Me eyes felt a little damp. 'I am so happy to see ye me Lord Timur, ye can never know how much. Danny is dead from a cowardly stroke.' I looked around fer Uri who was sitting and looking pale. 'Excuse me me Lord Uri is wounded and fadeing.'

Timur had frowned at me news and it changed to concern as he swiftly limped to Uri who was starting to slump. He supported him as I pulled away clothing. A soldier helped me get his mail off and the wound was exposed. It was a bad one, from the side and into the stomach area. I looked up at Timur. 'He is bleeding internally me Lord.' He must have heard the desperation in me voice and turned to a waitin soldier, 'Go fetch my physicians at once, no time is to be lost.' The Soldier sped away.

More physicians arrived from Subukii's army and things began to take on a semblance of order. I spoke some more with Timur, tellin him how Danny died and that we never found me wife. First, he looked purturbed and then I could see he was thinking. 'I have something I must do then we will talk again.' He limped over to some of his officers.

One of Timur's best doctors did the surgery on Uri and managed to stem the bleeding. I couldn't even assist I was much too tired and filthy. He was out of immediate danger but still at risk and I planned to sit at his bedside until he was safe.

Funeral rites, were held over several days for all those lost. Danny's body, was brought to me so that we could give him a Christian burial. I was surprised and honored when Timur attended. Bo'Orchu, Sengge who I was pleased to see living, and many other Mongols also attended. I found out many of the fallen, who had been left to die in the desert, had been saved by Timur's men.

I asked Lord Timurs permission to return to the village where the Afghan woman had died. When I told him how she had died and how she resembled Morgan he decided to accompany me.

With forty Turkic warriors in tow, Timur and I ambled back to that sorry site. We rode side by side and talked.

Timur smiled at me, 'It is good to have this time on our own my friend. I wish to be candid with you. I believe. No, I know that your wife is being held against her will,secretly in Asgabat. My dear brother in law is on the edge of panic, afraid of what I might do.' Timur sighed, 'For his sister's sake, I cannot and will not do anything but that doesn't mean that you and your Mongol friends cannot.' He gripped me arm, 'When we find out exactly where she is being held you will have my blessing. This is between you and I, publicly, I might have to scold you if any of Husayn's men die.'

'Thank ye me Lord ye do me a great service and I am honored to have yer friendship in this sticky situation.'

He smiled and then laughed, 'The fact that you can see this predicament as I do pleases me greatly. Look, we are arrived.'

As we moved through the village I looked about fer a sign of her grave. The place seemed deserted until one of the soldiers escorted the same old man from one of the huts. I dismounted and politely asked if he knew where the Afghan woman was buried. He took me arm and pointed. 'The soldiers laid her to rest under that acacia tree. It is one of a few shady places.' I began walking when Timur called fer me to wait. I turned back to watch him dismount. He grimaced when his bad leg hit the ground.

'The leg pains you me Lord?'

He nodded, 'It has its moments.' He grinned, 'I hear many are calling me Timur the Lame, it's catching on.' He turned to the old man who was standin slack jawed.

'You are the great Timur?' He went to his knees, which was very difficult for such an old man.

Timur took his hands, 'Do not kneel to me father,' he turned to the soldier, 'Help him up please.' The soldier jumped to obey. As this was going on, more old people were coming out of their huts. One hunched old woman using two canes made her way to Timur. She looked up with eyes almost covered with the yellow film of cataracts. Her voice was thin and reedy, 'My Lord, why are you here?'

She coughed and staggered a bit and Timur supported her on his arm. 'I came for one reason mother, but now I think I have another. Where are all your young people?'

'Taken my Lord, many months ago the shufta came and rounded them up, killing those that resisted and snatching babes from their mothers.' She turned her face into her shoulder as if trying to hide. 'They killed the babes too.'

Timur's face was dark with anger but he bent to kiss the old woman on her head. 'Things will change. I will see to it that you are supplied with goats, and chickens and young people to help you. There are displaced people that would happily live here. Now I must see this grave site, will you show me?'

The old woman led him to the tree and we followed. All I could think was 'Me lady ye didn't die in vain, even though it was a cruel death. I think you are here to watch over these people. Because of ye this will be a happy place once again.' All the graves were in this shady spot, which looked out over the surrounding hills and valleys. Timur and I stood fer some time paying our respects.

It was now time for retribution. The Mongols were ruthless and so was Timur. Husayn hid away in his palace as his city walls became an execution ground. Timur made sure he got the message. I watched as Farad had his tongue cut out. He had lied on his oath. His eyes were squeezed from their sockets, his moans echoing off the city walls. Then he was placed in an iron birdcage and hung high on the wall by the main gate. There he would die of thirst and exposure and rot to nothing. The great, self proclaimed, Emir Eban Samuli suffered a similar fate but only after continuous torture. His torture lasted some time because he was a stubborn man. The Mongols were more stubborn and after missing several pieces of anatomy he revealed the whereabouts of me wife. He too was left rotting on the wall on the other side of the gate. Their followers, more than two hundred still alive, were nailed to posts all along the wall and left to die. Their screams and moans would give many citizens sleepless nights. I was not as horrified as I would have thought. I had wanted revenge for so many reasons and now I had a measure of it. One of Bo'Orchu's men returned Morgan's sword to me. Samuli had made it his own for a moment in time.

The following night was dark. The moon would not show itself until early morning. With Bembe, Bo'Orchu and eight of his men, we climbed the wall. The crying of the dying gave us cover. Me wife's location was imprinted on me mind as we made our way through the city. No one accosted us. No one would dare, except those guarding Morgan. Timur had assured me that she would not be, killed. Husayn knew the penalty if it came to that and he needed anonymity when this was all over.

We paused in a dark alley to get our bearings, and I adjusted Morgan's sword hanging from me belt. I wasn't used to one there, mine was on me back. Bo'Orchu spoke softly, 'We should keep to the shadows now we are close.' I nodded, I could see the building we were going to and now we would watch fer lookouts. We spotted two, one on the roof and the other in shadows near the door. We only saw him because he moved. I dispatched Bembe to take the one on the roof and one of Bo'Orchu's men went fer the other. Things didn't go so well fer Bembe. He killed his man but the roof couldn't take both their weights, Bembe was a big man. They crashed through and all I could say was 'Oh shite!' as we raced fer the front door. With his man dead by the door the Mongol was waiting fer us. As soon as we were close enough he put his shoulder to the portal and we crashed through. There were more men in there than we had counted on but surprise was on our side. Me eyes were filled by a horrifyin scene. Morgan was strapped spread eagled on a filthy table and a man was tryin to extract himself from her as we entered. Bembe had landed on his feet and was swinging his ax at men all around him. The Mongols leaped to help and I went fer me wife. That scum still had his pantaloons around his ankles when I drove me sword into his back reaching his vitals. He let out a shriek and lay whimpering on the floor. I looked down on me poor wife, raped repeatedly and bruised beyond all measure. Her face was slack as I cut her loose and I was terrified that her mind was gone. I rubbed her hands and gently patted her cheek. 'Morgan, me sweet wife, can ye hear me?' A shadow appeared attackin me and I swatted it like a bug. I had paid no more attention to things around me but we must have won. Bembe was bringing me water and clean rags. We both wept as we bathed her. How men could rape a woman, let alone one lying in her waste, was beyond belief. They were less than the things that crawl in the dark. I picked her up in me arms as Bembe sloshed water across another table. I placed her on it and we continued to bathe her as best we could. There was a sense of reverence from all our men there and Mongols stripped clothing from themselves to help cover me wife. Her clothes were nowhere to be found.

Suddenly her eyes opened and she started flailing and screaming. I pulled her close, getting a split lip in the bargain, and whispered Morgan, over, and over again. Her thrashing finally stopped and then a small voice said 'Will?'

'Aye me love it's Will. Ye are safe in our hands now and no one is goin to harm ye again.'

She broke into a fit of sobbing and her arms felt like steel around me neck. She wasn't letting go.

Bo'Orchu asked if they should make a stretcher and I said no, I will carry her from this place. With men on each side and Bembe beside us, we left that awful house. One Mongol allowed himself, to clumsily, knock a torch from the wall and fire flared. He growled, 'The neighbors knew!'

We made our way through the city and nobody accosted us. The city watch passed in a rush towards the way we had come ye could hear the clanging of a bell behind us. Me wife was becoming heavy but I wasn't letting her go, Bembe offered and I thanked him but shook me head. The guards at the gate opened them and stood aside to let us pass. No words were said. Outside, a platoon of mounted soldiers and women with a horse drawn padded cart were waiting fer us. Women proceeded to take charge of Morgan. One spoke to me as they fought to pry her arms from me neck. 'Lord Timur has decreed that we and his doctors are to tend Morgan until such time she is physically well. You and your friends may visit after a time unless she becomes agitated, then you must leave.' She touched me arm with a concerned look, 'The psychological effects will far outweigh the physical.'

I took her hand in mine. 'Thank ye Lady I understand. May I accompany ye now?'

'It's best you do not and not for several days. Leave her now in the company of women.' She wiped a tear from me face and patted me cheek, 'Go now and get some rest. You are falling off your feet.' The cavalcade vanished into the darkness bearing me wife to safety.

Uri was awake when I went to see him. His color was much better. They had been feeding him meat broths, which helped replace blood loss, he wasn't permitted solids yet. He smiled when I sat on the edge of his cot. 'Did ye find Morgan?'

Aye we did. Then I proceeded to tell him all that had transpired including the executions of Samuli, Farad and all their men. His face was grim and angry when he learned of Morgan's ordeal. 'Those two ring leaders should have had to die even slower. They were foul men to be true.'

'We manage to find them in every part of the world, don't we. They were foul but trust me, they suffered greatly.'

'I can't quite believe Danny is gone!'

'I know, he always seemed invincible even when he had his head injury and a way was found to make him well. How many men would have been that lucky? only Danny.'

Uri smiled and then sobered. 'His luck ran out damn it and I already miss his mouth.'

I looked at him, 'Yer luck almost ran out too me friend. That was an ugly wound ye took and it would have been yer life in most parts of the world.'

He nodded, 'I have been wounded many times and this was the worst, besides my face.'

'That was ugly, this one was dangerous.' I kicked off me boots and got up on his cot beside him. Lying shoulder to shoulder, I don't know how long we chatted fer before one or both of us fell asleep.

A Nurse roused me, she was friendly enough but firm. 'Get back to your own room my Lord this man needs looking after without you laying on him.'

I smiled, yawned and said 'Yes maam' and left.

I was summoned to the women's wing. Morgan was awake and coherent. I bathed, combed me hair and dressed in clean clothing. I entered her room and saw her sitting up. She didn't smile but held out her hand. 'Will, I am so happy you are safe. Those nasty men were gloating about the trap set for you.'

I took her hand and sat on the edge of her bed as close as I could. 'I can't imagine what ye went through and ye were worried about me? Oh me love, No matter what, I thought of nothing but savin ye. Now ye are safe and I need to ask ye something.'

Her face seemed to darken and her hand trembled in mine. 'What is it.' I couldn't believe it but there was fear in her voice. I took her shoulders. 'Do ye want to return to England or stay? I will do whatever ye wish and Uri will tag along.'

She started to cry softly. 'Oh you sweet man, I thought you wanted to ask something else. Yes, I would like to go back to Haven. I can't look at this place in the same light as before. You said Uri would tag along, where's Danny?'

'Of course, you didn't know. Brace yer self Morgan dear, Danny is dead he died in the ambush.'

She just stared at me a sob escaping her lips. 'No, I didn't know. Please hold me Will.' She snuggled against me chest, 'Don't ever let me go.'

Over the comin weeks Morgan slowly healed. Me warrior woman was very different but I loved her deeply, though I did pray fer the day the old Morgan would return. Me heart wished one thing but me mind knew another. A semblance of the old Morgan could return but things were, forever changed, her view of the world of men, and between us. I accepted the fact that we might never be lovers again and it didn't bother me. Our love didn't need the physical to last, we were both growing a little older and we saw each other in many other ways.

Winter passed once again and spring arrived. Morgan was up, and about and so was Uri. He seemed as good as new. We found a warm sunny spot in one of the many gardens, and sat soaking in the warmth. People were coming along the path from out of the sun. We could only see shadows and I called out, 'Who is it?'

'It is Bembe and I have brought a guest.' A smiling Kareesh Al Saud descended upon us. 'I am very happy to see you all well.'

I gripped his hand, 'And you. Your injuries are all healed?'

Morgan took his arm and pulled him down onto the bench. 'You seem a little stooped.'

'Yes my dear, a legacy from one of the wounds. I get spasms once in a while.'

Morgan's lips pouted, 'I am sorry to hear that, it will make long rides difficult for you.'

He gave us a rueful look. 'My Silk Road days are over, I will retire here in Samarkand. It is dry and warm without being too hot and I can play at being a merchant if I get bored.'

Morgan smiled, 'You will get bored I know it.'

Bembe had taken up his place behind Morgan. She didn't want him there all the time, I could see it in her eyes but he was not letting her out of his sight again. I paused, looking at him. 'Bembe, what will you do if we return to England?'

'I will go with you!'

Morgan craned her neck to look up at him. 'It is a very different place Bembe. Cold and wet most of the time and the people might treat you badly and with mistrust.'

He looked sadly at her. 'You don't want me to come mistress?'

'That is not what I am saying my dear man. You are our close friend and would be welcome but you really must weigh your actions. We came here full of promise and now are retreating. I know that Will and Uri would not, except for my sake but the same could happen to you in a strange land. If you come to England, you will be tested many many times, perhaps for the rest of your life.'

'I will think on what you have said but I can't return to my own land and living here where black men are considered slaves, has its drawbacks.'

I smiled at him. You know Bembe, your father could be dead by now for all you know and you have friends in high places right here in Timur's court and amongst the Mongols. You have three valid options, not just one.' I grinned, 'Danny would say you are full of Shite and talk too much.'

Bembe started laughing, 'He always said I never talked.'

The day came, when we were summoned, to the palace. As we crossed from the women's palace to Timurs' I marveled at the military activity that was going on. A fine haze of dust hung in the air all over the city. Mongols and Turks were preparing to move. The cool reception area was a welcome relief from the dust. As our eyes adjusted I could see many contingents waiting to see their Highnesses. I was surprised at the number of Europeans.

The Vizier saw us and called. 'Sir Arthur and party please come this way!'

A Spanish Don glowered at us and whispered to his aide. 'They just got here and I've been waiting a day and a half. This Tamerlane wants to take care how he treats an ambassador of Spain.'

I smiled to me self and thought, 'Take care yer self Spaniard.' Then I thought, 'Timur the Great, Timor the Lame, Tamerlane, as the man grows so does the name.' I chuckled.

We entered into a large luxurious room to see Lord Timur and Saray sitting together on cushions.

Timur arose and held his arms wide to embrace each of us. 'Will my dear friend. Morgan, I am happy to see you well once more. Uri you have recovered? Are you well Bembe? Please join me.' He led us to a circle of comfortable cushions. A subtle way of making everyone equal like me da's round table.

Saray way laid Morgan, taking her hands in her own. Her smile was radiant. Did I say once that she was a plain woman? Well that smile made her truly beautiful. 'My Lady Morgan, I must apologize for my brother's complicity in what happened to you. I am sure he was duped as were all of you. The evil mongers are now punished and I ask for your forgiveness.'

'Of course I forgive you, for what? I don't know. Please my Lady I would like to put all this behind me.'

Saray held onto her one hand and led her away. 'Come, we shall have tea while the men talk.'

I smiled at Timur, 'Me Lord you are spending all this time with us and ambassadors are getting upset.'

He grinned, 'I find them much easier to read when they are annoyed, more difficult when they are polite and swarmy.'

'Swarmy? What a wonderful word me Lord.' Then we were all laughing. 'The armies are massing again, where to this time me Lord?'

'It will be a similar operation as the last, only this time against Khorezm and Urganj.' He smiled, 'A couple of weeks should see it done and the Empire grows.'

We chatted comfortably for nearly an hour and then Timur arose. 'Well my friends I have duties to perform so I must say goodbye and safe journey.' He turned to a servant, 'Please ask the Ladies to join us. Will, you still own my life, and know that you and your friends are always welcome here.'

Lady Saray and Morgan arrived and Timur bowed to Morgan. 'Look after your husband dear Lady and I hope you will return to see us one day.'

We had an open invitation though we all knew it would, never be used. This was it and I felt keen regrets at not being able to stay, chasing a whirlwind could be quite addictive. I bowed to the Lady Saray and took her hand. Kissin it I said, 'Goodbye me Lady,' and stepped back. We all took several paces backwards before turning to leave. The Lady Saray was lookin startled and a little pleased. I don't think anyone had kissed her hand before.

# **TERESE**

B o'Orchu was waiting fer us in the courtyard. 'I have been instructed by my Lord to see you all on board a ship.' He grinned, 'I find the duty to be quite onerous.' He ducked me swipe, laughing.

'Ye can't go into Egypt not with the present unrest, so where do we get a boat?'

'Lebanon, it will cut the land journey by days and many European traders land there and the island of Cyprus which is nearby.'

Turin was makin his way through the crowd. 'Salaam Alaikum Will. I heard you were leaving so I put my departure off a day to accompany you as far as Tehran.'

'Salaamu 'Alaikum my friend. How is yer shoulder? We will be happy to have yer company.'

'The shoulder could be better, I am glad it is not my sword arm. With exercise it should improve.'

I looked at both of them, 'Do we leave today or tomorrow?'

Bo'Orchu said, 'Tomorrow first light. You all need time to pack and say some goodbyes. I am taking twenty men. We will meet you at the north gate.'

Turin nodded, 'I only have fifteen men left.' He looked grim. 'Three cannot travel and the rest are dead. Anyway we will be there.'

I thought 'The Shah won't be happy, losing the best part of sixty men.' I hoped Turin could explain well enough to satisfy him. That young man did not deserve a career ender over this.

The air was still cool at the gate, the rising sun hidden behind the wall. Bo'Orchu was already there with his men and chatting with Sennge. So he was goin too, I liked that man. We rode over to them looking, down from our tall horses. Turin wasn't there yet so I quickly outlined me fears fer the captain's reception at home. Bo'Orchu nodded his understanding. 'We will pause at Tehran and I will ask an audience with the Shah. With me backing Turin's account he should be vindicated from wrongful command.'

'What of ye after ye have seen us safe? Lord Timur could be anywhere on this continent.'

Bo'Orchu chuckled. 'It might be difficult to catch up.' Then he sobered. 'We are to meet him at Astrakhan on the Caspian Sea. He will be holding council with members of the Golden Horde for several days. His saber rattling at Egypt was just a ploy for the present. He and Chagatai Khan have other plans. Keep all of this to yourselves please. If we miss him he will leave word of where to follow otherwise we wait for him there.'

I grinned at him, 'It's nice to have yer life planned out...' I heard clopping hooves and turned me head. Turin and the last of his men were approaching.

'Sorry to be late, I needed to say goodbye and honor the men left behind, they fought well.'

Bo'Orchu nodded, 'Yes they did as did all who died. Let us try to beat the heat for a couple of hours and be on our way.' We rode through the gate and out on the road for Tehran. Bembe was on a horse this time and didn't like it much. He would get used to it we couldn't have him running fer ten or twelve hour days. With horses mostly at the cantor we would make good time.

We were three days out and had just stopped to water the horses and have some lunch. The river we were beside was a pleasantly shaded muddy stream with water enough for the horses. I was picking out a plump date when Morgan shook me shoulder. 'Look over there.' Everybody looked where she was pointing. A score of vultures were circling on the air drafts, their quarry hidden by a hill. Ye could see more approaching. 'We should take a look, that's a lot of vultures fer an animal carcass, some will be on the ground already. I'll take Bembe and Uri to have a look. If it is important we will signal you from the hill top.'

Bo'Orchu nodded, 'We will stay comfortable right here. Don't worry we will come if you call.'

'Alright, let's go. Leave the horses, they need their rest.' The three of us climbed the hill. Some spots were difficult because of loose sand but we got to the top. An unsettling sight greeted us.

Hyenas, four of them, were circling a waggon laying on its side There were bodies of blacks behind it and one woman, standing alone, was swatting at the beasts with a rail torn from the waggon. She was on the edge of total exhaustion and was chained to the dead with nowhere to go. Then we heard the wail of a bairn. Bembe hied down the hill leaving us to catch up. I took time to signal the camp and saw them react. I was last down the hill and saw the hyenas were backing off except fer a large female. She wanted her prey challenging us with her hideous laugh and feinting at the woman. She misjudged Bembe who leaped through the air breaking her back with the ax. The animal's shrieks were silenced when he buried his ax in her skull. Seeing their leader go down the others scattered. Some vultures were quick to take the hyena's place but hopped and fluttered away like black gargoyles as we approached. The woman sat down hard. Her legs wouldn't support her any more. Uri was quick to support her and give her water, which she gulped greedily and Bembe followed the sound of the baby. The wailing infant was lying behind her in the shade of the wagon but amongst the bodies, the flies already annoying. Bembe crooned to the infant brushing tormenters away and brought the babe to the woman. She took it holding it to her breast with a small smile of thanks. The wailing stopped as the babe began to suckle. Ye could tell she was afraid, a handsome woman even under the sweat and dirt. Very dark and slender with full round lips and large almond shaped eyes. Bembe was attentive while Uri and I surveyed the destruction. The others rode up leading our horses and Bo'Orchu shouted, 'What happened here?'

'We don't know yet, we are trying to figure it out.' Then I saw the body of an Arab his legs crushed by the wagon, his throat cut, from ear to ear. A chest had been smashed open and the horses were gone. 'I think he ran afoul of thieves.'

Turin was circling the carnage looking over the ground. 'I think you are right Will. Several horses left this way two not carrying riders.'

Uri bent down and rubbed the sand, he stood up with a gold dinar between his fingers. He threw it to Bembe and scrutinized the dead men behind the wagon. They were chained together, along with the woman. Uri turned the head of one lead man. 'His neck is broken as is the one beside him. The others have many abrasions along with sliced throats. I think this man bought slaves and was returning home when attacked. He tried to run from them but failed dragging these men to their deaths. I'll bet he flashed too much gold and that did him in.' He looked at the woman, 'How did she survive?'

'I don't know, why don't we ask her?'

Uri gave me a dirty look. 'You may be a knight but don't get too cheeky.'

I was chuckling as I asked the woman. She didn't seem to understand Pharsi and then I saw her flinch from pain. 'Bembe, check her, I think she is injured. We have to free her from that damned chain.' I went back to the wagon and searched. A box lay in the dirt amongst the horse's traces. It must have been under the seat. Opening it produced a hammer and awl as well as a few other tools. I returned to the woman who, was now being tended by Morgan as well as Bembe. Her back was raw from being dragged but how had she survived havin her throat cut?

We prepared her ankle fer removing the shackle padding it as best we could with strips of cloth.

It was still goin to hurt like hell, after bein dragged by one foot it was raw and badly bruised. The rivet had to be driven out with hammer and awl and the first hit brought a squeak from her, after that she made no sound.

Bo'Orchu looked her over and said, 'We will camp by the river for the rest of this day and tonight. She is too, worn out to travel. We are going to get pushed out by scavengers any way.'

I looked around and there were many vultures on the ground eyeing us like we were a snack too.

Some maribu storks had landed and jackels were moving back and forth in the brush. Come night fall, the hyenas would be back if they weren't already there watching from the bush, after all they were the primary predator and would get the lions' share.

Bembe lifted the woman in his arms and Uri walked beside with the bairn, I led the horses.

That night sleep wouldn't come fer some time as I listened to the cackle of scavengers. As I began to feel drowsy Morgan snuggled up with a small snore. It woke me up again and I held her close with a smile.

I was bleary eyed as a cup of geen tea, was pushed into me hands. I sipped the scalding liquid and finally came around. Bembe and the woman were at the water a little upstream from the horse wallow.

She was bathing and washing her tight curly hair while Bembe swooshed a giggling baby through the water. I had a premonition but kept it to meself.

Tehran offered some fine cuisine and we took advantage of it while Turin and Bo'Orchu went to sort things out with the Shah. He had granted an immediate audience and I prayed things would go well. Turin was a favorite after all.

Bembe approached us with mother and child in tow. They had been shopping and she was wearing a colorful flowered robe. I noticed she had beaded bracelets on her ankles to hide the raw welt that marked her as a slave. He got right into it. 'Will my friend, you Morgan and Uri gave me my life back and I have had to make a difficult decision, I am going to stay. Serene and her child would never survive on their own. She has no documents whereas I do. She will be under my protection as my wife.'

My premonition was true. 'Serene is it? Ye can speak to her? Of course ye have our blessing we all wish ye the very best life can bring, don't we Morgan?'

Morgan smiled, 'You know I love you like a brother. You have guarded me and protected me for as long as we have known each other, I am going to miss you brother.'

Bembe dropped to his knees and took Morgan's hands pressing them against his forehead. 'biyete Inkosi-kaas.'

Morgan frowned, 'I asked you not to call me that.'

Bembe stared up at her. 'This is the last time we will see each other and I will call you that if I wish. You have always been my queen.'

There were tears in Morgans eyes, 'God bless you Bembe, go in peace and with our love.'

Bembe turned to me. 'I remembered a trade language from amongst the tribes and she understood a few words, not enough to tell me how she survived but that really doesn't matter, she did. I know her name and she is from a place called Sudan, for now that is enough.'

'Where will ye go? Ye could find a home in Timur's city. Travel to the Sudan could be dangerous as well as being dangerous from day to day with slavers about.'

'I think Samarkand, Lord Timur offered me a place in his guard. We would wait for a caravan going there I believe Captain Turin would help us.'

Later, just past noon, Bo'Orchu and Turin returned. Bo'Orchu grinned happily. 'All is well, the Shah is pleased and the Captain might even get promoted.'

Turin laughed, 'Mongols were ever famous for embellishing tales and I must say my friend is the best.'

I drew Bembe over and told Turin of his intentions. Turin grasped Bembe's shoulder 'Of course I will help. You can stay in my house until transportation can be arranged.' He looked at me, 'It is time for us to part my friend, duty calls. We have stood together you and I and I will cherish the memories. I never thought I would have a Christian friend Allah is mysterious in his ways.'

I grinned as I pulled him into an embrace. 'Aye, so is God. May your travels take you far and God bless.'

Turin mounted his horse, bent down to instruct Bembe where to go, and rode off. I watched him go with a pang. So many friends come and go.

We said our final goodbyes to Bembe Uta and Serene. Uri held the bairn fer a bit, he seemed to like it a lot. Our column moved out and I paused one last time to wave.

We stopped once again, only briefly, in Baghdad and then headed into new territory. We had to cross Syria to get to Lebanon. A torturous desert stood in our way and without the Mongols we might not have survived it. Finally, we were across and Damascus would be our next stop.

Tripoli was a large seaport in Lebanon and our final destination on this side of our world. Bo'Orchu put out feelers and soon came up with two ships to choose from, both going to Morocco where an English trader could be found. We heard a familiar voice and then saw a very familiar face and our minds, were made up. Baba's face had a stunned look when Morgan called out his name and then with his face beaming he came to hug us all. We introduced Bo'Orchu and Sengge who marveled at how small the world really was.

Baba held me at arms' length, 'did you all travel the Silk Road already? Where's Danny? He wasn't well the last time I saw him.'

'Danny regained his health only to die in battle. No, we did not travel the entire Silk Road God put someone in our path.'

Baba smiled, 'Who?'

'Have ye heard of Timur the Lame? I helped him get that way.'

Baba's smile turned into an Incredulous look, 'Who? Of course, I have heard of him, who hasn't. You must tell me everything when we are at sea. Now, damn it, I must see to my roster.'

I turned to me Mongol friends. 'Ye know, he was our first friend on this side of the world and it looks like he will be the last we see. I'm going to miss you more than anything or anyone. Bo'Orchu, ye are like a brother that I like.' I grinned and he laughed as he pulled me into an embrace.

'Come back and see us sometime Englishman, I will miss you too.' He handed me a box, 'Lord Timur asked that I give you this when we separated. That time is now my friend.'

I said me goodbyes to Sengge and the other Mongols as Bo'Orchu spoke farewell to Morgan and Uli.

They were quick to leave and for that, I was grateful. They didn't need to see me tears. It was time to bed down Storm and Taxeia and make them comfortable. We, and they, would have to get used to the sea once again. Morgan and I watched the recedeing shore and then I opened the box. Me eyes widened as I held it out for Morgan to see. It was filled with a King's ransom of diamonds and rubies.

# **EPILOGUE**

s we approached Haven I saw a familiar form at the distant gate, green scarf and all. First he watched and then began walking to meet us. Morgan looked at me, 'What now Will, are we going to put up our swords for a while? I hope so.'

I smiled, 'No more fighting dearest, at least not on purpose, I'm goin to visit friends and breed horses, Storm and Taxeia will help.' I grinned over at Uri, 'I'll make a horse lover out of you yet' I jumped down from Storm to embrace a dear friend.

**The End**

Printed in the United States
By Bookmasters